THE SWIMMING-POOL LIBRARY

Alan Hollinghurst was born in 1954. He is the author of one of the most highly praised first novels to appear in the 1980s, *The Swimming-Pool Library* (1988), and was selected as one of the Best Young British Novelists 1993. His second novel, *The Folding Star*, won the James Tait Black Memorial Prize and was shortlisted for the 1994 Booker Prize. His most recent novel is *The Line of Beauty*.

Alan Hollinghurst

THE SWIMMING-POOL LIBRARY

V

VINTAGE

Published by Vintage 2004

1 3 5 7 9 10 8 6 4 2

Copyright © Alan Hollinghurst 1988

The right of Alan Hollinghurst to be identified as the author
of this work has been asserted by him in accordance with the
Copyright, Designs and Patents Act, 1988

First published in Great Britain by
Chatto & Windus Ltd, 1988

Vintage
Random House, 20 Vauxhall Bridge Road,
London SW1V 2SA

Random House Australia (Pty) Limited
20 Alfred Street, Milsons Point, Sydney
New South Wales 2061, Australia

Random House New Zealand Limited
18 Poland Road, Glenfield, Auckland 10,
New Zealand

Random House South Africa (Pty) Limited
Endulini, 5a Jubilee Road, Parktown 2193,
South Africa

Random House UK Limited Reg. No. 954009

www.randomhouse.co.uk

A CIP catalogue record for this book
is available from the British Library

ISBN 0 09 946836 0

Papers used by Random House are natural, recyclable
products made from wood grown in sustainable forests.
The manufacturing processes conform to the
environmental regulations of the country of origin

Printed and bound in Great Britain by
Cox & Wyman Ltd, Reading, Berkshire

For Nicholas Clark
1959–1984

'She reads at such a pace,' she complained, 'and when I asked her *where* she had learnt to read so quickly, she replied "On the screens at Cinemas."'

The Flower Beneath the Foot

I came home on the last train. Opposite me sat a couple of London Transport maintenance men, one small, fifty, decrepit, the other a severely handsome black of about thirty-five. Heavy canvas bags were tilted against their boots, their overalls open above their vests in the stale heat of the Underground. They were about to start work! I looked at them with a kind of swimming, drunken wonder, amazed at the thought of their inverted lives, of how their occupation depended on our travel, but could only be pursued, I saw it now, when we were not travelling. As we went home and sank into unconsciousness gangs of these men, with lamps and blow-lamps, and long-handled ratchet spanners, moved out along the tunnels; and wagons, not made to carry passengers, freakishly functional, rolled slowly and clangorously forwards from sidings unknown to the commuter. Such lonely, invisible work must bring on strange thoughts; the men who walked through every tunnel of the labyrinth, tapping the rails, must feel such reassurance seeing the lights of others at last approaching, voices calling out their friendly, technical patter. The black was looking at his loosely cupped hands: he was very aloof, composed, with an air of massive, scarcely conscious competence – I felt more than respect, a kind of tenderness for him. I imagined his relief at getting home and taking his boots off and going to bed as the day brightened around the curtains and the noise of the streets built up outside. He turned his hands over and I saw the pale gold band of his wedding-ring.

All the gates but one at the station were closed and I, with two or three others, scuttled out as if being granted an unusual concession. Then there were the ten minutes to walk home. The drink made it seem closer, so that next day I would not remember the walk at all. And the idea of Arthur, too, which I had suppressed to make it all the more exciting when I recalled it, must have driven me along at quite a lick.

I was getting a taste for black names, West Indian names; they were a kind of time-travel, the words people whispered to their pillows, doodled on their copy-book margins, cried out in passion when my grandfather was young. I used to think these Edwardian names were the denial of romance: Archibald, Ernest, Lionel, Hubert were laughably stolid; they bespoke personalities unflecked by sex or malice. Yet only this year I had been with boys called just those staid things; and they were not staid boys. Nor was Arthur. His name was perhaps the least likely ever to have been young: it evoked for me the sunless complexion, unaired suiting, steel-rimmed glasses of a ledger clerk in a vanished age. Or had done so, before I found my beautiful, cocky, sluttish Arthur – an Arthur it was impossible to imagine old. His smooth face, with its huge black eyes and sexily weak chin, was always crossed by the light and shade of uncertainty, and met your gaze with the rootless self-confidence of youth.

Arthur was seventeen, and came from Stratford East. I had been out all that day, and when I was having dinner with my oldest friend James I nearly told him that I had this boy back home, but swallowed my words and glowed boozily with secret pleasure. James, besides, was a doctor, full of caution and common sense, and would have thought I was crazy to leave a virtual stranger in my home. In my stuffy, opinionated family, though, there was a stubborn tradition of trust, and I had perhaps absorbed from my mother the habit of testing servants and window-cleaners by exposing them to temptation. I took a slightly creepy pleasure in imagining Arthur in the flat alone, absorbing its alien richness, looking at the pictures, concentrating of course on Whitehaven's photograph of me in my little swimming-trunks, the shadow across my eyes . . . I was unable to feel anxiety about those electrical goods which are the general currency of burglaries – and I doubted if the valuable discs (the Rattle *Tristan* among them) would be to Arthur's taste. He liked dance-music that was hot and cool – the kind that whipped and crooned across the dance-floor of the Shaft, where I had met him the night before.

He was watching television when I got in. The curtains were drawn, and he had dug out an old half-broken electric fire; it was extremely hot. He got up from his chair, smiling nervously. 'I was just watching TV,' he said. I took my jacket off, looking at him and surprised to find what he looked like. By remembering many times one or two of his details I had lost the overall hang of him. I wondered about all the work that must go into combing his hair into the narrow ridges that ran back from his forehead to the nape of his neck, where they ended in young tight pigtails, perhaps eight of them, only an inch long. I kissed him, my left hand sliding between his high, plump buttocks while with the other I stroked the back of his head. Oh, the ever-open softness of black lips; and the strange dryness of the knots of his pigtails, which crackled as I rolled them between my fingers, and seemed both dead and half-erect.

At about three I woke and needed a pee. Dull, half-conscious though I was, my heart thumped as I came back into the room and saw Arthur asleep in the gentle lamplight that fell across the pillows, one arm sticking out awkwardly from under the duvet, as if to shield his eyes. I sat down and slid in beside him, observing him carefully, hovering over his face and catching again the childish smell of his breath. As I turned the light out, I felt him roll towards me, his huge hands digging under me almost as if he wanted to carry me away. I embraced him, and he gripped me more tightly, clung to me as if in danger. I murmured 'Baby' several times before I realised he was still asleep.

My life was in a strange way that summer, the last summer of its kind there was ever to be. I was riding high on sex and self-esteem – it was my time, my *belle époque* – but all the while with a faint flicker of calamity, like flames around a photograph, something seen out of the corner of the eye. I wasn't in work – oh, not a tale of hardship, or a victim of recession, not even, I hope, a part of a statistic. I had put myself out of work deliberately, or at least knowingly. I was beckoned on by having too much money, I belonged to that tiny proportion of the populace that indeed owns almost everything. I'd surrendered to the prospect of doing nothing, though it kept me busy enough.

For nearly two years I'd been on the staff of the Cubitt *Dictionary of Architecture*, a grandiose project afflicted by delay and bad feeling. Its editor was a friend of my Oxford tutor, who was worried at my drifting unopposed into the routine of bars and clubs, saw me swamped with unwholesome leisure, and put in a word – one of those mere suggestions which, touching a nerve of guilt, take the force of a command. And so I had found myself turning up each day at St James's Square and sitting in a little back office, disguising my hangover as a kind of wincing, aesthetic abstraction, and knocking box-folders of research material into shape.

Volume One was to cover A to D, and I was allowed to work on some of the subjects that interested me most – the Adams, Lord Burlington, Colen Campbell. I edited the essays of repetitive pundits, was sent out to the British Library or Sir John Soane's Museum to find plans and engravings; smaller subjects I was allowed to write up myself: I turned in an exemplary article on Coade Stone vases. But the Dictionary was a crackpot affair, a mismanaged business, an Escorial that turned into a Fonthill the longer we worked on it. I rang people up and there were parties from six till eight – which meant going on, and then some drunken supper and then, as often as not, the Shaft and acts in which the influence of the orders, the dome, the portico, could scarcely be discerned.

After I left Cubitts I felt hilarious relief at being no longer a cross between a professor and an office-boy – someone whose presence was explained as much by his name as by his interest in the arts. At the same time there was a slight sad missing of the slipshod office routine, the explanation over the first foul coffee of just where I'd taken whom, and what he was like in every particular. It was the sort of world that made you a character, and would happily, stodgily keep you one for life. And there was the subject too – the orders, the dome, the portico, the straight lines and the curved, which spoke to me, and meant more to me than they do to some.

I slipped away from Arthur next day and walked in the Park – it was perhaps the straight lines of its avenues that exerted some calming attraction over me. As a child, on visits to Marden, my grandfather's house, days had been marked by walks along the great beech ride which ran unswervingly for miles over hilly country and gave out at a ha-ha and a high empty field. Away to the left you could make out in winter the chicken-coops and outside privies of a village that had once been part of the estate. Then we turned round, and came home, my sister and I, spoilt by my grandparents, feeling decidedly noble and aloof. It was not until years later that I came to understand how recent and synthetic this nobility was – the house itself bought up cheap after the war, half ruined by use as an officers' training school, and then as a military hospital.

Today was one of those April days, still and overcast, that felt pregnant with some immense idea, and suggested, as I roamed across from one perspective to another, that this was merely a doldrums, and would last only until something else was ready to happen. Perhaps it was simply summer, and the certainty of warmth, the world all out of doors, drinking in the open air. The trees were budding, and that odd inside-out logic was evolving whereby the Park, just at the time it becomes hot and popular, shuts itself off from the outside world of buildings and traffic with the shady density of its foliage. But I felt the threat too of some realisation about life, something obscurely disagreeable and perhaps deserved.

Though I didn't believe in such things, I was a perfect Gemini, a child of the ambiguous early summer, tugged between two versions of myself, one of them the hedonist and the other – a little in the background these days – an almost scholarly figure with a faintly puritanical set to the mouth. And

4

there were deeper dichotomies, differing stories – one the 'account of myself', the sex-sharp little circuits of discos and pubs and cottages, the sheer crammed, single-minded repetition of my empty months; the other the 'romance of myself', which transformed all these mundanities with a protective glow, as if from my earliest days my destiny had indeed been charmed, so that I was both of the world and beyond its power, like the pantomime character Wordsworth describes, with 'Invisible' written on his chest.

At times my friend James became my other self, and told me off and tried to persuade me that I was not doing all I might. I was never good at being told off, and when he insisted that I should find a job, or even a man to settle down with, it was in so intimate and knowledgeable a way that I felt as if one half of me were accusing the other. It was from him, whom I loved more than anyone, that I most often heard the account of myself. He had even said lately in his diary that I was 'thoughtless' – he meant cruel, in the way I had thrown off a kid who had fallen for me and who irritated me to distraction; but then he got the idea into his head: does Will care about anybody? does Will ever really *think*? and so on and so forth. 'Of course I fucking think,' I muttered, though he wasn't there to hear me. And he gave a horrid little diagnosis: 'Will becoming more and more brutal, more and more sentimental.'

I was certainly sentimental with Arthur, deeply sentimental and lightly brutal, at one moment caressingly attentive, the next glutting him with sex, mindlessly – thoughtlessly. It was the most beautiful thing I could imagine – all the more so for our knowledge that we could never make a go of it together. Even among the straight lines of the Park I wasn't thinking straight – all the time I looped back to Arthur, was almost burdened by my need for him, and by the oppressive mildness of the day. The Park after all was only stilted countryside, its lake and trees inadequate reminders of those formative landscapes, the Yorkshire dales, the streams and watermeads of Winchester, whose influence was lost in the sexed immediacy of London life.

I found myself approaching the dismal Italianate garden at the head of the lake, a balustraded terrace with flagged paths surrounding four featureless pools, a half-hearted baroque fountain (now switched off) aimed at the Serpentine below, and on the outside, backing on to the Bayswater Road, a pavilion with a rippling red roof and benches spattered with bird droppings. Deadly as this place had always seemed to me, stony and phoney amid the English greenness of the Park, it was an unfailing attraction to visitors: loving couples, solitary duck-fanciers, large European and Middle Eastern family groups taking a slothful stroll from their apartments in Bayswater and Lancaster Gate. I sauntered across it, as much to confirm how I disliked it as anything else. Some desolate little boys played together more out of duty than pleasure. Queens of a certain age strolled pointedly up and down. The sky was uniformly grey, though a glare on the white frippery of the pavilion suggested a sun that might break through.

I was turning to leave when I spotted a lone Arab boy wandering along, hands in the pockets of his anorak, fairly unremarkable, yet with something about him which made me feel I must have him. I was convinced that he had noticed me, and I felt a delicious surplus of lust and satisfaction at the idea of fucking him while another boy waited for me at home.

To test him out I dawdled off behind the pavilion to where some public lavatories, over-frequented by lonely middle-aged men, are tucked into the ivy-covered, pine-darkened bank of the main road. I went down the tiled steps between the tiled walls, and a hygienic, surprisingly sweet smell surrounded me. It was all very clean, and at several of the stalls under the burnished copper pipes (to which someone must attach all their pride), men were standing, raincoats shrouding from the innocent visitor or the suspicious policeman their hour-long footlings. I felt a faint revulsion – not disapproval, but a fear of one day being like that. Their heads seemed grey and loveless to me as they turned in automatic anticipation. What long investment they made for what paltry returns . . . Did they nod to one another, the old hands, as they took up their positions, day by day, alongside each other in whatever station in their underground cycle of conveniences they had reached? Did anything ever happen, did they, despairing of whatever it was they sought, which could surely never be sex, but at most a glimpse of something memorable, ever make do with each other? I felt certain they didn't; they were engaged, in a silently agreed silence, in looking out endlessly for something they couldn't have. I was not shy but too proud and priggish to take up my place among them, and it was with only a moment's hesitation that I resolved not to do so.

I walked to the far end of the room, where the washbasins were, and looking in the mirror above them, commanded a view back along the whole enfilade of urinals and cabins to the door. I would only allow a minute or so for the Arab boy, if he hadn't come by then I would go, perhaps follow him to wherever he had gone, if he was still in sight. I affected to look at myself in the mirror, ran a hand over my short fair hair, did catch myself looking terribly excited, a gash of pink along my cheekbones, my mouth tense. There were footsteps on the stairs outside, but slow and heavy, and accompanied by short-winded singing, wordless and baritonal. Clearly not my boy. Disappointment was mixed, I realised, with a kind of relief, and I ran my hands unconsciously under the taps, switching quickly between the cold and the very hot hot. An elderly man had appeared behind me and, still tootling away in a manner that suggested all was right with the world, advanced to the urinals where he stood leaning forward, propping himself with a hand that grasped the copper pipe in front of him, and smiling sociably to the disgruntled looking fellow on his right. I turned round in search of the towel, and as I yanked it down and it gave out its reluctant click, the elderly newcomer said 'Oh deary me' in a speculative sort of way, and half fell forward, still gripping the pipe, while his feet, taking the stress from the new angle, slewed round and across the raised step on which he and the others were standing. Now half turned towards me, he lost his footing completely and slid down heavily, his head coming to rest on the porcelain buttress at the side of the stall, while his substantial, tweed-clad figure sprawled across the damp tile floor. From his fly, his surprisingly long, silky penis still protruded. He wore a self-chastising expression, as if he had just realised he had forgotten to do something very important. There was a slight foam about his lips, his facial expression became strangely fixed, his cheeks genuinely bluish in colour.

The man who had been at the adjacent place said 'Oh my Christ' and hurried out. All along the rank of urinals there was a hasty doing-up of flies, and faces that spoke both of concern and of a sense that they had been caught, turned in my direction.

I instantly pictured James, as he had described himself, kneeling over corpses on long train journeys, as a doctor honour-bound to attempt to resuscitate them, long after hope was gone. I also fleetingly saw the Arab boy, wandering off under the budding trees, and thought that if I'd never succumbed to this fantasy, I wouldn't be in this fix now. Still, I thought I knew what to do, partly from involuntary recall of life-saving classes by the swimming-pool at school, and I immediately knelt beside the old man, and punched him hard in the chest. The three other men stood by, undergoing an ashamed transition from loiterers to well-wishers in a few seconds.

'He didn't hang about, he knew the old bill'd do for him, soon as look at him,' said one of them, in reference, apparently, to their companion who had fled.

'Shouldn't you loosen his collar?' said another man, apologetic and well spoken.

I tugged at the knot of the tie, and with some difficulty undid the stiff top button.

'He mustn't swallow his tongue,' explained the same man, as I repeated my chest punchings. I turned to the head, and carefully lowered it, though it was heavy and slipped within its thin, silvery hair. 'Check the mouth for obstructions,' I heard the man say – and, as it were, echoing from the tiled walls, the voice of the instructor at school. I remembered how in these exercises we were only allowed to exhale alongside the supposed casualty's head, rather than apply our lips to his, and the alternate relief and disappointment this occasioned, according to who one's partner was.

'I'll go for an ambulance,' said the man who had not yet spoken, but waited a while more before doing so.

'Yeah, he'll get an ambulance,' the first man commented after he had left. He was well up on the other people's behaviour.

The patient had no false teeth and his tongue seemed to be in the right place. Stooping down, so that his inert shoulder pressed against my knee, I gripped his nose with two fingers and, inhaling deeply, sealed my lips over his. I saw with a turn of the head his chest swell, and as he expired the air his colour undoubtedly changed. I realised I had not checked in the first place that his heart had stopped beating, and had ignorantly acted on a hunch that had turned out to be correct. I breathed into his mouth again – a strange sensation, intimate and yet symbolic, tasting his lips in an impersonal and disinterested way. Then I massaged his chest, with deep, almost offensive pressure, one hand on top of the other; and already he had come back to life.

It had all been so rapid and inevitable that it was only when he was breathing regularly and we had laid him down on a coat and done up his fly that I felt shaken by a surge of delayed elation. I raced up the steps into mild sunshine and hung around waiting for the ambulance, unable to stop grinning, my hands trembling. Even so, it was too soon to understand. I told myself that I had scooped someone back from the threshold of death, but that seemed incommensurate with the simple routine I had followed, the vital little drill retained from childhood along with all the more complex knowledge that would never prove so useful – convection, sonata form, the names of birds in Latin and French.

The Corinthian Club in Great Russell Street is the masterpiece of the architect Frank Orme, whom I once met at my grandfather's. I remember he carried on in a pompous and incongruous way, having recently, and as if by mistake, been awarded a knighthood. Even as a child I saw him as a fraud and a hotchpotch, and I was delighted, when I joined the Club and learned that he had designed it, to discover just the same qualities in his architecture. Like Orme himself, the edifice is both mean and self-important; a paradox emphasised by the modest resources of the Club in the 1930s and its conflicting aspiration to civic grandeur. As you walk along the pavement you look down through the railings into an area where steam issues from the ventilators and half-open top-lights of changing-rooms and kitchens; you hear the slam of large institutional cooking trays, the hiss of showers, the inane confidence of radio disc-jockeys. The ground floor has a severe manner, the Portland stone punctuated by green-painted metal-framed windows; but at the centre it gathers to a curvaceous, broken-pedimented doorway surmounted by two finely developed figures – one pensively Negroid, the other inspiredly Caucasian – who hold between them a banner with the device 'Men Of All Nations'. Before answering this call, step across the street and look up at the floors above. You see more clearly that it is a steel-framed building, tarted up with niches and pilasters like some bald fact inexpertly disguised. At the far corner there is a tremendous upheaving of cartouches and volutes crowned by a cupola like that of some immense Midland Bank. Finances and inspiration seem to have been exhausted by this, however, and alongside, above the main cornice of the building, rises a two-storey mansard attic, containing the cheap accommodation the Club provides in the cheapest possible form of building. On the little projecting dormers of the lower attic floor the occupants of the upper put out their bottles of milk to keep cool, or spread swimming things to dry, despite the danger of pigeons.

Inside, the Club is mildly derelict in mood, crowded at certain times, and then oddly deserted, like a school. In the entrance hall in the evening people are always going to and from meetings, or signing each other up for volleyball teams or fitness classes. In the hall the worlds of the hotel above, and the club below, meet. I would always take the downward stair, its handrail tingling with static electricity, and turn along the underground corridor to the gym, the weights room and the dowdy magnificence of the pool.

It was a place I loved, a gloomy and functional underworld full of life, purpose and sexuality. Boys, from the age of seventeen, could go there to work on their bodies in the stagnant, aphrodisiac air of the weights room.

As you got older, it grew dearer, but quite a few men of advanced years, members since youth and displaying the drooping relics of toned-up pectorals, still paid the price and tottered in to cast an appreciative eye at the showering youngsters. 'With brother clubs in all the major cities of the world,' their names and dates incised in marble beneath the founder's bust in the hall, the large core of men who worked out daily were always supplemented by visitors needing a dip or a game of squash or to find a friend. More than once I had ended up in a bedroom of the hotel above with a man I had smiled at in the showers.

The Corry proved the benefit of smiling in general. A sweet, dull man smiled at me there on my first day, talked to me, showed me what was what. I was still an undergraduate then, and a trifle nervous, anticipating, with confused dread and longing, scenes of grim machismo and institutionalised vice. Bill Hawkins, a pillar of the place, I subsequently discovered, fortyish, with the broad belt and sexless underbelly of the heavy weight-lifter, had simply extended camaraderie to a newcomer.

'Hallo, Will,' he said to me now as I entered the changing-room and he came back, grunting and staring from a monster workout.

'Hi, Bill,' I replied. 'How're you doing?' It was our inevitable exchange, in which some vestige of a joke seemed to reside, our having the same name yet, by the difference of a letter, each being called something altogether different.

'Haven't seen you for a bit,' he said.

'No, I seem to have had quite a lot on,' I hinted.

'Glad to hear it, Will,' he replied, following me round the little maze of banked lockers. I found one that was free, slung my bag into it, and began to undress. Bill stood by me, amicable, massive, flushed, his head and shoulders still rinsed with sweat. There was a kind of handsomeness lost in his heavy, square face. He sat down on the bench, where he could politely talk while also watching me take my clothes off. It was typical of his behaviour, discreet, but not prurient: his was the old-fashioned ethos of a male community, delighting in men, but always respectful and fraternal. I knew he would never ask a personal question.

'That boy Phil's coming on well,' he said. 'Very nice definition. Said he was a bit loose after being off for a spell, but I should say he'd put on a centimetre or two this week alone.' Phil, I knew, was a lad he had a bit of a soft spot for; I'd seen him hanging around to count for him when he was on the machines, and because Phil was genuinely interested in his own body Bill was always able to engage him in earnest analyses of methods and results. I could see, too, that Phil, who was shy and stocky, might be a tricky proposition, and sensed some resistance in him to Bill's cheery and paternal chatter across the crowded shower room.

'Phil's all very well,' I suggested, 'but he's the plump type: he'll always have to work hard.' I pulled off my T-shirt and Bill shook his head.

'I'd like to see you do some more work,' he said with a sucking in of his breath. 'You've got the makings of something really choice.' I looked down, as it were modestly, at my lean torso, the smooth, tight tits, the little fuse of hair running down to my belt.

The swimming-pool at the Corry is reached down a spiral staircase from the changing-rooms. It is the most subterranean zone of the Club, its high coffered ceiling supporting the floor of the gym above. Corinthian pillars at each corner are an allusion to ancient Rome, and you half expect to see the towel-girt figures of Charlton Heston and Tony Curtis deep in senatorial conspiracy. Instead, a bored attendant paces around the narrow mosaic border of the pool in flip-flops. The water comes to within an inch or so of the margin, and any waves run over the floor, which glistens and, being uneven, holds little cold puddles. Some regulation, I suspect, stipulates how many turns around the pool the attendant must take each hour, for he combines his vigilance with relaxing in the spectators' seats and reading a book; after a longish spell of this he will then trot around the pool for a minute or two as if to make up his ration. I have never known, or known of, any occasion on which his services were needed.

The lighting of this dingy, dignified underground bath is not in keeping with its décor. Originally, old photographs show, branched neo-classical lampadaries spread a broad glare over the water, whilst at the corners shell-shaped cups threw an orangey glow upwards on to the grandiose mouldings of the ceiling. Until lately you could buy in the foyer upstairs a postcard, dating from not long after the war, showing white young men in the voluminous, mildly obscene, unelasticated swimming drawers of yore, about to jump in, and the sleek heads of those who had already done so dotted down the crowded lanes. On the back it said 'The Corinthian Club, London: The Swimming Baths (25 yards). Founded in 1864, the present fine building, housing a gymnasium, social rooms, and 200 bedrooms for young men, dates from 1935.' (James had immediately seen that this caption should be read with the clipped, optimistic tone of a Pathé news announcer.) In the recent past, however, coinciding with the outlay on a few tins of brown gloss paint, and the filling in of some of the cracks which continuous small subsidence and shifting of the ground brought about, the pool lighting had been redesigned. Away with the wholesome brightness of Sir Frank's original conception, and in with a suggestive gloom, blond pools of light contrasting with surrounding shadow. Small, weak spots let into the ceiling now give vestigial illumination, like that in cinemas, over the surrounding walkway, and throw the figures loitering or recovering at either end into silhouette, making them look black. Blacks themselves become almost invisible in the bath, the navy blue tiles, once cheery, now making it impossible to see, even with goggles, for more than a few feet under water. The luminous whiteness of the traditional swimming-pool is perversely avoided here: the swimmers loom up and down unaware of each other, crossing sometimes in the soft cones of brightness.

All this makes the pool seem remote from the rest of the world, but the impression is lessened by the PA system which interrupts its continuous relay of music – insipid pop on weekdays, classical on Sundays – to call members to the phone or to reception. It is the camp voice of Michael that one normally hears, wringing the wildest insinuations out of words such as *guest* and *occupant*. Those who know his ways greet each announcement with a delight unshared by the novice; in my first week at the club the disdainful announcement that 'Mr Beckwith has a man in reception' had brought a round of silly laughter as I walked, blushing, from the gym.

And the pool is a busy place. Except for certain mournful periods – early afternoons, Sunday evenings – there is a crowd: friends are racing, practised divers arch into the water making barely a splash, the agile avoid the slow, groups sit in a dripping line on the edge, feet flicking the water, cocks shrunken by the cold sticking up comically in their trunks. Miles of serious swimming are wound up in those twenty-five yards each day, and though some dally between lengths, of most you see only the heave of breaststrokers' backs, the misted goggles and gasping, half-averted mouths of crawlers, the incessant cleaving movements of their arms, and the bubbling wakes of their feet.

I went to swim most days, sometimes after exercises on the mats in the gym or a shortish turn in the weights room. It was a bizarre occupation, numbing and yet satisfying. I swam fast, alternating crawl and breast-stroke, with a length of butterfly every ten. My mind would count its daily fifty lengths as automatically as a photocopier; and at the same time it would wander. Absorbed in thought I barely noticed the half-hour – one unfaltering span of pure physical exercise – elapse. This evening I thought of Arthur a lot, running real and projected conversations through my mind as I tumble-turned from length into length through the cool, gloomy water. A week had gone by since we'd met, a week spent in bed, or trailing naked from bedroom to bathroom to kitchen; sleeping at irregular times, getting drunk, watching movies on the video. I was engrossed in him.

He was still strange to me, though, and much less predictable than I was. Perhaps he felt stifled in the flat. After hours of languid vacancy he would spring up and run from room to room, tapping door-frames and chair-backs as he went. Sometimes he ploughed through the stations on the hi-fi till he found some music to dance to, and would swarm around wearing nothing but my school straw hat, or a towel which he flirted about or shook like a fetish. I wasn't allowed to join in these dances: like the little circuits through the flat they had a secret, child's logic of their own, and to come near was to risk being kicked or jabbed by his swinging limbs. Then he would give up and fall recklessly on top of me on the sofa, panting in my face, kissing me, full of clumsy humour and longing.

We were so close that I was disturbed every time he span off into his own world: the sudden detachment, a spell broken, a faint fear of losing him altogether. On occasion he would laugh very loudly at something mildly funny, and keep on laughing as he slapped himself and pointed at my puzzled, cross expression. I couldn't understand where this laughter came from; it seemed to me some new nihilistic teen thing I was already too old for. I had seen kids in Oxford Street or on Tottenham Court Road laughing in the same cold, painful, helpless way.

In the end I would go out of the room and after a few moments he would follow me, suddenly silent. He would approach me intently, licking whatever part of me he came to first. Then he was no longer the dead soul from the amusement arcade or the windswept corner, and I had the infinitely touching sense of him quite apart from the crowd, slipping off to clubs and bars in pursuit of his own romantic destiny. I was moved by his singleness, and then wanted to smother it in sex and possessiveness.

He was most out of hand when we drank. Before he met me he had got through his evenings on a few Cokes and cans of beer, or whatever the men — terrible, he made them sound, as he nostalgically described them — bought for him as they chatted him up. Now he was exposed daily to my raw intake of wine, whisky and champagne. Whisky he sipped at suspiciously, and still had not got an adult taste for; but wine he loved, and he put back champagne as if it were lager, with awful belches and chuckles after each glass. Then his priority was to keep me informed of his condition: 'I'm a wee bit tipsy, William,' he would say almost at once. Then, 'Will? Will? You could call me pissed.' And a glass or two later, 'Man, I am wrecked, man.' It was when he grew quiet and gazed into the air, muttering 'Drunk again' as if in recollection of a mother chiding a father, that he was liable to change. As we hugged and nosed around each other, he would push me to arm's length and look me in the eye while he repeated something I had said. Odd words seemed to amuse or offend him, and he gave urchin imitations of my speech. 'Arse-hale,' he would drawl. 'Get orf my arse-hale.' Or if we were nattering in the kitchen as I woozily knocked up some supper, he would interrupt what I was saying and dance about shouting 'No, no, no – listen, no – "cunt-stabulareh,"' and double up with laughter. Sometimes I laughed graciously too, and did even posher imitations of his mimicry, knowing no one was listening. Sometimes I caught him and gave him what he was asking for.

So, the last couple of days, I had been closer with the booze, and it was all the nicer to have him loosened up but not cantering out of control. We had never been better together. Even so, the relief of being in the water again was intense; when he had made a phone call in the morning and said he'd go away for a day something inside me asserted 'That's right.' I lent him a shirt, perhaps I gave it to him – pink silk, it suited his blackness as much as it did my fairness – kissed him chastely, told him to come back when he wanted, and, when he had gone, went round opening windows (it was a coldish spring day). I put clean linen on the bed, and could hardly wait for night-time and getting in there for a good sleep all by myself. I kept stretching out my arms and legs, like one of those queeny Sons of the Morning in a Blake engraving.

After a while I took this further, and slammed through a set of pull-ups, press-ups and sit-ups – and then ached for the pool. So self-enclosed had my life been for the preceding week – broken only by five-minute trips to the local shop for cereals, tins and papers – that I looked on the public crowding the Underground platform with the apprehension and surprise that people feel on leaving hospital.

I came up dripping and panting from the pool to the changing-room. As I pushed open the swing door with its steamed-up little window designed, like those in restaurants, to prevent hurrying people from knocking each other flat, I heard the hiss of the crowded showers, and felt the warm, dense atmosphere of the place in my throat and on my skin. I sauntered along between the two files of hot jets whose spray danced up off the black tiles, shifting or suddenly cutting off as the men, naked or in their trunks, edged about, soaped a foot raised against the wall, gave their stomachs resounding smacks, or turned, as the doors to the outside world thwacked open, to see what beauty had arrived. Exchanging short greetings with a couple of chaps I scarcely knew, I chose a vacant position between a pale, ravaged looking youth with tattoos snaking up his arms and a huge dark brown man, six foot eight tall at a guess, very round and heavy, with an enormous childish face and not a hair on his head – or, I soon found, anywhere on his body. His sleek, heavy cock, cushioned on a tight, crinkled scrotum, stuck out from beneath a roll of fat. He was soaping himself vigorously, leaving a silky smear over his smooth, plump expanses of back and belly; and with cheery unselfconsciousness singing as he went about it. I nodded to him, as if to say that I could see he was happy enough, then, and he grinned back in a way that suggested a fond, exuberant disposition. I felt that he might stroke me as a golem does some little girl who trusts him, or inadvertently crush me to death. I set down my soap box and shampoo, let the water drum on my shoulders, and looked about.

At the Corry the men undress at their lockers, and then bring their towels to the duckboarded place at the end of the shower room. Often those who have swum still have their trunks on and some stud may allow a mocking minute of tension before the languid unknotting of the drawstring, and the peeling down of the tiny garment, freeing the cock and balls in one of the most mundane and heartstopping moments there is. An American guy, I thought, was doing this just now on the other side of the room; square and trim he stood breathing heavily and luxuriating under the water before turning his back and loosening his glittering briefs to reveal a firm hairless ass, milky white between the sun or sunbed-tanned zones of his back and thighs. I still had my really absurdly tiny black trunks on, and felt my cock protesting against their constraint, thickening up, and aching as it did so after the pounding it had lately been taking.

At first I used to feel embarrassed about getting a hard-on in the shower. But at the Corry much deliberate excitative soaping of cocks went on, and a number of members had their routine erections there each day. My own, though less regular, were, I think, hoped and looked out for. There is a paradoxical strength in display; the naked person always has the social advantage over the clothed one (though the naked person can forget this, as innumerable farces show), and under the shower I was reckless.

The effect of this on others, though, was not necessarily a good thing. It would be vain to pretend that all the men at the Corry looked like the stars of a physique magazine. There were gods – demi-gods, at least – but a place which gathered the fantasies of so many, young and old, was bound to have its own sorry network of unspoken loyalties, stolen and resented glances, ungainly gambits and humiliating crushes. This naked mingling, which formed a ritualistic heart to the life of the club, produced its own improper incitements to ideal liaisons, and polyandrous happenings which could not survive into the world of jackets and ties, cycle-clips and duffel-coats. And how difficult social distinctions are in the shower. How could I now smile at my enormous African neighbour, who was responding in elephantine manner to my own erection, and yet scowl at the disastrous nearly-boy smirking under the next jet along?

I first met James at Oxford, where he had heard of me but I knew nothing of him: it was at one of the little parties organised by my tutor at Saturday lunchtimes, with red and white wine, and nuts – genially queeny occasions where gay chaplains (chaplains, that is to say) and the more enlightened dons mingled with undergraduates chosen for their charm or connections, while one or two very old and distinguished people sat among the standing guests, holding audience and spilling their drinks on the carpet. I was feeling particularly full of myself: I had been fucking a French boy from Brasenose, it was a hot early summer in my second year, and I had the strange experience, on arriving in the crowded college room, of standing just behind my tutor and one of his graduate students who said to him, 'I hope you've asked young Beckwith; I must say I should think he's just in his prime this year . . .' before I watched the graduate's pleasure seep away in blushing discomfiture. James, in a crumpled linen jacket, open Aertex shirt, and baggy russet cords, was standing by the window. He looked very young, innocent, and yet mature, as he was already losing his fair, fine hair. His eyes, in contrast to his general colouring, were deep brown, and as my tutor introduced us James said 'Oh, how do you do?', indicating pleasure and surprise, and I said, in the rude way that I then thought brilliant, 'He has very beautiful eyes.'

I colour to remember how at first I assumed that James fancied me, so infatuated was I with myself. A few days later we met again at a cricket match in the Parks (my French boy having turned moody and hostile), drank beer together all afternoon, sat up late listening to Wagner, and I realised that what he liked was my company, and the fact that we felt the same about boys and music. We reached the stage of drunkenness where Brünnhilde's Immolation seems to last only thirty seconds or so, though each bar is still a miraculous revelation. When he turned off the gramophone, stood up and said, 'Well, you must go, darling,' I was smitten with friendship, moved especially that he did not want me to stay. After that we met almost every day of our undergraduate careers.

Tonight we were meeting in the Volunteer, my local gay pub. Mildly art-nouveau and metropolitan outside, with mysteriously opaque acid-etched windows, the Volunteer inside, after disastrous refurbishments, was an eternal parable of disappointment. A little back bar, favoured by the elderly, retained some period character, but the rest had been laid waste into the vast areas required for the mass jostling and cruising of a Friday or Saturday night. Round tables with beaten copper tops were aligned in front of the leather-covered tram which ran along the walls. In season, a fire burnt in the grate, the adjustable gas jets failing to kindle the synthetic logs. When it was lit the flames showed up the hundreds of fag-ends that had unthinkingly been thrown in.

The pub was at its least inspiriting in the early evening. Hardy regulars, resigned to hours of waiting, lounged at the bar or filled in time with the *Evening Standard*, inching their way down pints of lager, glowering at any newcomers and exchanging greetings in tones that suggested that things were pretty bad. And so they were. The Volunteer was a second-division gay pub, and while the glamorous and fashionable were chatting each other up in King's Cross or St Martin's Lane, a mood of provincial neglect settled over it. It seemed, as I bought my bottle of Guinness and retired to a corner, like the waiting-room of a station on a branch line where the last train was not expected for quite some time.

One of the barmen, very thin in very tight jeans, and with a lugubrious, made-up manner, wandered across to the door and stood looking out over the pavement, a lust-quenching advertisement to any potential drinker. 'Startin' to rain,' he said to no one in particular as he turned back into the bar. James, of course, had an umbrella and trotted in a minute or two later looking very respectable. He had just come from surgery.

'You look tired,' he said. 'Too much sodomy, I should say.' And then, as if in surgery, picking up my Guinness bottle: 'Take this tonic twice a day and have a complete rest: we'll soon have you back to normal.'

It was charming to see him, though looking (worthily, selflessly) tired himself. I didn't comment on this, for his overwork and his unfairly long spells on call depressed him and were making him look older. He sat beside me with his drink, and I ran my hand over his head, bald now to half-way back. He smiled, and put a kiss on my cheekbone.

'How are the ill?' I asked.

'Oh, fine,' he said.

'Anything interesting?' The bizarre things that people said and did in the consulting room were a staple of our conversation.

'Not really. The woman with the stones came back. And I had a lad in this morning with the most enormous donger.' James was obsessed by big cocks, many of which seemed to pass through his hands in his professional capacity – though all too few, I suspected, in his private one.

'How big?' I enquired.

'Ooh . . .' he gestured with his hands, like a fisherman – 'in its flaccid condition that is. Quite unbearably hideous youth, alas. He seemed to think there was something wrong with it – so I told him to go to the clinic.' He took a deep draught of beer. 'Fan-tastic cock, though,' he added wistfully.

I chuckled. 'You'd have been proud of me the other day,' I said, 'when I did a very heroic deed and saved the life of a queer peer.' And I related the incident in the Kensington Gardens bog. 'It was all due to you, darling,' I said. 'I remembered what you do on trains.'

'I'm impressed and proud,' James said. 'But a Lord – a Baron, or something bigger do you suppose?'

'Looked like a Baron to me,' I said – and with a silly smirk, 'anyway you wouldn't find a Viscount cottaging . . .'

'Not yet, you wouldn't,' James tartly rejoined. 'Has he been in touch since?'

'He has not. A man just came along when the ambulance arrived and ran about saying "Oh dear, my Lord" and that kind of thing. I imagine we may never find out who it was.' I looked at James. 'But to think you do that all the time. God, I felt wonderful afterwards . . .'

'Yes; you get over that, you'll find, should you ever do it again. But what about this boy? I suppose you'd better tell me.'

I must have bored James for many hours with the pitiless recollection of every detail of my sexual encounters. Often his response to my saying 'I met this fucking wonderful man last night' would be 'Thank you, I *don't* want to hear about it' – though this could never quite forestall at least a synopsis of the main events. The routine was a joke now, though behind it lay all his inhibitions, the uninvestigated secrecy of his own private life. Being a doctor, too, made him circumspect, as well as giving him a kind of authority for his lack of adventurousness. And even when I knew he had had some fling he would never mention it himself, so that lone events, which I suspected to be exceptional, could equally be interpreted as typical of a thriving sex life. Somehow he had made it impossible to ask him directly.

'What is there to say?' I for once replied. 'Except: total bliss, endless fuck, suck, schmuck.'

'You mean he's stupid.'

'He's no Einstein, I grant you.'

'So what do you talk about all the time?'

'I don't know, really. We have a kind of baby-talk – except all the words are rude – and we giggle a lot, and generally praise each other's personal appearance. We had a meal at the Testudo one night, and the conversation did run a bit thin. And I did something rather terrible.' I looked down in mock-confusion.

'Don't tell me.' He looked at me narrowly. 'Not Massimo?'

'Wasn't it too frightful of me? But I had to have him . . .'

'My God!' squealed James. 'You absolute bastard. How ever did you manage? I don't want to know.'

'We just slipped out the back, *not* in the lav, but actually in the sort of yard with the crates. Ever so quick.'

'But what about poor little whatsisname?'

'Arthur? Oh, he was sitting there waiting for me, all sleepy and unsuspecting. Actually, Massimo said he wanted to have him too, but I did draw the line there.'

'Was it like we always imagined?'

'Mm, was rather. Everything on the menu, you know; full helpings.' I leered helplessly. 'But I should have a go some time – I'm sure he's anybody's . . .'

'Thanks!'

'No, I mean, I'm sure there'd be no problem.'

'They do say, waiters . . .' murmured James, in a tone of smothered excitement. 'What's Arthur's . . . member like, incidentally?'

'Entirely delightful. Not your kind of thing, perhaps – short, stocky, ruthlessly circumcised, and incredibly resilient and characterful.'

James let a pause fall in which the brio of my testimonial edged towards embarrassment and then said, 'So you're in love with him, are you?' I took a professional sip of Guinness.

'I can't be, actually,' I admitted. 'We couldn't sit down and listen to

Idomeneo and feel a deep spiritual bond. It must just be an infatuation. Sometimes I don't feel I know him at all, which adds to the poignancy of the thing no end. And then Holland Park and my place is all a completely new world to him. He lives with all his family in a tower block. I said wouldn't his mother worry about where he was, but he said he often didn't go back home. They don't have a phone, so he couldn't let them know. But I imagine he's gone back there today – he had to go and sign on. But' – I drew round to it – 'you're quite right: it can't last. I don't want it to really – it's just been a heavenly week.'

We strolled off under James's umbrella to Westbourne Grove. One of the slight bores about James was that he was a vegetarian – so going out to dinner with him required careful planning. In the event we had a delicious Belpoori that cost almost nothing, served by a boy James ogled with a quite new kind of forwardness, while the rain lashed down outside. Perhaps it was the rain that made us reminisce, about beautiful Oxford contemporaries and how they had become bankers, or put on weight, or got married.

It was still raining when we left, so I suppressed my fondness for the Underground and took a lighted cab that was approaching. The cabby looked unimpressionable as I rather ostentatiously kissed James goodbye, and let my hand run down over his backside. He was so lovable, shy, manly, I couldn't see why he wasn't adored more, or more often. Yet if I couldn't do it there might be a reason others couldn't: he didn't project sex enough, he was too subtle a taste for the instant world of clubs and bars. We had slept together once or twice, but we were both funny with each other and did no more than kiss and cuddle.

'See you when all this is over, darling,' I said, and nipped from under his umbrella into the taxi, looking, as I always instinctively do, at the cabby's hand on the wheel to see if he wore a wedding-ring. I had had some good experiences with cabbies, and even straight ones could reach such a pitch of frustration, stuck in their cab and driving around mindlessly for hundreds of miles every day, that they were glad to come in for half an hour and talk filth, or you could show them a video and suck them off. This particular man, however, offered no temptation, and seemed to have become grafted into the grimy, bulging box of his cab.

As we left the crowded, shop-brightened streets behind us and crossed into the exclusive quiet of Holland Park I yawned and looked out with pleasure at the deserted pavements, glistening where a street-lamp stood, the overhanging budding branches of trees in front gardens, the unthinking stability which wealth lent the small mansions behind them, where occasional windows, with curtains it was felt unnecessary to draw, revealed books reaching to coved ceilings, figures holding glasses moving about, discreet lighting picking out pictures in dull gold frames.

I paid off the cabby at the gate, and jogged across the short gravel sweep to the door at the side of the dark house which gave access to the stairs to my apartment. A small lamp glowed above it, and the wet dripped down from the bare twigs of the creeper which surrounded the recessed porchway. My heart leapt when I saw there was a figure slumped in the shadow on the ground, sheltering from the rain.

It was with an unsteady lurch into jocularity that I said, 'Arfer, what the fuck are you doing there?'

'Man, I thought you was never coming,' he said in a tense voice, and sniffed heavily. 'I been sitting here fucking ages waiting for you.'

'But I didn't know you were coming back tonight.'

He didn't reply but stood up and moved towards me. I felt his heavy breath on my face, and annoyance that he was there. I suppose it was because he had frightened me. He gripped my upper arms with his long, strong hands, and pressed himself against me. The rain fell on us, but as I lifted my hands to embrace him, I realised that he was already soaked through, his body warming the damp clothes just as they were chilling him.

'Baby you're really wet,' I said in a practical tone. 'You should have said you were coming.' I freed myself and felt for my keys. 'Come in and take everything off,' I exclaimed, adjusting to the idea that he had returned, and not unmoved that he couldn't keep away. I stepped past him and unlocked the door, flicking on the light, and passing into the hallway at the foot of the back-stairs. He hesitated, then followed me in, his feet squelching in his sodden trainers, and pushed the door to.

I turned back to smile at him, already full of maternal goodwill. 'Baby,' I breathed . . . 'what the fuck have you done.' He sniffed, and ran the back of his hand across his nose and mouth. He winced under the light. There was a broad cut across his right cheek, clogged and dirty with blood. A purplish patina of blood could be made out on his black throat. Beneath a shabby old cardigan the upper right side of the pink silk shirt I had given him was soaked in blood, its new colour itself bleeding through the rain-wet material. I felt frightened again, unwittingly involved in something bad. There was something repulsive and careless about him, his nose clogged with bloody snot and his eyes tired from crying (though he tried to disguise this weakness with a mutinous look). But at the same time he was utterly defenceless: everything about him spoke of need.

We went upstairs. I felt relieved that no one was in the main part of the house. He followed me wearily, the wet corduroy chafing his thighs; I looked down hastily at the turn of the stair and saw his blurred brown footprints on the carpet.

In the flat, I helped him take off his clothes. He groaned and ached as I pulled his arm back to slide the shirt off. 'My fucking shoulder man,' he half-shouted, and I passed my trembling fingertips gently over his back and he breathed in suddenly when I brushed a bruise that was mysteriously welling up in the blackness of his skin. He was shivering and chilled, his lower lip hanging miserably. I pulled off his shoes and stood them on the doormat, becoming more practical, concerned only with immediate necessities. At the same time he grew more passive and inert. I pulled down his zip and tugged his tight, rain-slimed corduroys and his little briefs down over his ass and thighs; he managed to lift each foot as I pulled the wet, resisting trousers off, kneeling in front of him and glancing at his shrunken cock and his scrotum shrivelled up tight with cold and fear.

I propelled him to the bathroom and sat him down before attempting to clean and dress his wound. It was very painful, but he said nothing beyond the occasional ouch. I used some lint that I found in the cupboard, and stuck it down with several small Band-aids. When James was back I would ring him. I ran a hot bath and got Arthur to sit in it whilst I gently sponged water down his back, washed his flat muscular chest, lifted his arms and soaped his armpits and sides. Then I slid my hand between his legs and stroked his cock and balls. He lay back in the long, deep tub as if relaxing.

'Darling, what happened?'

'I got in a fight.' He looked at me crossly but sorrily. 'I wouldn't have come back here, only I didn't know where else to go. I didn't see why you should get mixed up with all this.'

'Who did you get in a fight with?'

'My brother – Harold. My big brother. He got this knife, he cut me with it – the fucking bastard cut me with it.' He looked at me with a kind of tired outrage. 'I can't go back there no more, my brother'll murder me. Only he don't know where I am, 'ere. I'll have to stay 'ere – for a bit, Will.' He splashed his hands down in the water. Blood was seeping out again through the lint of his dressing. He looked lop-sided and comical, and intensely distressed. Tears ran freely down his face and over the waterproof pink of the Band-aids. I dabbed at them with the sponge, and he shook his head, and winced, and winced again at the twisting of his wound that wincing caused. In my other hand, under the water, in spite of himself and his misery, his cock was hard. I wanked him slowly, the ripples slapping rhythmically against the side of the tub.

'Will,' he said, as if he must get it out before succumbing, 'I killed my brother's mate.'

2

I finished my fifty lengths and sat for a while at the shallow end with my feet in the water, my goggles pushed back on my head like a smoky second pair of eyes. Phil had come down from the gym and put on a brief and laborious display of butterfly: giving up towards the end of his last length he made some perfunctory strokes, then stood up and waded to the edge. I nodded and smiled at him.

'All right?' he said, as if he did not want to talk to me, or did not know how. I watched him in profile: a strong pleasant face which might barely change between leaving school and middle age, an incurious, dependable look. But he was coming on well. His tits now bulged out impressively; and as he raised his hands to his temples and pushed back his wet hair, his biceps doubled smoothly, sleek as coupling animals. He was the sort of boy who might be in the army, except that his weight-training suggested a labour towards some private image of himself, a solitary perfection. As often happens when I know someone else fancies a person I might otherwise have ignored, I realised that Bill's taste for him had made me want the boy too, and I looked at him lustfully and competitively.

It was getting late. I had deliberately taken my time in the gym, and spent a while joining in with some Malaysian boys, very supple and clever, who were training on the parallel bars. Old Andrews was coaching them – a man who still bore the stiffness of the drill square in his straight carriage and wiry limbs, and who, by a strange anomaly in the democratising ambience of the Corry, was always known simply as Andrews: Andrews himself wore this as the badge of an old-school sense of equality, though it sometimes sounded, in the mouths of the boys who, vaulting and balancing, literally passed through his hands, like an old-school formula of command. He was a difficult, demanding man, from whom those who used the gym a lot could win a tight-lipped affection. This evening his discipline was what I needed after the anxiety of home, and the oriental boys, with their intuitive sense of space and balance, and their wide, courteous smiles, provided a brief antidote to Arthur and our joint troubles. Then the nearly deserted pool, the water lapping at the edge, had tired me and calmed me more. I watched Phil spring up out of the bath, shoot me a little look, self-conscious but somehow, I felt, pleased, and amble off to the stairs. His trunks were becoming small for the weight he was putting on in the ass.

It would have been trite to follow him too soon, and I kicked about for a minute more. As I did so a head approached, old and large, held above the water, but given a sinister vacuity by pink-tinted goggles and a white rubber bathing-cap. Its progress was extremely slow, and each time it rode up and pale, heavy shoulders were seen, a weak opening of the arms, a nugatory kicking of the legs, had evidently taken place. When it got very close it submerged completely for several seconds, then came up looking at me, as it had clearly been doing beneath the water, stopped dead and lurched up to the full height of a plump, dripping, wheezing old man, with smooth, drooping breasts. When he pushed the goggles up on to his brow I knew for certain that it was his Lordship.

My curiosity about him delayed my surprise that he should already be out and taking exercise only ten days after a cardiac arrest. And on the other hand something abnormal in him made me feel that all his manifestations would be unpredictable and irreconcilable with each other. He stared at me, or through me, and I wondered what to say, to what extent recognition was taking place. He doesn't know at all who I am, I thought; he's just looking at a pretty young man; he would hardly be able to remember me. And to confirm this he seemed suddenly not to be there himself, appeared to die out of the scene in a moment. He turned and made off slowly to the steps at the corner of the bath; Nigel, the attendant, barely looked up from his book as the old boy hauled himself out and moved with heavy, wavering steps to the stairs. I gave him time to get up them, imagining already a further incident like that in the Kensington Gardens lavatory.

The shower-room was in its busy last shift: one of the sudden and unpredictable fluctuations in water temperature occurred as I came in, and there were cat-like yells as naked men leapt aside from the scalding jets. Darting movements of hands tried to regulate the taps, steam filled the air, and through it an impression of Bacchic pinkness was suffused, the colour of Anglo-Saxon flesh flushed by just tolerable heat. Warm from exercise I showered in water that was almost cold, and observed the strange variety of physical forms which were making their lingering transit back to the clean, clothed world.

His Lordship was upset by the temperature of his shower, and made feeble efforts to adjust it. He looked unhappy, the rubber cap, which he kept on, intensifying the babyish whiteness of his figure. He took tiny steps back and forth, and peered around with his mouth slightly open, revealing his lower teeth à l'anglaise. Beneath his round belly candy-striped bathing shorts sagged dispiritedly. It struck me I might often have seen him here before but, so selective was my vision, never paid him any attention until he had fallen down in front of me and made his claim to be taken care of.

Now he had chanced on one of the standard hard-on sessions of the shower, as on both sides of him and across the room three queens sported horizontal members which they turned round from time to time to conceal or to display, barely exchanging looks as they revolved. The old man took no interest in this activity, knowing perhaps from long experience that it rarely meant anything or led anywhere, was a brief and helpless surrender to the forcing-house of the shower. In a few seconds the hard-on might pass from one end of the room to the other with the foolish perfection of a Busby Berkeley routine.

I was interested to see what effect this would have on Phil, who was washing in a thorough, slightly over-hearty way; but though he glanced shyly at what was going on, his own simple little cock remained unstirred. A couple of Cypriot men, who talked loudly and securely in Greek, old friends with thick moustaches and frames rectangular with muscle, shampooed flossily opposite me; and some greyer specimens, voyeurs who came only for the showers, mooned hungrily at the other end of the room.

I was quite brisk, and followed his Lordship out to the drying area. He had a rough old towel, the grey of institutional laundering. He gathered it into a knot and dabbed at himself with it, breathing in a manner that was nearly a whistle, and seemed always about to become a well-known Mozartian tune. I paced around drying myself, then tied my towel round my waist in a kind of Polynesian skirt and couldn't resist saying to him, with a step forward and a bid for his attention:

'Are you feeling better now?'

'Hello, hello,' he said, not at all taken aback. 'Goodness me . . .' he looked around as if something interesting had just started happening somewhere else.

'I was surprised to see you swimming so soon after your . . . accident.'

'Like to swim you know,' he said promptly. 'Floating around in lovely, lovely water.' I waited for some recognition of the drift of my remarks. He wouldn't really look at me, though. 'Do you know, I've been swimming here for over forty years? Oh yes – up and down. I expect I've swum right round the globe by now – if you added it all together, you know. Splish-splosh, flippety-flop!' I identified already the abstracted tone with which he produced these inane jingling phrases, as if to prevent objections being made by filling up the space and time with nonsense. Yet somehow, at this stage, I wasn't going to let him escape.

'I was there, you know,' I remarked factually, 'in Kensington Gardens, when you were taken ill.'

He looked at me with a suddenly summoned attentiveness. 'I'm quite over all that nasty business now,' he said patiently.

'In fact,' I pursued, 'it was I who looked after you, you know . . .'

This seemed to knock him rather, and he started to shamble off into the changing-room and then to think better of it, coming back to me in a sideways manner. His eyes ran down my front and he looked at my long, gappy toes as he said 'You were the chappy that, er, puff-puff, bang-bang . . . I say, goodness me. My dear fellow!' He did not know what to do.

'Anyway,' I said, disappointed of a show of gratitude, 'I'm glad to see you've recovered' – and I moved away feeling foolish and a little cross.

It was the year of Trouble for Men, a talc and aftershave lotion of peculiar suggestiveness that, without any noticeable advertising, had permeated the gay world in a matter of weeks. Every bar and locker-room hummed with it, you picked it up on the Tube or waiting to cross the road. It was in the air and, had it been advertised, it could have been called decadent and irresistible. Re-entering the changing room I passed through a cloud of it, registering at first its quite bracing, outdoor quality before discovering the paler bluey-green femininity within.

I found my locker that evening was next to Maurice – a lean black boxer, straight, and one of the most attractive men in the Corry, with a high forehead and a mischievous, sentimental expression. I asked him about a match that was coming up next week, and he made a few feint swipes at me as he talked. I involuntarily flinched a centimetre or two, and my stomach muscles clenched. 'Don't worry, mate,' he said, 'I won't hit you – hard,' and he grinned and cuffed me round the ear. If only life were always so simple, I thought, as he tugged off his singlet and his Lordship, looking perturbedly about, came back into view at the end of the alley of lockers.

'I really am most frightfully obliged,' he said loudly when he saw me, and I readied myself, half-dressed, to conduct this conversation under the casual scrutiny of all the other men who were sitting and standing around us.

'Don't mention it,' I said brightly, embarrassed by the crass *double entendre* that might publicly arise. He came up closer, and Maurice stepped aside with a droll raised eyebrow.

'See you, then,' he said as he went off to the shower.

'What is your name?' his Lordship enquired, and then, with the forced Christian candour of one who has learnt the ways of teams and charities, 'I am Charles.'

'William,' I replied (though I am not often called that).

'William, I want to show you my gratitude. Heavens!' he added theatrically. 'It is to you I owe my presence here.'

'There's really no need. I did what anyone would have done.'

He raised a finger and knocked it on my chest. 'Lunch,' he said, nodding his head. 'You'll come to luncheon – my Club, nothing extraordinary, but it will do.'

'Well, that's very kind of you . . .' I felt drawn because I thought he was interesting and might have a distracting story to tell. If he were a nuisance I needn't see him again: there was also Arthur and the odder story of home and love and guilt, and I didn't know that I wanted to take on anything new.

'I think you should come on Friday,' he said. Then: 'Who knows, I may be dead by Friday. Perhaps better make it tomorrow – I should still be quick then.' It was a bizarre usage, which it took me a second or two to see; I had a fleeting image of him chasing me round a huge mahogany table.

'Well, that would be very nice.'

'Nice for me, William,' he insisted.

It seemed to be settled in his mind, and he wandered away holding his towel in front of him as though he expected to bump into something. I had to seek him out when I had finished dressing, to enquire which Club it was and what name would find him.

At home it was always very hot; the central heating throbbed away as if we feared exposure, and often, though high up and not overlooked, we kept the curtains drawn in the daytime, only a mild bloom of pinkish light penetrating into the rooms from outside. The creation of this climate was barely conscious, as people in crisis habitually transform their surroundings, the miserable sitting cold through the dusk without turning lights on, and the endangered, like Arthur and I, craving rosiness and security.

The penumbra helped us to hide from each other. As soon as the new terms were forced upon us by Arthur's coming back he must have felt as much as I did a sinking of the heart at our incompatibility. Inflicted with this new anxiety, we were afraid to annoy or burden each other. He spent much of the time asleep or sitting in a chair; and he bathed long and often. Very young and worried, he seemed to fear my resentment, and his gestures towards me took on a nervous respect; I would go to the dining-room and read alone, and he would come in with a cup of tea and touch me on the arm. If I had not been so fiercely and sexually in love with him, these days would have been utterly intolerable. And even so there were spells of repugnance, both at him and at my own susceptibility. Sex took on an almost purgative quality, as if after hours of inertia and evasion we could burn off our unspoken fears in vehement, wordless activity. Sex came to justify his presence there, to confirm that we were not just two strangers trapped together by a fateful mistake.

The immediate concern, the first night, had been to get him patched up. I lied to James on the phone, and felt the sudden sadness of complicity. I said that we had been fooling around in the kitchen and there had been an accident with a knife. He came over promptly in his car, and I went down to let him in. He adjusted with only slight awkwardness to his professional role, with a practical briskness which did not quite conceal his curiosity. Arthur was hanging about in my dressing-gown, apprehensive of a doctor; when I introduced them I assumed James would find him attractive, although the makeshift dressing on his cheek spoilt the general impression.

It had to be stitched and there was an injection. I watched, out of the way, James's absorption in the intimate, serious work, running through a long series of subcutaneous stitches and drawing the skin neatly together above. That way, he said, the scar would be smaller. Arthur shot me little tear-whelmed glances as it took place, and I looked on, firm and encouraging, as a parent might over some necessary ordeal of its child. I was touched, too, by James's expertise, his deft, slender hands holding Arthur's head, his intent application to a task that I could never perform for him. When it was done Arthur looked as if deservedly reproved, past the worst now, his face rueful and very swollen.

James washed his hands and said, 'I'll have that whisky.' As I poured it for him he shook his head disbelievingly. 'Don't do that again, Will,' he recommended. 'Bloody terrifies me.' I was struck by the uncertainty of it all: he clearly thought we had had a fight and made his own interpretation of what was itself a lie. It was almost amusing how far he was from the truth. 'I won't ask you how it happened.'

'Oh . . .' I waved my arm about. 'You know.' I saw that though appalled by it all he was also impressed: I took on the spurious glamour of a wildly passionate person, my dwindling agitation being read as the wake of a violent erotic upheaval. Arthur had gone to the bedroom, and I longed to tell James everything, to clear myself at once. Yet I feared his advice, the necessity of action it would entail. I remained standing up and kept the conversation short and superficial, so that he would have felt embarrassed to make any personal observations on the boy he'd heard so much about. I closed down on James in a graceless, scared way.

But it was once these practical measures had been taken that the impractical day after day of Arthur and me in the flat began. The only thing to do was nothing. Life this week was a black parody of life the week before. Then we had stayed in for pleasure; now we could not risk going out. I was free, but Arthur did not dare go out, and was nervous to be left alone. If the phone rang he looked ill with anxiety. Ordinary sounds, such as distant police sirens in Holland Park Avenue, took on for both of us a retributory grimness. I was shocked to find that my heart raced when I heard them, and the look we exchanged as they died away must have told him how frightened I was.

It had been wonderful after three days of this to go to the Corry, and when I got back I made no mention of Lord Nantwich and my own adventures. I saw at once that their secrecy would be essential to me. They were my right to a privacy outside this forced sharing of my home. Stepping into the roasting heat of the flat I found Arthur restive and relieved to see me. He came up and held me. He had altered his appearance in my absence, and undone his braids, though his hair still retained much of its former tightly combed and twisted nature and jutted out in wild spirals. The swelling of his face was going down and he had begun to look beautiful again, the protective dressing on his cheek almost decorative. Yet as he stood there in my old red jersey and my army surplus fatigues I felt a kind of hatred for him and his need to disguise himself in my things.

There was a pretty bad half-hour after that, when I was not in control of myself. I poured myself a drink, though I did not give him one – and he didn't seem to mind. My whole wish was to throw things around, make a storm to dispel the stagnant heat, assert myself. Yet I found myself fastidiously tidying up, tight-lipped, not looking at him. He followed me helplessly around, at first retailing jokes from the television, dialogue from *Star Trek*, but then falling silent. He was confused, wanted to be ready to do what I wanted, but found he could only annoy me further. Then I hurled the stack of newspapers I was collecting across the floor and went for him – pulled the trousers down over his narrow hips without undoing them, somehow tackled him onto the carpet, and after a few seconds' brutal fumbling fucked him cruelly. He let out little compacted shouts of pain, but I snarled at him to shut up and with fine submission he bit them back.

Afterwards I left him groaning on the floor and went into the bathroom. I remember looking at myself, pink, excited, horrified, in the mirror.

I took all my clothes off and after a few minutes went back into the sitting-room. I don't know if it was just his confused readiness to take what I gave him, or if he really understood the absolute tenderness that I now felt for him as I picked him up and dumped him on the sofa; but he held me very tight as I lay down beside him. I was the only person he had; the very melodrama of the case had repelled me before, but for a while I allowed myself to accept it. I had been disgusted by his need for me, but now it moved me, and I burbled into his ear about how I loved him. 'I love you too – darling,' he said. It was a word that he could never have used before, and the tears poured down my face and smudged all over his, as we lay there and hugged, rocking from side to side.

There were several occasions of this kind, when I was exposed by my own mindless randiness and helpless sentimentality. I made a point of going out to the baths each day, and while I was there, talking to friends, exercising, looking at other men, I could see with more detachment how these scenes weakened my authority. I was eight years older than Arthur, and our affair had started as a crazy fling with all the beauty for me of his youngness and blackness. Now it became a murky business, a coupling in which we both exploited each other, my role as protector mined by the morbid emotion of protectiveness. I saw him becoming more and more my slave and my toy, in a barely conscious abasement which excited me even as it pulled me down.

The Corry featured in these days as a lucid interlude – with an institutional structure that time in the flat entirely lacked. I tended to stay late or go to a bar afterwards, not for sex, but for the company of strangers and for talk about sport or music. Walking back up the drive and feeling for my keys I even felt reluctance to plunge back into my private life, its unsterilised warmth in which sensation seemed both heightened and degraded. Yet going to the bathroom to hang up my wet towel and swimming trunks, I could be touched unexpectedly by the sight of Arthur's few possessions, and his muddied cords, stiff where they had dried, tangled up with my silk shirt on the airing-cupboard floor, had me sighing and wincing at their pathos – even if, the next morning, I wished I had never seen them and that I had myself to myself. Perhaps we should have burnt them: the empty, crumpled tubes of his trousers, the blood-stained pink of the shirt, were evidence of a kind. We were such inexpert criminals.

At the Corry, too, I could more easily examine the question, which we barely asked each other, and certainly never answered, of what we were going to do. The present impasse was unbearable, its resolution unimaginable. I insisted on Arthur telling me what had happened and why, but though we went through it several times a strange opacity came over him, the facts seemed not to tie up. I determined that his brother, like Arthur, had no work, and had got his girlfriend pregnant, that their father found out Arthur was gay, that there had been fights, that the brother, Harold, had a friend who was a drug-dealer, who had been inside more than once, and who had got Harold involved in the business, that the friend had stolen money Arthur was saving in his mattress in the room the brothers still had to share, that he had denied it, that there had been a fight, and that it had gone desperately wrong, that Harold, uncertain who to side with, had drawn a knife, Arthur had been wounded but had grabbed the weapon and, in one sudden, unintended, irrevocable moment, had slashed the friend's throat – all this on a late rainy afternoon in a ruinous house in the East End, bombed out in the Blitz and still standing. This last detail, as if to give verisimilitude to an otherwise incoherent narrative, had been something he had learned at school. But the other details, produced with fluctuating expressions of sulkiness and hopelessness, a lurid compendium of miseries, were unstable from day to day. I felt I pressed him to the edge of his articulacy, and at the same time as I sought to protect him appeared to him dangerously inquisitive, threatening to topple the beliefs and superstitions which were the private structure of his life, and which had never before been exposed.

The one thing I did not question was that he had killed this man, Tony; but to accept this was to admit that I knew nothing about how murder worked in the real world. No reports in the papers? No newsflash on the radio? Arthur knew about these things from experience: Tony was a wanted man, a criminal treated with violence by the police and revulsion by the older community. And then it seemed that violence against a black would rarely reach the national press, that radio silence could envelop the tragedies of the world from which he came. This silence also intensified his fear. It made the prospects now as uncertain to him as the background of the event was to me. Were the police looking for Arthur? How had Arthur's parents reacted? Would they, while throwing him off, silently thwart the course of justice? Or would they, or Harold at least, independently seek him out to administer some justice of their own?

It did not take me long to fear the consequences to myself of any of these possible events. If it had not been for our week of love I would perhaps have been frightened of Arthur too; but I was never even critical of his crime. A rare, unjustified trust kept me on his side. Even so, that part of the road, with its parked cars and spring trees, which could be seen from the windows took on an ominous feel. I scanned it as one looks at a photograph with a glass to make out half-decipherable details, but its mundanity was unaltered: it rained and dried, wind blew scraps of litter across, children walked dogs – dawdling, looking in at the houses, nosey for details, but only as people always, routinely are. I'm not sure what form I expected the threat to take; a police car actually stopping outside, a powerfully built black man darting up the drive? I had several dreams of siege, in which the house became a frail slatted box, shadowy and exquisite within, the walls all cracked and bleached louvres which fell to powder as one brushed against them. In one dream Arthur and I were there, and others, old school friends, a gaggle of black kids from the Shaft, my grandfather tearful and hopeless. We knew we had no chance of surviving the violence that surrounded us, closing in fast, and I was gripped by a nauseating terror. I woke up in the certain knowledge that I was about to die: the bedsprings were ticking from the sprinting vehemence of my heartbeat. I didn't dare go back to sleep and after a while sat up and read, while Arthur slept deeply beside me. It took days to lose the mood of the dream, and its power to prickle my scalp. The neighbourhood seemed eerily impregnated with it, and its passing made possible a new confidence, as if a sentence had been lifted.

That Thursday I had my lunch with Lord Nantwich. I told Arthur I had a long-standing arrangement and he made a point of saying, 'Okay man – I mean you've got to lead your own life: I'll be all right here.' I realised I'd been apologising in a way and I was relieved by his practical reply.

'You can always have some bread and cheese, and you can finish off that cold ham in the fridge. Anything you want me to get you?'

'No, ta.' He stood and smiled crookedly. I didn't kiss him but just patted him on the bum as I slipped out.

I'd put a suit on, smarter perhaps than I needed to be, but I enjoyed its protective conformity. I so rarely dressed up, and not having to wear a suit for work I seldom took any of mine off their hangers. My father had had me kitted out with morning suits and evening dress as I grew up and I had always relished the handsomeness of dark, formal clothes, wing-collars, waistcoats over braces: I looked quite the star of my sister's wedding when the pictures appeared in *Tatler*. But I rarely wore this stuff. I had always been a bit of a peacock – or rather, whatever animal has brightly coloured legs, a flamingo perhaps.

I was a bit late so I took a cab – which also solved the problem of finding Wicks's. My father was a member of the Garrick and my grandfather a member of the Athenæum, but otherwise I was unsure about London Clubs. I could easily confuse the Reform and the Travellers', and might well have wandered into three or four of them this morning before hitting on Wicks's. Cabbies, through a mixture of practicality and snobbery, always know which of those neo-classical portals is which.

'I've come to see Lord Nantwich,' I told the porter in his dusty glass cabin. 'William Beckwith.' And I was told to make my way upstairs to the smoking-room. As I climbed the imposing stairway, lined with blackened, half-familiar portraits, a mild apprehensiveness mingled with a mood of irresponsibility in my heart. I had no idea what we might talk about.

Entering the smoking-room I felt like an intruder in a film, who has coshed an orderly and, disguised in his coat, enters a top-secret establishment, in this case a home for people kept artificially alive. Sunk in leather armchairs or taking almost imperceptible steps across the Turkey carpets, men of quite fantastic seniority were sleeping or preparing to sleep. The impression was of grey whiskers and very old-fashioned cuts of suiting, watch-chains and heavy handmade shoes that would certainly see their wearers out. Some of those who were sitting down showed an inch or two of white calf between turn-up and suspenders. Fortunately, perhaps in recognition of the dangers involved, almost no one was actually smoking; nonetheless the room had a sour, masculine smell, qualified by the sweetness of the polish with which fire-irons, tables and trophies were brought to a blinding sheen.

Lord Nantwich was sitting at the far end of the room, in front of one of the windows which looked down on the Club's small and colourless garden. In this context, unlike that in which I had last seen him, he appeared almost middle-aged, robust and rosy-cheeked. I approached him self-consciously, although I reached his chair before his gaze, which wandered halfway between the cornice and a book he had open on his knee, distinguished me.

'Aah . . .' he said.

'Charles?'

'My dear fellow – William – goodness me, gracious me.' He sat forward and held out a hand – his left – but did not struggle to get up. We shared an unconventional handshake. 'Turn that chip-chop round.' I looked about uncertainly, but saw from his repeated gesture that he meant the chair behind him, which I trundled across so as to sit in quarter-profile to him, and then dropped into it, the elegance of the movement overwhelmed by the way the springing of the chair swallowed me up.

'Comfy, aren't they,' he said with approval. '*Jolly* comfy, actually.' I hauled myself forward so as to perch more decorously and nervously on the front bar. 'You must be dying for a tifty. Christ! It's quarter to one.' He raised his right arm and waved it about, and a white-jacketed steward with the air of a senile adolescent wheeled a trolley across. 'More tifty for me, Percy; and for my guest – William, what's it to be?'

I felt some vague pressure on me to choose sherry, though I regretted the choice when I saw how astringently pale it was, and when Lord Nantwich's tifty turned out to be a hefty tumbler of virtually neat gin. Percy poured the two drinks complacently, jotted the score on a little pad and wheeled away with a 'Thank you, m'lord,' in which the 'thank you' was clipped almost into inaudibility. I thought how much he must know about all these old codgers, and what cynical reflections must take place behind his impassive, possibly made-up features.

'So, William, your very good health!' Nantwich raised his glass almost to his mouth. 'I say, I hope it wasn't too horrible . . .?'

'Your continuing good health,' I replied, able only to ignore the question, which drew improper attention to what had passed between us; though I also felt a certain pride in what I had done, in a British manner wanting it to be commended, but in silence.

'What a way to be introduced, my goodness! Of course I know nothing about you,' he added, as if he might be exposing himself, though morally this time, to some degree of danger.

'Well I know nothing about you,' I hastened to reassure him.

'You didn't look me up in the book or anything?'

'I don't think I have a book to look you up in.' My father, I thought, would have looked him up straight away; in Debrett, as in *Who's Who*, the volumes in his study always fell open at the Beckwith page, as if he had been checking up credentials that he might forget, or that were too remarkable to be readily believed.

'Well that's splendid,' Nantwich declared. 'We've still got everything to find out. What utter fun. When you get to be an old wibbly-wobbly, as one, alas, now is, you don't often get the chance to have a go at someone absolutely fresh!' He took a mouthful of gin, confiding in the glass as he did so a remark I could barely make out as it drowned, but which sounded like 'Quite a corker, too.'

'It's an agreeable room, this, isn't it,' he observed with one of his unannounced changes of tack.

'Mmm,' I just about agreed. 'That's an interesting picture.' I tilted my head towards a large and, I hoped, mythological canvas, all but the foreground of which receded into the murk of two centuries or so of disregard. All that one saw were garland-clad, heavy, naked figures.

'Yes. It's a Poussin,' said Nantwich decisively, turning his gaze away. It so evidently was not a Poussin that I wondered whether to take him up, whether he knew or cared what it was; if he were testing me or merely producing the philistine *on-dit* of the Club.

'I think it could do with cleaning,' I suggested. 'It appears to be happening in the middle of the night, whatever it is.'

'Ooh, you don't want to go cleaning everything,' Nantwich assured me. 'Most pictures would be better if they were a damned sight dirtier.' Mildly dismayed, I treated it as a joke. 'Bah!' he went on. 'You get these fellows – women mostly – doing all the old pictures up. No knowing what they'll find. And then they look like fakes afterwards.'

I saw he was dribbling gin from his glass onto the carpet. He touched my outstretched hand. 'Whoopsy!' he said, as if I were being a nuisance. His gaze drifted into the middle distance and I too looked about, a little at a loss for talk.

'Actually, I love art,' he announced. 'One day, if we get on quite well, I'll show you my house. You're keen on art, I should say?'

'I do have quite a lot of time for it,' I conceded; then, fearing he might think my tone was rude, I enlarged a figure of speech into an observation. 'I mean, I don't have a job, and I have plenty of time to go to galleries and look at pictures.'

'You're not married or anything are you?'

'No, nothing,' I assured him.

'Too young, I know. You've been up to university, of course?'

'I was at Oxford, yes – at Corpus – reading History.'

He drank this in with some more gin. 'Do you like girls at all?' he asked.

'Yes, I like them quite a lot really,' I insisted.

'There are chaps who don't care for them, you know. Simply can't abide them. Can't stand the sight of them, their titties and their big sit-upons, even the smell of them.' He looked down the room authoritatively to where Percy was dispensing Sanatogen to a striking likeness of the older Gladstone. 'Andrews, for instance, cannot tolerate them.'

It took me a moment to work this out. 'In the gym?' I said. 'Yes, I'm not surprised – he seems very much a man's man. You must know Andrews then,' I lamely concluded. But I had lost my host already; I saw that he attacked questions with excitement but abandoned them within seconds. Or perhaps they abandoned him.

'If you'll give me a hand I do think we might go through now, so that we can get a good seat. They're like hyenas here. They eat everything up if you're not in there quick.' I lifted one of his elbows as he pushed himself up with the other, his whole frame shaking with the effort. 'Let's have a look at the Library,' he said, as if speaking to someone who was very deaf, winking at me in a musical-comedy way. 'That'll fool them,' he explained, in a voice only slightly quieter. Then, returning the stare of a nonagenarian wild-dog in the chair nearest the door, 'We have a history of self-abuse in duodecimo – but it's probably *out*.'

The dining-room was a far finer place. There was a long collegiate table in the middle, and smaller tables, set for two or four, allowed for more private talk around the walls. Contemporary copies of Hogarth's *Rake's Progress* hung in a double rank opposite the windows, and the famous full-length Batoni of Sir Humphry Clay, Roman statuary behind him and garlands of dead game at his feet, dominated the end wall. Beneath it the dining-room staff were arranging plates, tureens and cheeses at an immense funerary sideboard. The ceiling had an Adamish rosette at its centre, and from it hung a fairly elaborate crystal chandelier which had been conspicuously converted to electricity. Yet despite the tarnished brilliance of the room, some residual public-school thing, quintessential to Clubs, infected the atmosphere. The air retained a smell of cabbage and bad cooking that made me apprehensive about lunch.

'Here we are, splendid, splendid,' whistled Lord Nantwich as he chose the corner table which was most sequestered and afforded the best view.

'Not quite the first, I see; or are they still having breakfast? You can get a good breakfast here: kidneys. For me they do a black pudding – though they won't often do it for all the old farts in here. I enjoy a good understanding with the staff. Been coming here since I was a lad, of course, and damn good tuck and tack. What do you want?' he demanded, as a busy little waiter-boy arrived with menus that seemed to have been typed out on a pre-war Remington, with all the capital letters jumping up into the course above.

When I looked across from my menu I saw that his Lordship was staring at, or rather through, the reddening and nervous boy. 'Derek, isn't it?' he said at last.

'No, sir, I'm Raymond. Derek's left, sir, in fact.'

'Raymond! Of course – forgive me, won't you?' begged Lord Nantwich, as if pleading with a society woman.

'That's all right, sir,' said the boy, smoothing down his order pad, and Nantwich turned his attention briefly to the card. More silence followed, and Raymond felt moved to add: 'I saw Derek this week, as a matter of fact, sir. He seems all right again now . . .' but he trailed off as Nantwich was evidently not hearing him. 'Thank you, sir,' he added inconsequently.

'Now what's Abdul got for us today?' Nantwich ruminated.

'Pork'd be very nice, sir,' said Raymond dispassionately.

'I will have the pork, Raymond – with carrots, have you got? And the boiled potatoes – and I want a whole *estuary* of apple-sauce.'

'See what I can do, sir. And for your guest, sir. Any starter at all, sir?'

My mind recoiled from Brown Windsor soup to prawn cocktail to melon. 'No, I think I'll just have the trout – with peas and potatoes.'

'Bring a bottle of hock, too, Raymond,' my host requested; 'cheapest you've got.' And the moment the boy turned away, added, 'Delightful child, isn't he. Quite a little Masaccio, wouldn't you say? Nothing compared to Derek, mind you, but I like to see a nice little bumba when I'm eating.'

I smiled and felt oddly bashful; and the boy was pretty ordinary. I also felt a guest's obligation to charm, and was aware that I was giving nothing. How loaded dirty talk is between strangers, seeming to imply some sexual rapport between them, removing barriers which in this case I was interested in preserving.

'Do you live in London all the time?' I asked him partyishly.

He thought about this: 'I do, though I'm often elsewhere – in my thoughts. At my age it doesn't matter where you live. *Passent les jours, passent les semaines*, as the Frenchman said. I blank a lot, you know. Do you blank?'

'You mean, just let your mind go blank? Yes, I suppose I do. Or at least, I like letting my mind wander.'

'There you are. You see, I've had such an interesting life and now it's so bloody dull and everyone's dead and I can't remember what I'm saying and all that sort of thing.' He seemed to lose his thread.

'What is it you think about mostly?'

'Ooh, you know . . .' he muttered broodily. I crudely assumed he meant sex. 'I'm eighty-three,' he said, as if I had asked him. 'And how old are you?'

'Twenty-five,' I said with a laugh, but he looked sad.

'When I was your age,' he said, 'I was hard at work. When I stopped working you hadn't even been born.' His eyes seemed to unveil in the curious way they had, and to concentrate on my face – or rather on my head, which he held in his gaze as if in his hands; it was with the appraisal of a connoisseur that he pronounced his expert, cupidinous sentence: 'Youth!'

One younger yet arrived at this point, with wine. It was very inferior stuff, though Nantwich knocked it back with enthusiasm. Then 'Ah, here is Abdul!' he exclaimed. From the swinging kitchen door a very black man entered the dining-room pushing a domed platter on a trolley. He was perhaps forty, well built, with fierce, deep-set eyes and a moustache that lent a subtle violence to his expression; his thick lips, black at their edges, were red where they curved into his mouth, and his colouring was intensified by the pressed white linen of his chef's pyjamas and apron and the battered funnel of his chef's hat.

I watched Raymond go up for a respectful word with him, and Abdul, casting a glance in our direction, began to wheel the trolley around to where we were sitting. Various other lunchers, wandering in, nodded to him as they looked for their places; and as the hour got under way another boy of a similar tartish blond appearance came to join Raymond.

'Good afternoon, my Lord,' said Abdul punctiliously.

'Aah, Abdul,' replied Nantwich with satisfaction. 'Thou bringest the meat unto us, the spices and the wine.'

'It's a pleasure, sir,' Abdul assured him with a formal smile.

'My guest is called William, Abdul.'

'How do you do,' I said.

'Welcome to Wicks's Club, Mr William,' said Abdul with a hint of servile irony, lifting the lid off the lean and tightly bound leg of pork on the trolley. Flicking his eyes across to Nantwich he commented, 'Your guest is not having the pork, my lord.'

He had a strong presence and I looked at him casually as he cut the meat (which looked slightly underdone) into thick juicy slices. His hands were enormous, though dextrous, and I was attracted by the open neck of his uniform, which gave no suggestion that he wore anything beneath it. As he concentrated the lines of his face deepened, and he poked out his pink tongue.

Nantwich proved to be a voracious eater with poor table manners. Half the time he ate with his mouth open, affording me a generous view of masticated pork and apple sauce, which he smeared around his wine glass when he drank without wiping his lips. I attended to my trout with a kind of surgical distaste. Its slightly open barbed mouth and its tiny round eye, which had half erupted while grilling, like the core of a pustule, were unusually recriminatory. I sliced the head off and put it on my side-plate and then proceeded to remove the pale flesh from the bones with the flat of my knife. It was quite flavourless, except that, where its innards had been imperfectly removed, silvery traces of roe gave it an unpleasant bitterness.

'Tell me why you don't have a job,' Nantwich asked after we had busied ourselves with our food for an uneasily long time. 'We all need a job of work. Christ! Without a job doesn't one just go do-lally?'

'It's because I'm spoilt, I'm afraid. Too much money. I wanted to stay on at Oxford, but I didn't get a First, though I was supposed to. I did work for a publisher for two years, but then I got out.'

'I mean, if you want a job I'll get you one,' Nantwich interrupted.

'You're very kind . . . I suppose I should do something soon. My father thought he could get me a job in the City, but I couldn't face the idea of it, I'm afraid.'

'Your father?'

'Yes, he's chairman of, oh . . . a group of companies.'

'Your money comes from him, then?'

'No, as it happens, it's all from my grandfather. He's very well off, as you can imagine. He's settling his estate on my sister and me. We get it all in advance to avoid death duties.'

'Capital,' said Nantwich; 'as it were.' He munched on for a bit. 'But tell me, who is your grandfather?'

I had been supposing, somehow, that he knew, and I took a second to rethink everything in the light of the recognition that he didn't. 'Oh – er, Denis – Beckwith,' I then hastened to explain.

Again the sudden emission of interest. 'My dear charming boy, do you mean to say that you are Denis Beckwith's grandson?'

'I'm sorry, I thought you knew.' Often the intelligence met with a less enthusiastic reception. Then Nantwich's interest had gone. 'I suppose you come across each other in the House of Lords,' I ventured. He had half turned and stared out of the window. When he swung back he leaned close to me and I smelt the pork in his mouth as he said:

'That chap is a very interesting photographer, indeed.'

'Really? I don't think . . .' Then I saw that it was one of his conversational hairpins. I followed his glance across the room to where a dapper man, with crisp gold hair going grey, was sitting at the central table. Nantwich made a kind of diving or salaaming motion with his hands, and the man nodded and smiled.

'Ronald Staines, you must know his stuff, of course.'

'I'm not sure that I do.' I was sure he must be a dreadful photographer. 'What sort of thing does he specialise in?'

'Oh, very special. You must meet, you'd love him,' said Nantwich recklessly. I suffered a twinge of the mildly oppressive sensation one gets when one realises that the person one is talking to has *plans*.

'Actually, there are lots of people, not yet dead, that I'd like you to meet. All my society is pretty bloody interesting. Falling to bits, of course, ga-ga as often as not, and a coachload of absolute Mary-Anns, I won't deny it. But you young people know less and less of the old, they of you too, of course. I like young people around: you're a bonny lot, you're so heartless but you do me good.' After this bizarre outburst he sat back and lapsed into one of his vacant spells, occasionally emitting an 'Eh?' or giving a shrug. I wondered what his complaint was: not just senility, clearly, as he could be sharp and to the point; was it hardening of the arteries, some slowly spreading constriction that brought on his spasmodic torpor? I knew that I must judge it by medical criteria, although I reckoned that he took advantage of his condition to further the egocentric discontinuities of his talk.

Looking around the room I saw clear cases of other such afflictions, and thought how people of a certain kind gather together as if to authenticate a caricature of themselves – their freaks and foibles, unremarkable in the individual, being comically evident in the mass. As spoonfuls of soup were raised tremblingly to whiskery lips and hands cupped huge deaf ears to catch murmured and clipped remarks, the lunchers, all in some way distinguished or titled, retired generals, directors of banks, even authors, lost their distinction to me. They were anonymous, a type – and it was impossible to see how they could cope outside in the noise and race of the streets. How much did they know of the derisive life of the city which they ruled and from which they preserved themselves so immaculately and Edwardianly intact? As my eyes roamed across the room they came to rest on Abdul, who stood abstractedly sharpening his knife on the steel and gazing at me as if I were a meal.

After doing more than justice to bowls of family-hotel trifle we made our slow progress back to the smoking-room. As Percy poured coffee we were joined by Ronald Staines. He was dressed entirely properly, but there was something about the way he inhabited his clothes that was subversive. He seemed to slither around within the beautiful green tweed, the elderly herringbone shirt and chaste silk tie which plumped forward slightly between collar and waistcoat. His wrists were very thin and I saw that he was smaller than his authoritative suiting. He was a man in disguise, but a disguise which his gestures, his over-preserved profile and a Sitwellian taste in rings drew immediate attention to. It was a strikingly two-minded performance, and, though I found him unattractive, just what I was looking for in the present surroundings.

'Charles, you must introduce me to your guest.'

'He's called William.' I held out a hand which Staines shook with surprising vigour. 'We've been getting on very well,' Nantwich added.

'Don't fret, my dear, I'm not going to break anything up. Ronald Staines, by the way,' he said to me. 'With an "e".' He pulled up a chair, not risking to ask if he could join us. 'And how did you get involved with Charles?' he asked. 'Charles has some terrible secret, I'm sure – his success rate with the *ragazzi* is quite remarkable. He always has some very, very handsome young man in tow.'

I had always been a sucker for this kind of thing, out of vanity, and liked to allow the old their unthreatening admiration.

'You're bloody lucky he hasn't got his camera with him, William,' said Nantwich. 'He'd have you stripped off in a moment and covered in baby oil.' I got the impression of a long-lasting relationship conducted in a bitchy third-person.

'I have seen photographs of you, though, William,' Staines recalled.

'Surely Whitehaven did one, or am I wrong? – little swimming things, and a stripe of shadow covering those dreamy blue eyes? So talented, that young man, though some of his stuff can be a little . . . strong. Not this one, mind you: I saw it in that New York exhibition – there have been several, I know, but last year, in a kind of abattoir in SoHo . . .'

'He's Beckwith's grandson,' said Nantwich, as if to discount the possibility which Staines was outlining.

'Of course,' exclaimed Staines in a curiously condescending way; 'how interesting!' – turning his head aside to suggest a sudden loss of interest. 'My dear, I've done some pieces which will delight you. I wouldn't be in the least surprised if they delighted William as well – I'm certainly delighted myself. They're a new departure, newish anyway, and rather religious and full of feeling. One's a kind of *sacra conversazione* between Saint Sebastian and John the Baptist. The young man who modelled Sebastian was almost in tears when I showed it to him, it's so lovely.'

'How did you do the arrows?' I interrupted, remembering Mishima's arduous posing in a self-portrait as Sebastian.

'Oh, no arrows, dear; it's before the martyrdom. He's quite unpierced. But he looks ready for it, somehow, the way I've done it.'

'How can you tell it's Sebastian, then,' said Nantwich emphatically, 'since the only thing that identifies Se-bloody-bastian is that he's got all those ruddy arrows sticking up his arse?' This seemed a fair criticism, but Staines ignored it.

'You'll admire the Baptist, though,' he added. 'An Italian lad, a porter at Smithfield, in fact – a more virile Saint than one normally sees, perhaps, quite sort of hairy and rough. Are you interested in photography?'

'I am, rather,' I answered, 'but I don't know a lot about it. I used to take photographs when I was at Oxford, but they're nothing special, I don't suppose.'

'Hold on to them, William, hold on to them!' he warned. 'Never destroy a photograph, William; it's a bit of life sealed in for ever. If you become famous, which I've *no* doubt you will, people will want to see them. I'm being rediscovered myself, and I promise you they'll buy anything. To be honest, I've sold a lot of tat lately, but at Christie's they like it. I'm a sort of period figure, you see, and put something in those big photography sales and you find the aura of the famous names rubs off on you. Their catalogue person calls me "the unacknowledged master of post-war male photography in Britain". I fetch a price, now, you know. But then, and this is what I'm saying, I feel *absolutely awful* about it, I just want to have them all back.'

'I've told William he must come and see your studio,' Nantwich declared.

'My dear, of course. Let me just get a bit straight and I'll be thrilled to see you. I've got a big job of work on *à ce moment*, but when that's finished. And who knows, I might do a few little pickies of you – fully clothed, needless to say. I think you'd make an interesting subject for me. It's such a very English look, that, the pink and gold number and the long, straight nose. None of your Master Whitehaven anonymous stuff, though. It's a character study I want.' For the second time I had the sensation of being somehow professionally appraised.

'Well, we'll see,' I said, pleased to think of sitting again, but not keen to be rushed into some shady deal.

'How's the big job of work coming on?' Nantwich asked with suspicious casualness.

'Wonderful to have met you,' piped Staines, with a switch of conversational direction worthy of Nantwich himself. We shook hands again and he was already leaving us. 'Take care, Charles,' he advised.

My host was silent for a moment or two. 'Bit of a cunt,' he said. 'But still really frightfully good.' He looked very weary now, and I too prepared to leave.

'Thank you so much for lunch, Charles; I have enjoyed it.'

He turned a surprised gaze on me. 'You like the old Club?' he asked. 'Not too bad, is it?' Fine hair-veins branched merrily over his pinkish cheeks, but his dark eyes were sunken and his big head looked heavy with impending sleep. I thought how I had seen him dead on the lavatory floor. I felt quite fond of him, and was glad that I had belonged to him and not to the talkative, rather sinister Staines. 'I do hope we'll have another little chin-wag soon,' he said. 'I'll see you at the baths, of course.' Again it seemed inconceivable to me that this man could be capable of physical exercise. As if reading my thoughts he explained: 'I find the water most . . . therapeutic. Swimming, if you can call it swimming, is the only thing that makes me feel young. Floating around, splish-splosh, flip-flop . . .'

Downstairs again on my way out, I stopped off for a pee. The lavatory was off the hall, down a corridor where lesser but brighter portraits were hung, late Victorian and Edwardian mostly, the flashy brushwork making the sitters seem all the more roguish and *parvenus*. Staines was coming out as I entered, and uttered a 'Whoops,' though he did not otherwise indicate that he knew me. As I stood at the urinal, along the front of which ran a tilted glass plate to prevent the old buffers from piddling on their shoes, a voice said, 'Enjoy your meal, sir?' It was Raymond, our waiter, who I had not realised was there. He caught my eye in the mirror as I glanced across.

3

I did so regret it was the Central Line I used most. I couldn't get any kind of purchase on it. It had neither the old-fashioned open-air quality of the District Line, where rain misted the tracks as one waited, nor the grimy profundity of the Northern Line, nor the Piccadilly's ingenious, civilised connexiveness. For much of its length it was a great bleak drain, and though some of its stops – Holland Park, St Paul's, Bethnal Green – were historic enough, they were offset on my daily journeys by the ringing emptiness of Lancaster Gate and Marble Arch, and the trash and racket of Tottenham Court Road, where I got out. Somewhere, I knew, the line had its ghost stations, but I had given up looking out for their unlit platforms and perhaps, in a flash from the rails, the signboards and good-humoured advertisements of an abandoned decade.

I had been waiting now at Holland Park for a long time. I was far too familiar with its typical social mix: girls with pearls and pink stockings, some arrogant-looking Italian youths and a grand, pouchy old couple were also waiting, though the train they would get into would be quite heavily peopled with blacks and Indians coming in from Acton to the West End. That was the saving grace of the Central Line, the way that beyond Shepherd's Bush and Liverpool Street, it veered off at either end to outlying towns to the north. I stood for a minute or more with my toes over the platform's edge, looking down into the concrete gully where a whole family of nervous, sooty little mice shot back and forth as if themselves operated by electricity. Then, thinking again about the abolished stations at the British Museum and Wood Green, I wandered along and looked, tourist-like, at the Underground map. It was a clever piece of work, all the lines being made to run either up and down, from left to right, or at forty-five degrees, so that the whole thing became a set of dissolving and interpenetrating parallelograms. It was perhaps only of that very stretch of the Central Line which I always travelled that its fastidious rectilinearity gave a true picture: from Shepherd's Bush to Liverpool Street the line had that Roman straightness which I so admired above ground and which below contributed to the great speed the trains sometimes got up. In rush-hour congestion though, the trains collected behind each other, and there would be long, numbing waits in the tunnels. Then I hated the Underground.

My fondness for it was anyway somewhat forced, and my concern with the smaller details of its history and performance had been worked up artificially to give it some faint aesthetic interest after I had been banned from driving. (Unhappily, I had had a few too many glasses of Pimm's when I was caught by my blind spot, twitching out to overtake and smacking into a little old car that was trundling past me, invisible in either of my mirrors . . . My mother was now using my Lancia for her forays into Fordingbridge and for her occasional journeys up to London from the ranch in Hants.) So I made the best of the Tube, and found it often sexy and strange, like a gigantic game of chance, in which one got jammed up against many queer kinds of person. Or it was a sort of Edward Burra scene, all hats and buttocks and seaside postcard lewdery. Whatever, one always had to try and see the potential in it.

Before going to the Corry I cut down through Soho Square to a cinema in Frith Street. It wasn't so much to see a film as to sit in a dark, anonymous place and do dark, anonymous things. Arthur and I had got wrecked on tequila the night before, the bottled romance of Mexico, as it described itself. The evenings had been getting longer lately, in two senses, and we both needed a little help with our own bottled romance. As it was he had become brash and giggly and fallen into an open-mouthed, stertorous sleep during the first five minutes of the Royal Command Performance. Deeply drunk myself, I roamed off to bed, and the next morning, when I woke groaning and groping at nine, dimly remembered looking at myself with immense self-satisfaction in the hall mirror and giving a barely prophetic rendition of 'Nessun dorma' seven or eight times.

As always when I had a bad hangover I felt criminally randy, but Arthur, whom I found still lying on the sitting-room floor, his chin sticky with a dozer's saliva, spent the morning alternately shitting and vomiting (which was painful for him) and walking very slowly from one item of furniture to another, his lower lip drooping and with a funny look about him which I realised was his equivalent of pallor.

Though it was not much fun, this hangover created a minor drama in our life and we reacted to it with disbelieving shakings of the head, exaggerated winces and a vocabulary honed down to 'man', 'shit' and 'fuck' produced in gasps or cracked whispers. Then Arthur, with a comical ungainliness, as if he were running a three-legged race with an invisible partner, would canter off to the lavatory once more. Later I got

47

him to go to bed and went out, still quite speedy from the drink and in the mood for what sex-club owners call an experience.

The Brutus Cinema occupied the basement of one of those Soho houses which, above ground-floor level, maintain their beautiful Caroline fenestration, and seemed a kind of emblem of gay life (the *piano nobile* elegant above the squalid, jolly *sous-sol*) in the far-off spring of 1983. One entered from the street by pushing back the dirty red curtain in the doorway beside an unlettered shop window, painted over white but with a stencil of Michelangelo's David stuck in the middle. This tussle with the curtain—one never knew whether to shoulder it aside to the right or the left, and often tangled with another punter coming out – seemed a symbolic act, done in the sight of passers-by, and always gave me a little jab of pride. Inside was a small front room, the walls bearing porn-mags on racks, and the glossy boxes of videos for sale; and there were advertisements for clubs and cures. In a locked case by the counter leather underwear was displayed, with cock-rings, face masks, chains and the whole gamut of dildoes from pubertal pink fingers to mighty black jobs, two feet long and as thick as a fist.

As I entered, the spotty Glaswegian attendant was getting stuck into a helping of fish and chips, and the room stank of grease and vinegar. I idled for a minute and flicked through some mags. These were really dog-eared browsers, thumbed through time and again by those rent-boys who had the blessing of the management and waited there for pick-ups; curiously incredible stations of sexual intercourse, whose moving versions, or something similar, could be seen downstairs. I looked at the theatrical expressions of ecstasy without interest. The attendant had a small television behind the counter which was a monitor for the films being shown in the cinema; but as there was no one else in the shop he had broken the endless circuit of video sex and was watching a real TV programme instead. He sat there stuffing chips and oozing, batter-covered sections of flaky white cod into his mouth, his short-sighted attention rapt by the screen, as if he had been a teenaged boy getting his first sight of a porn film. I sidled along and looked over his shoulder; it was a nature programme, and contained some virtuoso footage shot inside a termite colony. First we saw the long, questing snout of the ant-eater outside, and then its brutal, razor-sharp claws cutting their way in. Back inside, perched by a fibre-optic miracle at a junction of tunnels which looked like the triforium of some Gaudí church, we saw the freakishly extensile tongue of the ant-eater come flicking towards us, cleaning the fleeing termites off the wall.

It was one of the most astonishing pieces of film I had ever seen, and I felt a thrill at the violent intrusion as well as dismay at the smashing of something so strange and intricate; I was disappointed when the attendant, realising I was there and perhaps in need of encouragement, tapped a button and transformed the picture into the relative banality of American college boys sticking their cocks up each other's assholes.

'Cinema sir?' he said. 'We've got some really hot-core hard films . . .' His heart wasn't in it so I paid him my fiver and left him to the wonderful world of nature.

I went down the stairs, lit by one gloomy red-painted bulb. The cinema itself was a small cellar room, the squalor of which was only fully apparent at the desolating moment in the early hours when the show ended for the night and the lights were suddenly switched on, revealing the bare, damp-stained walls, the rubbish on the floor, and the remaining audience, either asleep or doing things best covered by darkness. It had perhaps ten tiers of seats, salvaged from the refurbishment of some bona fide picture house: some lacked arms, which helped patrons get to know each other, and one lacked a seat, and was the repeated cause of embarrassment to diffident people, blinded by the dark, who chose it as the first empty place to hand and sat down heavily on the floor instead.

I had not been there for months and was struck again by its character: pushing open the door I felt it weigh on sight, smell and hearing. The smell was smoke and sweat, a stale, male odour tartishly overlaid with a cheap lemon-scented air-freshener like a taxi and dusted from time to time with a trace of Trouble for Men. The sound was the laid-back aphrodisiac pop music which, as the films had no sound-track, played continuously and repetitively to enhance the mood and cover the quieter noises made by the customers. The look of the place changed in the first minute or so, as I waited just inside the door for my eyes to accustom themselves to the near dark. The only light came from the small screen, and from a dim yellow 'Fire Exit' sign. I had once taken this exit, which led to a fetid back staircase with a locked door at the top. Smoke thickened the air and hung in the projector's beam.

It was important to sit near the back, where it was darker and more went on, but also essential to avoid the attentions of truly gruesome people. Slightly encumbered with my bag I moved into a row empty except for a heavy businessman at the far end. It was not a very good house, so I settled down to watch and wait. Occasionally cigarettes were lit and the men shifted in their seats and looked around; the mood faltered between tension and lethargy.

The college boys were followed by a brief, gloomy fragment of film involving older, moustachioed types, one of them virtually bald. This broke off suddenly, and without preamble another film, very cheery and outdoors, was under way. As always with these films, though I relished the gross abundance of their later episodes, it was the introductory scenes, buoyant with expectation, the men on the street or the beach, killing time, pumping iron, still awaiting the transformation our fantasy would demand of them, that I found the most touching.

Now, for instance, we were in a farmyard. A golden-haired boy in old blue jeans and a white vest was leaning in the sun against a barn door, one foot raised behind him. A close-up admired him frowning against the sun, a straw jerking between his lips. Slowly we travelled down, lingering where his hand brushed across his nipples which showed hard through his vest, lingering again at his loose but promising crotch. On the other side of the yard, a second boy, also blond, was shifting bags of fertiliser. We watched his shirtless muscular torso straining as he lifted the bags on to his shoulder, traced the sweat running down his neck and back, got a load of his chunky denim-clad ass as he bent over. The eyes of the two boys met; one close-up and then another suggested curiosity and lust. In what seemed to be very slightly slow motion the shirtless boy ambled across to the other. They stood close together, both extremely beautiful, perhaps eighteen or nineteen years of age. Their lips moved, they spoke and smiled, but as the film had no sound-track, and we heard only the cinema's throbbing, washing music, they communicated in a dreamlike silence, or as if watched from out of earshot through binoculars. The picture was irradiated with sunlight and, being fractionally out of focus, blurred the boys' smooth outlines into a blond nimbus. The one in the vest appeared to put a question to the other, they turned aside and were swallowed up into the darkness of the barn.

Where did they get them from, I wondered, these boys more wonderful than almost everything one came across in real life? And I remembered reading somewhere that a Californian talent-spotter had photographic records of three thousand or more of them ranging back over twenty or thirty years and that a youngster, after a session in the studio, mooching through the files, had found pictures of his own father, posed long before.

In the meantime there were other arrivals at the cinema, though it was difficult to make them out; while the sunlit introduction had brightened up the room and cast its aura over the scattered audience in the forward rows, the sex scenes within the barn were enacted in comparative gloom, allowing the viewers a secretive darkness. I tugged my half-hard cock out through my fly and stroked it casually.

One new entrant tottered to the deserted front row, which in this tiny space was only a few feet from the screen. There was a rustle of papers, and I could see him in silhouette remove his coat, fold it neatly and place it on the seat next to that in which he then sat down. The rustling recurred intermittently, and I guessed he must be a man I'd seen at the Brutus the very first time I went there, a spry little chap of sixty-five or so who, like a schoolgirl taken to a romantic U picture, sat entranced by the movies and worked his way through a bag of boiled sweets as the action unfolded. A fiver from his pension, perhaps, and 30p for the humbugs, might be set aside weekly for this little outing. How he must look forward to it! His was a complete and innocent absorption in the fantasy world on screen. Could he look back to a time when he had behaved like these glowing, thoughtless teenagers, who were now locked together sucking on each other's cocks in the hay? Or was this the image of a new society we had made, where every desire could find its gratification?

The old man was happy with his cough-drops, but I wanted some other oral pleasure (the Winchester slang 'suction', meaning sweets, I realised was the comprehensive term). Not, however, from the person who came scouting up to the rear rows now, one of the plump, bespectacled Chinese youths who, with day-return businessmen and quite distinguished Oxbridge dons, made a haunt of places like this, hopping hopefully from row to row, so persistent that they were inevitably, from time to time, successful.

The man on the end of the row had to shift, and I realised I was to be the next recipient of Eastern approaches. The boy sat down next to me, and though I carried on looking at the screen and laid my hand across my cock, I was aware that he was staring at me intently to try and make out my face in the darkness, and I felt his breath on my cheek. Then there was the pressure of his shoulder against mine. I gathered myself emphatically, and leant across into the empty place on the other side. He sprawled rather, with his legs wide apart, one of them straying into my space and pressing against my thigh.

'Leave off, will you,' I whispered, thinking that a matter-of-fact request would do the trick. At the same time I crossed my legs, squashing my balls uncomfortably, to emphasise that I was not available. The sack-lifting boy was now sliding his finger up the other one's ass, spitting on his big, blunt cock and preparing for the inevitable penetration. As he pressed its head against the boy's glistening sphincter, which virtually filled the screen in lurid close-up, I felt an arm go along the back of the seat and a moment later a hand descend unfalteringly on my dick. I didn't move but, sensing the power that speech had in this cryptic gathering, I said loudly and firmly: 'If you come anywhere near me again I'll break your neck.' A couple of people looked round, there was an 'Oooh' from the other side of the room, spoken in a uniquely homosexual tone of bored outrage, the tentacles withdrew, and after a few moments, compatible perhaps with some fantastic notion of the preservation of dignity, the advancer retreated, earning a curse from the man at the end of the row, who was forced to get up again, attempting to conceal his erection as he did so.

Exhilarated by my control of the situation, I spread myself again; the boy duly came over the other's face, and very pretty it looked, the blobs and strings of spunk smeared over his eyelids, nose, and thick half-opened lips. Then, abruptly, it was another film. Half a dozen boys entered a locker-room, and at just the same moment the door from the stairs opened and something came in that looked, in the deep shadow, as if it might be nice. It was a sporty-looking boy with, evidently, a bag. He was not sure what to do, so I bent my telepathic powers on him. The poor creature struggled for a moment . . . but it was hopeless. He stumbled up towards the back, groped past the businessman (I heard him say 'Sorry') and sat a seat away from me, putting his bag on the seat between us.

I let a little time elapse and distinctly heard him swallow, as if in lust and amazement, as the boys stripped off and, before we knew where we were, one of them was jacking off in the shower. Something made me certain that it was the first time he had been to a place like this, and I remembered how enchanting it is to see one's first porn-film. 'Christ! They're really doing it,' I recalled saying to myself, quite impressed by the way the actors seemed genuinely to be having sex for the pleasure of it, and by the blatant innocence of it all.

I then proceeded by a succession of distinct and inexorable moves, shifting into the place between us and at the same time pushing his bag along the floor to where I had been sitting. I sensed some anxiety about this, but he carried on looking at the screen. Next I slid my arm along the back of his seat, and as he remained immobile I made it as clear as I could in the dark that I had my cock out and was playing with it. Then I leant over him more, and ran my hand over his chest. His heart was racing, and I felt all the tension in his fixed posture between excitement and fear, and knew that I could take control of him. He had on a kind of bomber jacket, and under that a shirt. I let my hand linger at his waist, and admired his hard, ridged stomach, slipping my fingers between his shirt buttons, and running my hand up over his smooth skin. He had beautiful, muscular tits, with small, frosted nipples, quite hairless. My left hand gently rubbed the base of his thick neck; he seemed to have almost a crew-cut and the back of his head was softly bristly. I leant close to him and drooled my tongue up his jaw and into his ear.

At this he could no longer remain impassive. He turned towards me with a gulp, and I felt his fingertips shyly slide on to my knee and shortly after touch my cock. 'Oh no,' I think he said under his breath, as he tried to get his hand around it, and then jerked it tentatively a few times. I continued stroking the back of his neck, thinking it might relax him, but he kept on feeling my dick in a very polite sort of way, so I brought pressure to bear, and pushed his head firmly down into my lap. He had to struggle around to get his stocky form into the new position, encumbered by the padded arm between our seats; but once there he took the crown of my cock into his mouth and with me moving his head puppet-like up and down, sucked it after a fashion.

This was all very good and with my hangover I felt it with electric intensity. But I was aware of his reluctance, and let him stop. He was inexpert, and though he was excited, needed help. We sat back for a while, my hand all the time on his shoulder. I loved the nerve with which I'd done all this, and like most random sex it gave me the feeling I could achieve anything I wanted if I were only determined enough. There was now a fairly complicated set-up on screen, with all six boys doing something interesting, and one of them I realised was Kip Parker, a famous tousle-headed blond teen star. I ran my hand between my new friend's legs and felt his cock kicking against the tightish cotton of his slacks. He helped me take it out, a short, punchy little number, which I went down on and polished off almost at once. God he must have been ready. After a shocked recuperation he felt for his bag and went out without a word.

I'd had a growing suspicion throughout this sordid but charming little episode, which rose to a near certainty as he opened the door and was caught in a slightly brighter light, that the boy was Phil from the Corry. He had smelt of sweat rather than talcum powder and there was a light stubble on his jaw, so I concluded that if it were Phil he was on his way to rather than from the club, as I knew he was fastidiously clean, and that he always shaved in the evening before having his shower. I was tempted to follow him at once, to make sure, but I realised it would be easy enough to tell from seeing him later; and besides, a very well-hung kid, who'd already been showing an interest in our activities, moved in to occupy the boy's former seat, and brought me off epically during the next film, an unthinkably tawdry picture which all took place in a kitchen.

On the train home I carried on reading *Valmouth*. It was an old grey and white Penguin Classic that James had lent me, the pages stiff and foxed, with a faint smell of lost time. Wet-bottomed wine glasses had left mauve rings over the sketch of the author by Augustus John and the price, 3/6, which appeared in a red square on the cover. Nonetheless, I was enjoined to take especial care of the book, which also contained *Prancing Nigger* and *Concerning the Eccentricities of Cardinal Pirelli*. James had a mania for Firbank, and it was only out of his love for me that he had let me take away this apparently undistinguished old paperback, which bore on its flyleaf the absurd signature 'O. de V. Green'. James held the average Firbank-lover in contempt, and professed a very serious attitude towards his favourite writer. I had long deferred reading him in the childishly stubborn way that one resists all keen and repeated recommendations, and had imagined him until now to be a supremely frivolous and silly author. I was surprised to find how difficult, witty and relentless he was. The characters were flighty and extravagant in the extreme, but the novel itself was evidently as tough as nails.

I knew I would not begin to grasp it fully until a second or third reading, but what was clear so far was that the inhabitants of the balmy resort of Valmouth found the climate so kind that they lived to an immense age. Lady Parvula de Panzoust (a name I knew already from James's reapplication of it to a member of the Corry) was hoping to establish some rapport with the virile young David Tooke, a farm boy, and was seeking the help of Mrs Yajnavalkya, a black masseuse, to set up a meeting. 'He's *awfully* choice,' Mrs Yaj assured the centenarian *grande dame*. Much of the talk was a kind of highly inflected nonsense, but it gave the unnerving impression that on deeper acquaintance it would all turn out to be packed with fleeting and covert meaning. Mrs Yaj herself spoke in a wonderful black pidgin, prinked out with more exotic turns of phrase. 'O Allah la Ilaha!' she reassured the anxious Lady Parvula. 'Shall I tell you vot de Yajñavalkya device is? Vot it has been dis thousand and thousand ob year? It is *bjopti*. *Bjopti*! And vot does *bjopti* mean? It means *discretion*. S-s-s-s-s-s-s-s-s-s-s-s-s-s-s-s-s-s-s- s-s-s-s-s-s-sh!' It was such a long 'Sh!' that I found myself quietly vocalising it to see what its effect would be.

'Quiet, Damian,' the woman opposite me said to her little boy. 'Gentleman's trying to read.'

It was about nine when I reached home. The tall uncurtained window at the turn of the stairs still let in just enough of the phosphorescent late dusk to make it unnecessary to turn on a light. I enjoyed a proprietorial secrecy as I walked slowly and silently up, as well as the frisson of bleakness that comes from being in a deserted place as darkness gathers. There was something nostalgic in such spring nights, recalling the dreamy abstraction of punting in the dark, and the sweet tiredness afterwards, returning to rooms with all their windows open, still warm under the eaves.

The door of the flat was slightly ajar, which was unusual. I was inclined to keep it shut as I was (or had been) often the only inhabitant of the house, the businessman in the main floors below being frequently abroad. And I had occasionally witnessed Arthur pushing it to, or checking as he passed through the hall that it was closed. My heart sank as I nudged it open and heard Arthur's voice, not addressing me – he could not possibly have known I was there – but talking quietly to somebody else. The door of the sitting-room, which was open, hid whatever was going on; the light from that room fell across the further side of the hall.

My first assumption was that he was on the telephone, which would have been reasonable enough except that he had said he hated the phone. For a sickening moment I felt that I was being somehow betrayed, and that when I went out he rang people up and carried on some other existence. A plan was afoot of which I was the dupe; he had not killed anybody at all . . . Then I heard another voice, just odd syllables, high – it sounded like a young girl. I heard Arthur say 'Yeah, well I expect he'll be back here soon.' I made a noise and went into the room.

'Will, thank God,' Arthur said, half rising from the sofa, but encumbered by the heavy breadth of my photograph album, which lay open across his lap and across that of a small boy sitting beside him and leaning over it as if it were a table. It was my nephew Rupert.

Rupert had had longer than me to work out what to say. Even so, he was clearly unsure of the effect he would have. First of all he wanted it to be a lovely surprise: he stared up at me, mouth slightly open, in a spell of silence, while Arthur, too, looked very uncertain. Again I found myself suddenly responsible for people.

'This is an unexpected pleasure, Roops,' I said. 'Have you been showing Arthur the pictures?' I thought something might be seriously wrong.

'Yes,' he said, a little shamefaced. 'I've decided to run away.'

'That's jolly exciting,' I said, going over to the sofa, and lifting up the photograph album. 'Have you told Mummy where you've gone?' I held the heavy, embossed leather book in my arms, and looked down at him. Arthur caught my eye, frowned and expelled a little puff of air. 'Blimy, Will,' he said confidentially.

Rupert was then six years old. From his father he had inherited an intense, practical intelligence, and from his mother, my sister, vanity, self-possession, and the pink and gold Beckwith colouring that Ronald Staines had so admired in me. I had always liked Gavin, a busy, abstracted man, whose mind, even at a dinner party, was still absorbed in the details of Romano-British archaeology, which was his passion and career, and who would have had nothing to do with the way his son now appeared, in knickerbockers and an embroidered jerkin, with a Millais-esque lather of curls, as if about to go bowling a hoop in Kensington Gardens. Philippa had a picturesque and romantic attitude to her children (there was also a little girl, Polly, aged three), and Gavin allowed her a free hand, concentrating his affection for them in sudden bursts of generosity, unannounced treats and impulsive outings which disrupted the life of the picture-book nursery at Ladbroke Grove, and were rightly popular.

'I left a note,' Rupert explained, standing up and beginning to walk around the room. 'I told Mummy not to worry. I'm sure she'll see that it's all for the best.'

'I don't know, old chap,' I demurred. 'I mean, Mummy's jolly sensible, but it *is* quite late, and I wouldn't be surprised if she were getting a *bit* worried about you. Did you tell her where you were going?'

'No, of course not. It was a secret. I didn't even tell Polly. It had to be very very carefully planned.' He picked up a Harrods carrier-bag. 'I've brought some food,' he said, tipping out on to the sofa a couple of apples, a pack of six Penguin biscuits and a roughly sawn-off chunk of cold, cooked pork. 'And I've got a map.' From inside his jerkin he tugged out an A–Z, on the shiny cover of which he had written 'Rupert Croft-Parker' with a blue biro in heavy round writing.

I went into the bedroom and rang Philippa. A maid, Spanish by the sound of her, answered the phone; they had a fast turnover of staff, and if I had been Philippa I would have been led by now to ponder why. Almost immediately she came through from another extension.

'Hello, who is this?'

'Philippa, it's me, I've got Roops here.'

'Will, what the hell do you think you're playing at? Can't you imagine how worried I've been?'

'I thought you would be – that's really why I'm phoning . . .'

'Is he all right? What's been going on?'

'I gather he ran away. Didn't you see his message?'

'Of course not, Will, don't be so bloody silly. He doesn't leave messages. He's six years old.'

'I'm sure I left messages when I was six and I wasn't nearly so clever as Rupert.'

'Will, we are talking about my baby.' (I suppressed recall of the song of that name by the Four Tops.) 'Look, I'm coming round straight away.'

'OK. Or give it a minute or two. We haven't really had a chance for a little chat yet.' I was aware that Rupert had entered the room.

'Are you talking to Mummy?' he said, with a solemn look on his face. I nodded as I carried on listening to Philippa, and winked at him. I sat on the edge of the bed and he came and leant beside me and slipped his arm around my back.

'You can have a little chat with him any time you like,' his mother asserted. 'It's gone nine o'clock – it's way past his bedtime. We were supposed to be going to the Salmons for supper – I had to ring and say there was this crisis, we couldn't come. It's just ruined everything.'

'I'll bring him over if you like,' I offered, the problem of Arthur and visitors suddenly surfacing in my mind.

'No, that would take far too long. I'll come in the car.' She put down the receiver as I was about to make another suggestion.

'Is Mummy coming round here?' asked Rupert, his expression an intriguing transition between petulance and relief.

'She'll be round in a minute,' I confirmed. And it would not be very much more than that. I walked abstractedly towards the door. He trotted round, looking up at me.

'Was she frightfully cross?' he asked.

'I'm afraid she was a bit, old chap.' I made a plan. 'Look, you can keep a secret, can't you?'

'Of course I can,' he said, assuming a very responsible air.

'Well, look. What time was it when you left home?'

'About six o'clock.'

'And what did you do then?'

'First of all I went for a walk. A really long walk, actually, up that very steep path, you know – where the homosexuals go.'

'Yes, indeed,' I muttered.

'And then down to the bottom where we went roller-skating that time. And then all the way round to the top again. And then' (he raised his arm in the air to designate the main thrust of his campaign) 'all the way down here. I rang the bell for quite some time, but I could see there was a light on, and *at last* that African boy came down.'

'Did you tell him who you were?'

'Naturally. I told him I had to come in and wait for you.'

'Well the thing is, love, that that African chap wants us to keep it a secret that he's here. So what we're going to do is hide him away when Mummy comes round, and pretend we've never seen him. All right?'

'Quite all right by me,' Rupert said. 'Has he done something wrong, then?'

'No, no,' I laughed naturally. 'But he doesn't want his mother to know he's here – just like you, really. So if we don't tell anybody at all, then she'll never find out.'

'Good,' said Rupert. He was clearly dissatisfied.

We went into the sitting-room. 'I think it would be better if you stayed in the bedroom, darling,' I said to Arthur. 'This child's mother is coming round. We've agreed to keep it all a secret.' He left the room directly, and I heard him shut the bedroom door. 'I expect Mummy will be here any moment,' I said.

My nephew was determined and casual. 'Can we go on looking at the pictures?' he asked.

'All right,' I agreed. Then another thought struck me. 'How long were you here before I arrived?'

'I was here for about twenty minutes – before you arrived.'

'Perhaps best to pretend to Mummy that I found you on the doorstep. Otherwise she'll wonder how you got in – or why I didn't ring her sooner.'

He looked at his large, rather adult watch. 'Yes, that's fine,' he said. We sat down side by side, and I lifted the album on to my knee. It was one of a set in which my grandfather had had all his loose and various collection of snaps, taken over a long life, mounted. He had had more volumes bound than he needed and gave one to me. It had the generous proportions of an Edwardian album, many, many broad dark grey pages, tied in with thick silk cords which knotted at the edge outside, the whole protected with weighty boards covered with green leather, tooled with flowers around the border, and with a pompous but impressive 'B' beneath a coronet in the centre.

'How far did you get?' I asked, offering to open it halfway through.

'Let's start again,' Rupert urged. We'd once spent an hour looking through this album together, and I had had the impression that he was committing it to memory, working out the connections. It was a sort of book of life to him, and I was the authoritative expounder of its text.

The early part was fairly random, this scion of the family photograph collection being merely the duplicates and duds. There was me with a cap and a brace on my teeth, at my tother; there were Philippa and I in our bathing costumes in Brittany (a windy day by the look of it); me in my shorts in the garden at Marden, my grandfather and my mother in deckchairs behind, looking cross. 'There's Great Grandpa, look: I don't think he was in a very good mood, do you?' Rupert giggled, and banged his heels against the front of the sofa. 'Then it's Winchester.'

'Hooray!' cried Rupert, who, though an independent child, was still strongly patriotic about such things as the school from which, one day, he would doubtless run away.

'Now can you find me in this one?' I asked. It was my first-year College photograph. I looked along the rows so as not to give him any clues; but I need not have troubled. It was with only a slight diffidence that he brought his finger down on me, standing in the middle of the back row. I looked utterly sweet, short-haired, and rather sad, giving the impression that my mind was on higher things. That this was not the case was made clear by the next photograph, of the swimming team. It was posed by the pool, where the springboard was anchored to the concrete; three boys stood on its landward end so as to make a two-tiered composition. The Matheson Cup, the perfectly hideous schools trophy which we had won that year, was held aloft by Torriano, the boy in the centre of the back row. But the most noticeable thing about the picture was what by then could fairly have been called my manhood. I had on some very sexy white trunks with a red stripe down the side; and I remember how, when the picture went up on school NoBos, with a list for people to sign who wanted a copy (normally not even all the members of the team in question), there was an unprecedented demand, and the trunks themselves, of which I was crazily fond, disappeared from the drying-room overnight and I never saw them again. On my face, rounder and saucier then, there was an expression of almost disturbing complicity.

Rupert's finger came down, hesitatingly though, on me. 'That's you,' he said. 'Who's that?'

'That's Eccles,' I said reflectively, haunted for a second by the already period-looking photograph, in which the faces took on a greater clarity as time went by. The boy's stocky body and outward-bulging thighs were untypical build for a swimmer, but he used to move with a bucking, concentrated energy. With his sleek black hair, long pointed nose and a smile showing his small, square teeth, he looked impishly young and, with his head tilted slightly to one side, would give, for as long as the picture survived, an impression of unqualified charm.

'Is he the one that changed his name?'

'Yes, that's right.'

'Why did he?'

'Well, it wasn't so much him as his father, I suppose, or his grandfather even. He was Jewish, and before the war Jewish people changed their names so that people wouldn't know. His real name was Ecklendorff.'

'Why didn't they want people to know what their name was?'

'It's a long story, old boy. I'll tell you another time.'

'Yes,' he frowned, turning the page. It was Oxford now – the matriculation photograph, posed in the stony front quad at Corpus, the pelican on top of the sundial appearing to sit on the head of the lanky, begowned chemist at the centre of the back row. I looked rather anonymous in it and once Rupert had identified me we moved to some colour snaps of a summer picnic at Wytham. There I sat, cross-legged on a rug, shirtless, brown, blue-eyed – perhaps the most beautiful I had ever been or ever would be. 'That's you,' cried Rupert, splodging his forefinger down on my face as if recording his fingerprints for the police. 'And that's James! Isn't he funny?'

'Yes, isn't he a scream.' James had on his panama hat, was quite drunk and had been caught at an unflattering angle (one I had never seen him from in real life), so that he looked lecherously seedy.

'And is that Robert Carson um Smith?'

'Smith-Carson, actually, but jolly good all the same.'

'Was *he* a homosexual?'

'Certainly was.'

'I don't like him.'

'No, he wasn't very nice really. Some people liked him, though. He was great friends with James, you know.'

'Is James a homosexual, too?'

'You know perfectly well he is.'

'Yes, I *thought* he was, but Mummy said you mustn't say people were.'

'You say what you like, sweetheart; as long as it's true, of course.'

'Of course. Is *he* a homosexual as well?' he chimed on, pointing to the remaining person in the picture, the blazered, boatered man-mountain, Ashley Child, a wealthy American Rhodes scholar whose birthday, as far as I could remember, we had been celebrating.

'A bit hard to say, I'm afraid. I should think so, though.'

'I mean,' Rupert looked up at me cogitatively, 'almost everyone is homosexual, aren't they? Boys, I mean.'

'I sometimes think so,' I hedged.

'Is Grandpa one?'

'Good heavens no,' I protested.

'Am I one?' Rupert asked intently.

'It's a bit early to say yet, old fellow. But you could be, you know.'

'Goody!' he squealed, banging his heels against the front of the sofa again. 'Then I can come and live with you.'

'Would you like that?' I asked, my avuncular rather than my homosexual feelings deeply gratified by this. And really Rupert's cult of the gay, his innocent, optimistic absorption in the subject, delighted me even while its origin and purpose were obscure.

I was saved from the sexual analysis of the next set of pictures, the Oscar Wilde Society Ball, by the doorbell ringing. (The dress-note that year had been 'Slave Trade', and the spectacle of predominantly straight boys camping it up to the eyeballs would have been confusing to the child's budding sense of role-play.)

It was not Philippa but Gavin who had come. 'Sorry about this, Will,' he said. 'Has he been a frightful bother?'

'Not a bit, Gavin. Come in. We were just having a talk about homosexuality.'

'He is frightfully interested in that at the moment, although he can't have the least idea what it *is* — can he? It must be the effect of his overbearing and possessive mum. Odd what little children get up to; I was a committed transvestite at his age. But that seemed to get it out of the system,' he added hastily.

'I'm surprised the overbearing mum let you come to collect him,' I admitted.

'Got a bit of a head,' said Gavin, in a way that suggested this was a known euphemism.

The reunion with his son was a low-key affair, conducted by both as if nothing had happened, while Gavin and I carried on a pleasant conversation over the child's head. 'At least this little escapade has saved us from dinner at the Salmons,' he conceded. 'That man is the most insufferable little twerp. I'd better just give Philly a call, if I may.'

'Yes, of course.' The phone was in the bedroom. 'But you will be back home in no time at all.' I tried to disguise my sudden swerve of attitude. 'I mean, if you *really* want to, then do . . .'

'Thanks. Where is the phone?'

'Oh, I'll show you.' I felt extremely anxious, and as Gavin followed me across the hall, I turned and addressed him outside the bedroom door in an unnaturally carrying tone: 'I suppose you want to confirm to the child's mother that I have been a responsible uncle and not encouraged him in hard drugs or any other dangerous abuse.'

Gavin smiled at me politely, sensing he was missing a joke. 'Partly that, but also I'm going to have a little talk with our runaway before he goes home to be eaten alive.'

'Yes, do save him from all that,' I gabbled. 'So you're *ringing* to say you'll not be coming straight home.'

'Quite so.'

I paused, considering how I could possibly disallow this. 'Right,' I said with a nod, opening the door resolutely and going into the room. To take another person in there was in itself disquieting; it made me conscious of how unaired it was, and of the fetor of socks and semen which would never have been allowed to accumulate in the Croft-Parkers' dustless Regency sleeping quarters. Dirty clothes amassed on chairs and on the surrounding floor. The wardrobe doors were open.

This was the most alarming thing to my eye, as I had imagined it as the only place in which Arthur could reasonably have hidden. As I went into the room I was ready, if need be, to find him merely sitting there, or standing around, waiting. Though a surprise, it would not have seemed so remarkable; only my failure to warn Gavin would have been thought odd. But to warn him would have been a treacherous concession. I showed Gavin the phone, on the bedside table. The curtains were closed, as always, but I had put on the overhead light, and as the duvet was thrown into a heap at the foot of the bed, the rumpled green sheets and pillows showed their shamingly stained and fucked-over countenance; Gavin remained standing as he phoned.

I wandered back into the hall, where Rupert was standing, an expression of the utmost apprehension on his face. 'Isn't that boy . . .' he mouthed, his eyebrows raised and then biting his lower lip, which I laid my finger across in a gesture of silence. The bed came down to within an inch or two of the floor. He must be behind the curtains.

'Thanks, Will,' said Gavin as he emerged, with a slightly amazed look.

'Everything OK?' I enquired, with extreme casualness.

'We'll be off now, young feller.'

I saw them to the door of the flat. 'Thanks, Will,' said Gavin again. 'See you soon. You must come round or something . . .' He laid a hand fraternally on my shoulder.

'Bye, Roops,' I said, expecting my normal kiss but getting instead a handshake; which, nevertheless, I recognised as a sign of greater intimacy.

Farce is always more entertaining to watch than to enact, and I was relieved to hear the house door slam and a car start. I turned back to the bedroom, crossing to the window as I said, 'It's all right, they've gone.' But when I tweaked open the curtains, it was my own face, with a silly hide-and-seek smirk on it, that I saw reflected in the window. 'Funny,' I said aloud. There was a rustle behind me, and I swung round to see the flung-back duvet heave, lurch upwards, and after a further convulsion, bring forth Arthur. He had been curled up there like a young stowaway, his flexible body folded so as to be almost imperceptible. He hammed up his recovery rather, flustered at the alarm, boastful of his ingenuity. 'Man, you didn't know where I bloody was!' He fell back giggling, then clutched his head, still leaden from his hangover.

I sat by him on the bed and drummed my fingers on his belly. 'I'm surprised you let him in,' I said, 'after all the never going out.'

'He just kept ringing the bell, man. I stuck me head out the lav window, and there was this little nipper. He must a rung the bell ten times, fifteen times. So I thought, no 'arm in a little kid. So I went down. Very sure of 'imself, he was, come up 'ere, asked me who I was and that. Just a friend of Will's, I said.' He looked up into my eyes. 'Anyway you come back after a bit.'

'How's your face feeling?' I asked. 'James says he'll come tomorrow and take the stitches out – just the ends, apparently, and the rest all dissolves.'

'Not too bad.'

I ran my hands over his soft half-open mauve lips. His tongue slid up and licked my fingers. I had certainly never fallen in love more inconveniently, and more and more I wanted it to end. Even when he spoke, in his basic, unimaginative way, I felt almost sick with desire and compassion for him. Indeed, the fact that he had not mastered speech, that he laboured towards saying the simplest things, that his vocal expressions were prompted only by the strength of his feelings, unlike the camp, exploitative, ironical control of my own speech, made me want him more.

Loving him was all interpretation, creative in its way. We barely used language at all to communicate: he sulked and thought I was putting him down if I made complicated remarks, and sometimes I felt numb at the compromise and self-suppression I submitted to. Yet beyond that it was all guesswork; we were thinking for two. The darkened air of the flat was full of the hints we made. The stupidity and the resentment were dreadful at times. But then in sex he lost his awkwardness. He showed his capacity to change as I rambled over him now with my fingertips and watched him glow and gulp with desire; his clothes seemed to shrivel off him and he lay there making his naked claim for the only certainty in his life. It wasn't something learnt, I suspected, from the guys before me who'd picked him up and fucked him and fucked him around. It was a kind of gift for giving, and while he did whatever I wanted it emerged as the most important thing there was for him. It was all the harder, then, when the resentment returned and I longed for him to go.

After James had taken out Arthur's stitches we took the Tube to the Corry together, leaving Arthur to do – whatever he did when I wasn't there.

'He watches telly most of the time, I think,' I said.

'Does he read or anything?' James wanted to know.

'He once asked me to buy him some War Picture Library comics, but I just couldn't bring myself to do it in our local newsagents.'

'I can see it would sort ill with *Apollo*, *Tatler* and *GQ* – but I expect newsagents get used to the strangest combinations of taste. They have to look on patiently while kids thumb through *Men Only* and *Penthouse* and end up buying the *Beano* and the Bucks Fizz fan mag. I saw someone the other day buy the *Spanking Times* and the *Amateur Yachtsman*, for instance . . .'

'That's not so odd – and isn't a spanker some sort of rope or something?'

'A sail, I believe – as in the limerick which ends "haul up the top sheet and spanker".'

The train moved a few yards out of Queensway station and then stopped abruptly. 'Could you ever get into spanking?' James asked in the selfconscious silence that ensued. I was obliged to live up to it.

'Not in a serious way. I put our young friend over my knee from time to time, but . . .' In fact, drunk one night and recalling an evening when I had been picked up by a Polish workman who got me to whip his ass with his thick leather belt, I had made Arthur half kneel, half lie over the corner of the bed and given him several strokes of my old webbing corps-belt from school. I knew he would have let me go on, but excited though I was I dropped it.

'I just can't see the point of it,' complained James. 'Does Arthur actually like it?'

'I think he does rather. I mean it gives him a hard-on, and all that.' The man beyond James looked up in a bothered way as the train started again. With James I often reverted to the flaunted deviancy we practised at Oxford, queening along the Cornmarket among the common people (as we more or less ironically called them), passing archly audible comments on boys from the town who took our fancy: 'Quite go for that', 'Don't think much of yours, dear', 'Get the buns on that'. James had worked up a cult of an overweight black youth, with a central gold tooth and a monstrous, lolling member.

'What's he really like?' he asked, as we hammered into Lancaster Gate and the racket of the train spaced out and slowed. 'I mean, is he a nice sort of person?'

'He is, actually, very nice, I think.' I felt entirely penned in by not being able to speak of all the things that made the set-up so strange, and which, depriving Arthur of initiative, made him a non-social being. 'Very nice in bed, certainly.'

James and I both saw how crass this comment was. 'But what happens when you go out? I assume you've tired of each other's company sufficiently to go to the pub or the flicks or whatever.'

I longed to tell him, whom I could completely trust; but my trust to Arthur, enforced by the whole way I was living my life, had become an unbreakable code to me, that is to say a principle of honour as well as an enigma. I merely shrugged.

'And that fight, for God's sake.'

I shrugged again. Could he really believe the fight story? 'It's all pretty much a mystery to you, isn't it?' I said, both proud and pained at the unplanned and inexplicable way things stood. There was nothing I could adduce in evidence of Arthur's charm. 'Sometimes I just put my arms round his shoulder and burst into tears.'

'I'm not surprised,' was James's comment.

At the Corry the mood was perverse. A few bull-necked mutants were hogging the weights, the room was crowded, and crossness was given voice to. Bradley was training for a contest the following week, and did so many presses that he lost count and, red-faced and shuddering, insisted on starting again. Others, who worked out for more trivial reasons, forced to stand around, lapsed from their normally passing and formal chat into extended conversations, like housewives with shopping waiting for a bus.

'I *know* – well, that's what *she* said.'

'But have you seen her since?'

'Only briefly, and then I couldn't say anything, because of course you-know-who was in attendance.'

'I really *like* her actually; from what I've seen of her, that is.'

It was the typical transsexual talk of the place, which had been confusing to me at first and which had thrown poor James into deep dejection when he innocently overheard a boy he had a crush on talking of his girlfriend. It was all a game, any man in the least attractive being dubbed a 'she' and only males too dire for such a conceit being left an unadorned 'he' or, occasionally, sinisterly, 'mister' – as in the poisonous declaration 'I trust you won't be seeing Mister Elizabeth Arden again.'

'You know that new girl behind the bar?' one square-jawed athlete enquired of his bearded companion.

'What, the blonde, you mean – no, she's been there a while.'

'*No*, not her, no, the dark one with big tits.'

'I'm not sure I've seen *her*. Nice, is she?'

It was conversation thrown out with a complex bravado, its artifice defiant as it was transparent. I half listened to it as I waited, and looked around at the dozens of bodies, squatting, lying, straining, muscles sliding to the surface in thick-veined upper arms, shoulders bending and pumping, the sturdiness of legs under pressure, the dark stains on singlets that adhered to the sweating channel of the back, the barely perceptible swing of cocks and balls in shorts and track-suits, with, permeating it all, the clank and thud of weights and the rank underarm essence of effort.

When I finally got a chance at the bench I realised I felt strangely weary, and going in a rotation with three other guys I slightly knew, cut my ration each time from ten to eight lifts. After a couple of turns I saw that Bill was watching me. 'I only made that eight, Will,' he said, with a worried look.

'Hi, Bill. Yes, I'm doing them in eights now.'

I watched him thinking and deciding not to censure what he obviously saw as an absurd infringement of tradition. 'Well, everything going okay, Will? Too many people here, I think. Too many people. It's getting ridiculous. Never used to be like this.' I agreed that it was inconvenient, and suggested that the club was hungry for the money more membership must bring. 'Very true, Will. But the interests of the members there are already have to be considered. It's supposed to be democratically run, you know, this place.' He looked around mournfully. 'Seen young Phil lately?' he asked with slight bashfulness.

I hadn't seen him here the previous evening, and I was left uncertain if it had been him in the cinema. 'I haven't, actually. Has he been neglecting his training?'

'He may have been coming in earlier,' Bill assured himself. 'There may be some other gym he goes to, too. I don't know. He needs to keep in trim, though. Very nice little body, that.'

'Not so little,' I suggested, remembering the beautiful hard heaviness in the dark. 'What does he do, anyway?'

'He works in a hotel actually,' Bill declared, proud to know this fact, which might be taken as the token of a fuller intimacy than was, evidently, the case.

'How extraordinary,' I said, my image of Phil as a military figure distorted by this notion, but settling into a new image of him, still in uniform however, marching along an upstairs corridor with a tray of coffee and sandwiches held at shoulder height. 'Which one, do you know?'

'Not sure about that, Will,' Bill admitted. 'One of the big famous ones, I think.'

James had been swimming diligently while I was in the weights room and when I went down to the pool he was hanging by his elbows in the deep end, in spasmodic conversation with a person I hadn't seen before. By a silly convention I always affected a censorious attitude towards men he might actually be getting somewhere with. I stopped by him at the end of my first length, pretended to adjust the strap of my goggles, and raising my eyebrows (an effort doubtless diminished by the goggles themselves) declared, 'I don't think much of yours, dear,' before plunging on.

Up in the showers afterwards he was standing beside the same person, and the reason for it became clearer. The boy, very brown all over, except for a pink triangle above the crack of his ass, was thin and wiry, though not quite unattractively so, his colour glamorising (as it can do a nondescript Italian or Arab) what would have been a meagre body if pale. There was something strained about him, particularly his gaunt, narrow head, hollow-cheeked and with short dark curls. His sunken eyes were a cold blue, made the more striking by his tan; when he turned round I saw that he had shaved off all his pubic hair, which added a kinky and intenser nakedness to his salient, sideways-curving, pink-headed and very large cock.

The conversation was not fluent. The youth would pass some bland comment, and James would try to reply with adequate enthusiasm or insouciance. 'See you,' said the youth, abruptly turning off his shower and going off to dry. 'Yes, see you,' said James, managing to make it seem a careless possibility, though the smile faded off his face in a way that showed it was not spontaneous. He had effectively been put down, as it is impossible to go padding out after someone in simulated sportsman-like ease when they have just said goodbye to you. I crossed over and took my place beside James.

'Who's your friend?' I enquired. He merely gave me a sceptical look. 'Why don't you go after him?'

'I don't think I care for him.'

'Oh come on! He looked to me as if he quite cared for you – if Dame Tumescence is anything to go by.'

'Another time, perhaps.' He shampooed his receding hair in a listless fashion. 'I see Miss Manners is having a ball.' It was one of James's almanac of nicknames.

'She is the end, that one,' I agreed, glancing at the man in question, one of that breed of middle-aged queens whose strategy, as they become uncontestably unattractive, is to cultivate a barging, unsmiling manner, sensitive to imagined infringements of their rights and never getting out of anyone's way. Like James's 'Miss Marple', a portly man who wore his glasses even in the shower and would blunder round and round the changing-room in his underwear for thirty or forty minutes, his spectacles misting up from the heat of his body, he was one of the odd crew at the Corry who, knowing no one there, existed in a kind of unseemly limbo of paranoia and repression. James, who himself occupied the club in a highly fantastical way, had catalogued many of its members with fantasy names. Some of them confused me – Miss De Meanour and Miss Anthropy were impossible to distinguish, whilst a pair of boneheaded identical twins could be referred to indiscriminately as 'Biff'. There was no doubt about 'Miss World', however, the hilariously vain queen of uncertain years, known to me also as Freddie, who came into the shower now, casting off his towel as if it were the hungrily awaited climax to a striptease.

'Hullo, *Will*,' he said as he came alongside, his tanned, creased, sinewy body swivelling balletically. He spoke in a carrying, recital manner, as if testing some primitive broadcasting machine. 'How are *you*? You're looking wildly wicked and young.'

'I *am* wildly wicked and young,' was the best I could do before I, as the French say, saved myself – inevitably bumping into Miss Manners as I did so.

'Clumsy little slut!' he hissed, with such venom that I couldn't help laughing.

On the train home I carried on with Firbank. I was on *Prancing Nigger* now, though I shared James's preference for its other title, *Sorrow in Sunlight*. How Miami longed to lift up Bamboo's crimson loincloth! 'She had often longed to snatch it away.' I lolled into reflection on Bamboo's charming words, 'I dat amorous ob you, Mimi'; and as I approached the house they were becoming a catchphrase of the sort I sometimes keep nonsensically saying to myself and anyone else for days on end, or singing in the style of Handel arias or Elvis Presley songs. I found myself muttering it, with mounting intensity and irrelevance, when I came into the flat, called out, searched round and found that Arthur had gone.

4

Charles Nantwich's house was in a street off Huggin Hill, so narrow that it had been closed to traffic and was no longer marked in the London A–Z; it was a cobbled cul-de-sac obstructed at its open end by two dented aluminium bollards padlocked to the ground. Halfway down on the left rose the tall façade of purplish London brick, the dormers behind its upper parapet looking out over the roofs of the surrounding semi-derelict buildings. It was an elegant post-Fire merchant's house, prosperously plain, the only ostentation the door-case, with its delicately glazed fanlight and heavy projecting hood, the richly scrolled brackets of which were clogged with generations of white gloss paint. Much of the glass in the tall windows appeared to be original: warped, glinting and nearly opaque. I waited opposite for a minute, surprisingly taken back, by its air of secrecy and exclusion, to the invalidish world of Edwardian ghost stories, to a world where people never went out.

Though close to Cannon Street, Upper Thames Street and the approach to Southwark Bridge, this little knot of side streets was very quiet. Drivers avoided the narrow gauge of its alleyways, and much of it seemed to have been given over to somnolent trades – a bespoke tailor, a watch repairer. One or two of the premises were warehouses; some had battened-up windows or displayed bleached and cracked signs for businesses long defunct. Though the buildings were eighteenth or seventeenth-century, the streets were medieval, and, sloping quite steeply towards the Thames, gave the unsettling feeling that they could not long avoid being swept away. Skinner's Lane, ending in a wall topped with spikes like spurs, half hidden amid tufts of brilliant yellow alyssum, had a mortal mood to it, and gave Charles's residence the eccentric rectitude of a colonial staying on, unflaggingly keeping up appearances.

I rang the bell twice before the door was opened by a man in shirt-sleeves and an apron, who let me in and then seemed to think better of it. 'His lordship expecting you, is he?' he asked suspiciously.

'Yes, William Beckwith. He asked me to come for tea.'

'First I've heard of it,' the man said unsmilingly. 'You'd better wait here.' He went off with an ambiguous tread, his sergeant-majorish bearing infected with an ambling carelessness.

It was a narrow, dark hall, the stairs going up ahead to the left, an old-fashioned coat-and-stick-stand, of the kind on which one could conceivably sit, behind the door, and a high, marble-topped table against the opposite wall. On it was a salver with letters stamped for the post – one to the bank, another to a person called Shillibeer with the outlandish address of E7. Above it was a gloomy mirror in a gilt frame. The rest of the panelled walls were covered with pictures, hung one above the other to the cornice, and ascending the stairs too, where their glass collected some light from an upstairs window. There were oils, water-colours, drawings, photographs, all mixed up. There was an unusually large David Roberts of a Nubian temple, choked almost to the eaves with sand, with blue-robed figures giving a sense of its stunted, colossal scale. I was looking at a lovely pastel head of a boy which hung beside it, when the door at the back of the hall opened and Charles and the paramilitary butler appeared in it, issuing from a brighter room beyond, which cast new light over the bizarre, threadbare rugs on the floor.

'Rosalba,' said Charles, shuffling forward before greeting me. 'My dear William. I do hope Lewis wasn't rude to you. He can be most cantankerous at times. Can't you, Lewis?'

Lewis had a look of being above such things. Following patiently behind, his square moustached head, with its cropped greying hair, indicated no emotion. 'You never said he was coming.'

'Oh, nonsense, nonsense – I told you days ago I would be having an interesting young guest for tea for two. My word, you're jolly brown, young fellow.' We stood now in front of the mirror and I looked in, needlessly, to confirm what he was saying. We were having an early May of wonderful weather, and I was already as dark as some of the half-caste boys I showered with at the Corry. My hair, though, grew lighter, and my eyes too, as I met my own glance, appeared arrestingly pale. It was that faintly depraved effect I admired in James's thin friend at the baths. Charles laid a hand heavily on my shoulder. 'Kind of sand-brown isn't it. Jolly good, jolly good.' He also indulged the mirror's grouping of us for a moment, his eye flinching from the stare of the taller Lewis, who hung about behind us. There was evidently a strange, and I thought pathetic, story behind all this.

'Let's go into the library,' Charles said, pushing me forward as a kind of support. 'We'll have tea in there, Lewis, please.'

'You do realise I'm cleaning the silver?' Lewis complained.

'Well, it won't hurt to have a break – and I'm sure you'd like a cup yourself, you know. Then you can get back to cleaning the silver; what's left of it.'

Lewis gave him a calculating nod, and retreated without a word. We went on into the room on the left of the front door.

Library seemed a grand term for a room that, like all the rooms in the house, was modest-sized; but it was stuffed with books. Some were housed in a handsome break-fronted bookcase with Gothic windows; others furnished shelves and tabletops, or were stacked up like hypocaust pillars across the floor. If the room had once been panelled, it was no more. The walls were white, and above the door a pink and grey pediment had been painted, perhaps as a *trompe l'oeil* relief; within it classical figures posed, and it was almost with embarrassment that I noticed that exaggerated phalluses protruded in each case from toga and tunic.

'Funny little chaps, aren't they?' said Charles, who was ho-humming his way towards a chair. 'Come and sit down, my dear, and we can have some chit-chat. I've had no one to talk to for ages, you see.'

We sat on either side of the empty grate in which a huge jug of bulrushes and peacock feathers stood. Above the mantelpiece, with its little brass carriage clock, hung a life-size chalk drawing of a black boy, just the head and shoulders, a slight smile and large, speaking eyes conveying happiness and loyalty.

'So, have you been at the Corinthian Club today?'

'No – I prefer to go in the evenings. I'll drop in after I leave here.'

'Hmm. There's more going on in the evenings, wouldn't you say. Actually, I think it can get too crowded. And some of the people are so rude and hasty, don't you find? Some young thug called me an old wanker the other day. What do you do – argue or try to be witty? I said I'm way past that, I can assure you. But he didn't smile, you know. It's so terrible when people don't smile. It seems to be a new thing . . .'

I pictured the old boy's determined, naked totterings around the changing-room. He was terribly vulnerable, I now saw. A few days before, when I ran into him and he invited me to tea, he was feebly trying to open the wrong locker (it was the old confusion between 16 and 91). He clearly had no recollection of where he had left his clothes, and was wholly dependent on the little disc attached to his key. As he fumbled and muttered to himself the tenant of 16 came up, a trim little student I'd seen around. 'No dear, you're 91 and I'm 16,' he said impatiently, and found himself equipped with a joke – 'give or take a year or two.' Charles didn't understand at first, and as 16 propelled him away I felt an unusual upsurge of kindness for him as against the sexy complicity with the boy that I would normally have encouraged. I came to Charles's rescue, suspecting he would allow me to be gently protective. When he didn't, at first, even recognise me, I knew that it was necessary.

'I suppose the place must have changed a lot?' I blandly hazarded. But he wasn't with me; he even screwed up his eyes as he stared through me, perhaps reliving some hurtful episode. I let a few moments pass, looked over the spines of black-bound art folios – *Donatello*, *Sandro Botticelli*, *Giovanni Bellini* – which lay on the table beside me. My grandfather had them too, in the library at Marden, and I recalled childhood afternoons looking at their fine-toned sepia plates; they must have been a special series in the Thirties.

'You're not cold, are you, William?' Charles suddenly asked. I assured him I was fine, though the sunless room was surprisingly cool after the glare of the streets. 'We don't get any sun here – only in the attic. Those houses block it out. We're very cut off here, of course.' It was an odd remark to make of a house almost in the precincts of St Paul's Cathedral, but as I looked out of the window I knew what he meant. The ear picked up a constant faint rumble of traffic, but the little clock sounded far louder; no one passed by outside and it was hard to imagine a breeze ruffling the papers strewn about in the rich stuffy air of the room where we sat. 'It's a shady little street,' he added. 'In the old days it was known as Gropecunt Lane, where the lightermen and what-have-you used to come up for the whores. There's a reference to it in Pepys – I can't find it now.'

'It's a beautiful house.'

'Do you like it? It's a very special house, more special than you might think. I bought it at the end of the war – it was all knocked to hell round here of course by the bloomin' Blitz. I was wandering about with Sandy Labouchère, seeing the extent of the damage. This was several years later but there was still all the rubble, covered in flowers and so on – frightfully pretty, actually. Look at this little street, he said – this little bit seemed to have survived OK. Down we came. You could do that up, Charles, he said. You wouldn't believe the state it was in, broken windows and plants and things growing out of it. We asked about it in a little grocer's there used to be over the road.' He paused and looked around rather bashfully.

'It is now very sadly closed, but the grocer's son . . . my dear William, you cannot imagine how handsome he was . . . seventeen, big strong lad of course, carrying sacks of flour – it was like pollen on his hair and hands, big strong hands of course. Well, my dear, said Sandy afterwards, if you don't buy it I will, just for that, you know. Of course, that was him all over.'

I smiled at the story, though I hadn't the least idea who Sandy Labouchère was. It was Charles's most sustained utterance to date, and in the chair of his own little library he was far more in command than in his wavering and insane peregrinations outside. Or at least so it seemed until Lewis came in with the tea.

'He joined the merchant navy and went sailing about all over the place,' Charles said, looking at Lewis picking his way among the books, but referring, I imagined, to the beautiful grocer's boy. 'Thank you, I'm sure William will pour if you'd like to put it down here.'

'I'm sure he will, sir,' said Lewis, slamming the tray on to the table between us. The wide china cups with their twig-like handles jumped in their saucers. 'He looks the type who'd pour out very nicely, sir, in my opinion.' He was sulking terribly about something. Charles reddened with irritation and anxiety.

'You're ridiculous today,' he muttered. I felt awkward watching this going on, but also detached, as one can be witnessing people mired in their own domestic quandaries.

'He's wildly jealous,' Charles explained when we were alone again and he was raising his teacup between two tremulous hands. 'Oh, he's making my life a misery.' His big jovial head looked at me pathetically.

'Has he been with you long?'

'I'd give him his notice but I can't face the idea of interviewing a replacement. Someone in your own home, William – it's such a, such a thing.' I thought inevitably of Arthur, and swallowed guilt with my strong Indian tea. 'But I do need someone to look after me, you know.'

'I'm sure you do. Isn't there an agency?' Charles was fingering the biscuits, unable to decide which he wanted.

'I always try to help them.' He spoke almost to himself. 'One day I'll tell you the whole story. But I can tell you now, he is not the first. Others have had to go. If I can't entertain a young man to afternoon tea . . .'

'You mean I am the cause of all this, it can't be.' He nodded at me as if to say that he too found it incredible – indeed, as if not sure that I believed it.

'He is not normal,' he explained. 'But he will have to get used to it, when you come again.'

I thought for a moment about the implications of this. 'I don't want to make things worse for you,' I insisted. 'We could have tea somewhere else.'

'It's important to me that you come here,' Charles said calmly. 'There are things I want to show you, and ask you, too. It's quite a little museum I have here.' He looked around the room, and I politely did the same. 'I'm the prime exhibit, of course, but I'm afraid I'm about to be removed from display; returned to my generous lender, as it were.' How does one treat such baleful jokes from the elderly? I looked blank, as if not with him – and so perhaps showed that I knew it to be true.

'I'm sure you must have some fascinating things. Of course I still don't know anything about you. I still haven't looked you up.'

He grunted, but his mind was clearly running on to something else, so that he broke through my following platitudes: 'Come on, let me show you around.' We were still on our first cup of tea. He had begun to push himself out of his armchair and I jumped up to help him. 'That's what it's all about,' he confirmed mysteriously. 'Don't worry, we'll come back here – want to take a biscuit with you?'

I gave him my arm and we made for the door. 'So much stuff in here,' he complained. 'God knows what it all is ... books, of course. Need more shelves but don't want to spoil the room. Still, it won't matter soon.' In the hall he hesitated. His suited forearm lay along my bare brown one, and his hand gripped mine, half-interlocked with it. It was a broad, mottled, strong hand, the knuckles slightly swollen by arthritis, the fingertips broad and flattened, with well-shaped yellow nails. My hand looked effete and inexperienced in its grasp. 'Straight across,' he decided.

The room we entered was a panelled dining-room with a carved overmantel and a leafy frieze picked out in gold, an effect rather like paint-sprayed holly at Christmas-time. It had the sleepy acoustic quality that some rooms have which are rarely, if ever, used.

'This is the *salle à manger*,' announced Charles. 'As you can see that slut Lewis never bothers to dust in here, because I haven't actually *mangé* in it for years. It's a jolly nice table, that, isn't it.' It was indeed a very handsome Georgian oak table with ball-and-claw feet, and in the middle stood a silvery statuette of a boy with upraised arms and Donatellesque buttocks, an incongruously kitsch item.

'That little bit of nonsense is by the same chap who did the willies in the other room. We'll see some more of his stuff, but come over here first.' He led me – or I led him – towards a sidetable where a green baize cloth covered a square object, perhaps a foot high and eighteen inches long; it might have been a picture in a stand-up frame. He leant forward and tugged the cloth away. It was a display case of dark polished dowling, rather British Museum in appearance, within which stood a tablet of pale sandy stone, a couple of inches thick. On its smooth front face three contrasting heads were incised, full profile, in shallow relief. I inspected it appreciatively, and looked to Charles for information. He was nodding in satisfaction at having turned up something interesting. 'Fascinating, isn't it. It's a stele showing the King Akhnaten.'

I looked again. 'And who are the other two?'

'Ah,' said Charles with pleasure. 'They're King Akhnaten as well.' He chuckled, though it could by no means be the first time he had explained its mystery. 'It's an artist's sketch, like a notepad or something, but done straight on to the stone. You know about Akhnaten, do you?'

'No, I'm afraid I don't.'

'I thought not, otherwise you would see the significance of it straight away. Like so many bizarre-seeming things, it has its logic. Akhnaten was a rebel. His real name was Amonhotep the Third – Fourth, I can't remember – but he broke away from the worship of Amon (as in Amonhotep) and made everyone worship the sun instead. Something I'm sure you'd agree with him over,' he added, patting my wrist. 'But such apostasy was not in itself enough. *Oh* no. He had to change the way he looked as well. He shifted the court from Thebes, where it had been for God knows how long, and set it up at Tel-el-Amarna . . .'

'Aha,' I said, remembering there had been a battle of that name.

'As it was all made out of mud, it didn't survive the end of his régime by long, sad to say. But there are bits and pieces in museums. There's a thing like this at Cairo. You haven't been to Cairo. And there's this one, which has one more head on it. You can see how the artist changed the king's appearance until he got the image which we know today.'

Looking again, I could see, reading Arabically from right to left, how the wide Pharaonic features were modified, and then modified again, elongated and somehow orientalised, so that they took on, instead of an implacable massiveness, an attitude of sensibility and refinement. A large, blank, almond-shaped eye was shown unrealistically in the profile, and the nose and the jaw were drawn out to an unnatural length. The rearing cobra on the brow was traditional, but its challenge seemed qualified by the subtle expression of the mouth, very beautifully cut, with a fuzz of shadow behind the everted curl of the upper lip.

'It's wonderful,' I said. 'Where did you get it?'

'In Egypt before the war. Made my trunk pretty heavy . . . I was coming back from the Sudan for the last time.'

'It becomes more wonderful the more you think about it.' I could not have delighted him more.

'I'm so glad you see the point. For a while it was quite an icon to me.' The point, as I saw it, was that you could take an aesthetic decision to change shape. The king seemed almost to turn into a woman before our eyes. 'A chappie came from the Louvre and wrote a thing about it. It doesn't yet have the Pharaonic beard, you see – you know, the ugly, square beard – which he does have in most of the remaining statues, even the female Pharaohs, whatever they were called, are shown with beards – perfectly lifelike, though, wouldn't you think?' Charles loved making these misogynistic gibes.

'So what happened to him?' I asked.

'Ooh – it all came to an end. They went back to worshipping boring old Amon. The whole thing only lasted about twenty years – it could have happened within your lifetime. There are those who say it was a bad thing – like Methodism, someone once declared – but I disagree. Cover him up again will you?' I put the sun-worshipper back into his millennial darkness.

The drawing-room was behind the dining-room and had larger plate-glass windows that brought in all the light they could from a tiny paved garden bounded by a tall whitewashed wall. The room was papered a pale green and had a suite of white and gilt chairs, tables, and a square, spindly-legged sofa. A plumply cushioned modern armchair on one side of the fireplace looked at a portable television.

'I'll sit down, my dear,' Charles decided. 'It's so tiring, talking.' He took the comfortable seat.

'Really, I should go,' I said.

'No, no – I don't mean that. And look at this fine picture; and there's more to show you.'

I sat on the fragile, entirely unupholstered sofa. 'Well you must say when you want me to go.'

'It's another of my icons.' He looked from me to an oval portrait which hung above the fireplace. From its mandorla of gilded oak leaves a livery-clad negro turned towards us. A sky of darkening blue was sketched behind him, and the shadowy form of a palm-tree could just about be made out. He appeared to be an eighteenth-century colonial servant; evidently a favoured one. 'It's Bill Richmond,' Charles explained.

No wiser, I stood up to look more closely at the pugnacious brown face with its thick lips, flat nose and short curly hair. It frowned ironically from the crimson and gilt of the high-necked footman's coat. 'I'm afraid he's not as pretty as the King Akhnaten,' I said.

'He wasn't in a pretty business, poppet. Well . . . he was a man with several lives: first of all he was a slave, then he got brought back to England by a General whatsaname in the War of Independence. He found him in Richmond, which is where his name comes from. Bill was one of those big strong lads we like so much, so the General trained him up as a boxer. He became quite well known for a while – along with Molineux, of course, that Byron sparred with. They were the first of their kind to break out, really – they were good fighters, so they made a figure in the world. Don't he look kind of sad, though.'

'Very sad. He don't – doesn't look much like a boxer, either.'

'No. You see, he became a valet or what-have-you to some Lord. When he'd done with fighting he just carried on in service. Hence the livery. It makes for a good picture but a sad story. I'm sure the artist must have scaled him down, too. Byron says, when he met him later in life, that he was a great strong fellow. I'll look it up for you some time. I believe he used to work in Molineux's corner too.'

'You don't know who it's by?' But Charles seemed to have lapsed into reflection on the fate of Bill Richmond, and wore a nostalgic expression as though he had known him personally. As ever, I let it pass; I was learning not to worry about silences in the conversation. I was happy to ponder his treasured artefacts and the secret metamorphoses that they enshrined.

'A last leg, and a question,' he proposed. 'Both rather special.' I took his arm again and we went out into the hall. 'Are you interested in boxing? That's not the question, by the way.'

'I suppose I am,' I said. 'I boxed a bit at school.'

'Oho! You be careful. You don't want to get that pretty nose broken.'

'I don't do it any more. Don't worry.'

'It's been a great interest of mine. You'll have to find out about all that side if you go into this.'

I looked at him humorously. 'Go into what?' He was unlocking a door under the shadow of the cantilevered stairs and groping for the light switch.

'Come down here. Whoopsy! That's it.'

In front of us a narrow staircase ran steeply down between unplastered rubble walls. It was a squeeze for us side by side, and I tended to be half a step behind, as he, one hand on the rope banister, committed himself with a heavy, lurching tread to each new stair.

'This is the most remarkable thing,' he said in a tone of enthusiasm. 'Oh, he'll like this, won't he. There's no other house in the world that has anything like this. Come along in, come along in.' He took on for a moment the air of a horror-film villain, muttering gleeful asides while leading his victim into the trap. The stairs turned a corner, and we went down two or three more steps and under a rough wooden lintel into a cool, mildewy darkness.

Various fleeting ideas, tinged with alarm, went through my mind as I stood and brushed at my upper arm where it had rubbed against the chalky staircase wall. Then Charles found the second light switch and the darkness fled, revealing a squarish quite lofty cellar room. Though it contained nothing at all there were two remarkable things about it. The walls, which were plastered and painted cream, had a continuous frieze running round, which, being above head height, looked tastefully classical at a glance but, like the library over-door, were homosexual parodies when inspected close to. And the floor, uneven, pitted in places, was a mosaic.

We made our way along the walls on old drugget, through which the roughness of the floor obtruded, so that I was afraid of Charles stubbing his toe or even twisting his ankle. On the further side of the room he stopped. 'You see it best from here,' he explained. The colours were very subdued, the white almost a light brown, the reds rusty like dried blood. 'Now, what do you make out?'

I thought about it; it was evidently a Roman pavement – a relic of some riverside palace or temple? I knew nothing about Roman London, had forgotten all but a handful of images from some illustrated lectures that Gavin had given several years before. In the top quarter was a large bearded face, with open mouth and the vestiges of neck and shoulders above a broad rent in the fabric where the tesserae merged into the restorer's grey cement. To the left at the bottom stylised fish shapes, like an emblem of Pisces, could be made out, sliding past each other; and to the right, and above, the upper parts of two figures could be seen, the one

79

in front turning to the one behind with open, choric mouth as they dissolved into the nothingness beyond the broken edge of the pavement.

'Nobody is quite agreed on what the figures are,' Charles conceded hospitably. 'The chappie at the back could be Neptune but he could be the Thames god with an urn or whatever. Then these are little fishes, *évidemment*; and here are these young boys going swimming.'

I nodded. 'Swimming, you think, do you? Isn't it a bit hard to tell?'

'Oh no, swimming. That's the whole point. This is the floor of a swimming-bath, do you see. There used to be a great baths here, in the very early days. There were springs. The water soaked through the gravel and what-have-you until it hit the London clay and then out it came!' He seemed delighted at this trick of geology, as if it had operated for his special benefit.

'And what's happened to it now?'

'Stuck it in a pipe,' he replied with breezy contempt. 'Led it away. Buried it. Whatever. This little bit of the baths is all that's left to show how all those lusty young Romans went leaping about. Imagine all those naked legionaries in here . . .'

I did not have to look far to do so. The scenes around the walls were as graphic an imagining as Petronius could have come up with. 'I think your friend has given us his impression,' I said.

'Eh? Oh, Henderson's pictures, yes.' He laughed hollowly. 'They're a trifle embarrassing, I'm afraid — when eggheads come to look at the floor, you know. They think they're going to get caught up in an orgy.' We both looked up at the section nearest us, where a gleaming slave was towelling down his master's buttocks. In front of them two mighty warriors were wrestling, with legs apart, and bull-like genitals swinging between. 'Quite amusing though, too, *n'est-ce pas*?' He looked down pointedly at my crotch. 'They used to fairly *turn me on*. But needless to say it was a long time ago.'

I didn't want to pursue this vein, and strolled reflectively along to where the two boys ran, as Charles saw it, towards the water. Or perhaps they were already standing in water, lapping round their long-eroded legs. They were intensely poignant. Seen close to, their curves were revealed as pinked, stepped edges, their moving forms made up of tiny, featureless squares. The boy in full-face had his mouth open in pleasure, or as an indication that he was speaking, but it also gave a strong impression of pain. It was at once too crude and too complex to be analysed properly. It reminded me of the face of Eve expelled from Paradise in Masaccio's fresco. But at the same time it was not like it at all; it could have been a mask of pagan joy. The second young man, following closely behind, leaning forward as if he might indeed be wading through water, was in profile, and expressed nothing but attention to his fellow. What did he see there, I wondered – a mundane greeting or the ecstasy which I read into it? That it was merely a fragment compounded and rarefied its enigma.

Charles rested his hand on my shoulder as I bent over it. 'Jolly fellows, aren't they?'

'I was thinking they were rather tragic.'

'My dear what I want to ask you is this.' Feeling the physical weight of him on me, I was sure for a moment that he had some physical demand in mind. Would I let him take my clothes off, or kiss me. A don at Winchester had asked a friend of mine to masturbate in front of him, and though he didn't, such things can harmlessly be done. I stood up straight and looked away over his shoulder. 'Will you write about me?'

I caught his eye. 'Well – how do you mean?'

He looked down, quite bashfully, at the bathers. 'About my life, you know. The memoirs I've never written, as it were. I assume you can write?'

I felt touched, and relieved; I also felt that it was quite impossible. 'I did once write two thousand words on Coade Stone garden ornaments.'

'Oh, it would be much more than that.'

'But I don't know anything about you,' was a second reservation.

He smiled. 'I thought you might be interested to find out, as you say you haven't anything else to do. I could pay you, of course,' he added.

'It's not that, Charles,' I said, resting my hand in turn on his shoulder. He looked almost tearful at having brought his idea to a head and facing possible disappointment.

'Before you say anything else I want to ask you, take time to consider it. Because, though I say it myself, I think it would prove to interest you a very great deal. It wouldn't be an immense amount of work, in a sense. I've got masses of papers. All my diaries and what-have-you since I was a child – you could have it all to read.'

It seemed at first a monstrous request, although I could see it was quite reasonable in a way. If he had had an interesting life, which it appeared he had, he could not possibly hope to write it up himself now. If I didn't do it, nothing might come of it. It was partly because I idly disliked any intrusion into my constant leisure – my leisure itself having taken on an urgent, all-consuming quality – that I instinctively repelled the idea. But it was not, after all, impossible.

'I'll think about it, of course,' I said non-committally. 'Give me a few days.'

He was extremely grateful. And of course he would be able to see the shape and possibilities of the whole project, when I had barely begun to imagine what it might entail. Suddenly he looked drained again. 'We'll go upstairs, my dear, and then you'd better push off.'

We left the Romans in the dark, and climbed to the hall, where I handed my host over to a silently hostile Lewis. He held him there, almost by force, in the picture-lined gloom, and together they watched me fumble with the lock, and let myself out.

When I arrived in the changing-room Phil was drying: not the preliminary stand-up towelling but those final points to which he paid so much attention, and which were executed sitting down. Naked on the bench, legs wide apart, one foot raised in front of him, he rubbed his towel carefully between each toe, and patted powder (I looked, yes, Trouble for Men!) into the dry pink crevices. I approached him at an angle – noticed how his ass spread on the cheap deal of the bench, showing just a shadowy hint of hair between the buttocks, admired the band of muscle which had begun to harden above his hips, and coming round him and picking a locker not far away, glanced down at his cock and balls trailing on the edge of the seat. He looked up at me for a second with his dark, bright, expressionless eyes.

'Hi, Phil.'

'Hullo,' he said, glancing up again. There was something more than usually inhibited about his manner, and his selfconsciousness came out in a flush. I was casual in the extreme, walked over to the mirror, looked with satisfaction at myself, and at him. Though I was ostensibly chasing a speck of dirt in my eye, my gaze searched the mirror in more depth, to find his attention flickering time and again towards me.

I came back and started undressing. I was so completely accustomed to undressing in changing-rooms that the act had lost that charge which it had for me elsewhere. Still, I felt a small warm amorous hum as I pulled off my shoes, tugged down my jeans and caught Phil's fleeting inspection of my cock. I stroked it with a single indolent gesture as if to set it free, and to present it to the boy who, with surely affected indifference, was sitting in front of me, pulling on his white ankle-socks.

'How's the hotel?' I asked.

'Oh, er, okay,' he said, surprisingly unsurprised that I should know about it. 'Hard work,' he added.

'What do you do in it?'

'In the hotel, you mean?'

'Indeed.'

'Oh. Everything, at one time or another. At the moment I'm waiting.'

'Mm, me too,' I agreed. But he was clearly not a person that I could win over with collusive bad jokes. I feared for a second he might take it up literally; his ignoring it suggested that he had understood what I meant – but was incapable of indicating the fact. More silence followed, in which I felt that I had the upper hand. He was now standing and putting on his old-fashioned and manly white underpants.

'Going to work out?' he asked. It was his first unsolicited remark to me, and despite its consummate blandness it had the air of being the final fruit of a long internal quest for something to say.

'That's right: nothing heavy, you know.' I was in shorts and singlet now, and tying up my white plimsolls. 'I'm not aiming to have a beautiful physique like yours.'

Something masculine in him momentarily bridled, though the new pleasure of being called beautiful, which must have been the secret purpose of all his body-work, won over and he smiled with shy pride. 'Do us a favour,' he said. It was a moment at which a more experienced person could well have turned to admiration of my own, less ambitious, build.

As I prepared to go off into the gym I asked him, 'What hotel is it you work in, actually?'

He was prefacing every remark with 'Oh' as if unsure of the way statements might begin. 'Oh . . . the Queensberry, yes.'

'Not far from here, then.' I took my key from the lock.

'No.'

'Well, see you.' I was making off down the alley of lockers and would soon have been lost to his view, when he said:

'Yeah, you ought to come over some time.'

I half turned and grinned: 'I'd like that.' He didn't grin back; in fact he looked very serious – and there had been something about the way he said 'you ought to come over some time,' casual and comradely and yet pondered, or even rehearsed, that convinced me that this was the same uptight, hungry boy I had blown in the Brutus, and that he needed my help, had passively picked on me as the one to show him what it was all about. I held his gaze a little longer, thinking of saying, 'Well, how about tonight?' Arthur-less, I was moronically ready for it, but somehow I deferred. I sensed he was relieved when I said, 'Next week some time?'

'OK.' He lifted his right hand a few inches off the bench in a strangely touching, almost secret wave. Two other hearty figures pushed past me, coming in red and sweaty from the gym. 'How're ya doin', Phil boy,' said one of them in the routine American disguise of some British queens. I went on into the gym, believing that some kind of agreement had been made, that it filled his thoughts now as it did mine. Then for a few minutes I made myself think about something else, concentrated on my exercises on the mat, stretching and limbering up. Because I was so easily moved by people, I had learned to distance myself, just in those moments when I felt them taking hold: I made myself regard them, and even more myself, with a careless, almost cynical detachment. But as I gathered, spread and folded up my body now, endeavouring to feel alive all over, ready and independent, I saw Phil again, in one of those odd *coups d'oeil*, typical not only of his hesitant mobile manner but of so much of gay life, where happiness can depend on the glance of a stranger, caught and returned. Aptly enough, I was lying on my back, with my legs in the air, wide apart. Between them I saw him pass the open gym door, his bag in his hand, his shirt-sleeves rolled up in tight bands around his biceps. He went by, but a second or two later stepped back again, and peeped into the gym. Our eyes met, I raised my head, he looked for a moment longer, and then, moved perhaps by the secrecy which characterised his doings, without smiling, turned and went off. As I sat up it was as if a fist squeezed my heart and cracked a tiny flask at its centre, saturating it with love.

An hour or so later I found James in the shower. He held out his hands to me in a pathetic gesture; the fingertips were white and puckered.

'A long time, eh?' I commiserated.

'There's just been nothing, darling. I don't know why I bother.'

'Nor, I confess, do I.' James, in his maudlin way, was waiting around for something worth looking at to stroll in. 'How long, as a matter of interest?'

He had no watch on. 'It may be as much as half an hour.'

'You must be jolly clean, anyway.' I pulled off my trunks, and noticed him peek, with the neutralised sexual interest that existed between us, at my dick.

'Spotless. But enough of me. How are you?'

'In a strange position.'

'Tiring of His Speechlessness the Khedive of Tower Hamlets?'

'Oh – no, that's all over ages ago.'

84

'Oh . . .' A veneer of commiseration covered a discernible pleasure at the news. I chose not to expand on it.

'No, it's my queer peer, you remember? He wants me to write his life.' James gave me an old-fashioned look.

'Whitewash, I imagine?'

I considered this. 'I think not, actually. He talks of handing over diaries, telling all.'

'But what is there to tell?'

'I think a lot. I've just been to see his memorabilia. It's all very suggestive. He was in Africa for a long time, I gather. It's the queer side, though, which would give it its interest. I have the feeling that's what he wants made known.'

'What's his name?'

'Nantwich, Lord, Charles.'

'Oh really,' said James irritatingly. 'Well it would be interesting, then.'

'You know about him?' I stumbled. Because he had come into my life up the back-stairs, I had fatuously assumed that no one else could have heard him announced.

'A certain amount. He's the sort of chap who crops up in the lives of other people. Kind of diplomatic-artistic, Harold Nicolsony circles. In fact, he must be about the last person in those circles not to have had his life written. You must do it.'

'Well, I'm glad I asked you. I'll get reading.'

'He's surely incredibly old.'

'Eighty-three, he claims. He wanders rather, and it's hard to tell what's what and what, as it were, isn't.'

'What's his house like, frightfully grand?'

'Frightfully grandish. Very nice, actually – stuffed with pictures, blacks, for the most part. He has a somewhat terrifying servant who's horrible to him and looks like a criminal. I must say I've become rather fond of the old boy. He has a Roman mosaic in the cellar and there are rather awful decorations of Romans with great big willies, Tom of Finland *avant la lettre*, but not what you expect to see in the homes of the aristocracy. Lord Beckwith, certainly, would frown on them . . .'

'It's too exciting. I'll look some things up for you when I go home.'

I didn't sleep well that night. It was hot enough to sleep without any covering, but I woke in the small hours feeling just perceptibly cold. The day's spasm of emotion for Phil recurred and recurred, and the prospect of the Nantwich book, which was alluring, was also oppressive;

suppressed guilt and helplessness over Arthur, as well, added their weight, and as the first light felt its way around the curtains, all the things which showed promise seemed only troublesome, agitating the white sheet of a future imagined without them. I started to fantasise over Phil, but didn't have the heart for it, had at last no sensation of sex, somehow, in my person. I dozed off, and dreamt of having tea with him in the British Museum; there was a mood of intense restraint between us, and when I woke I could not believe that we could possibly become friends.

Uncharacteristically, though the birds were cheeping from four in the morning, I lay in bed slovenly and indecisive until eleven o'clock. By then I had more or less resolved not to write Charles's memoirs, and to keep my life clear of interference from the demands and misery of other people. Even so, the vacuity of a whole wasted morning showed me how much I needed demands to be made. Sleepier for having overslept, I shaved as the bath ran, the steam repeatedly obscuring my image in the mirror. At first flushed with the heat of the water, I sprawled in the bath till it cooled. I remembered sharing a bath at school with the house tart Mountjoy (it rhymed with 'spongy') and the long talk with my housemaster, Mr Bast, which had ensued. Mr Bast had taken the opportunity, in that zealous, companionable way which housemasters have when they rediscover the pastoral nature of their vocation, to criticise the lack of one in me. 'You've got a good brain, William,' he said; 'you're good at games – and I can see why the other boys find you attractive (oh yes, I know all about that). But you should have better things to do with your spare time than messing around with Mountjoy. You lack vocation, William, that is what troubles me.' At that disaffected age, I felt it was a lack to be proud of. In the following weeks I messed around with Mountjoy far more than before. 'This is my vocation,' I would tell him, as we met up after books and sloped off over Meads for a quick one.

I was nearly asleep when the phone rang; I lurched dripping into the bedroom, sheltering myself in an enormous bath towel. It was James.

'There are various references in Waugh's *Diaries*,' he said.

'To Nantwich, you mean?'

'Yes. They're mostly only glancing – he must have known him at Oxford, and after. There's no Oxford diary of course. The most interesting one is before Waugh goes to Africa: "Dinner with Alastair, who returns to Cairo on Sunday. We ran over the Abyssinian plan again. Later we were joined by Charlie Nantwich. He was quite drunk, having been at Georgia's. Georgia says he is having a liaison with a Negro waiter at the Trocadero, and it is not going well. We pretended to know nothing. He passionate about Africa, beauty, grace, nobility etc of Negroes. He gave me copious advice, which I promised to remember. A. very quiet."'

'Amazing,' I said. 'Is that all about him?'

'That's the main thing. Quite juicy, isn't it? Dearest, you must do this. You are going to, aren't you?'

I rubbed at my legs with the towel. 'Actually, I've just about come to the decision not to.'

'Well I think you're mad.'

'I know.'

'Look, he's obviously selected you specially. You're *meant* to do it.' In James a scientific mind coexisted with a fantastic and romantic belief in Providence. 'And you've got fuck-all else to do. And you can write – your essay on Coade Stone vases was heart-breaking. And you're very keen on the grace, nobility and so forth of Negroes. It's an ideal opportunity. If you don't do it, some other creep will get on to him. Or worse, the old boy will die. It would be an inestimable advantage,' James concluded, 'to do it while he was alive, to talk to about it all.'

'You've obviously thought about this far more clearly than I have,' I said flippantly but truthfully.

'I'd do it myself, but you know how it is – the sick to heal . . .'

'I agree there are reasons for doing it. I've just been preoccupied with the reasons for not doing it.'

'It's too pathetic. I know you think you're too grand to do any work, but you've got to commit yourself to something. Otherwise you'll end up an old-young queen who's done nothing worthwhile. Famous last words of the third Viscount Beckwith: "Fuck me again".'

I smirked and half-laughed. 'I thought my last words were to be "How do I look?"' James, himself in his grandest mood, was doing his occasional lecture, for which he stood in, it struck me, as an updated version of Mr Bast. 'It's just the thought of it going on for years and years, and perhaps not being interesting in the least.'

'There is also the thought that it will undoubtedly be a bestseller. Come on, he was obviously testing you out at his house – what did you think of the pictures, how did you react to the statue of King Thingamy.'

'There's no doubt of that, and he obviously fancies me.'

'Surely you can handle *that*, my dear,' James objected silkily. 'I mean, you may have to pleasure him once or twice. Mostly with these very old queens they just ask you to go swimming in their pool, or they burst into the bathroom by mistake when you're having a bath. They just like to have a look, you know.'

'For God's sake, James, I'm not bothered about all that. It's me that's doing him a favour in the first place. He's already seen me in my birthday suit several times. He hasn't got a pool. That's why I know him.'

'Promise me you'll do it. Write the book, I mean.'

'But darling, you know how it is,' I squirmed. Instinctively I was playing with myself. 'I mean, I hate the idea of tying myself down. I want to go out all the time and – you know.'

'As far as I know, writing books does not preclude having sex. Admittedly some great authors have gone without: Jane Austen, for example, never partook of coition while she was working on a book. Bunyan, too, I believe, wrote the whole of *Pilgrim's Progress* without a single fuck. But no such restraints need apply to you. Why, within half an hour of finishing your day's work you could be in some back room, buggering away like nobody's business.'

I quite enjoyed these sarcastic smacks. 'Anyway, I don't have to make my mind up yet. I said I'd let him know in a few days. It's partly that I've never done anything like this – you know, there must be so many professional biographers. I'm completely inappropriate.'

'Do you think he doesn't know that? He knows he could set any of the latter-day Mrs Asps on to it. He's chosen you because he thinks you will understand. After all, you saved his life once; now he wants you to do it again.'

'Don't get carried away with the poetic justice of the whole thing,' I requested. 'Look, I've got nothing on, and I've made the carpet all wet.'

'All right. But I thought I'd better set you straight on this one. I'm late for my visits as it is – boils, babes, buboes, they're all being kept waiting. That shows you how important I think it is.'

'Okay, dear. I'll speak to you soon.'

'Okay. Just think what fun it will be choosing your author's photograph for the dust-jacket.'

'Mm – I hadn't thought of that.' We were both laughing as we hung up.

Three days later I left St Paul's station, and skirting round the back of the Cathedral headed for Skinner's Lane. The weather was still hot, but windless and grey: there was a glare in the sky, but I cast no shadows on the pavement. The lane itself and the house were smaller than in my thoughts.

I rang the bell and prepared myself and my expression for the curt reception by Lewis and the subsequent pleasure of Charles in seeing me and knowing that I would take on the work. Over the phone I had agreed at least to look at some of the material; I was to tell him in a month if I thought that I could turn it into a book. 'I know it's queer,' he had said. 'I'm not famous. But the book could be.' As before, nothing happened, so I rang again, stepping back as I did so into the street, in the way that callers do, both to nerve themselves for an encounter and to lessen the embarrassment that comes from being one of the street users who is seeking admittance to the private realm of the house. The windows were as opaque as before, but because I now knew what waited behind them I looked at them as if I could see through them into the friendly cluttered library and the silent dining-room.

There was still no response, and I found myself complaining under my breath, 'You did say four o'clock.' There was no one else about, though after ringing the bell a third time and also, to command attention but not to seem importunate, knocking soundly a couple of times, I looked round again to see if I was still alone. A middle-aged man had now appeared at the end of the lane, and as he passed and went into one of the derelict properties across the way I felt obliged to go through a minimal pantomime of impatience and perplexity. This involved trying the door with the flat of my hand and finding that it was unlocked and gave, slightly, inwards. I pushed it half open; and darted in.

In a voice quite unlike my own, I called out 'Hello'. There was no reply. The library door, on the left, was open, so I went cautiously in. It looked untidier than before, with papers and cuttings spread on the main table: this I attributed to Charles's search for material for me. I was surprised, as I turned to leave, by the sudden rising, yawning and shaking of a large black cat. It had been lying in Charles's armchair by the fire and stared at me for a moment with something close to enmity before looking away, licking itself, and carrying on as if I weren't there. It was a beautiful animal, tall and slender, with a nose both broad and long, and erect, triangular ears; it seemed a ceremonial more than a domestic cat, and its voiceless indifference to me heightened my sense of unease and irreality.

I did not try the dining-room but went, knocking and looking in, to the drawing-room at the back. It was empty and orderly, with folded newspapers, a sewing-basket and a darning mushroom on a side-table – things that a masculine household must have. From here a door was open into the kitchen, which I had not seen before. With its wall-cupboards with frosted glass sliding doors, its stoneware sink, round-topped Electrolux fridge and green enamelled gas-range, it resembled a colour plate from my dead grandmother's just post-war copy of *Mrs Beeton*; the plugs, which were of black Bakelite and only two-pinned, perfected the image. At a small table under the window Charles and Lewis evidently ate their meals. The pans and plates of a modest lunch stood untouched in the sink.

I felt a strong desire to loiter and look, but also, in case I was observed, to appear not to. And I began to worry about Charles. If Lewis was not around the old fellow might have collapsed undiscovered. I had not noticed whether there were bells in the rooms. I might be alone in the house with a cat and a dead man. It was an idea I did not find wholly unattractive. I strolled back through the hall, glancing at the pictures; hesitating at the foot of the stairs I peered at a little sketch of a dragoman, just a few swift lines that denoted turban, smile, sword and curled-up shoes. As I turned I saw a figure move beside me. My heart leapt and continued to pound when I realised it was only myself swivelling towards the dim old mirror I had looked in before. The gloom made it more mysterious and nervousness quickened my reaction. I did not wait to look at myself, but started to climb the stairs.

I never wore metal-tipped or noisy shoes, preferring to sneak around unheard. Still, the treads of the stairs themselves so moaned and cracked as I went up that there was no chance of being furtive and I climbed boldly, two at a time, to the first floor. In the silence as I stood at the top I heard another dull noise, faint but heavy, and the indistinct sound of a voice talking. It seemed to come from the room at the back of the house, the one above the drawing-room, which would very likely, I thought, be Charles's own bedroom. I didn't want to interrupt what might have been a private rite, but I acted on a more reasonable belief that something must be seriously amiss. When I pushed open the door and went in it was at first impossible to say which was really the case.

'Charles,' I said clearly.

'For God's sake!' The reply was desperate, muffled and close at hand. 'Open the bloody door – *please*!' I can only have taken a second to work this out, but already there came the pent-up banging I'd heard before. I crossed the room to a smaller door whose handle I tried and a moment later turned its stiff brass key; it was a door which was rarely locked, but which, gratifyingly, still could be if need be. Charles was not gratified. He had retreated to the other side of what was evidently a little dressing-room, with a chest-of-drawers, an open wardrobe, and a corner washbasin against which he leant, red in the face, his tie and collar undone, a look of both apprehension and fury on his face. He made me think of a boxer, penned in his corner, honour-bound to make a final and fatal sortie. He had no idea who I was.

'Where's Lewis?' Though questioning me he seemed to look through me. He was out of breath. 'Has Graham gone?'

I went towards him with my arms open, but he stepped forward with no purpose of greeting or reconciliation. He lurched past me, though I turned to support him and in the event merely pawed at his shoulder, and followed him closely into the bedroom. There he grappled with a chair which was lying on its side on the floor; the stooping and the effort seemed too much and I stepped around him to help. 'Charles, it's William.'

He took no notice of this until he had righted the chair, and dropped on to it heavily. Then he looked at me silently and intently. 'They've gone,' he said, after a while in which I squatted in front of him and watched him with an anxious smile. 'They locked me in there – or Lewis did. He didn't want me to get involved. Look at this room.'

Already Charles was struggling to his feet, though he reached towards me, and I felt he had gone through a transformation, and while doubting its logic, accepted that I was there. I held his considerable weight against me, while his left arm draped round my shoulders and we tottered towards the bed like a pair of drunks. When we got to it he held out his other arm in an eloquent gesture of amazement and desolation.

Actually in the bed, its wide featureless face absurdly crowned by a panama hat, lay a full-sized human effigy. It was only the rudimentary dummy that schoolboys make to suggest their sleeping forms in the near-darkness of an abandoned dorm, but in the light of a summer afternoon the bunched-up bedding and clothes of which it consisted were revealed as glaringly offensive. Its lolling pillow of a head was meant not to deceive but to warn. Looped around it, and displayed over the bedcover, was an Old Wykehamist tie, ineptly knotted, which made me remember, for a second, how my mother used to stand behind me at the mirror each morning to knot my tie when I was a little boy. Red rose petals were scattered artistically around, and where the heart of the effigy might have been there was a rust-red stain on the white bedspread that did resemble the colour of long-dried blood. I reached for a little bottle on the bedside table: it was vanilla essence.

After we'd looked at it for a bit, I let Charles turn, and sit down on the edge of the bed, and then yanked the doll apart, casting its hat on to an armchair and rolling up the tie. 'You recognise that tie,' said Charles, with surprising detachment. I smiled. 'What a pickle, eh?' And indeed it was the general state of the room, in which a fight had clearly taken place, that had shocked me when I first entered it. The composition on the bed had been in bizarre, attentive contrast to the slewed pictures, toppled knick-knacks and pillaged drawers of the rest of the room. 'I can't take another of these melodramas,' Charles said.

Though I was deeply curious, I felt a strong reluctance to ask Charles what had taken place, or to probe the humiliation he had undergone. I helped him to take off his jacket and shoes, and laid him down on the pillow that had recently imitated his head. As if entranced, he was asleep within seconds.

5

The first instalment of Charles's papers was crammed into an old briefcase. Carrying it on the Underground, I felt like a young schoolmaster, taking home a bag bulging with books and essays. It was heavy, as I lolled in the crowded train, holding it by its charred leather handle, which had been strengthened with black insulating tape and was slightly sticky to the touch.

At Tottenham Court Road a young man got on whom I recognised and placed within a second or two as the wiry person that James had fancied a while ago in the showers. He was even more deeply tanned than before, and there was something unsettling about this, as there was about his big, protuberant cock, very emphatic in his light cotton trousers, and the contrast of its fatness with his thin, taut body. He had a sports bag over his shoulder, and the clean gleam of his forehead confirmed that he had come from the Corry and a shower. He stood opposite me in the doorway, and we held each other's gaze for a long moment before each modestly looked away, though with the evident intention of looking back again after a few seconds. And so the sudden precipitation of sex had begun.

At Oxford Circus many people got off, and I dropped into the seat next to the door. Many people also got on, so my view of the boy was blocked. He remained standing where he had been; when I looked across through the glass screen that shelters the seats from the door I saw only the bums and palms of standing passengers flattened witlessly against its other side. I was heightening the drama of the pick-up by making him follow me.

This was impossible at Bond Street, where even more people got on. The seat I had taken was marked for the use of the elderly and handicapped, but had another claimant come, a figure like Charles, for instance, I would have been prepared to leave the train, when my stop came, with a lurching gait or limb held awry to designate my previously unguessed incapacity. As it was there were merely ordinary commuters and shoppers, though one of the strap-hangers, a man whom I spotted eyeing the erection which even the shortest journey on tube or bus always gives me, inclined to swing or jolt towards me as the train lost or gained speed, and the pressure of his knee on mine, and of his eyes in my lap, irritated me when what I wanted was the boy I could no longer see, and whom I dreaded getting off, unnoticed, at a stop before mine.

It was not until we had passed through the desert of Lancaster Gate and Queensway that there was a major upheaval; at Notting Hill Gate the seat beside mine became empty and the remarkable and inevitable thing happened, as my older admirer, smirking and hesitating, seemed about to take the seat beside me, and the boy from the Corry, materialising suddenly in front of me, and appearing as it were in second place, managed to slip by, almost risking having the older man sit on his lap, and occupied the seat towards which his rival was already lowering his suited rump. Confusion and apology were inadmissible in so bold an action, and he wisely comported himself as if there had never been any question of anyone but him sitting beside me. I drummed my fingers on my knees, and turned to him with a slow, sly grin. The other man's face grew clenched and red, and he barged away to another part of the car.

Only thirty seconds or so were left before we reached Holland Park, though I could decide, as I had done on occasion before, to stick with somebody I was cruising right through to a station miles beyond my own, where, if the cruise was unsuccessful, I might find myself marooned in a distant suburb, with boys mending their push-bikes on the front paths, shouts of far-off footballers on the breeze, and beyond, the fields and woods of semi-country.

So, as the train began to slow up, I tentatively gathered Charles's bag to me in a hint, which was reversible if need be, that my stop was next. I was relieved to see, while we agreed that the Corry was indeed too crowded these days, that he also bent forward, ready to stand up. As we elbowed our way out and started along the platform I spotted my other suitor again, savouring the last seconds he might ever see me, and looking almost nauseous as the train pulled away past us and bore him off.

'Do you live round here, then?' I said to the boy, across another funny kind of distance.

'Not exactly, no,' he said, with something complacent about him that brought back to me my original impression that he wasn't very nice. I smiled interrogatively. 'I thought I might come and check out your place, actually,' he explained.

After some efficient sex, we had a glass of Pimm's and sat on the window-seat in the evening sun. The air was streaming with seeds, to which Colin was sensitive, and after sneezing and screwing up his eyes for a few minutes, he announced that he had to go. I was not sorry; my mind was already running on to the prospect of opening the bag and getting a feel of what lay ahead. When I closed the door of the flat behind Colin, there the bag was, where I had propped it on a chair before making a grab at him. Retrieving it now, I saw how disrespectful I had been to cast it so hastily aside for the sake of that good but rather professional and chilly trick.

I took the bag into the dining-room, tugged open its straps and pulled the contents on to the table. I closed the window to prevent papers from blowing round; since Arthur's disappearance I had been a fiend for light and fresh air.

The main part of the archive was a set of quarto notebooks, bound in brown boards, rubbed and worn at the edges — most of them with a clear ink inscription on the front cover; 'Oxford, 1920' and '1924: Khartoum' were the first two I picked up. They were written in a fast, elegant and not especially legible hand, in black ink, and there were odd items tucked between the pages — postcards, letters, drawings, even hotel bills and visiting cards. There was also a fat five-year diary, of the kind which can be locked, with other letters and documents, and a large buff envelope bulky with photographs. I drew up a chair at once to look at these, as I believed they would be, although enigmatic, the keys or charms to open the whole case to me.

There were snapshots, group photographs and studio portraits, all mixed up together. A mounted picture of a set of cocky young men was captioned 'University Shooting VIII, 1921' in the amateur Gothic script still favoured at Oxford for matriculation and team photos. After a bit I was sure that one of the standing figures, a big boy with swept-back glossy hair and an appealing smirk, must be Charles. The face was far leaner than now, and his whole person seemed well set-up; I had seen him less and less in control of his life, and was surprised for a moment to find a young man who would have known how to have a good time. He appeared again in a more studied portrait, where he was less handsome: the spontaneity and camaraderie, perhaps, of the shooting photo had animated him into beauty.

Most of the pictures, however, derived from his African years. There were predictable snaps of Charles on a camel, with the Sphinx in the background – a tourist memento explained by the inscription on the back, 'On leave, 1925'. Most of them, though, clearly – or, in many cases, fuzzily – depicted life in the field, and were full of reticent authenticity.

Typically, they showed groups of natives, largely or wholly naked, standing round under dead-looking trees, gazing at flocks of goats or herds of cattle. In some Charles appeared, in shorts and sola topi, flanked by robed, shock-headed men of intense blackness. There was one heavily creased photograph of an exquisitely soulful black youth, cropped at an angle, where presumably another figure in the picture had been scissored off. After the scene in Charles's bedroom this gave me a mild unease, as if it might be a magical act of elimination.

In only one picture did a woman appear prominently. This was a very old-fashioned studio item, in which Charles, still young, and beautifully dressed, leant over the back of a little gilt sofa, on which a pretty, thin-lipped woman was sitting. Behind them the balustrade and pillars of the photographer's set made as if to recede into a romantically hazy background and to confer on the couple the flushed transience of a Fragonard. Such arcadian hints, however, seemed to have been ignored by the sitters, who appeared tense, and though skilfully grouped by the artist, curiously separate. Had there been a woman in Charles's life, then, an episode of which this was the unhappy reminder? It seemed more probable that it was a sister; and there was a troubled quality about the eyes of both sitters that suggested some family connexion. Did the people in wherever it was that they hailed from talk of the melancholy and ill-starred Nantwiches? It was certainly time to do that basic research which Charles had already several times recommended to me.

I returned the photographs to their envelope: most of them had no annotation on the back, and though suggestive and informative in a general sort of way, they did little to enlighten me. I did not know how thoughtfully Charles had collected them for me, but it was quite possible that his had not been a very thoroughly photographed career. Evidently doing this job would be as much a matter of probing his memory for links and identifications, as of reading his personalia and getting up the history of the Sudan.

I flipped about through the notebooks, picking on odd sentences, getting caught for a paragraph, but feeling irritated, almost piqued by the way the life in them went parochially on. I suppose I expected them to fall open at the dirty bits, but they were discreet enough to fall open at records of duties, quarrels with officials, guest-lists for parties. More than that, I expected there to *be* dirty bits, and the slightly repellent introduction to the trivia of colonial existence gave me sudden doubts. It was the awful sense of another life having gone on and on, and the self-importance it courted by being written down and enduring years later, that made me think frigidly that I wasn't the man for it.

It was really the present which reassured me. Charles's life now was so incoherent, such a mixture of fatigue and obsessive, vehement energy, of knowing subtlety and juvenile broadness, of presence and absence, that he gave me the hope which the books withheld. The more recent incident at his house, for instance, was excellent copy. From what I could gather, he had been locked in the dressing-room by Lewis, not as a punishment but to protect him, and prevent him from interfering while Lewis fought with another man in the bedroom. This man was a previous employee. I asked Charles why he had come to the house, and rather guessed that he had been invited as a possible replacement for Lewis. Lewis, as I already knew, was a model of jealousy, and I could easily imagine his slothful, sarcastic violence breaking out if his pitch was queered. Yet if he had fought for his devotion to Charles, why had he then attacked him through the schoolboy voodoo of the effigy? Like all the other miscellaneous symptoms, it made sense to Charles himself. He castigated himself after he woke up and we went down to the kitchen and made tea. 'It was bound to happen,' he felt. But he was unable to explain it to me. 'Lewis was a damn good scrapper,' he said several times.

The phone rang. When I answered it, a formal and affected voice said, 'Is that William?'

'Speaking.'

'I have Lord Beckwith on the line for you.' Some thirty seconds elapsed before my grandfather picked up the receiver. He had become so very grand that he commanded servants to do even the simplest things for him. His butler was an efficient, humourless man, almost as old as himself, one of a race virtually extinct, stifled by their own correctness. He would never, one felt, have locked his employer in his dressing-room. This was the first time, though, that he had been commissioned to dial my number, and I felt that slight anxious remoteness that thousands must have experienced during my grandfather's life in government and the law.

'Will? How are you, darling?' This was the other side of his magnificence, the unhesitating intimacy and charm that, more than the talent to command, had meant power and success. His endearments were not amative or effete, but manly like Churchill's, and gave one a sense of having been singled out, of having value. His 'darlings' were not public, like Cockney 'darlings' or the 'darlings' we queens dispense, but private medals of confidence, pinned on to reward and to inspire.

'Grandpa. I'm extremely well – how are you?'

'I feel somewhat overwhelmed by the heat.'

'Is it as hot up there?'

'No idea. Hotter, I should think. Look, I'll be in town all next week – will you take me out to lunch?'

'You're sure you wouldn't rather take me out?'

'I always take you out. I thought we could change it round for once. Of course, I'd suggest coming over to Holland Park, but you can't cook, can you?'

'Not at all, no.' It was our customary bluff, shy patter. 'You'd regret it deeply. I'll take you somewhere very expensive.' And besides, I felt the demands of an ever-intensifying privacy. Very few people came to the flat; I had whittled my social life down almost to nothing. Since my grandfather had more or less bought the flat for me, I churlishly resented any interest in it on his part; he had not been to it since its previous owner had left. Beneath our joky talk lay the awareness, which neither of us would ever have mentioned, that he had given his money to me already. 'It's so nice to be paid for!' he expanded.

Going back to the journals later on I found that they had changed; some of them had noticeably long entries in them, but not, in the two or three I studied, to tell the story of a very complex incident, or gather up several days' entries. The entries were anyway irregular, and periods of more than a week sometimes elapsed between them. The longer passages, which might start with a routine description, gave way after a paragraph to an earlier period recalled in detail, like a story. One of these, I noticed from the names, was about Winchester, though it had been written up in the course of a visit to the Nuba Hills. I saw Charles retiring from the company of his boorish companions to sit at a little camp table in his tent and reconstruct, amid the boulders and thorn-bushes of Africa, an episode of his English life.

At the time Winchester itself had been recorded in the five-year diary. It was written in a studied, microscopic hand, with tangling ascenders and capital letters which emerged from snake-like scrolls. On the bordered title-page the printer's lettering (again, that effortful Gothic) announcing 'This diary belongs to: ————' was outdone by the looping tendrils with which 'The Hon. Charles Nantwich' was laboriously rendered in the manner of the signature of Elizabeth I. At a cursory look this diary was unreadable in more senses than one. With a schoolboy's typical mixture of secrecy and conventionality the entries (which could only cover three lines per day) were written almost entirely in abbreviations.

What was more interesting was to see how, over the five years at the school, the hand had changed, casting off the juvenile fanciness for later, adolescent, affectations. Equally illegible, the writing came to look less monkish and stilted, and took on a passionate, cursive air. Certain characters, 'd', for example, and 'g', became the subject for worried stylistic amendment and experiment. Little 'e's, in particular, were restless – now Greekly sticking out their pointed tongues, now curling up in copperplate propriety. I remembered people at school attaching similar prestige to handwriting, though I never did much to adjust my own frankly careless scrawl.

I would certainly have been too slovenly to have stuck, as Charles had done, to the virtually useless annotation of my life in a book for five years. It was one of those changeless schooltime occupations, which have no function beyond themselves, and I was touched to think of Charles as a prefect fitting in the details of match scores and books each evening on the same page that he had used as a new man, his eye flicking back each year over the slowly accumulating trivia. There must have been so much more, for the book showed only the self-imposed thoroughness of the dull-witted or the lonely. I had no doubt that Charles's wits had been quick; and if he was lonely, then his thoughts would not have been taken up with fixtures and Latin verbs, he would have been living in his imagination.

The next time I saw him was in the pool, where I was thrashing up and down as usual and nearly bumped into him in the underwater gloom. He was not swimming, but floating just off the deep end: head back, hands on hips, his body seemed to be buoyed up by the white balloon of his stomach, and his legs hung down at an angle below. He was quite still, and his pushed-back goggles gave the impression that his eyes had rolled back into his head, while his body was abandoned to a trance. Though to my mind he looked dead, there was something wonderfully natural about the way he just lay on and in the water, as though on a half-submerged lilo; among the heavy swimmers and divers he seemed serenely disengaged, and I was amused, when I realised who it was, that he inhabited the water in a way that was all his own. At every other turn I saw him, from underwater; and he revolved occasionally with little flips of the hands, like some benign though monstrous amphibian. I left the pool without disturbing him.

In the hallway, as I was leaving, I found Phil hanging around. It was the first time I had seen him since the day we had made our tentative assignation, and I felt a not quite pleasant choking and thumping of the heart. I had wondered – as Bill used to do – where he had been all week, though I suspected I had altered my own pattern slightly so as not to see him, as though, like a bride and groom, our contract would somehow be spoilt if we met before the appointed hour. He was sitting now on one of the long upholstered benches, leaning forward, his forearms on his knees, reading a leaflet from the Club rack, which carried information about concerts, plays and events. I came on him in profile, before he realised I was emerging from downstairs, and saw at once that he was merely killing time. He turned the leaflet over and over in his hands, and as he shifted there was a swift sleek gathering and relaxing of the muscles of his upper arms, left uncovered by a pale blue T-shirt. His bag was on the floor at his plimsolled feet. When he saw me he at once stood up, with a look of strained matiness.

I grinned and changed gear. 'Hi, Phil!' I went towards him with one arm extended, and touched him on the shoulder.

'Hi,' he replied. A smile fled across his face. It was clear enough that he had been waiting for me but there was a childlike wariness to our greeting, like that of schoolboys introduced to each other by their parents.

'How have you been? I didn't see you downstairs.'

'Oh, I was there,' he said. 'Earlier on.'

He picked up his bag. It was impossible for either of us to say 'Well, is this it, then?'; instead we found ourselves going towards the door together. A close follower of Corry form might have seen it as an interesting development – a suspicion confirmed by Michael, at the reception-desk, who said, 'Goodnight, gentlemen' in a tone of bitter reproach. It was about 8.30 and in the winter 'Goodnight' would have been the instinctive word; but Phil and I strolled out on to the street to find the sky still bright, the pavements and the buildings warm. The slow, late expanses of a high summer evening were before us.

I carried on talking and, without hesitating, turned not towards the station but in the direction of the Queensberry Hotel. We reacted differently to the slight panic of the occasion, he shutting up completely and looking very serious, whilst I carried on with unnatural brightness and ease.

'Mm, it's good to be out in the open air,' I said. 'What a beautiful evening!' He seemed unable to find a reply to this. 'It gets so crowded in there,' I expanded.

'Oh – yes . . .' he said, catching and letting go the conversational straw. We walked on, and I came very close to him for a step or two, as one does walking with a friend: our upper arms brushed and then parted once, twice, with a gentle lurch in my stride. When we had started touching, everything would be all right, I told myself. 'Yes,' he added, 'it can get very crowded.'

I turned towards him with a broad, calculated grin. 'That's because chaps like you hog the weights all the time.'

Perhaps because he had heard such complaints before, he seemed to take this as a genuine sarcasm. 'No, it's not that,' he insisted – which, of course, it wasn't. 'No, it's because they let so many new members in.' Still I carried on grinning at him.

'You must be on the weights a lot, though,' I said. 'The way you're filling out, my dear . . .' I thought it was important to drop in a casual endearment, but he showed no response to it.

We had about a ten-minute walk to Phil's hotel, and an uncomfortable amount of it was spent in silence, with both of us looking about with affected interest at the buildings, the shops, the parked cars. Normally, if I was leaving a pub or nightclub with a pick-up, and taking a cab or a tube to his place or mine, we had both of us been drinking, time sped by, and we were openly set upon sex. I had rarely felt as sober as I did on this summer evening walk; each speechless step seemed more fateful than the last; and deeply embarrassing doubts began to occupy me. I was so lucky in general, so blessed, that my pick-ups were virtually instantaneous: the man I fancied took in my body, my cock, my blue eyes at a glance. Misunderstandings were almost unknown. Any uncertainty in a boy I wanted was usually overcome by the simple insistence of my look. But with Phil I had let something dangerous happen, a roundabout, slow insinuation into my feelings. Though I very much wanted to fuck his big, muscly bum – and several times dropped behind a step or two to see it working as he walked – my stronger feeling was more protective and caressing. It was growing so strong that it allowed doubts not entertained in the brief certainties of casual sex. If I had got it all wrong, if going back to his place meant a drink in the bar, a game of chess, a handshake – 'I've got an early start tomorrow' – the evening would be agony. Already I dreamt up headaches, queasy tums, excuses for dullness and an early escape; and I was so tense that as I did so I even began to feel the symptoms.

In Russell Square I grabbed him by the upper arm (its instant, globed hardness was thrilling) and pushed him from the pavement through the gate into the garden in the middle, half-running beside him, and conducting him not down the path under the gigantic plane trees but close along by the hedge that screens the lawns from the street.

'Sorry,' I said, letting go of him, my fingertips trailing for a second down the length of his arm. 'I just saw someone I wanted to avoid.'

'Oh,' he said, not without excitement, and looking back over his shoulder. 'Who was it?'

I did not answer, but kept on walking. He had not yet come into view, but when we both looked round again a few moments later, we glimpsed, through the gap of the gateway behind us, the familiar figure of Bill from the Club go past, smartly got up in maroon slacks and a dark green short-sleeved shirt. His burliness made his fast walk seem the more flustered and ungainly.

A strange look went over Phil's face. 'Oh, it's Bill,' he said, with an awkward little laugh.

'Yes. Did you want to see him?' A split second after this reasonable-sounding dissimulation I thought that perhaps he did.

'Oh – no. Is he a friend of yours?' Phil asked.

'I suppose he is, yes. I often see him at the Corry. He's a very decent sort. Very decent.' I sounded quite unlike myself. 'You must know him too,' I added.

'Oh yes.' He said this rather weightily, and we walked on, crossing the lawn now that the danger was past. It would have been disastrous for the three of us to have met, but my success in avoiding it was soured by wondering what Bill was doing in Russell Square anyway. No reason whatever that he shouldn't be there, of course. But he lived in Highgate; and he had been coming from the direction of the Queensberry Hotel.

The Russell Square Gardens have three wonderful fountains at their centre. Water, shot upwards in high single jets, falls on to huge concrete discs, raised only a few inches above the surrounding paving, and flees away over their concave surfaces into a narrow channel beneath their rims. They are unusable in any but the stillest weather, for even a light breeze fans the falling water away, drenching the paths and benches. Although it was late for such things, they were still working now, and we stopped to look at them without a word.

The westering sun shot through the upper zones of the planes, picking out the flaky pastel trunks and branches amid the motionless green and gilt of the leaves. Below was a dusky gloom through which people moved, breathing the warm, dusty summer smell. And the fountains pounded upwards, as if to cling to the light, and fell with only the slightest wavering of pulse on to the wide grey discs in front of us.

Phil must have seen them far more often than I had, but he seemed content to stand and watch. Their mesmerising, impersonal play was a relief. Then first one, and then another, in three downward jumps, was switched off. A painful feeling of emptiness and ordinariness came over me. I turned ruefully to Phil, and looked him up and down for several seconds. As we walked on I wondered if I shouldn't have used the moment to put an arm around him, even to kiss him.

As we crossed the road to the hotel, though we both became more tense, there was a perceptible shift of power: we were entering his territory. 'We'd better go round the back,' he said. 'We're not supposed to be out front when we're off duty.'

'No, sure,' I said; then enquired, 'When are you back on duty again?' If it was any moment now, it would alter the whole imaginary campaign.

'Oh, from midnight,' he said. 'That's why I'm here. I don't live here, you see, but when you're on night duty they give you a room. I'm on nights all this month.'

'I see. Where do you live normally?' I had a hunger to know these facts and to read things into them.

'Oh, up in Kentish Town. There's a staff house there — it's known as the Embassy. Because of all the foreign staff,' he explained needlessly.

We went along by the huge Edwardian façade of the hotel, and I glanced nervously up at its convulsed top stages: balconies, bows, gables, turrets, executed in a sickly mixture of orange brick and dully shining beige faience. Then we cut down a narrow street that sheared at an angle across the corner of the hotel site and revealed the undecorated plainness of its back parts.

Phil pulled open a door with a window in it, and we penetrated into a horrible area of store-rooms, rumbling boilers and stacked wicker laundry-baskets. It was like the subterraneous parts of the worst schools we used to play matches against. There were frequent fire doors which closed the corridor into hot, brightly lit sections. When we climbed to the floor above, which was the main floor of the hotel, we were treading for a few yards on patterned hotel carpet, and there were brass wall-lamps and prints of eighteenth-century London. Then we were in the service area again.

We passed by the open door of a kind of rest-room: the curtains were drawn, and there was a semi-circle of once stylish wooden-armed easy-chairs, of the kind where the seat cushions collapse through the supporting rubber straps, and a television, in front of which a man in the hotel's dark blue uniform was squatting. The air was dead with smoke and there were large, bar-room ashtrays on the floor, piled high with fag-ends.

'Hi, Pino!' said Phil. The man looked round; he had very curly dark hair, dull, handsome Spanish looks – about thirty years old.

'Hey Phil! How you work this thing? Is not on.' He slapped the sides of the cabinet with the palms of his hands, as though trying to revive a drunk. Then looking round again and seeing me, he got up.

'Pino, this is Will. He's just a friend of mine.' We shook hands.

'You a friend of Phil's?' he asked, as though to confirm what a good fellow I must be. 'Phil is very nice boy. Is very very nice boy.' He rocked about grinning and laughing at this, sliding a light punch at Phil's chest and capering backwards. 'Phil elp me this mornin with the bang.' Though he was much Phil's senior, he behaved like a child in his presence, and Phil, able at last to show me a place where he belonged, responded by showing how accustomed he was to this person I did not even know.

'You helped him with the what?' I asked.

'The van. I'm teaching him to drive the hotel van. But you're not much good, are you, Pino?'

Pino found this even more amusing. 'He very nice boy,' he repeated. It was hard to tell if he was crazy about him himself or merely recommending him to me. He sounded like someone trying to sell his sister to a tourist. 'You have drink?' he said.

I glanced hastily at Phil, and said 'Oh, er – no thanks,' while Phil himself said, 'Yes, we're going to have a drink upstairs.'

My heart sank at the prospect of sitting in some stuffy hotel bar with the boy I was in love with and an imbecile Spanish waiter; I thought for a second that Phil must have chickened out of our encounter, and grabbed at the Spaniard as a chaperon. But Pino was suddenly solemn, and extended his hand again.

'Very nice to meet you, Weel,' he proclaimed. We shook hands once more. 'I go to watch *Call my Bloff*.' As we left he resumed his persuasion on the television. 'You fockin, fockin thing!' he went on amiably.

'That's where we watch television,' Phil said when we were outside. He led me on to a staircase and we climbed right to the top, perhaps eight floors up. We took the stairs two at a time, and all the while I had this wonderful ass in my face; I had a hard-on by the time we reached the first floor. The attic corridor was hot and low-ceilinged, with dormer windows wide open and the traffic noise from far below nostalgically audible. Phil persuaded a key from the tight front pocket of his cords, and let us in to a small bedroom. 'This is it,' he said.

The room was furnished with a single bed, a bedside cupboard with a lamp, and a low cheap dressing-table with a mirror in which, standing, one could see only the region of one's crotch; there was also a chair and a curtained-off hanging cupboard. I closed the door behind me and we both put our bags on the floor, side by side. The tension was terrific, and I could hear the rapid shushing of my pulse in my ear. I knew everything was up to me.

'Well . . .' I began, but at the same moment he turned away towards the window; his face was stiff with embarrassment and fear. He stood there, looking out.

The mood of delay snagged me temporarily. 'Do you often entertain people here?' I asked, the words coming out with a quite sarcastic edge.

'Oh – er, no,' he replied, half turning his head but still shyly concealing his face. I took the three or four steps it required to cross the room and stand beside and slightly behind him. Outside, beyond where the light from our window fell, there was a deep inner well. The roof in which these rooms were built dropped steeply away, and facing us across the void were other similar dormers, unlit, their windows open into shadowy stillness. Above the roofline the sky was amorously transformed by the pink glare of the London dusk.

I put my arm around Phil's shoulder. He immediately began talking. 'We can go on the roof,' he said. 'During the day the staff sunbathe up there. There's a really good view.'

Nothing was going to get done unless I took command. Lifting my other hand I gripped his jaw, turned his head towards me and kissed him. Slowly, clumsily, as if being brought back to life, he swivelled round, put his arms around me and then held me extremely tight. I had wanted to kiss him for such a long time that I clung on, forcing my long, pointed tongue to the back of his throat; pulling out and biting his lips till I tasted the blood on my tongue. He was powerless and amazed. When I drew my head back a string of saliva swung between our mouths and I wiped it brutally from his chin. He had gone a deep, searching red.

I tugged out the bottom of his T-shirt and slid it up over his rhythmic stomach. The T-shirt was very tight, so I only pushed it into a roll under his armpits and stretched across his hard, jutting tits; I twisted his nipples between my thumb and forefinger and then, holding his eyes with a passionate stare that at once felt almost cruel, I grabbed at his crotch, fumbled and tore open his fly, and pulled down his trousers and underpants to his knees. Through all this he stood, arms away from his sides, impassive, like a child in a doctor's surgery, or someone being measured for a suit. He made no gesture towards me, except by a curious, serious facial expression: this was what he'd heard about, this was what he wanted us to do.

His cock remained as inert as it always had in the showers: circumcised, wrinkled, self-contained as the rest of him; it seemed equally to await discovery. I held it in the palm of my hand and ran my thumb backwards and forwards over it as if it had been a pet mouse. Nothing happened – or if anything, it shrank a little. I was taking things too fast.

I stepped back, tugged off my shoes (shabby old suede lace-ups which were never unlaced, a lazy affectation which I believed to be overtly sexy), unbuttoned and flung off my white cotton shirt, and with a hint of suspense, undid my fly and yanked off my trousers. Phil's eyes were mesmerised by mine, and seemed reluctant to go down on my nodding dick. Then he too suddenly got undressed, and stood away from the window, his head bowed under the sloping ceiling. His body looked fantastic, highly developed, everywhere convex, hard and innocent. His whiteness was broken only by the red blotch of an insect bite in the tender, creased skin at his waistband.

I was much more gentle with him now, stroking, kissing and nibbling – smiling, too, and making small pleasurable noises. And he began to respond, imitating me at first, but then making it up himself. Several times, though, it simply came to a stop, we stood back for a moment, seeing each other as we most often had before, in the showers or the changing room, naked and restrained. Perhaps the fact that the restraints of the public space had been taken away made us feel unnatural, inept at using our freedom.

The small bed was like being at school or university. It wouldn't encourage changes of position, but was all right for any simple sex act. When Phil and I rolled about our legs or our shoulders were hanging over the edge, increasing the precariousness of the situation: there was a strangely constricting need to cling together. Then he was on the point of falling on to the floor, his stomach muscles ridged to hold himself horizontal as I hauled him back by the waist, his head lurched upwards and our skulls cracked together quite painfully. The next day I had a perceptible bruise. Things were not working out with the instinctive ease I'd imagined. But I felt it was important to get on with it, and after a while and some laughter to relax him (though it also brought back an inhibiting normality) I turned him over and started to nose around his bum. It was deeply beautiful, creamily smooth when slack and when he clenched his buttocks almost cubic with built muscle. There was still the dust of Trouble for Men on the hairs in his crack, which I oiled back with my tongue, and sniffed through the dry smell of the talc to his own rectal smell – a soft stench like stale flower-water. His asshole was a clean pale purple, and shone with my saliva.

He rolled over, feet swinging above my head, and snuggled down beside me again, hugging me and resting his chin on my chest, putting off the looming fuck. My cock did look thick and threatening between his thighs, nudging its head up under his balls. Though he wanted to go through with all this he seemed baffled by some deeper incapacity. The childlike embraces were spontaneous, but the kisses, and the stroking of my cock, were acting, and made me an actor too.

There followed a weird, long nothingness – perhaps an hour and a half of lying together, holding each other, barely whispering a word, occasionally shifting and rubbing against each other fiercely, but only for a few seconds. At one point blood-warm water ran suddenly from my ear and dried along my neck. Later, both our stomachs moaned at the same time: we had had nothing, couldn't have managed anything, to eat. I felt I had lost all the command I'd had in the cinema, the certainty that made each seduction, as James drily remarked, 'an act of Will'. Then Phil sat on the edge of the bed and said, 'I've got to get ready.' I'd been waiting for this moment, staring at the angle of the dormer embrasure, lining up the chair and the edge of the open window, first with my right eye, then with my left. I lay on the bed, and watched him put on dark socks, clean Y-fronts, a laundered white shirt, dark blue trousers with red side-tapes like the soldier I still wanted him to be. Then he took the shirt off again, and smiled at me sweetly as he put on his high-collared blue uniform jacket over his bare skin. I was stunned by his body, but thrilled to see him dressed up, warm and hard, privately beautiful in his uniform. He sat down again to lace up soft-soled black shoes, and leant over me before going and kissed me with a charming assumed air, as if I were a country girl with whom he had enjoyed a night of passion before riding off to join his regiment at dawn. At the door he paused and buffed up his shoes on the backs of his trouser-legs in a schoolboyish way. 'I'll be along soon,' he said.

When he had gone I jumped up and walked around stretching, flapping my hands as championship swimmers do before taking up positions. I gazed out into the warm, still night, and heard twelve strike somewhere far off, just as I used to at Oxford and so rarely did in London. I also peered at the one picture in the room, which I'd not been able to make out from the bed. It was an Aerofilms view of Ludlow – the circuit of the roofless castle, the silver loop of the river, the massive church tower foreshortened at the head of its street-long shadow. It had that vacant quality that the photographs of chateaux and provincial towns have in the compartments of French trains: sunlit prospects of places one will never visit and which could never look the same again. Then I settled down to read about Charles's doings long ago.

We have been in Dekatil two days now, pleasantly busy with tax matters, crop inspections & medical help. I think perhaps this is the fulfilment of my dream, or the nearest I can hope to come to it.

The Nuba people are enchanting, with an openness & simplicity sadly lacking among the people of the north: indeed the contrast with the past few months could hardly be greater. Those swathed Muslim figures seem from this distance to be the embodiment of restraint & secrecy, whereas here no one wears a stitch of clothing, with the exception of a rare string of beads about the waist. I saw one pair of adolescent boys – very tall & elegant – sauntering along with their fingers intertwined, wearing scarves of red cotton tied round their upper arms. One old man, too, had a watch, & encouraged people to ask him the time, which had to be done in a very respectful manner. Then he wd listen to its ticking, & give a knowing & superior smile.

It is this, which I hardly dare to call innocence, for fear it might not be, or that I do not understand, which has moved me particularly, & has given me a sense of contentment, almost of elation, even when doing the repetitive chores of the DC. The beauty of the men is so openly displayed that it seems a reproach to lust. I felt anger & something akin to remorse last night when I thought of how this noble, graceful people has, until so recently, been stolen into slavery or mutilated into eunuchry.

Also last night, a dream of Winchester (the events are vague to me now, but the mood was powerful); & all day I have been haunted by it, & felt the intensity of its passions all over again. Not the forgettable saturnalia (which of course I have not forgotten) but the adoration and devotion. I thought mainly, needless to say, of Strong & of Webster. If the truth be told it is them that I think of most often, when I turn out the light, when I wake here, in the hour or so before dawn, when all the night warmth has gone, & for a short spell, until the light begins, the cool wind blows & I unroll the blanket at the foot of the bed. At the same time my memory of them warms me, stealing out from somewhere within and permeating my person. Though it is usually accompanied by excitement, it is not in essence a sexual thing (that is Ross or Van Orde in Mob Lib, or Chancey Brough out at Burford or B. Howard in my rooms after the Commem Ball – or any of the others who stock my private case of lust – its dog-eared pages!) No, with Strong & (more) with sweet Webster, it was the dumb love, the somehow utterly graceful restraint . . . I wonder often, having no idea, having dreaded even to find out, what all those boys are doing now, hate to think that I remember them alone, while they – Brough where?, in the City? Webster doubtless in some easy colonial office – pass their days among casual acquaintances, returning home by train or trap in the evening to young wives, working out their plans . . .

Strong I remember first in the bidets, in my first week in College (it might even have been my first day). In spite of everything to the contrary in the domineering, exalted ethos of the school, the bidets startled me from the beginning by their democratic nature – boys of all ages bathing in the same room, knees drawn up in the shallow tin baths. We'd had nothing like it at Mr Tootel's. I recall how Strong, whose figure was pretty well though not excessively attuned to his name, stood up dripping & came and stood beside me. I was not used to taking my clothes off in public: I hung back with my hands clasped in front of me rather than climb into the scummy water out of which this prefect had just arisen. There was something repugnant to me in the water: it was one of the many moments when the sweet, civilised certainties of home were trampled by the stronger, medieval laws of school. 'Get in, baby,' said Strong with a sceptical look, drying himself brusquely. Still I hesitated, and I think I was only able to do it because I felt suddenly unaware of myself in the senior boy's presence. Certainly it never struck me that I could be seen in a sexual light myself. I looked at Strong, and at his red, thick prick, which was thickly overgrown with black hair, as were his legs, all matted & streaked down with the bathwater. I had never been in the proximity of a mature boy before. I suppose I must have stared rather obviously – not out of lust but interest. I think, though I cannot be sure, that Strong took this as a kind of sign, and perhaps he was aware of the spell he had cast. I was not aware of it myself, only now I see that it was the first time that something happened that wd recur with me – a kind of loss of selfconsciousness in the aura of a more beautiful or desired person. My eyes were entranced, & devoured what was before them. In retrospect I think I see the selfconscious way Strong finally wrapped his towel round his waist and called out boisterously to another prefect, 'Bloody new men!' I felt a thrill of mastered shock at his language.

After that I always got straight in the water: that too was because I had passed through some kind of initiation. I knew that one day I should leave the water for other men younger than myself. I remember how the little islets of scum used to float between one's legs & hang around one's kit.

I was made to learn my notions, never imagining that they were useless to anyone older than the prefects who tested us on them. I memorised them religiously, & will never forget them, I suppose. My pleasure when challenged for the colours of Chawker's hatband and came out with the symmetrical 'plum-straw-plum-light-blue-plum-straw-plum' was so obvious that the prefect, Stanbridge, tweaked my ears, & made me falter, though not fatally, in reciting the Seven Birthplaces of Homer.

What I was much slower to learn were the notions that weren't written down, the notions people got into their heads. It wasn't long before Stanbridge and other, less senior men in the dormitory, started brocking me. 'Oh, he's quite a little tweake, isn't he?' Stanbridge would say sarcastically, sitting on my bed & patting me with a hand whose gentleness was suddenly disguised with mocking roughness. I was frightened in the near dark. I didn't know what a tweake was – all I could think of was how Stanbridge tweaked my ears. There was a suppressed excitement in the other men, who gathered around, taking their lead from Stanbridge, emboldened to knowing sarcasm by their numbers. 'You *are* a tweake, aren't you, Nantwich?' said Morgan, a fat, ugly, Welsh quirister, reviled by the others but being allowed, too, into the menacing conspiracy around me. 'Tell us the truth.' He spoke in a false, loving way, stroking my hair. The truth of the matter was I did not know what was going on, but my heart knocked in my breast and I felt sick. I longed for the morning – chapel, & being in my toys again, especially for the discipline and concealment of chapel and books.

This torture, which was mental more than physical, went on for some time. Then one night Stanbridge had been to the public house and came in very late. Talk had died out, and it felt as if most people were asleep. He came over to my bed & put his hand down under the blankets. I shrank away, but he reached for me, and felt me fiercely. He was a wiry, humourless, red-headed boy. Then he got into the bed too, though he was fully clothed, & still had his shoes on: their hard leather soles scraped my feet. He was very heavy & strict, though he had some sense of the danger, & kept on saying 'Sh' to me, though I had not dared to say a word. He made me bite on a handkerchief while he buggered me. I cannot remember much about it except that I cried and cried, in a soundless, wretched way, & the hot pain of it, & an agonised guilt, as if it had all been my fault, about blood on the sheets – though no one ever said anything about it. Later it became obvious to me that other men in the dormitory had known about it. I was deeply aware that it was not a thing that could be appealed against. Also after that the teasing stopped, & I was shown a companionable respect. And we all learnt, when the Second Master himself came to the dormitory late at night a few weeks later, that Stanbridge's brother had been killed in France: Stanbridge himself became clouded about & supported by the decent & entirely artificial respect that we young gentlemen accorded to the bereaved. Every week brought news of the deaths on the battlefields, often of Wykehamists who were fresh in the memories of dons & boys, & many of whom had been lavishly adored.

Things did not pick up with Strong until the next term, when he had me as his valet. I put up a slight resistance to this idea, because there was something unnatural in being sweated. In the holidays I had servants of my own, so it seemed absurd to become a paid lackey in the term. Yet Strong was very businesslike & pleasant in his proposal. Although he was a College man he had, I now knew, the reputation of not being very bright. I should say what he looked like: solidly built, with a wide, square face, cleft chin, square nose, dark, deep-set eyes, a heavy beard for a schoolboy, & thick, curly hair that was almost black. His father was a banker, not a country person, but he had lived mostly with his mother near Fordingbridge. He had rather bandy legs, & walked on the outside edges of his feet. I did not particularly need the money I got from being his valet but all the men who were valets agreed that the money was why they did it.

It soon became clear that he was very fond of me. He would make me clean his shoes & make his bed & cook his toast in Chambers over the coal fire. I did not really begin to fall in love with him until he became more obliging, calling me to him for no reason other than to have me there, or question me about something I was supposed to know – all this of course very shy & inept although it had to me the fascination of authority. But then other boys noticed that he had a softness for me, and brocked us both, so that I, who had been as unconscious as ever of anything erotic, suddenly learnt what was going on &, by some profound power of suggestion, what my feelings actually were. As soon as they said we were always together, I glowed that our secret had been revealed – although until that moment I had not known the secret myself. At first there were fighting denials, but the pleasure of affection overrode them, a pleasure oddly shared by the other boys, who were both catty and collusive. All was well in Chambers, but we were awkward when alone. I was soon idolatrously in love, & I believe he was too. One afternoon in Cloister Time when the whole College was out on war work at a farm beyond St Catherine's Hill, digging potatoes, he took me off for a walk through the fields. We walked along arm-in-arm though he was much bigger than me. I had an intense sense of privilege & occasion, though I don't think I envisaged anything particular happening. Nor did it. He said it wd be awfully sad when he left, but he wanted to join the War, & play his part. Then he said how perfectly furious he had been when he had heard what Stanbridge had done to me. He would have done something about it, only Stanbridge's brother being killed had made it impossible. I said I didn't mind, really; but he said he would never have done a thing like that. When we got back to the potato field, there were remarks. Somebody said, 'You look a bit stiff, Strong' & somebody else said, 'You two look fairly tweaked.' There was a general impression that we had made love to each other, which was pruriently celebrated by the other boys, as if on the morning after a wedding. I blushed & was delighted at this. I remember sifting through the barely damp forked earth with my hands, picking out the potatoes, the dirt packing behind my nails, & not in the least minding that we hadn't.

Strong died the following year. A splinter from a shell lodged in his head, & he spent some time in a mental hospital near St Albans. I used to think about him & imagine him raving: apparently he was sometimes quite insane. And then it was read out that he'd died. About a month later I received a letter saying he'd left me £50. It wasn't in his will, but he had told his mother when he was in hospital that he wanted me to have something, & she had suspected then that he was going to die. She came over to have tea with the Second Master, who told me all this.

By then things were beginning to turn round. The worship I felt for bigger boys, the heroic ones already taking on beauty as their leaving drew near, & the glamour of the Army glowed about them, was as strong, or almost so. But by the time I was 16 my eyes swung about & saw the younger boys. The emotions were far more complex, for being senior I had power, which I could use over them & then luxuriously abdicate in making my feelings clear. The idolatry was to do with not having – it was idealised, & above lust, which was catered for anyway by incessant parties, mutual pleasurings & painings. For two years or so we were utterly abandoned. An intoxicating, almost deranging mood possessed us. Of course there were one or two men who never joined in, who slept or pretended to sleep whilst the rest of us writhed round in passionate couplings or orgiastic free-for-alls. A boy called Carswell was our Lord of Misrule, an incredibly lusty little chap. We looked forward to night-time like some kind of animal that sits out the day, listless & almost blind; then as we undressed for bed a light came into our eyes. Not that we didn't frig in the day-time too. Our conversation was as salty as we could make it, and there was excitement to be had in seizing brief opportunities for lust in ever more public places. The occasional exposures, as when Carswell was conspicuously brought off in Chapel, must have opened the eyes of the dons, if they didn't know already, to the occupational depravity of the College men. Oh there will never again be a time of such freedom. It was the epitome of pleasure. When I sink back into the mood of those days, & then think of what happened afterwards, I am amazed. Those who were not killed are running the country & the empire, examples of righteousness, & each of them knowing they have done these unspeakable things. I suppose it is a part of the tacit lore of manhood, like going with whores or getting drunk, which are not incompatible with respectability and power.

Webster was not a College man – he was in Phil's – so my infatuation with him was bound to be more poetic. He was a well-made little fellow, smooth & brown, with luxuriant curly hair, & he had a beautiful sad expression. His father was a wealthy rum-distiller from Tobago, & his mother was English, & had aspired to give him the best education she could. He was the first negro I had ever known, & in the beginning I suspected he must be slow. Later I found he had a sophisticated, literary mind: he was inclined to be solitary & read a great deal. In his first summer I saw him one day at Gunner's Hole, lying on the bank in his swimming-drawers, buried in some history book. His colour, among the trees, the green water & the faded grass struck me like a Gauguin.

I found that he went to swim whenever the school's stiff regimen allowed, and if the weather was fine. I had never had much time for it, though it had its erotic side; but I started to swim too. He was a much finer swimmer than I, it should be said, but I was much bigger & could sometimes beat him as we thrashed round the bend together. At the end of our races he gasped & gave his dazzling smile and I lounged beside him in the water, or put my arm round his shoulders, saying 'That was damned close' but thinking inside 'I love you, I love you, I love you.' When we climbed out on to the bank I was fascinated by the way the water stood off him, leaving him no need to dry himself with a towel, and when he shook his head, the droplets flew away, leaving his black cushion of hair barely damp. Though his head hair was so thick, the rest of his body, though he had passed into manhood already, was virtually without hair, & on the frequent disinterested occasions I contrived to touch him I found his skin as smooth as a dream. It was the beginning of all this thing. In a way it was like my admiration for Strong, but now transformed by a stronger, even ethical power. I formed the impression that I was in the presence of a superior kind of person.

Now this was a very strange impression to form. Here at Dekatil, surrounded by the radiant darkness of the Nuba, with not another white man for hundreds of miles, I am continuing to act on it. Does anyone else feel it, or understand? Did anyone then, at Winchester? It was the wildest apostasy. It was the greatest revelation. It affected one's view of everything.

It did not do so at first, it is true. It was something deeper than articulate thought – a twilight luxuriance of my own, a heretical fantasy. I did not even put up much of a fight when other men commented on our being together, & called him cruel, unthinking names. Perhaps I did not even want them to share the secret or to know how wrong they were. And the manners that were making us men kept the boys from insulting him to his face. Webster himself was scrupulously courteous, & considerately friendly to mild men who spoke to him.

By a strange coincidence, the incursion of this black-skinned boy into my life was paralleled by the quartering of a goodish number of American soldiers at Winchester in the last year of the war, among them a squad of negroes. They excited a great deal of comment, appearing as they did in the profession which at that time we venerated above all others. One night in my last term I had gone on a secret escapade with some friends to the Willow Tree, & several of the soldiers were in the bar. They were noisy, but not I suppose dangerous or even unfriendly. After a while a tall, burly negro in the group came over & asked if we knew where he could get a girl for the night. We were all awed by his colour and his quiet but resonant voice, & we said we were sorry, we had no idea. 'Well, what do *you* do?' he wanted to know. There was something sarcastic beneath his respectful tone, and we blustered priggishly & inadequately. I suddenly thought how strange it was for a working man from America to be faced with these effete, distinguished youngsters of another colour, almost another language. I doubt if any of us, despite hints some of us put about, had ever had a girl anyway. He nodded at us contemptuously & said 'I know what you fucking do.' It was a word we sometimes used, but to hear it used against us by someone from the class where rough language (& 'fucking' itself) were known to thrive, was a shocking & belittling experience.

Later on, before our group left, I went to the pissoir in the back yard of the pub, a narrow room with a gutter & a powerful smell of Jeyes' Fluid (it is the same smell in the latrines here – it brought the memory flooding back on my very first day in the Sudan). I had just begun to relieve myself when another figure came in to the shadowy, twilit urinal, and squeezed past me to stand at a position further along. Of course it was the negro soldier. As he urinated copiously he made noises of pleasure and satisfaction, & then began talking quietly & confidentially, as if we were old friends. He said how he had a beautiful girlfriend in Wilmington, Delaware, how lonely it was being a soldier, how he wanted some action (this in a very loaded voice). I felt terrified but also thrilled that he was talking to me. Everything about him was strange, forceful; he was utterly his ordinary self yet to me he was abrasively, rankly new. I could think of nothing to say. I turned to look at him, at least to say goodbye. He stirred some primitive instinct of hospitality in me. I saw his eyes in the gloom, and his teeth. He was looking at me, grinning. My eyes darted about & I just made out that he was stroking his penis. He took his hands away from it & reached towards me, leaving his brutal, aching sex massive and erect.

I fled from that pissoir & joined my half-drunken friends for the walk back to College, the awkward, well-tried climb back in, my head ringing with the unutterable shock of it. It had been too sudden an offering of what I too deeply desired. I never saw the soldier again. A thousand, thousand times I've wished I had . . .

I was asleep when Phil came in, and I woke to feel him sitting on the bed, taking his shoes off. I reached out to touch whatever part of him was nearest (it was his right knee) and mumblingly asked him the time (it was six o'clock). I was ready to snuggle down with him for his off-beat, shift-work sleep, but in a few moments he was lying on top of me, kissing me.

The taste of his breath was remarkable, especially since I had just woken and was babyishly vulnerable to him: there was whisky, and laid over it, to conceal it from me as much as from the guests and management, there was peppermint. He was quite slavish with his hands and tongue, and he licked me, lapped at me, in a deaf, drunken homage for several minutes. Then he sat back on his heels, astride me, and unbuttoned and took off his tight little jacket. I stretched out my arms and dreamily stroked his shoulders and tits, smiling in a stupid, sleepy way that he seemed to find just as sexy as I intended.

6

I found James leaning in a corner of the foyer, lips pursed over the score.

'Taking it a bit seriously, aren't you darling?' I said.

'Darling.' We kissed drily, rapidly. 'No, it's frightfully good, actually.'

'Well, I'm glad you're going to enjoy it.' I gazed around despairingly at the white tuxedos and bare shoulders. It was far too hot to be in an opera-house, and I had come along in what was virtually a pair of pyjamas – a super-light African cotton outfit, the queenery of which was chastened by a hint of martial arts.

'Everybody's looking at you,' said James, who, adorably, was wearing a suit and tie. 'God knows what Lord B. will think.' He had a pleasantly snobbish respect for our family; my grandfather was very fond of James, whom he saw as a humane and practical person, with charming manners and a keen interest in the arts.

'I despise them all,' I protested, turning away from a macabre trio of queens, very got-up with gloves and velvet bow-ties. 'The way some of these creatures look at you, you feel as though you're being violated – ocularly.'

James was a little embarrassed, had not yet slipped out of the responsibilities of the day, was to be on his best behaviour, and yet also, I knew, longed to side with extravagance. I was in a mood of atrocious egotism, brought on by what had turned out to be absolute adoration from Phil, but I seemed to sense, as I looked across the hall and up the long mirrored stairway, a further perspective, in which James and I were together as we had been in the past.

'They might pay less attention to you,' he said, 'if you didn't look like something out of the *Arabian Nights*. You appear to have an erection, as well.'

'Of course I've got an erection. I'm in love.'

James gave me a comically shrewd look. 'Oh God. And who's the victim this time?'

'What a horrid thing to say!' I swept the audience with another glare. 'He's a boy from the Corry, actually – a body-builder – short – dark hair – called Phil.' Just saying that made me wish I were with him even more. I glanced at James and saw a look of terrible anxiety pass over his face.

'I wonder if it's anyone I've seen there,' he said. Then: 'Ah – here's Lord B.'

My grandfather, looking very fine with sleek, grey hair and sun-browned face, was making his way courteously through the crowd. 'James. Very good to see you.' They shook hands and grinned. 'Turning in, old boy?' he said to me. 'I could have a bed made up in the box.' At the same time he shook me by the scruff of the neck, insisting on his joke even as he showed he did not mean it. The glow of mutual appreciation permeated my mood. We started upstairs.

'Did you have a sleep after lunch?' I enquired.

'I think I probably did drop off – how about you?'

'Mm – I spent all afternoon in bed,' I replied truthfully.

'Frightfully good lunch, though. Do you know this restaurant, James?'

'Where did you go?'

'The Crépuscule des Dieux.' He chuckled. 'It ought to be just up your street . . .' He meant, because of Wagner, though he can't have been unaware of the discreetly homosexual style of the whole place, the waiters in tails with long white aprons, the rich older men treating their bored and flirtatious young dolly-boys. 'Not the food for you, though, perhaps – all swimming in blood!' James loathed jokes of this kind but he managed a disgusted smile. He'd passed a demanding New Year at Marden once, subsisting entirely on roast potatoes and Stilton, and pretending indifference as chargers of pheasant, goose and almost raw beef were borne in by the staff.

Upstairs, my grandfather remembered the name of the doorman who walked along the corridor with us, saying, just at the last moment, 'And how's your wife, Roy?' (Roy being the man's surname rather than his Christian name).

'I'm afraid she died, my lord,' Roy said in a well-seasoned way. Here was a test for my grandfather, for a merely courtesy concern had turned on him and presented him with a real little tragedy. I stood and watched him pat the man on the back in a brotherly way, and nod his head impressively.

'They're pretty terrible, these bereavements,' he said. 'And it doesn't get any better, I'm afraid.' As Roy said, 'No, my lord,' he was already leaving him, having done the convincingly human thing and yet not involved himself in the least. He pulled the door to and placed us, him in the middle, and James nearer the stage.

My grandfather was a Director of Covent Garden, and I had seen many operas with him from this same box. Yet I never felt it was a good point to watch the performance from: for the privacy and elevation of the box we paid the cost of seeing the orchestra, a view into the wings and an imperfect vantage on the upper stage. The privacy, anyway, was an ambiguous thing, since the eyes of the stalls dwelt on the boxes as though on the balconies of a royal residence. I was aware of the bad effect this had on me – an affected unawareness of the rest of the house, exaggerated laughter and enthralment in the remarks of my companions. I did not like myself much for this – indeed the box represented to me in some ways the penalties of exposure, discomfort and pitilessness which were paid for privilege. Tonight I sprawled over the red plush sill and let James and my grandfather talk until the lights went down.

It was *Billy Budd*, an opera I recalled as a gauche, almost amateur affair, and I had not in the least expected to enjoy it; and yet, when Captain Vere's monologue ended and the scene on board the *Indomitable* opened up, with the men holy-stoning the deck and singing their oppressed, surging chorus, I was covered in goose-flesh. When Billy, press-ganged from his old ship, sang his farewell to his former life and comrades – 'Farewell, old *Rights o' Man*, farewell' – the tears streamed down my face. The young baritone, singing with the greatest beauty and freshness, brought an extraordinary quality of resisted pathos to Billy; in the stammering music his physiognomy, handsome and forthright and yet with a curious fleshy debility about the mouth, made me believe it as his own tragedy.

None of this should have surprised me. I had not heard any music for a few days, and I was all charged up, glowing and gratified, so that my sense of everything was heightened. I felt every phrase of the music in a physical way, as if I had turned into a little orchestra myself.

In the interval we had champagne, though James would only take a drop, saying it would give him a headache. He was prone to bad headaches, often of a nervous kind (for instance, when he had a clear weekend after being on call for two or three weeks he would spend it supine in a darkened room, a hand pressed to his brow). The heat and intensity of a theatre always brought on a bit of a head for him too. I think he concentrated exceptionally hard – at a concert he would either follow the score or his knuckles would be white with tension – whereas I, though I was gripped and appalled by the opera, blubbing again at the despair of the poor little Novice, his body and spirit broken by his flogging, had also had periods of several minutes' duration when I had paid no attention at all, thinking about Phil, and sex, and what I was going to do later.

My grandfather looked at me apprehensively. 'Are you enjoying it, darling?' he asked.

'I think it's wonderful,' I said. 'It's a funny old production, but there's something quite touching about that.'

'Mm – I agree. Quite unchanged since the very first performance, of course. It's a museum piece, still being used after thirty years. We had a lot of talk about a new production, but we felt the loot could be better spent on something else.'

'Yes.' I was on for more champagne already.

'What do you think, James?'

'Oh, I'm enjoying it,' James said, with an emphasis that suggested reservations. His eyes were darkly rimmed, he looked sallow with lack of sleep, and I wondered what it would be like to come to the crowded unreality of a theatre after a day's long concentration on illness and misery.

'I don't know if it's a piece you especially care for.'

'It's always more moving and impressive than you expect,' James said, as so often echoing my own feelings; but our solidarity brought us to the edge of difficult terrain. What he would want to talk about would be the suppressed or (in his usual term) deflected sexuality of the opera. We must all have recognised it, though it would have had an importance, even an eloquence, to James and me that would have been quite lost on my grandfather. He had spent all his adult life in circles where good manners, lofty savoir-faire and plain callousness conspired to avoid any recognition that homosexuality even existed. The three of us in our hot little box were trapped with this intensely British problem: the opera that was, but wasn't, gay, the two young gay friends on good behaviour, the mandarin patriarch giving nothing of his feelings away.

I decided to brave it, and said: 'It's an odd piece, though, partly the sex thing, of course. Claggart's bit about beauty and handsomeness could win a prize for general ghastly creepiness. He's sort of coming out with it and not coming out with it at the same time.'

My grandfather hesitated diplomatically before saying: 'That was very much Forster's line actually. Though I don't think it's generally known.'

'Did you meet Forster?' James blurted in reverence and surprise.

'Oh, only occasionally, you know. But I do clearly recall the first night of *Billy Budd*. Britten himself was in the pit, of course. It made a fairly big impression, though I remember opinion was very divided about it. Many people understandably didn't altogether care for the Britten–Pears thing.' James looked blank and I frowned, but my grandfather went on. 'There was a party afterwards that Laura and I went to and I had quite a long chat with old Forster about the libretto.'

'What was he like?' asked James. My grandfather smiled wearily – he did not care to be interrupted. Then James looked mortified.

'He seemed satisfied with it, but there was something distinctly contrary about him. I was quite surprised when he openly criticised some of the music. Claggart's monologue in particular he thought was wrong. He wanted it to be much more . . . open, and sexy, as Willy puts it. I think *soggy* was the word he used to describe Britten's music for it.'

I thought this was extremely interesting, and my grandfather looked pleased, as if he had belatedly discovered the use of something he had dutifully been carrying about for years. I felt matters had subtly changed, an admission been made. But then that 'understandable' dislike of Britten and Pears – there was a little phrase I might myself take on through life, wanting to forget it or to disprove the unpleasant truth it hinted at. I tilted out the last of the champagne and watched James talking to his host. I seemed to see him as a boy, a shy but exemplary sixth-former reporting to a master. The open score on the sill of the box was like a book in a portrait codifying some special accomplishment, the entry to a world of sensibility where he had found himself when young, and to which, hard-working and solitary, he must still have access.

I was smiling reflectively, perhaps irritatingly, at him as we were joined by Barton Maggs, one of the most assiduous and proprietary opera-goers in London and abroad, on his interval tour of the nobs.

'Oh dear, oh dear – Denis, Will . . .' he nodded upswept, sandy eyebrows at us.

'Do you know James Brooke? Professor Maggs . . .' He discharged a further nod at James. He seemed to be out of breath, getting round everybody in time, and his weight was emphasised by a too tight and youthful seersucker suit and white moccasins on small womanly feet.

'Fair to middling, I'd say, wouldn't you?' he proposed.

'We were just saying how good we thought it was.' Maggs had no sense of humour and no awareness either that we would instinctively treat him with irony.

'Oh dear – it's funny, isn't it, I always think how funny, there not being any women in it. Some people claim not to notice.' He looked around as if *anything* might happen.

'You couldn't have *women* in it, though, could you. I mean, it takes place on a *ship*.' I felt that just about summed it up.

My grandfather engaged with it drolly. 'Still, I think you want a sort of Buttercup figure, don't you, Barty – selling tobacco and peppermints to the crew . . .'

'Perhaps Captain Vere's sisters and his cousins and his aunts could be brought in,' I said. 'I'm sure they'd quell any mutiny.'

'Oh yes, h'm. I do miss hearing a good soprano though,' he said, and looked almost bereft, as if Britten had let him down in not providing the display of palpitating femininity that so many homosexuals crave. The warning bell was already ringing and he busily took his leave.

My grandfather was reminiscing about Forster again (matter which was all new to me as well, so that I asked myself why I had never as it were interviewed him about his past) when James broke in a second time. 'I say, isn't that Pears down there?' We all turned to look.

Pears was shuffling very slowly along the aisle towards the front of the stalls, supported by a man on either side. Most of the bland audience showed no recognition of who he was, though occasionally someone would stare, or look away hurriedly from the singer's stroke-slackened but beautiful white-crested head. Then there was the protracted and awkward process of getting him along his already repopulated row. James and I were mesmerised, and seeing him in the flesh I felt the whole occasion subtly transform, and the opera whose ambiguity we had carped at take on a kind of heroic or historic character under the witness of one of its creators. Even though I felt he would be enjoying it, I believed in its poignancy for him, seeing other singers performing it on the same stage in the same sets as he had done decades before, under the direction of the man he loved. It had become an episode in his past, just as the blessing of Billy Budd was in the memory of the elderly Captain Vere. Indeed, gazing at Pears, who was doubtless embarrassed and uncomfortable as he finally regained his seat, I reacted to him as if he were himself an operatic character – just as I had entered with spurious, or purely aesthetic emotion into Charles Nantwich's war-time adolescence, and the loss of his shell-damaged idol in a Hertfordshire mental hospital. It was an irresistible elegiac need for the tendernesses of an England long past.

Then the lights went down, my grandfather said curtly, 'I don't give him long,' and we all applauded the orchestra.

I didn't see Phil the following night as he was going for a drink with some friends and I couldn't face the boredom and frustration of it. Besides, I would have been out of place, and a puzzle to his mates, who didn't know – it was so soon, they couldn't yet know – that he was gay. 'Why don't you go and see your friends,' Phil had suggested to me, and I had retorted, 'But, dearest, I don't have any friends' – a hyperbole which expressed a surprising truth. There were people I was glad to see, but almost no one I would seek out, or invite for a meal or a drink. Instead, I sat up in the dining-room with a bottle of Scotch and Charles's Oxford diary:

October 26, 1920: After a groggy start, over to Sandy's rooms. He was as bad as I was, & said had he made a fool of himself with Tim (he couldn't remember a thing after we left the Grid). I said probably, but Tim was surely used to it by now. S. had an eggnog & got dressed & didn't look too foul; I read a letter from his mother out loud to him, imitating the prim tones of a schoolmarm (perhaps I shouldn't have done?). She has the fantastic impression that S. *does not drink*. Back to Oriel & the others were already waiting for us – Tim Carswell, Chancey Brough, Eddie Lossiter & the rest. The rest went off in Hubert's car with much honking and shouting, which made me doubt the wisdom of going – head less clear than a bell, & it was a dank, foggy morning so the ground wd be heavy going. Tim seemed fine with Sandy, but when we got in Eddie's car he suddenly got out and went to sit in front with Eddie, so it was S., Chancey & me in the back. Ch was bursting with vulgar health, his skin, close up, had a waxy smoothness like church candles. I felt how big he was, squashed up next to me – his trousers immaculately white & straining. S., who thinks him so handsome (as well as a boor), cd barely be fagged to speak to him; whilst I, who don't think he's handsome, chatted to him happily enough – the usual thing. Tim & Eddie were madly earnest in front & talked about the League of Nations all the way to Witney.

Tom Flew had brought the dogs in his van, & since a couple of other friends of Eddie's joined us at Witney (one of them I thought I'd seen before, fair & amiable with a broken nose), they went on the last bit in the car, while Chancey & I took a ride in the van. The smell, as ever, was asphyxiating, & what with the lurching of the van I thought I was going to bring up the excellent kidneys and bacon Matthew had fixed for me earlier on. Old Tom himself, in his dog-carcd, dog-mouthed, dogshit-coloured cap & hacking jacket, stank as bad as the dogs. He kept turning round while he was driving & swearing at them through the cage. Then they wd yap & whine, panting all the while in a rank, warm, excited sort of way. I was quite glad to be penned up against Chancey (we had a buttock each on the passenger's seat) for he at least smelt of shaving-soap & hair-lotion.

We stopped just in time. Tom's boy (who improves on acquaintance – farcically rustic, of course, but his hands are magnificent, an octave and a half, I shd think) said there had been a fair few hares – but he'd been kicking about in the lane for hours, marking the spot, & it seemed fairly hopeless. At this stage I wd have been glad to find myself back in Oxford, & Sandy was pretty tragically keen on the idea of bed, a darkened room & a bottle of aspirins. Still, off we set, for what turned out to be an utterly futile morning's sport, with poor visibility, a kind of clinging drizzle in the air, the mud making things very tricky, & not a sniff of a hare less than several hours old. Eventually Tim called off & we toiled through to another road, up which Tom's boy miraculously appeared in Hubert's car, looking absolutely terrified, with the lunch in the back.

This was Hubert's idea, rather than go over to the public house as normal where we had felt less than welcome before when S. was very drunk & indiscreet (not to say made up like a Regent Street margery); but the question was, where to have it? Some said in the car & Tim said we cd take it to the house of someone he knew not far away, but Eddie's friend with the broken nose said he owed that someone a thousand pounds, so that wd never do. Then Tom's boy suggested what he called the Old Castle, which was in the wood we cd see not far ahead, looming out of the mist. Tom said he thought it wd be acceptable to us – it was designed for just this, he said. The boy opined that it was an old place, but Tom scorned this vigorously & said it was just a 'make-believe', a 'fairy-tale castle', so we gathered it was some kind of folly or woodland lodge.

We went on up the lane & then cut along the side of a field. The fence at the edge of the wood was no more than a few rotten posts, sticking out of the bracken. Many of the trees were dead or decrepit, & there was a surprising number of yews, which made the wood even darker. It must have been deathly quiet when free of people like us, swearing and pranking about. Sandy & I rather fell back & came on after the others, arm-in-arm, enjoying the melancholy mood, I thought, until S. said 'God, I feel sick!' & I realised his was the silence of a man who's had too much the night before. I cd see too that he felt anxious about Tim, from the way he pretended to pay no attention to him & then I wd catch him looking at him through his eyebrows – full of humiliated fondness.

The Castle was a funny old place, smaller than I'd expected & completely irregular. There was a hall in the middle, with a dark panelled room off it at the back. On either side half-collapsed walls made off into the wood, & were cunningly topped with small trees to look like authentic medieval ruins. Some of the windows were pointed, some round, some square, & through the ivy you cd see that the walls were patterned with huge pieces of vermiculated stone – not, I think, the usual builders' material, which is drilled artificially, but the real thing, brought from some volcanic site. The whole surface of the little Castle was freakish & grotesque, with the hairy fingers of long-dead creepers, the dull gloss of the ivy, the arrow-slits, & the rough, labyrinthine lava. S. & I slid our fingers into the inviting little passages, & lots of woodlice & things came scampering out. At the back we went through an arch into a little dank yard, with ferns lolling from the walls, a heap of old beer-bottles in one corner, & the ash & half-burnt logs of a fire that had been lit there long ago. It was strange that whoever had camped there had not gone inside – we had found it unlocked, & there was a huge blackened chimney-breast in the hall.

When S. & I went in the others were already flinging the picnic around as if it were a hare & they were dogs. There were some long trestle-tables, with benches, & at either end colossal Arthurian chairs made out of whole trees. The entire thing was like some mad college hall, except with pigeons flopping around, & more bird-droppings than usual on the tables. There were other bits of furniture too, hideous Victorian things too big to destroy, like a carved cupboard with a ruched scarlet curtain (all torn & stained) & an old S-shaped loving-chair, where 2 people cd sit acceptably side-by-side with a balustrade in between. 'This is a queer old dive,' said Chancey to me, in a confidential sort of way. 'Do you think so?' I said. 'I was just thinking how like home it was.' I cd see he didn't know quite whether to believe me.

It was a lesson in manners at lunch. Hubert & Eddie were particularly abandoned, cramming ham & gherkins into their mouths, slopping drink about, & behaving in a thoroughly aristocratic fashion. When Tim got up, Hubert spread mayonnaise on the bench, hoping he'd sit down in it, but Sandy, of course, who rather grandly partook only of a bread-roll & a glass of champagne, shouted out to him just in time, & earned some sullen gratitude. I ate, I think I can say, in a perfectly decorous fashion, with a slight sprawling over the table in deference to the occasion. But Chancey was a paragon of etiquette, wielding cutlery like a born lady in his rugger-player's hands. He never relaxes, & seems constantly aware of his inferior station, though everyone else would gladly forget it. 'Of course, we never had champagne at home,' he confessed to me – so I made him drink from the bottle till the foam ran down his chin. All the while Tom & his boy sat by the door eating in silence, Tom taking frequent top-ups from a bottle he seemed to have established as his own, & saying 'None for the boy' whenever Eddie proffered a glass in his direction. Poor Tom's boy! I soon felt revived by the drink & looked at him with more interest. His clothes were all too small, which made him look wretched and absurd at the same time as showing how large he was. Only his tweed cap was big enough, & threatened to come down altogether over his wide, if incurious, gaze. I had quite a vivid idea of him wrestling with me & throwing me about.

After a while people wandered outside, Tom was reluctantly pulled back into action, holding on to his bottle & advising against any further sport in the afternoon. S. retired to the car & Chancey & I strolled into the little back room, with glasses in our hands, as though we had been at a party at a house in town, & were going to look at the pictures. And there were pictures. The room had a bowed church window, which looked as if it had been ripped out of a much older building, with rather lurid stained glass & in the middle two medallions with portraits of sweet, curly-headed little boys in ruffs, haloed in urine-coloured light. There must have been some curious family tale behind it. 'A fine pair of fairies,' quoth Chancey, with ill-judged humour.

Then something very strange began to happen – or perhaps it had really begun to happen much earlier on. Ch had walked back across the room, scuffing the plaster & rubbish that covered the floor where part of the ceiling had collapsed. Rainwater must have built up above it, & indeed the whole room, with the somewhat sepulchral effect of the stained glass, felt hideously damp & had that sad mouldy smell that must have meant the beginning of the end for the old Castle. I turned around myself & found Chancey looking at me in the queerest way, his glass stiffly held out in one hand at an angle, so that the contents were very slowly running out down the stem & dripping on to the floor. Outside I heard Eddie shouting 'Charlie' & then Tom's boy saying 'They've all gone, sir.' There were whoops & whistles from the wood & Tim, presumably, tooting on his horn. I smiled quizzically at Chancey, wondering no end about the possibility of all this, though I didn't really think I cd go through with it, & went back into the hall. The door was open, but the party had been cleared away, apart from a dozen empty Bollinger bottles which had been left where they had fallen. There was no one there.

I went & sat in the old loving-chair, rather appalled by its hackneyed readiness for the occasion, & after a moment Ch came back in, & walked over with the same intent look on his face. As he sat down I noticed, as I hadn't been able to help noticing earlier in the van, how terrific his private parts were, & now he was conspicuously more excited. As old Roly Carroll wd have said, 'you cd see the copper's 'elmet'. I looked at them coming towards me, & felt that frightful inner convulsion of lust, my heart in my mouth & blushing like a rose. The mud, too, spattered up his boots & over his white breeches as tight as a trapeze-artist's, had some strangely unsettling effect on me.

But as soon as he sat down he changed tack completely, & went on about his wretched family as if nothing had happened. How hard his father had worked, & what his mother had done to give him a good education, & how people like Eddie looked down on him because he had been to a school he'd never heard of, & how – & this was the unearned climax to his peroration, which went on for a good 5 minutes while I said nothing whatever – I was the only person who showed him any true consideration, & thought about his inner life. Now this fairly astonished me, as, without being callous, I had never for a moment imagined he had an inner life & frankly, the glimpse he had just afforded me of it was none too appealing. There is nothing worse than making a bid for someone's body & getting their soul *instead*.

I looked at him in a contemptuous way, I fear. There we were, side by side, gazing past each other, our elbows resting on the rail between us. 'Enough of this,' I said & clasped his hand in mine, our elbows wobbling on the rail as if we were Indian arm-wrestlers. Then suddenly he seemed to panic, & was hugging me boisterously. We clung to each other for some while, leaning over the little fence, which was less than comfortable. He said many extravagant things about me, most of which, on reflection, were apt enough, & which people don't say to me sufficiently often . . .

How amply misnamed is the loving-chair! I suggested we have a walk outside – partly because there was no refuge if anyone came back to look for us – so off we went, & he got going once again on how he thought Tim didn't trust him, was it because he knew about his 'real nature', & so forth. I told him about Tim at school & what he had been like then, whatever censorious woman-chasing attitudes he took on now. 'I must have buggered Tim Carswell at least 500 times,' I said, calling up a random figure which can't have been far from the truth. Poor old Chancey was fairly shattered at this. 'I've missed out on my youth,' he said, rather melodramatically.

When we got into a particularly thick knot of yews, I caught his arm & we set to it. I knew he had to have me, which was very painful (after so long without anything of this kind) though over quickly. I was quite unaroused throughout, had had quite enough of it all by the time he was waxing melancholy and emotional, kind of victorious & guilt-laden at the same time. It was only afterwards – only now – I saw the beauty of it.

We eventually found the others back where we'd started & ready to give us up & go home without us, which wd have been an intolerable price to pay for so little pleasure. Loud were the exclamations & I suppose widespread the obvious conjecture. Only Sandy actually said, as I climbed into the car where he had been resting all this while, 'Poodlefaking with Chancey Brough, eh? You wicked little slut.' Later, on the journey, though with Tim this time on the other side of me, Chancey, feeling all rejected, having chosen to ride in the front, Sandy said, his eyes closed & I had thought asleep, 'So tell me about our bourgeois Priapus, Charlie,' quite loudly, so that I had to tickle him & fight all the way back to College . . .

It was the middle of the evening, and not too late, I thought, to ring Charles up. I was amused to see that there were two C. Nantwiches in the directory, and that mine did not choose to distinguish himself from his namesake in Excelsior Gardens, SE13. The phone was answered at once by a brusque-sounding man, evidently Lewis's replacement; I was relieved that Charles had found someone and felt ashamed of my self-centred neglect of the old boy. 'I'll see if his Lordship's in,' said the man, which struck me as an especially absurd formula in this case. Charles came on almost immediately.

'Hello! Hello!' he was going. He had evidently started talking before picking up the receiver.

'Charles! It's William . . . William Beckwith.'

'My dear. How frightfully pleasant to hear you. Are you reading my stuff?'

'I certainly am. I was just ringing to say how terrific I think it is.'

'Are you enjoying it, then?'

'I think it's wonderful. I've just read about you and Chancey Brough in the woods near Witney.'

'Oh . . .?' I chose not to elaborate on something he appeared, at least, to have forgotten. But I was very struck that, as well as the Winchester stuff, which, despite its period, spoke for me too, down to the very details of places and customs, there was a much less expected fore-echo of my own life in the episode of the Old Castle. I had been to the same place, Pevsner in hand, on an architectural drive with my tutor. The end whose beginning Charles had witnessed over sixty years before was near at hand: the roof had fallen in, the stained-glass windows were boarded up, a barbed-wire fence surrounded the site and red and white signs said 'Danger – Falling Masonry'.

'And I also wanted to find out how you were.'

After a silence he said: 'Are you coming to see me again?'

'Of course, I'd love to – there's so much I want to talk to you about.'

'Don't come tomorrow.'

'No, all right.'

'You're pretty interested in my story, then, are you?' he said with a chuckle. 'Quite a tale, isn't it?'

'It may be too much of a tale for me to tell . . .' I said with pussyfooting kindness.

'My dear, I think it would be a good thing,' Charles pursued as if he had not heard (and perhaps he hadn't), 'if you went down to Stepney on Friday. Have a little parley with old Shillibeer at the Limehouse Boys' Club. Friday's the big night – it would save me telling you . . . so much. It's a seven o'clock start, of course.'

'Er – yes, all right . . .' I said.

'And come and see me at the weekend? It's lonely as bloody hell here' (he whispered the last three words as if there had been ladies present). 'My new man will have to meet you . . .' Then the line went dead. He had simply, impractically, absent-mindedly, hung up.

I lay back on my bed and thought about the many lives of Charles Nantwich – the schoolboy discovering black beauty, the frivolous undergraduate beagling, drinking and ragging, the dreaming District Commissioner in the Nuba Hills, the old man who had forgotten the functions and protocol of the telephone.

When I suggested an evening in Limehouse to Phil he was less than enthusiastic. 'Why don't you go?' he said.

'I am going.'

'Oh, right. I think I'll stay in, though.' He looked worried by the idea.

'I'd have to get back here to be on duty – so I couldn't drink or anything.'

We were in his little attic room at the hotel again, and he licked me and fiddled with my nipples as though to make me forget that this fractional disobedience was taking place.

'I probably won't be there very long,' I said. Although we had been together a lot in the previous week I had privately told him nothing about the Nantwich affair. 'I've just got to talk to some old man about something – I don't imagine there'll be much to it.'

Phil stayed silent. It would soon be time for him to go to work, and I felt him already preparing to abstract himself. Tonight this distancing gave me a little qualm, and as he sat up to get dressed I pushed him back roughly and fucked him hard and fast, his asshole still tacky with spunk and grease from our slower, longer lovemaking just before. As he cleaned up afterwards and looked out his laundered clothes there was still a reserve in his manner, nothing so strong as resentment, but the first suggestion of an independence which it was only dignified that I should allow. All the same I felt unhappy. While he sat on the end of the bed with his back turned to me and pulled on his socks, I looked baffledly at his compact physique. Then he was sitting very still and I caught his eye in the gloomy recess of the dressing-table mirror.

'Man, I really do love you,' he said, both as if it were a discovery and to reassure me and chide me for being silly just because he didn't want to go on a journey to Limehouse (a journey whose only conceivable interest for him would have been that of being with me). To show goodwill he came back upstairs a few minutes after leaving and quite startled me as I stood naked looking out at the stars. He had brought me, under cover of Room Service, a tray with a smoked salmon sandwich and a glass of Drambuie – things which hardly went together, but which had touchingly been chosen for their luxuriousness.

The following evening, after an early swim, I went on east on the Central Line. The City had already evacuated, and though the train was crowded to Liverpool Street there was only a scattering of us left for Bethnal Green, Mile End and beyond. All the other people in my car – Indian women with carrier-bags, some beery labourers, a beautiful black boy in a track-suit – looked tired and habituated. When I got out at Mile End, though, other passengers got on, residents of an unknown area who used the Underground, just as I did, as a local service, commuting and shopping within the suburbs and rarely if ever going to the West End, which I visited daily. I felt more competent for my mobility, but also vaguely abashed as I came out into the unimpressionable streets of this strange neighbourhood.

I was a touch nervous as well: it was my first independent research into Charles's life and finding myself doing it I also found myself precipitately involved in the project. I had brought a notebook with me on which I had even written 'Nantwich' in bold letters. But I had no idea what I was going to write in it, who 'old Shillibeer' was or what to expect from him. I remembered seeing a letter addressed to him at Charles's house, the unusual name. It was a Dickensian or Arnold Bennettish sort of name, with a patina of East End commerce and grime to it. It had a portly, self-made propriety about it as well as a coarse, bibulous slur. I rehearsed things I might say to him, and anticipated hostility or dislike.

And then coming out this far – though only this far – symbolised for me uncomfortably how I had fallen short in helping Arthur. It was only a few weeks since his disappearance and I had done nothing about him and already was so absorbed in someone else that I didn't even think of him for days at a stretch. There was nothing I could do, of course. I didn't know where he lived, and I could hardly report the disappearance of a murderer to the police. Saying that to myself gave me a shock, made me flush and my heart race. The awful fact, which I had grown domestically used to while we were together, struck me badly when I came on it suddenly, from some way off. It was as if, sweeping a distant view with binoculars, I glimpsed the violent act and came back to it hurriedly, sharpening the focus with trembling hands.

I had left far too much time for my journey to the Boys' Club and dreading to arrive conspicuously early I walked by on the other side of the street, crossed over Commercial Road and went briskly along to St Anne's church, whose bizarre and gigantic tower I had seen from the distance. The day had grown heavier as it grew older, and the early evening light was neutral and overcast as I crossed the churchyard. The leaning birches along the path gathered a further gloom to them, and I gazed up through their branches at the giant uprearing of masonry beyond.

A slight noise like a snapped stick made me look sideways and peer at where, under the young trees, a youth was sitting on one of the table-tombs, elbows on knees, flicking and stripping a long twig in his hands. I could make out no expression, and barely hesitated in my walk, continuing to the north door, which I had no doubt would be locked, and then, with affected nonchalance such as I would have shown equally under the gaze of a mugger or a pick-up, sauntered up the half-open fan of steps beneath the tower, my absorption in its weightlifting baroque disturbed and strained by my awareness of the boy.

There is always that question, which can only be answered by instinct, of what to do about strangers. Leading my life the way I did, it was strangers who by their very strangeness quickened my pulse and made me feel I was alive – that and the irrational sense of absolute security that came from the conspiracy of sex with men I had never seen before and might never see again. Yet those daring instincts were by no means infallible: their exhilaration was sharpened by the courted risk of rejection, misunderstanding, abuse.

The church was thoroughly locked and the west door, with fine grit and year-old leaves driven against it, was clearly never used. The abandoned mood, and the mental image I had of the vast, dusky interior, made the church somehow repugnant to me, monolithic, full of dead sensibility. I turned and casually took in the figure sitting under the trees. It was hard to see, but I had the feeling he was looking at me, picking at the bark on the stick in his hands in an indolent, time-wasting way. I trotted down the steps and turned back across the churchyard.

When I got close to him, he was looking around as if unaware of me, as it might be waiting for his mates to show up. But the solitude of the churchyard made this altogether unlikely – it was not a thoroughfare, but a sequestered rendezvous. On the other hand, if he was on the lookout for sex, he had chosen a spot where he might have gone unseen all evening. There was something desolate and adolescent about his singleness, and I was not surprised to see that he was only sixteen or so. He did not meet my gaze as I walked past him, but when I was just beyond he said, in a pure Cockney voice, "'Ere, got a light?"

It was faintly incredible too to have this oldest of pick-up questions put to me, though I suppose all techniques have their freshness and wit when one is very young. I span round with a welcoming grin. 'No, sorry,' I said.

He met my smile with a shy blue gaze. 'Never mind,' he said. 'I ain't got no fags.'

This could have been a calculated snub, expressed in the strange symbolic style of the streets. Still, I kept on grinning, to show I didn't mind, and so perhaps to stir his worse contempt. He looked away, and I took in his appearance: tight old jeans, a blue T-shirt with a horizontal pink stripe running under the arms, baseball boots; a slender build, a roundish face touched with acne about the mouth, heavy dark blond hair, naturally oily, swinging forward like that of a Sixties model. I scuffed around in the dry, unmown grass beside him, my cock lurching into a hard-on which he could hardly fail to notice. His own genitals were pinched up tight in the crotch of his jeans, and he squeezed the swelling outline of his cock with the palm of his hand.

'Live round 'ere, do you?' he said, squinting up at me provocatively and sarcastically. I smiled again and shook my head. 'Thought not,' he said, looking away and snapping the stick up now in his hands. My uneasy imagination saw in this some covert allusion to 'faggot'. Still, I was determined to have him. It was partly the insolent way he sat and spoke, his overvaluing of his own charms itself making him more sexy. But it was also his youth, and the boredom and randiness of the mid-teens, that got me going. It brought back to me the time, like the erotomaniac nights and days that Charles evoked in his diary, when life was all hanging about and fantasy. It was the mood of long car journeys through France with my mother map-reading for my father, whilst Philippa and I fought or slept in the back seat and I dreamt of men. Then we would arrive at some cathedral town and I would climb out of the car attempting to master an overwhelming erection. During the trip I was drawn compulsively to public lavatories where the drawings and graffiti confirmed my sex-obsessed but impractical view of things, their mystery heightened by repeated but incomprehensible words of argot. As our family group strolled through the square in the evening, dressed in beautiful light clothes, I would drag behind, my gaze searching out the bulging flies of the lads gathered round the war memorial, the clenching buttocks of the boys who slammed the pinball machines just inside the doorways of bars.

I didn't have much time. 'Do you?' I said.

He stood up and began to wander off. 'Eh?'

'Live round here . . .'

'What d'you think?' he said. He had this tight, mean, logical talk, highly defensive and dull. I followed him, feeling more and more at a disadvantage – old, too, as people over twenty are to their juniors. He reached the low wall by the road, and turned round, stroking the outline of his quite big dick. Just along the street people were waiting at a bus-stop. It was no place for a scene. I came up close to him and put my hand on his shoulder, and he smiled in a way that for the first time revealed his nervousness.

'Come on,' I said, seizing this advantage. But immediately he closed down again; it was with studied shrewdness that he said:

'How much money 'ave you got, then?'

I nodded my head and chuckled ironically – the only way was to behave like him. 'Just enough for myself,' I said.

"sthat so? Well you'll need a lot more than that if you want a nice bit of bum round 'ere' – almost in a whisper, as if trying to keep the great bargain he was offering me a secret from the group at the bus-stop.

I'd had enough. I dropped my hand, half-turned and jumped over the wall. 'Bye-bye,' he called cheerily as I waited to cross the road – and chose a bad moment that meant I had to run; a van honked at me. I felt the boy's absolutely unfriendly eyes on me, and annoyance and humiliation, and, as I turned up the road to the Club, conflicting urges to dismiss him as rubbish and to run back and pay whatever he wanted. I saw myself pissing over him, jamming my cock down his throat, forcing my fingers up his ass – disturbing images with which to enter a Boys' Club. I resented his ability to resist me, and that I had no power over someone so young.

The Club building must formerly have been a Nonconformist chapel. The bulk of it was built of a rebarbative grey stone, with mean pointed windows; tacked on in front and at the side were modern extensions in red brick, with metal-framed windows (the frosted glass spoke of changing-rooms) and peeling white trim. It was, as Charles had said, a big night, and the lino-tiled hallway was full of family people – rather got up, I suspected: mothers with arms crossed anxiously under their bosoms, and fathers showing the suppressed pride of parents at a speech-day. Many youngsters were rushing about, and the sense of private occasion made me feel more than ever out of place. I went over to the glass-fronted NoBos and communed for a second with my reflection before scanning the lists of activities, notices about excursions, and team photographs, routinely seeking out the faces of pretty boys (of which there were several) and those inevitable glimpses of underwear up the rucked short-legs of seated footballers. Then, in the next frame, there was a larger notice, printed in an old-fashioned and distinguished way, announcing that on this very day, in contests of three rounds each, the London and Home Counties Boys' Club Boxing Championship would be decided, and the winning team presented with 'the Nantwich Cup'.

I felt how slow and incurious I had been now that I saw this evidence of Charles's further influence and philanthropy. Of course he hadn't sent me all this way merely to speak to the mysterious Shillibeer; I was amused and impressed that there was more to it, as well as getting the uneasy feeling that Charles was orchestrating his revelations with some expertise. I became convinced that when the line had gone dead two nights before it was a deliberate foreclosure on his part, and that back in the City he would now be nodding expectantly. Coming hard upon the grotesque and momentary episode in the churchyard it made me feel just a little out of control. I heard applause and a voice raised beyond the swinging green doors into the hall. I went in, trying to look as if I knew what to expect.

The ring was raised in the middle of the room, which still had its galleries on three sides, supported on thick wooden pillars. Seating rose in scaffolded tiers around the ring, leaving a kind of ambulatory under the galleries, through which I could walk almost unnoticed. Up above, too, the place was packed, and I hoped I would be allowed to drift around rather than getting penned in a seat for the evening. I loitered in one of the aisles, leaning against the stepped edge of the temporary arena. The man whose feet were by my elbow leant over and said, 'You want a seat?' – making accommodating gestures and showing how he and his party could squeeze up. But I declined. The dinner-jacketed MC completed his announcement and stepped down, a balloon-bellied referee in white shirt and trousers that lacked any visible means of support squeezed between the ropes, and a few moments later the first couple of lads sprang into the ring.

There's something about boxing which always moves me, although I know it is the lowest of sports, degrading the spectator as much as the fighter. For all its brutality, and the danger of those blows to the head, those upward twisting punches that are so tellingly called cuts and which tear the fronds of the brain known as the *substantia nigra*, an inner damage more terrible than that of pouchy, sewn-up eyes, mangled ears and flattened noses, it has about it a quality that I would not be the first to call noble.

Boys' boxing, of course, is not nearly so awful. The bouts are short, the refereeing paternal and attentive. Any moderately heavy punch is followed by a standing count, and fights are swiftly brought to an end if there are signs of stunning or bleeding. It maintains too, in some ideal, Greek way, an ethos of sport rather than violence. In the hall tonight the Limehouse supporters far outnumbered the St Albans visitors – and the place was small enough for individual voices shouting their encouragement to be heard, just as they might have been decades before in hymns or prayers in the same building. But when the fights were over, and the referee held the boys' huge gloved hands in his smaller fingers, jerking aloft the winner's arm as the result was announced, there was a touching mood of friendship, the boys embracing, patting each other clumsily with their upholstered fists, clasping the hands of the cutmen and the trainers in their gentle paws.

In the first fight, between two fourteen-year-olds, the Limehouse youngster had started well, but it was a sloppy affair, the St Albans boy always retreating to the ropes and clinching with his opponent rather than putting up a fight. In the second break I strolled off round the back and came in again on the side where the judges' table was, just below the ringside. A lean sixty-year-old man, with no forehead and grey pointed sideburns that curved across his cheeks like a Roman helmet, was standing talking with some parents in the audience. When he turned round I saw the words 'Limehouse Boys' Club' on the back of his sweatshirt. Just as the bell rang I said, 'Excuse me, can you tell me where I can find Mr Shillibeer?' He looked at me stonily, not out of aggression but out of slowness.

'Bill? Yeah, he's out the back somewhere, I should say. Try over there, through the blue door. *Come on Sean, let 'im 'ave it,*' switching without notice to the really important matter and showing in his wild single-mindedness that he had already forgotten me.

It seemed a foregone conclusion, anyway, and as the sporadic engagements of the final round began I slipped away and made for the blue door. It was a fire door, and had a window of wired glass in it, through which I saw, as I pushed it open, two figures approaching down a corridor: a boy in pumps, singlet, shorts and gloves, and the massive, stocky figure of Bill Shillibeer – Bill, that is to say, who had befriended me years before at the Corry, and whose courteous adoration of Phil I had been privy to over the last few months.

'Hallo, Will,' he said as usual.

'Hi, Bill . . .'

'His Lordship said you'd be coming down. This is Alastair, by the way.' He rested his hand on the boy's head.

'Hello', I nodded. Alastair blinked, shuffled and pummelled the air in front of him, breathing in and out like a steam train. I laughed with relief that Phil had not come with me.

'It's a big night for us,' said Bill, 'hosting the Nantwich and being in the finals. We're placing a lot of hope in this young man.' Looking at Alastair, I was not surprised. Unlike the scrawny little bruisers of the first bout, here was a boy, older, certainly, broad-shouldered, with some unconscious charismatic glow to him. Bill's hopes, too, cannot all have been sporting. His protégé had a handsome, square-jawed head, pink and gold colouring like my own, and instead of the bog-brush haircuts of his team-mates a trendy coiffure, cropped short and close at the sides, with sprouting golden curls on top: he looked like the inmate of a penitentiary as imagined by Genet. Along his erotically plump upper lip ran the licked blond wisps of his first baby moustache. I felt a churning of lust for him, and the mood of the churchyard, which had abated a bit among the mums and dads, crazed me again. 'Come and see him do his stuff,' said Bill – and we went back into the hall as the bell for the end of the first fight rang out.

I didn't know if Bill was being very cool and ironic, or if he assumed I would know that he was Shillibeer and that he played a part in the Nantwich feudal system. For the moment he was too engaged with the boxing, running across to speak to Alastair's father (who was biting his cheek with anxiety in the second row) and showing how he belonged by making fluent, familiar remarks – 'All right, Sean? That's the stuff!' 'You gotta watch that left, Simon' – all with a slightly forced or stagey air, brought on by the tension of the occasion (for Bill was a shy, sober man) and perhaps by my presence there.

We had seats right at the front, by the Limehouse corner, and the floor-level view of the ring, the scuffling of feet on the canvas, the alarming lurch of the ropes towards us when one of the boys fell against them, made it a disturbingly immediate spectacle. When Alastair's name and age and weight were called out, Bill subsided to the seat beside me and seemed exhausted by his anticipation on the child's behalf. 'He's darned good, he's *darned* good,' he said to me. Then the bell rang.

He was paired with a black boy, heavier than him but less agile. Alastair, who had hyped himself into a state of dancing aggression by the time that the two of them touched their white-knuckled gloves together, moved about with wonderful deftness, rather keeping himself to himself at first, but darting in for arhythmic, chancy jabs. Like many boxers I'd seen, people like Maurice at the Club, Alastair was not physically large; his shoulderblades and scruff, uncovered by his royal blue singlet, were not packed with muscle, and his upper arms, though long and powerful, lacked the volatile, easy massing that many ordinary working boys could muster. He ambled in for a swift succession of blows, left, right, left, that sent his opponent on to the ropes, half tripping as he fell backwards. As the referee sprang between them, conjuring an eight-second standing count with the deaf-and-dumb gestures of the ring, the voices rose for Alastair – his father loud and abrupt, and the juvenile babble of his team supporters and mates. One trio of teenage stylists bawled their encouragement while grinning and chewing, selfconscious, acting manly, caring and not caring. After a little more capering about the round ended.

Bill was on his feet in a second, propelled by sheer anxiety and commitment. The helmet-whiskered man was planning to do the mopping and pepping up, but Bill snatched the stool and bounded up between the ropes, pushing his boy into the corner with an awkward, forceful accolade. I looked up at them and half caught Bill's remarks, a mixture of love and surprising complaints. 'You're letting him off, you're letting him off,' he said. 'And don't forget your fists' – useful advice that was followed by dogmatic, nodding one-worders, as he sponged Alastair's flushed, upturned face, wiping brusquely at the unspoilt features, and running his sopping embrace around the boy's shoulders and up the shorn, gold fuzz of his neck. 'Beautiful,' he said. 'Great. Smashing.' Alastair just nodded back, saying nothing, staring entranced at Bill, breathing in keenly through his nostrils. When the bell rang, Bill popped the gumshield back into his mouth, swelling and spreading the pink lips into a fierce sneer. Then, as the referee bobbed backwards to the ropes, they were off again.

The second round was unspectacular at first; the St Albans boy was by no means unattractive, I decided, if of a rather slow-witted, suspicious expression – and he managed to place a couple of good body-shots under Alastair's guard, shots that were rare in this kind of fight. Then Alastair sent through a vicious jab to the black boy's face, where we heard not only the muffled smack of the glove but beneath it a strange, squinching little sound, as of the yielding of soft, adolescent bone and gristle. As the boy fell back Alastair followed up, before anyone could stop him, with a second blow of punitive accuracy. Cutting the air between them with his arm, the referee held Alastair off, gestured him away, and as he did so caught up his left glove in his hand. Across its blancoed surface, smeared by the impact of the second blow, was the bright trace of blood.

Bill turned to me with a look of relief. 'He's done it,' he said. 'They'll have to stop it now. Yes, he's done it.' The shouts in the hall were modified with a sympathy easily accorded to the loser, and Alastair, himself looking rather stunned, cheated somehow by his own victory, jogged about in the ring, punching the air, which was all that was left for him, and showing he had hardly noticed, he needed a fight. After brief deliberations between the ref and the officious, serious judges (this was their life, after all) the unanimous decision was announced. Then Alastair relaxed, hugged and patted his opponent with a careless fondness, and did his lively round of thanks and handshakes. I was moved by the propriety of this.

Bill of course went off with his champion, and after I'd watched the opening of the next fight, which didn't promise to go so well for Limehouse, I wondered what the hell I was doing and sloped off too through the audience and out by the swinging blue doors. Through another door on the right I heard the familiar fizz of showers and felt the familiar need to see what was going on in them.

There was such an innocence to the place that they saw nothing suspicious in my presence there – nothing either in Bill's, who, freed from adult prerogatives, absorbed himself with earnest complicity in this little manly world. The mood here also was one of pure sportsmanship, of candid bustle, like a chorus dressing room. Both teams shared the facilities, and Alastair and his opponent sat side by side on a bench, Alastair undoing, with patient, soldierly tenderness, the bandages that bound the black boy's hands, and then offering his own hands to be undone, his wrists lying intimately on the other's hairless thigh. The black boy wore a plaster woefully along his already puffing cheekbone.

'I'd have a shower, lads,' said Bill professionally. Watching the lads undress I felt, as perhaps Bill always felt too, not only randy curiosity but a real pang of exclusion, in every way outside their world. The shower was a perfunctory business and soon Alastair was back by us, towelling himself with surprising unselfconsciousness for a sixteen-year-old. I realised why it was, when, after tucking his long-skinned dick into cheap red knickers, and pulling on a grey jersey and those baggy, splotch-bleached jeans which look as though a circle of kids have jacked off all over them, he said to Bill: 'I got to go and see my girlfriend.'

Bill grinned at him wretchedly. 'Don't do anything I wouldn't do,' he said.

[7]

At my prep school the prefects (for some errant Wykehamical reason) were called Librarians. The appellation seemed to imply that in the care of books lay the roots of leadership – though, by and large, there was nothing bookish about the Librarians themselves. They were chosen on grounds of aptitude for particular tasks, and were known officially by the name of their responsibility. So there were the Chapel Librarian, the Hall Librarian, the Garden Librarian and even, more charmingly, the Running and the Cricket Librarians. My aptitude, from the tropically early onslaught of puberty forwards, had been so narrowly, though abundantly, for playing with myself and others, that it was only in my last term, as a shooting, tumid thirteen-year-old, that I achieved official status, and was appointed Swimming-Pool Librarian. My parents were evidently relieved that I was not entirely lost (urged absurdly to read Trollope I had stuck fast on Rider Haggard) and my father, in a letter to me, made one of his rare witticisms: 'Delighted to hear that you're to be Swimming-Pool Librarian. You must tell me what sort of books they have in the Swimming-Pool Library.'

I was an ideal appointment, not only a good swimmer but one who took a keen interest in the pool. A quarter of a mile from the school buildings, down a chestnut-lined drive, the small open-air bath and its whitewashed, skylit changing-room saw all my earliest excesses. On high summer nights when it was light enough at midnight to read outside, three or four of us would slip away from the dorms and go with an exaggerated refinement of stealth to the pool. In the changing-room serious, hot No 6 were smoked, and soap, lathered in the cold, starlit water, eased the violence of cocks up young bums. Fox-eyed, silent but for our breathing and the thrilling, gross little rhythms of sex – which made us gulp and grope for more – we learnt our stuff. Then, noisier, enjoining each other to silence, we slid into the pool and swam through the underwater blackness where the cleaning device, humming faintly, swung round the sucking tentacle of its hose. On the dorm floor in the morning there were often dead leaves, or grassy lumps of mud, which we had brought in on our shoes in the small hours and which seemed mementoes of some Panic visitor.

I told Phil all or some of this when he asked me about swimming, and showed him my Swimming-Pool Librarian badge (brass letters on red enamel, with a bendy brass pin) which, along with my preliminary life-saving badge, I still had and kept in a round leather stud-box on my dressing-table. The box itself, aptly enough, was a gift from Johnny Carver, my great buddy and love at Winchester. Phil was round at my place for the first time, and it seemed to arouse a curiosity in him which had been almost abnormally absent before.

'It smells so rich,' he said.

'That onion flan, yesterday – my old socks . . .' I apologised.

He was close enough to me now to laugh at anything. 'No, no. I mean it smells expensive. Like a country house.'

I still dream, once a month or so, of that changing-room, its slatted floor and benches. In our retrogressive slang it was known as the Swimming-Pool Library and then simply as the Library, a notion fitting to the double lives we led. 'I shall be in the library,' I would announce, a prodigy of study. Sometimes I think that shadowy, doorless little shelter – which is all it was really, an empty, empty place – is where at heart I want to be. Beyond it was a wire fence and then a sloping, moonlit field of grass – 'the Wilderness' – that whispered and sighed in the night breeze. Nipping into that library of uncatalogued pleasure was to step into the dark and halt. Then held breath was released, a cigarette glowed, its smoke was smelled, the substantial blackness moved, glimmered and touched. Friendly hands felt for the flies. There was never, or rarely, any kissing – no cloying, adult impurity in the lubricious innocence of what we did.

'Are you into kids?' Phil asked.

'I'm into you, darling.'

'Yeah, but . . .'

'You know it's illegal, our affair. Officially, I can't touch you for another three years.'

'Christ,' he said, as if that altered everything, and paced around the room. 'No, I think kids can be quite something. After fourteen or so. I mean I wouldn't touch them when they were really *small* . . .'

'No – but a little chap who's already got a big donger on him, gets a hard-on all the time, doesn't know what to do with this thing that's taking over his life – that's quite something, as you say.'

Phil grinned and blushed. One of the reasons he loved me was that I put these things into words, legitimised them just as I was most risqué. He was encouraged by this *franc-parler* to explore the new possibilities of talk,

141

sometimes in so reckless a way that I thought he must be making things up. The men at the Corry came in for particular attention. 'I really dig that Pete / Alan / Nigel / Guy', he would quietly celebrate as we dressed after a shower, or emerged on to the evening streets again. The wonderfully handsome, virile and heterosexual Maurice seemed to excite him in particular. 'What a pity he's *straight*, man,' Phil would say, with charming and earnest shakings of the head.

It was a touching advertisement for free speech. But at the same time it caused me a twist of jealousy. If he was getting into this kind of mood about Alan, Nigel and the rest, who knows what might not happen when I wasn't there to receive his confidences but Pete or Guy in person was, with queeny smile, easy tumescence and buttock-appraising eye? In the pool one evening I'd introduced him to James, who had clearly fallen parasitically for him at once; but I saw no danger there. There were more reckless propositioners, like the laid-back Ecuadorian Carlos with his foot-long Negroni sausage of a dick; his (successful) opener to me had been: 'Boy, you got the nicest dick I ever see' – a gambit only really useful to those who are pretty well set up themselves. And a few days ago, as we were all drying, I had heard him, forgetful or careless of this, say to Phil: 'Hey, you got a really hot ass, boy,' and watched Phil redden and ignore him – and say nothing of it to me.

I probably needn't have worried. We were having such a good time ourselves. Most of the days I spent at the hotel, where I got to know Pino and Benito and Celso and the others. Late evenings and nights were passed in sleep and sex in that transitory little attic room with its picture of Ludlow from the air. Phil would sleep until eleven or so each morning, but the fabulous weather went on and for the heat of the day until we hit the Corry at six, we were up on the roof in the sun.

It was a narrow, gravelled island we had to lie on, guarded by glazed brick chimneys and, running along the sides, a prickly little gothic fence of iron finials and terracotta quatrefoils. Beyond this, on either side, the roofs fell steeply away, caught up here and there into dormers, and punctuated with parapets and turret-like protrusions. On the left we looked out into the upper branches of our close neighbours, the plane trees in the square; from here the road, in the gulf between them, was lost to view, though we heard its rumbling and squealing far below, and in the silence between the lights the distant slap and splash of the three fountains in the public garden. On the right we looked down on the bulk of the hotel, its inner wells, ventilation shafts and fire-escapes. Beyond all this we were in the company of other tall buildings – the humourless monoliths of the Senate House and the deserted Centre Point, the green dome of the British Museum Reading Room – beyond which the pretentious corner cupola of the Corinthian Club could just be discerned. There was no one much about on these eminences, on all the surprising secret acres among the water tanks, the escape-ways and the maintenance ladders. The hotel roof itself we always enjoyed alone.

We spread towels over the softening asphalt, and lay on them in our swimming-trunks, at first, but later, when no one threatened to disturb us, naked. We fed each other's bodies with sun lotions – a low-screen one for most of me, but for Phil, who was just starting on his tan, and for my hitherto untanned bum, one with a high protection factor, which needed (I suggested) almost continuous reapplication. We were very happy on the roof, sometimes reading, sometimes stroking and exciting each other, mostly just soaking up the sun. Phil would rub my tits or my cock, or send his fingertips over me more gently than tickling, whilst the sun beat on my closed eyelids like summer lightning over crimson lacquer. When I opened my eyes the sky would be so bright it looked almost dark. Then I would turn over and doze for an hour with my face half-buried between the spread cheeks of his ass.

And we talked – hours of particular, loving banalities. I insisted on how his opinions mattered, and developed and construed his platitudes into aperçus he was far from entertaining himself. Because I was in love with him, and had brought him out, I believed in a core of redeemable talent and goodness in him. I had found him frowningly reading the *Daily Telegraph* but had nudged him on to *The Times*, which we pulled apart on the roof for him to read the news whilst I dawdled over the crossword, or tried to decipher the misprint-coded concert notices. One day I read a review of a Shostakovich concert that I had been booked to go to with James, and realised with a lurch of guilt that I had stood him up. I had rushed back to the hotel with Phil instead – he would have been sitting on my face just as the 'terminal introspection' commended by the reviewer was at its most abysmal.

Not that Phil was stupid, but he had made his way in the world without the constant love, the lavished education I had had. Indeed, being lonely, he had read a surprising amount – Hardy, *The Forsyte Saga*, Dorothy L. Sayers, John le Carré, *Wuthering Heights* – but without forming any ideas about the books. Intermittently, on the roof, he was getting through *The Go-Between*.

'What d'you make of it?' I asked.

'Oh, it's okay. It's a bit boring in places, when he's fighting with the plants and stuff. Ted Burgess is all right, though. I imagine him looking like Barry at the Club.' He smiled wistfully. When at last he finished the book he said he didn't think much of the ending.

'Well the idea is that seeing Ted and Marian shagging in the barn so freaks him out that he can never form a serious relationship with anybody when he grows up.' He was clearly dissatisfied with this.

'That couldn't happen, could it?'

'I suppose it is pretty unlikely,' I agreed. 'Still, in a general way it holds good. I expect you had something momentous in your childhood. It's the whole gay thing, isn't it. The unvoiced longing, the cloistered heart . . .' He looked at me cautiously and was struggling into some unpromising anecdote until I climbed on top of him and kissed him quiet.

We did a lot more of this, and a lot more reading, on his first weekend off, when he came to Holland Park. Its 'country-house' smell and the established presence of my things subdued him rather. He gazed abashed at my Whitehaven picture and, with an access of solemnity, embarked on a reading of *Tom Jones*. I was glad of his self-reliance; and companionable hours passed with him, sprawled in an armchair with his book, and me behind him, at my writing-table, going through Charles's papers and looking up now and again with a sudden rush of the blood at his powerful figure and sober head, his face, full of thoughts, turned from me in a lost profile.

The quiet, slightly contrived domestic mood made me think of Arthur again, and I couldn't help being grateful for the open windows, the normality, the cool of the new set-up. Not that there weren't things I missed. It was fine, making love to Phil, and I was obsessed with his body. But he lacked the illiterate, curling readiness of Arthur, his instinct for sex. Both of them were teenagers over whom I had many advantages; both of them watched me for the moves I would make. But where with Arthur, when I did move, there was an immediate transport, a falling-open of the mouth, a mood of necessity that was close to possession, with Phil there was a more selfconscious giving, callow at times and imitative. When I was rough with him it was to break through all that.

Phil's affection expressed itself too in a kind of wrestling, which was sweatily physical but which wasn't quite sex. There were no rules and it generally involved him in his pants and me in nothing at all, clinching wildly on the sofa or wherever we happened to be, tumbling on to the floor, straining, twisting and squeezing at each other but showing enough decorum not to knock things over. I suppose all this assertion of muscle was his familiar shyness, and silly as it was it had something authentic of him in it, which was beautifully exposed over those few seconds when our eyes at last held each other's, he fell into a silent slackness of submission and the ragging and bragging dissolved into tenderness and release.

I had had a brief talk with Bill after the boxing. The contest itself went on and on and through much of it I sat around in the changing-room while Bill exhorted or solaced his team and a succession of teenaged boys got dressed in front of me. Sometimes fathers, who fancied themselves as boxing pundits, came in with brothers or friends, and lectured, berated or praised their bruised progeny. Bill's behaviour with the fathers was torn: longing to be smoothly accepted as a mentor and character, he also resented the parental intrusions into the bond of trainer and pupil. Then Limehouse lost the cup, and Alastair was not the man of the match (to whom a specially tinny trophy, redolent of prep-school sports, was presented). In an overlong speech, the sadistic-looking head of the judges, a thin-lipped man with oiled, old-fashioned hair, said how close it had been, and praised the generosity of Lord Nantwich, 'who not only gave this magnificent cup, but 'elped the Boys' Club movement in so many and varied ways.' It was regretted he was not well enough to be there himself. The audience showed appreciation in a hearty fashion, and the Cup, a kind of baroque tureen with handles in the form of upward-reaching youths, was presented amid generous applause to the ferocious, broken-nosed little tyke who captained the St Albans gang. Bill could not contain the mood of futility which overcame him. I imagined he would be taken for a consolatory drink by friends, fellow trainers, even, illicitly, the older of the boys. But they were all frightfully busy. The place drained and grew quiet.

I took him for a beer at the nearest pub, a cavernous saloon where a few men gazed stunned at a television above the bar.

'Never mind, Bill', I said, bringing back two pints to a corner table he had chosen.

'Oh, thanks, Will. Thanks a lot. Cheers.' He picked up the glass and sucked off the frothy head of the beer — then set it aside with an apprehensive look. 'It's a long time since I've had one of those,' he said.

'Really? Would you like something different?'

He was shocked at having seemed ungrateful. 'No, no, no. It's great. It's just I don't drink much these days. Used to, though; if you know what I mean.' There were more sadnesses in him this evening than I'd known about before. He took a tentative sip. 'Still, even I need cheering up sometimes,' he said, as though he were widely known as a figure of high spirits.

'There's always another time,' I condoled feebly. 'The sport's the thing.' He shook his head in self-denying acceptance of what I said. 'To tell you the truth, I was quite surprised to find you here. I didn't realise that was your name. I had this idea you were called . . . Hawkins,' I added, laughing at my own absurdity.

Bill looked at me earnestly. 'I can explain that,' he said, in the tone of one who has just dreamt up an alibi and is about to test it on a sceptical CID man. But he didn't do so. 'I will explain it to you one day. You're quite right though. At the Corinthian Club I'm Hawkins, but down here with the lads I'm Shillibeer – Shilly Billy, they call me. All in good fun, of course.'

'You're a dark one,' I said flirtatiously, and he looked pleased. 'But tell me about the Nantwich Cup.'

'The Nantwich? Well, his lordship established it in 1955. He did a lot for this Club – he paid for those new changing-rooms. He used to come down a good deal himself, but we don't see much of him nowadays.'

'So you've been coming here a long time.'

'Thirty years or so, I suppose.' Bill picked up his drink, then put it down again. 'No, Hitler knocked it about, you see. It used to be the Congregational Church for this area, but it was burnt out in the Blitz. The old club building was completely destroyed, but they say it was much too small anyway. Then his lordship says, I'll put up the money if you can find somewhere else and convert it. That was all done, of course, when I started coaching here.'

'But not the changing-rooms, I guess.'

'That's right. There was just an outside latrine at the back. The lads'd get all their kit on at home. Or else they just had to change in the gym.'

'I suppose he's always been interested in boxing,' I asked.

'Lord Nantwich? Oh, he loves it, yes. I believe he used to be quite a fighter himself. I think that's why he was interested in the Boys' Clubs – boxing's always been at the heart of the Clubs. It's what holds them together, and the kids respect the boxers, of course. Some of the lads spend all day at the Club. It's what gives meaning to their lives; they don't hang around the streets, you know, that lot. What do you do, by the way, Will, if you don't mind me asking?' We had got on for years without such questions being put.

'Ah. Nothing, I'm afraid.' I tried to make the best of it. 'Not until now, anyway. Now I'm going to write about Lord Nantwich.'

Bill looked perplexed. 'How do you mean?'

'His life. He's asked me to do his biography.'

'Oh yes . . .' He weighed this up and looked again at his untouched drink. 'You'll be a kind of ghost writer, don't they call it?'

I hadn't thought of this. 'I don't think so, no. It'll just be by me. I think he thinks he'll be dead by the time it comes out. That's why I'm trying to find out all about him.'

Bill still looked disturbed. 'He's a wonderful man, Lord Nantwich,' he said. 'That's one of the things you'll find out.'

'You see, I didn't know until today that you even knew him.'

'I didn't even know until yesterday that you did.' He did not smile, and I suspected some slight friction, or horripilation of jealousy like that of the cattily possessive Lewis. 'He knows a huge number of people,' he said more tolerantly. 'How did you get caught up with him?'

It seemed disloyal to tell the truth so I said simply that I had met him at the Corry.

'He doesn't go *there* very often these days,' said Bill, as if to imply that in that case I had been exceptionally lucky.

'No, it was fortunate. The thing is, Bill, I would value your help – what you know about him. I would acknowledge it of course in the book.' He appeared satisfied by this. 'I suspect you may be a leading witness.'

'You make it sound like a trial or something,' said Bill. I picked up my beer and looked at him interrogatively. 'Do you want me to tell you now?' he asked, clearly uncertain, as I was, about how biographers worked.

'Not now,' I smiled. 'But I'd like it if we could get together soon. You're not touching your drink.'

'I'm sorry, Will. I'd like to in a way, but I think with the mood I'm in tonight it wouldn't be a good thing. It's never a good thing, to be honest, when I go back on the booze. Somehow it always lands me in trouble.' Looking at his ungainly muscularity, I wondered if it nursed and suppressed an instinct for violence. Perhaps his self-denial had been painfully learnt, and was the clue to a double life whose difficult side was all in the past.

We walked together through bleak, twilit streets to the Underground, and rode into town on the Central Line. Over, or rather under, the noise of the train and in the near-emptiness of the carriage he confided in me. His confidences, though, were not about himself: they were the secrets and crises of others that he had observed. He told me feelingly about how the boy Alastair's mother had died of leukaemia, and the struggles of the father to look after him properly. He said how Roy, at the Corry, had come off his motorbike and severed a tendon in his knee. Something more came out about the Nantwich Cup too – how Charles had created it in memory of a friend of his who had been killed, though Bill was vague about the details, and when I asked him how *he* had met Charles, assumed a kind of dignified obtuseness, as though so intimate and critical a subject could not be so lightly approached. Could there have been something between the two men? It was the recurrent problem of imagining them twenty, thirty years earlier – before I was born, when Charles was the age that Bill was now, and Bill was Phil's age. He was looking forward then, building up his body like a store, a guarantee of his place in the future. Now the future had come he still hoarded and packed it. It sat opposite me, massive, gathering bullishly at the shoulders, the open shirt showing a broad V of black hair, the thighs splayed ponderously on the slashed and stitched upholstery of the banquette. I knew I could never love it or want it, but it was an achievement, this armour of useless masculinity.

As we travelled west, through lit City stations like Bank and St Paul's which I thought purposeless at night till I recalled that Charles, for one, would need them, that here and there in the City that was emptied for the weekend, people, eccentric or indigenous, still lived, my thoughts deserted Bill (though I still looked at him), and fled on down the rails to Phil. We were nearly at Tottenham Court Road, where Bill would have to change for the Northern Line, when he said, with tense cheeriness: 'How's young Phil getting on these days?'

I didn't know how much he knew. Phil and I had been discreet, though together, at the Corry; but it was hard to tell what, in the crowded complex of the Club, had been seen, guessed or overheard. I gave a smile which could be read as a happy admission or an amiable ignorance. 'All right, I should say,' I offered neutrally.

The old bashful earnestness crossed Bill's face, and as the train fiercely slowed and the inertia carried him towards me he said bravely: 'I loves that boy.' His innocence and embarrassment were revealed in the relish he summoned up in his tone, and even more in the tortured affectation of saying *loves*. The train abruptly stopped, tilting him backwards as he rose, and he bustled off with a sad and hasty goodbye.

June 9, 1925: Back in London after nearly 2 years, & everyone complaining about the heat. Unable to wear shorts, open shirt & topi, I begin to see what they mean. The town, after Cairo & then Alexandria, is strikingly brisk & convenient – also much smaller, in detail if not in plan, than I'd expected; I've been going about with the sort of pleasure I used to have on getting back to Oxford after the vac, checking that it's all there (which in fact it isn't).

At Brook St, Sandy had called already before I got in, & left a message, in his inimitable style, on a page torn out of a book; it was in French, & highly, if florally & indirectly, improper, about how 'il y a une chose aussi bruyante que la souffrance, c'est le plaisir', & so on. I was tantalised at the end of the page & only then turned to the message, which was florally and indirectly improper, but in English. I sat for a while in the little morning room, with the old brass clock ticking busily away, & some lovely calceolarias, & Poppy's picture looking down sternly, & thought of all the days that have passed there since I went to Africa, with no more happening than occasional visits from Wilson with a duster. It was deliciously calming, like an Egyptian nobleman's tomb, where the guide angles the sun in off an old piece of tin-foil, & the departed embrace the gods on the walls.

After that a round of visits of a dutiful kind before seeking out Sandy at his bizarre address in Soho. For a while I thought I wasn't going to find it, but after ringing at one house where I was welcomed by a vast, fair woman with pink feathers I heard his characteristic whistling of 'La donna è mobile' from way up above & stepping back saw him leaning over a balcony between 2 palm trees. He dropped down a key, & I made my way up. It was wonderful to see him & despite joyful exclamations I cd think of nothing to say at first, so we hugged each other for ages until we needed a drink.

It is quite the oddest place, with the balcony which is like a tiny garden, & inside a high, cool studio with steps going up to a kitchen on one side, & to a bedroom on the other. Beyond the studio you can climb out on to a roof where Sandy apparently sunbathes naked with his friends & where there is a fine view of the old Wren church with its bulbous spire. We had some American cocktails with all sorts of muck in them & got frightfully drunk.

Later on a friend of his came up (he had his own key). He is called Otto Henderson, an artist, & apparently very well in with Cocteau & the Parisian world. I fear I showed I knew nothing about it all. He, I gather, is a keen practitioner of Sandy's bare-bum sun-worship, as his mother, who is Danish, comes from a family of pioneering nudists. He was very interested to hear about the tribesmen of Kordofan, & wanted to know how they went on when they became amorously excited. He is a striking-looking fellow, with thick fair hair, shifting eyes & huge lyrical moustaches. His clothes, on another, wd have been enough to incite nudism – a boisterously checked jacket, bright yellow trousers & a bow-tie with dogs on it.

I rather liked him, but I was sorry not to have Sandy to myself. We all went on to a dingy little chophouse, the idea of which, apparently, was to reintroduce me to the epitome of English culture. Between us we made a thoroughly English nuisance of ourselves, & Sandy & Otto regaled me with the news of London life, Otto showing a thorough familiarity with all our old friends & treating me as if we had been at school together. Timmy Carswell has married, 'extremely well' Otto assured me. I felt a little pang, and a little gloom, too, which I dashed away with some more of the sour red wine we'd ordered. Sandy – who at the House had really I suppose been madly in love with Tim – cursed him obscenely & teetered into maudlin reminiscence. I sat back and looked around the restaurant while this was going on, though I cdn't avoid remembering Tim and his angelic beauty at 15. It was not nice to think of female fingernails doodling over his smooth man's body.

June 15, 1925: Odd – though perfectly natural – how going away disconnects one from life. Everything has gone on at such a pace. Sandy painting his pictures, & clearly more or less living with the effusive Otto – and this puts me in a strange position. The paintings themselves I do not understand, & have been thinking about over this week, when I've seen him often. Their colours are unnatural, & their subjects are peculiarly distorted; but above all they are large. It is not a largeness I can claim to like, or even believe in. Their largeness is the largeness of Sandy's own gestures, of his drinking, of his fantastical filthy talk – it is not the largeness of large pictures. He has an extraordinary study of Otto, naked to the waist, seen from somewhere right down on the ground, so that he towers up above, his chin turned heroically, all the features exaggerated almost into brutality. It's larger than life-size. It's ridiculous, I can't help myself feeling. But I know that that might be because Otto is himself ridiculous. S. is so absorbed in him, so greedily goes on about him, that I feel his thoughts are not really with me any more. His manner is wilder than ever, but beneath it all there is restraint & even boredom between us.

About Africa, about everything that has happened to me, he shows no curiosity. I fear he even finds me a dull dog.

June 18, 1925: On Friday I had a meeting with Sir Arthur Cavill – early evening at the Reform, whisky-and-soda, talk about nothing in particular. He appeared almost embarrassed to touch on the purely routine matters we were supposed to discuss. I liked him – austere, detached at first, fastidiously bachelorly – & was not surprised when keen feelings flashed under the surface of his conversation. At the end, after many formalities, he talked briefly about Meroe, & the first time he had seen the pyramids there. It was as if both of us, lightly warmed with drink, suddenly felt our spirits freed. For a moment we were very far away from Pall Mall, & though little was said we shared an exalted almost *tender* glance.

June 23, 1925: Last night a bizarre encounter. I was at Sandy's studio in the afternoon when without a word he & Otto tore off their clothes & clambered on to the roof. I sat around reading about Lawrence of Arabia and Queen Marie of Rumania in the *Times Literary Supplement* until I had mustered the insouciance to join them. They are brown as what – Corsicans? – all over, but of course I need not have felt ashamed. Otto seemed to respect me more when he saw how sunburned I was. 'We must go to the Tropics,' he said to Sandy, 'and run around like the darkies.'

I wished we were there too. It felt selfconscious & absurd lying up on the leads as if we were laundry, & there was something so prurient about the nudity when I compared it to days on tour when all our party wd stop at a river, & the men strip off their shirts & drawers to wash them & spread them on the boulders to dry. I nursed those little idylls to myself, & thought of sitting among the bushes with my pipe while the men dived & splashed, or roamed through the muddy shallows. Then we were many miles from civilisation; here I made strategic play with the tepee of the paper while Otto & Sandy brazened it out in a strange discipline of their own.

In the evening we wandered down to Regent Street. All along by the Café Royal people were swarming around & there was a mood (which *was* quite oriental) of clamour & grime with underneath it a great passive summery calm. Life in England is so little of the streets that it was delicious to loiter. There were fantastical characters about, & several girlish young men, at intervals, waiting & waiting. One felt how this corner of Town has seen so much of that kind of thing. Across the road in the monumental mason's showroom, the angels hovered with outstretched wings and lilies in their hands: they seemed to reproach us mutely through the plate-glass windows – or perhaps they cast some benediction over us.

Inside the Café there was an unreal, subaqueous atmosphere, early lights burning though it was still hot & bright outside, & layers of smoke drifting above the marble tables. I hadn't been there since I was an undergraduate & it seemed as unlikely to me now as then that England cd have come up with somewhere so thoroughly democratic, where I, a Lord after all, might share a table with a bookmaker. Actually it excites a rather corrupt & non-democratic emotion in me – of the daring 'chic' of slumming it. I think Sandy feels this less, & goes there as a bohemian & for the fun.

It was fun, too, & we drank champagne and smoked Turkish cigarettes & sprawled on the benches. Eddy St Lyon was there with an actorish young man & winked at us hugely across the room; he has aged extraordinarily & looks ripe with corruption & self-abuse. At the next table some roughish characters were playing dominoes, a thick-set older man, a kind of foreman with his gang. S. was clearly somewhat preoccupied with one of them, eighteen or so, with grubby, sun-bleached hair & broad features: there was something both delicate & brutal about him, with dark stains spreading from the armpits of his shirt & preternaturally powerful, dirty hands that showed a surprising refinement when he pushed the dominoes out, or raised his beer-glass to his lips. When the glass was empty, S. reached over and half-filled it with champagne. The boy smiled candidly, revealing a broad gap in his front upper teeth which made me swallow & tingle with lust, & the 'foreman' looked across with pride and gratitude, as if we had somehow helped the boy with his education. When their game was over, S. told the youth that he wanted to draw him, & they arranged a time & shook hands on a price; I began to see how the mixed nature of the clientele worked to everyone's advantage. After this Sandy rather basked in his own *savoir-faire*, & we ordered another bottle of champagne.

I had noticed a solitary figure sitting across the room, also drinking freely, even heavily. He was slender, & beautifully dressed, of indeterminate age but clearly older than he wanted to be. He must in fact have been about 40, but his flushed appearance & what may well have been a discreet *maquillage* gave him an air of artifice & sadly made one feel that he must be older, not younger. He was not only by himself but in some heightened, almost dramatic way, alone. He squirmed & twitched as if a thousand eyes were on him, & then composed himself into a kind of harlequin melancholy, holding out his long ivory hands & admiring his polished nails. His gaze wd wander off & fix on some working-boy or freak until an appalling rasping cough, which seemed too vehement to come from within so frail & flower-like a body, convulsed him, doubling him up into a hacking, flailing caricature. After these attacks he sat back exhausted & quelled the tears in the corners of his eyes with the back of his trembling hands.

Otto took notice of this & said in his know-all familiar way: 'Old Firbank seems to be in a bad condition.' I asked him more, & he told me that the man was a writer. 'He writes the most wonderful novels,' said Otto, 'all about clergymen, & strange old ladies, & – & darkies: you really ought to read him.'

Sandy was standing up. 'Let's go & join him,' he said. I demurred, but it was no use. Poor Firbank looked quite alarmed as this boisterous trio of young men converged on him. But I saw there was something pathetically like relief in his reply to Otto's greeting, as if, when we gathered about him, the world cd see at last that he had friends.

There was a similar contradiction in his reaction when Otto, fixing him with a manly & companionable smile, began to recite a poem – some nonsense about a negress 'frousting in the sun, thinking of all the little things that she had left undone' & a good deal of hey-nonny to follow. Firbank seemed to shudder & smile at once (I learnt subsequently that he was the author of this doggerel) & when it was finished said in a kind of airy gasp: 'How wonderful it must be not to wear a tie!'

He had a curious & characteristic action of sliding his hands down his legs (which were twisted round each other more often than is customarily possible) until he was gripping his ankles & his head had virtually disappeared beneath the table. When he straightened up his breath came more raspingly than ever – or he wd cough again, & burst into a suppressed purple under the powdered finish of his flat, high cheekbones. Physically I found him terrible to be with, & conversation too was well nigh impossible; but there was something fascinating about his exquisite self-preservation & the reckless drinking & coughing which threatened to tear the whole thing apart.

As if he knew what I was thinking he said, with a hint of pride, 'I'm going to die, you know, quite soon.' This didn't seem at all unlikely, but when I none the less havered, he insisted that his 'Egyptian fortune-teller' had confirmed it. When he next left the country – for France, quite soon, & then to winter in the desert villages around Cairo – he wd never return. It was a childish & theatrical moment, difficult to respond to seriously, & yet, like occasional lines in melodrama, mordantly moving & true. 'I don't want to die,' he added.

I was beginning to see why he did not attract drinking companions, & wondering whether we too might not be moving on, when he invited us all to go & hear the negro band at the Savoy: 'It's the most wonderful music there is,' he said. So we knocked off the rest of the champagne at giddy speed, & lurched out into the street: I assumed we wd walk, but our author's pedestrian performance was as wayward as his sessile one: it combined the futile caution of the drunkard with a true instinct for elegance – if of a somewhat decadent kind. With each step he rippled upwards, from foot to head, whilst appearing somehow to steer & balance himself with low-down oscillations of his hands: again I was reminded of wall-paintings in Egyptian tombs – there was so *linear* a quality to him. We hailed a cab in Piccadilly Circus & as he slumped into the smoky compartment beside me he exhaled his new resolve: 'We must have the most heavenly talk about Africa.'

Phil agreed to come with me to visit Ronald Staines, and since we were at my flat I dressed him myself. I forbade him underwear, and forced him into an old pair of fawn cotton trousers which, tight on me, were anatomically revealing on him. The central seam cut up deeply between his balls, and his little cock was espaliered across the top of his left thigh. A loose, boyish, blue Aertex shirt set this off beautifully, and as I followed him downstairs I was thrilled at my affront to his shyness, and could hardly wait for the strapping I would give him when we got back. All along the pavement in the beating sunshine I kept letting my hands knock him, my fingertips trail over him as they swung.

We crossed over Holland Park Avenue and were strolling north up Addison Avenue when there was the slap-slap of running sandalled feet behind us, and my little nephew Rupert was prancing along beside us.

'Roops – this is a pleasure,' I said. 'Are you running off somewhere again? You don't seem very well kitted out if you are.' He had on smartly pressed shorts with an elasticated waistband and a T-shirt advertising the previous year's Proms.

'No, I'm just going for a walk,' he said. 'It's such a lovely day—one would hate to stay indoors!'

'One would indeed,' I agreed. 'Roops, this is my friend Phil, who's staying with me for a bit.'

'Hello,' he said breezily, and then gambolled along backwards in front of us, so as to get a good look at the two of us. I thought it must be like being filmed, walking towards an ever-receding camera, and I put on silly faces to make him laugh. When he decided he liked us he dropped into place between us, and we swung along hand-in-hand. He was as touching and confidential as ever, and I felt we must look like a young couple that by some dazzling agamogenesis had produced this golden-haired offspring.

I was keeping an eye out for the house numbers and we were already nearly there. 'We're going in here, darling,' I said, and Phil looked up a shade apprehensively while Rupert, disappointed that our meeting was over so soon, took on a serious air, not quite understanding what was going on, and glancing from one to the other of us, as though some decision had to be taken.

'Why don't you come round for tea one day?' I suggested. 'If old Pollywog will let you.'

'Yes, I will,' he said. But something else was clearly worrying him and he tugged on my hand and led me off to several parked cars' length away. He looked around carefully, and I knew what he was going to talk about. For a moment I thought he was going to tell me he had seen Arthur, and I felt that perhaps life would suddenly become quite different. 'What ever happened to that boy?' he asked.

'Oh, he went away a bit ago,' I said plausibly, as if it were a lie.

'Did he manage to run away all right, then?'

'Oh yes—he got clean away.'

'Have you heard where he went to? Did he go abroad?'

'Funnily enough, old chap, I don't know quite where he is. It was all top secret, you know. I hope you didn't tell anyone about it?'

'No,' he whispered, shocked that I could imagine that.

'As a matter of fact,' it struck me, 'if you should see him I'd quite like to know. It would have to be really hush-hush, though. Keep your eyes skinned when you're going for a walk or anything' (here he rubbed his eyes quickly, carrying out my orders at once) 'and if you do see him, and you're really sure it's him, why don't you give me a ring?'

'All right,' he said. I was glad I had made a little game or experiment out of it, and began already to look anxiously forward to it.

We went back towards Phil, who had been left in the middle of the pavement. I grinned at his fidelity, his cleanness, the plump relief of his . . . copper's helmet. Rupert shook hands with both of us and made off, looking about like anything. When he was out of view Phil and I walked up the short flagged path to the front door of Staines's house; it was the left-hand portion of a spacious 1830s villa, with a woody privet-hedge (the kind with rooms inside it large enough for a child to hide in) round the garden, and curtains at the downstairs windows drawn in a degenerate way suggestive of late rising and afternoon TV.

Staines came to the door and welcomed the two of us with the air of a man who has a good appetite. As I thought when I had met him before at Wicks's, there was someone strangely passionate and slavish holed up inside his immaculate clothes — today an almost transparent suit of sour cream Indian silk.

'I'm so glad Charles got *you*,' he said.

'Thank you,' I replied. 'Do you mean there have been others?'

'Oh, there was a frightfully *old* young man with bad breath who ran a printing press. He was around a lot last year, looking at everything. Happily Charles got rid of him, for being too snobbish.'

We went through into a drawing room with heavy theatrical curtains held back by tasselled cords, and floor-length windows open on to a terrace; a lawn and a huge weeping beech were visible beyond. A zealous sense of good taste pervaded the room: unread classics in the bookcase showed the uniform gilding of their spines, and the flowers could have graced a wedding of minor royalty. On a Sheraton side-table lay a vast, tooled portfolio; a crowd of framed photographs surmounted a mahogany writing-desk and gave the impression of a glamorous and sentimental past. Phil, trained to accommodate the whims of guests, seemed uncomfortable to be a guest himself. He hung back awkwardly, unable to get his hands in his pockets.

'And what do you do?' Staines asked him.

'I'm a waiter.'

'Ooh.' There was a peculiar silence. 'Well, I'm sure you won't have to wait very long,' he said encouragingly, appraising Phil's physique with an artful glance. 'Are you a friend of Charles's too?'

'Oh, no — I'm just a friend of Will's.' It became clear to me that Staines did not know why he had come, but was, as I had expected, glad that he had.

'Quite so! Well please, make yourself absolutely at home. I'm afraid there isn't a pool – but you may like to sunbathe outside with Bobby' – he gestured tritely towards the garden – 'or whatever!'

'I think Ronald and I will have things to talk about, darling,' I said. 'But do sit in on it if you want.' I felt a shiver of possessiveness and cruelty, as if I were some vile businessman addressing his wife. We all went to the windows and stepped out. To the side there was a gathering of expensive garden furniture, chairs with curved wicker arms and flowered cushions, a long, unfolding sun-bed, and a glass-topped table with a jug of Pimm's and a matching set of Deco beakers: there was something ideal about it, as if it were in a catalogue. Beyond, at the edge of the terrace, stood tubs of alpine plants – dwarf conifers, lichen-yellow, and wiry tufts of heather leading their perfectly senseless existence. 'We can all have a drink,' said Staines. Then round the corner from the garden Bobby appeared.

Bobby was – what? – thirty-five? He had been deeply indulged, had eaten too much, drunk too much, and his face and body were the record of it. I could see at once what sort of a child he had been: the loose mouth, the cheap, unblinking, china-blue eyes, the lock of glossy blond hair that he pushed back as he ambled towards us – all were features of a school tart, as it might be Mountjoy, aged by a decade and a half (and where was Mountjoy now?). His clothes made the idea inevitable: a crumpled white shirt, plimsolls, and baggy white flannels held up round the waist with what I recognised (from James having one the same) as an Old Gregorians tie. When we were introduced he said 'Hullo' in a plummy, straight manner and extended a hot damp hand with plump, double-jointed fingers and long chalky nails. I thought confusedly of theories of the humours, and could not imagine intimacy with a man with such hands. 'So you're going to do old Charles,' he said, and chuckled as though Charles were a delinquent like himself. 'Well, good luck is all I can say.'

He had pitched into the subject with charmless suddenness, but I was obliged to ask him more. 'The old boy's not all there, you know. I shouldn't wonder if there was some mental thing. The mother was quite barmy, of course. Whole lot of them were *pretty odd*.'

'The previous Lord Nantwich, Charles's father, was a gifted poet,' Staines reassured me formally, dispensing the Pimm's in little dribbles and sploshes as the fruity garnish fell in. 'He wrote plays in verse for his servants to perform. My grandmother used to know him – which is how I came to meet Charles, you see. He dandled me I think would be the word – longer ago than even I can remember.'

'Where did the family come from?'

'Oh, they still lived in Shropshire. They had a house in town, but they never came down. I don't think the old man appeared in the House of Lords once. They were madly out of touch with the modern world – no telephones or anything – and I suppose that's why they became a bit queer. Charles was *devoted* to his mother; they wrote to each other every single day. And there was Franky, of course. Has Charles told you about him?'

'Charles has told me almost nothing.' (Should I be writing this down? The 'Nantwich' notebook still had nothing in it, except for some scribbles on the back page where I had tried to get a biro to work.)

'Well some time I'll recount that sad, sad tale. Suffice it to say, William, that *Franky* was Charles's big brother, and would have come into the title in the normal course of events. He was a nymphomaniac, if a man can be. They used to say the farmworkers at Polesden sewed up their fly-buttons. He was always getting them in a corner and making them do things. And of course in those days you *could* – I may be embroidering a little but I think I'm right in saying that virtually any, you know, working-class lads could be had for . . . not more than ten shillings. They needed the money, dear. It's too amusing really, or was until one of Franky's boys got nasty and *simply* smashed him to pieces. That was what finally turned their poor mother's mind, I should think.'

'And the uncle,' Bobby prompted impatiently.

'Oh, the *uncle* – yes, Charles had this heavenly uncle who everyone thought was a terrific lady's man, and carried on very chivalrously and was seen a lot with the great beauties of the day and *all that*. But really, of course, he was nothing of the kind; and used to tool about with guards – on the train, I mean; well, the other sort, too, I dare say. So there was really a lot of *that sort of thing* going on there. Compared with the rest, Charles was quite the white sheep of the family.'

Bobby dropped on to the sun-bed. 'They all liked a "bit of rough",' he said, with the same pompous dissimulation, as if he were a policeman reporting the language of an offender in court. 'I must say, though, Charles's "gentleman's gentlemen" are the end. Who's he got at the moment, some other old lag?'

'I believe there is someone new,' I said. 'I haven't met him yet. Lewis I met. He seems to have been rather unsatisfactory.'

Staines looked hesitant, even troubled. His account and Bobby's would not be the same, I knew, and where Staines spoke with affection, Bobby refracted matters through a kind of slothful contempt. Now he said: 'You know how he gets them, don't you. Bloody motors out to Wormwood Scrubs or wherever and when he sees someone likely coming out, he picks them up and offers them a job. Ridiculous way of engaging a person.'

'It's not quite as simple as that,' Staines said. 'Charles has a lot of feeling for the underdog, the underchap as it were. He's made great friends that way, and changed the whole course of people's lives. Sometimes it just doesn't work out. One doesn't know quite what *goes on*, of course, but they tend to become very possessive and jealous, and then there's usually trouble. Oh dear! Look, come inside, William, and let me show you some things.'

We were going in, and I dithered on the sill as to whether I could leave my darling Phil with Bobby. Phil looked resigned – or perhaps actually didn't mind: I had been surprised and shamed by his tolerance of people to whom I took an unhesitating dislike. But Staines seemed to sense the problem, and turned back. 'Come along too,' he called, extending his arm and dropping his wrist in a perfect Shuckburgh.

'I'll stick by the booze,' said Bobby, gruffly.

If the drawing-room had the unnatural, aspiring look of a room about to be photographed, the room where the photography actually went on had a cultivated air of clutter, as if the clean and discrete camera should lay claim to the turmoil, the evident symptoms of art, of a painter's studio. Empty drums of developing fluid accumulated around an ostentatiously full waste bin, a dramatic spot picked out the workbench where the only painterly act, the touching up of prints with a fine brush, took place. Otherwise it was a deserted theatre – of the acting or of the operating kind. The powerful lights, with their silvery reflecting umbrellas, were switched off, and as the curtains were closed I had a quick recall of school play rehearsals in vacated classrooms, gestures made with imaginary props, embarrassed boys swallowing syllables, the sense of a final achievement lugubriously remote. Nonetheless I looked around admiringly and just as I still naughtily mount the pulpit when I visit a church, clutched Phil to me histrionically in front of one of the heavy unrolled backdrops of eggshell cartridge-paper. The lens of the crouching camera eyed us enigmatically, daring us to move. Phil grinned, and only saw too late what I was playing at.

'Actually, over here is where I would want to shoot you, William.' Behind the sheet of paper, at the rear of the studio, was a setting of another kind, a painted canvas flat showing a balustrade, a curtain tumbling down above, and a hazy impression of parkland beyond. It was similar in kind to the scene in the mysterious early photograph of Charles with a woman – though such backdrops must have been common in photographers' studios all over the world before the war. 'I picked it up from a demolition site out at Whitechapel,' said Staines, coming up behind me to look at it, and resting a ringed hand on my shoulder. 'It's not all I picked up there, either, if you must know.' I smirked. 'No, I'm going to use it for my kind of *Edwardian* pics. So touching. You did say you'd do one of them didn't you – you've got just the looks for it. Nothing naughty, nothing naughty *at all*.'

'I should be pleased to,' I decided.

'But first I want to look out some pickies of old Charles and others. It's all in the most frightful mess. Really I need someone – well, someone like you really – to come and sort out the *archivi*. It's been a help selling lots of stuff, but still.'

Together we tugged out the wide shallow drawers in which hundreds and hundreds of photographs were laid up. Crazed, silky sheets of tissue-paper interleaved the older prints and, pulled back, revealed anonymous society faces of the Forties – I supposed – sulking, or smiling complacently. Some I wanted to look at more closely, but Staines dismissed them and hurried on; or if he told me about them they were people I had never heard of. It was depressing to think of the scene of Charles's life crowded with such glossy Mayfair figures, the women with their jutting busts and lacquered lips, the men with their conceited crinkly hair.

'This is all Bond Street stuff,' Staines reassured me. 'Some of it's *brilliant*, but it's not what we want.' So Phil and I carried the trays of photographs through into the drawing-room – and I asked if we could see the new work too, the martyrdoms and butcher's boys. Staines went off to hunt for other things, letters he might have had, while Phil and I sat like spoiled children on the sofa by the empty fireplace and looked through it all. There was something wanton about the way he let us rummage, and about the muddle of the system. I felt each picture encourage a question, or hint at some urgent, tawdry secret.

Phil, of course, had no idea what we were looking for. But he was very quick to spot that the subject of one photograph, taken from an odd angle so that he seemed to turn into a kind of naked coastline, was Bobby. And Bobby turned up quite a bit, in soulful vigil at a window, or in his whites, more dazzling then, against a bright white wall in Tunis, or, less convincingly, leaning into lamplight over an old book. There were some camp fantasies – Bobby as sailor; or as Airforceman, with perched cap and oiled kiss-curl. In one, dated eighteen years ago, he appeared, wearing only sandals and a cincture of vine-leaves, between two classical garden statues. Staines could have had no difficulty in inducing that expression of tossed-back pagan pleasure: degeneracy was already evident in the luscious good looks and the unclassical softness of his body. It seemed that Bobby must have run off with the much older man, by then perhaps an acclaimed society portraitist with the entrée to country houses. I imagined Bobby being pampered and disapproved of by their hostesses, and, though the Sixties were beginning, posing for the adoring Staines in the artistic, Sicilian manner of an earlier age.

When Staines came back, empty-handed, I asked him about Sandy Labouchère and Otto Henderson. 'There *is* a picture of them,' he said, 'somewhere. I didn't actually know them much – I'm too *young*, you see, really to be of use to you . . . They were a gruesome couple when I met them: Labouchère was a hopeless drunkard, and so was Henderson. They stuck together, more or less, painting the most extraordinary pictures, morbid to a degree and full of decadent young men twice as large as life – in *all* respects. Otto was really a cartoonist, of course, though sometimes he managed to get work in the theatre. I saw some strange opera he did, with the most shaming caryatids and things, and slaves. It had the most uncomfortable-looking furniture in it; I remember one critic said, "Mr Otto Henderson was responsible for the *misère-en-scène*".'

'What happened to him?'

'Do you know, he may well still be alive. I haven't heard of him for an age: he was living, the last time I had news, in a basement in Earl's Court, I think it was, with a sort of *sect*. When his friend finally drank himself to death, poor old Otto did become a bit queer. I've got a painting by Labouchère, by the way, if you'd like to see it. It's rather specialised, so I keep it stored away.'

'I would be interested.'

'It *is* rather amusing.' Staines warmed to the idea. 'Why don't you, um, *Phil*, come and help me with it, and William can get on with the photographs.' I let them go and soon after came on a picture of Charles: it was just the sort of thing I wanted for my book. Aged perhaps fifty, thickening but handsome, he was sitting in a high-backed chair in front of the big pedimented bookcase in the library at Skinner's Lane. Leaning round the chair, proffering a glass on a salver, was a white-jacketed black. He was surely supposed to be looking at his employer, but had been caught as, for a second, he followed the direction of his gaze, and showed to the camera a shy, devoted smile.

I put out various other pictures, of people who were beautiful or eccentric enough to ask about and who I hoped might have a place in the crazed mosaic of Charles's life. In one of the drawers I was surprised to find a stiff, creamy envelope, embossed 'Staines, Photographer. New Bond Street', containing a set of enigmatic, rather beautiful nudes: a thin young man, turning away his head, or slatted by shadow from a venetian blind, or crouched apprehensively on the bare floor of the studio. The boy's face was always partly hidden, and his personality obscured in the sinister melancholy of the compositions. Even so, I knew who it was from the distinctive curve and mass of his cock – Colin, James's Corry pal whom I had had on that hot afternoon at my flat a few weeks before.

I had started to get a bit excited about this, when I felt a presence in the room. Bobby was standing at the french windows, looking at me expressionlessly. I started tidying up, shuffling together the pictures I wanted. 'Ronny not here?' Bobby said; he already sounded a little drunk.

'No, he's gone to look for something.'

Bobby let a weary smile on to his lips. 'I should come with me, if I were you.' I took this as a bald proposition, but when he had crossed the room to the door, and turned and said, 'Oh, come on,' I felt that it wasn't, and that some kind of trick had been played on me.

We went through the hall and into the studio, Bobby for a moment halting and blocking my view before letting me too see what was going on. Staines, stooping over the tripod, his right eye jammed into the viewfinder, was aware of us, and flapped his left arm behind him to keep us back and have us observe professional etiquette while he was concentrating. 'Try not to smile,' he said. Leaning against a tall white plinth, shirtless, his skin lubricated, almost glittering in the studio lights, the top button of my trousers undone, Phil grew suddenly guilty and selfconscious. That deep and telling blush of his that I loved pumped up into his cheeks and forehead and into his short back and sides, and soaked downwards, over the strong shaft of his neck, fading into his glossy chest.

On the way home we stopped off at the Volunteer, and had a beer outside on the pavement, caught up in that sad, erotic mood of an early evening in summer – working people going home, the first queens coming into the pub, dusty tiredness mixing with anticipation. I gazed up and down the street, said little, and from time to time looked ironically at Phil, I think shocked to find how easily he could be manipulated, slightly sick with a feeling that perhaps I wouldn't be able to keep him. That afternoon I had turned him into pornography, and I was shaken to find Staines following my own instinct so literally, so instantaneously; proud, too, but with the unease of a sexual braggart. Phil himself had an air of compromised but defiant success about him.

As we turned into my road he was hobbling and said, 'Will, I'm busting for a piss.' The tight waistband of my trousers squeezed cruelly on his bladder, swollen with a couple of pints of lager. By the time we had entered the house and climbed the stairs he hardly dared move, and clutched at himself with a babyish moan of need. I unlocked the door and as he slipped in caught him by the arm and made him stand where he was. Then I knelt down and undid his shoes and pulled his socks off: he was jiggling on the spot, gasping 'Man, hurry *up*!' But instead of letting him go I led him on to the lino of the kitchen, and he stood there, obedient and desperate. I took off his shirt, and undid the top button of his trousers, restoring his porno image – some tough, cocky, bemused little tart. His dick was already half-hard from the desire to piss, and as I kissed him, and bit him, and licked his tits, I whispered to him to let it go. I slipped my hands between his legs and squeezed his balls, and watched his eyes widen as he overcame his inhibition. He looked grateful, almost ecstatic, as the first shy stain blossomed in his lap, his cock jacked up under the thin skin-tight cotton, and then it was all happening, it pumped out, on and on, his left leg darkening and glistening as it drenched down. An abundant, infantile puddle spread on the lino, and when he had finished I went behind him, pulled down his trousers, pushed him to the floor and fucked him in it like a madman.

Later we shared a bath with foam up to our ears, like they always discreetly have in films. Phil needed some slacks and falling fondly back now on my notion of him as my little soldier, I gave him my old army fatigues. He padded about in them, and rummaging in the pockets brought out some loose change, a spunk-stiffened hanky, and a folded white card. I looked at the card, which bore a national insurance number, and on the other side the name 'Arthur Edison Hope', and his address.

8

Next day I was earlier at the Corry than usual, swimming with the lunchtime set before going east to Charles and then, alarmingly, perhaps futilely, beyond. Phil was back to work on an awkward split shift, and I would see him in the evening, over at the hotel.

The shower room was crowded, so that I had to wait at the entrance with one or two others, anxious to be through and in their offices again, eyeing the more determined lingerers with a sceptically raised eyebrow. The gross-cocked Carlos cooed 'Hey, Will' and beckoned, so I jumped the queue and joined him under his nozzle, his rose. 'Is very busy,' he acknowledged, 'but I like to see the boys.' Here was the conscience of the Corry in a phrase. He soaped my shoulderblades in halting, appreciative arcs, slowly moving further down my back, and I began to get a hard-on.

Andrews the gym instructor was across the way, austerely washing his head with coal tar soap. With his wiry, pre-war, slightly bowlegged body and his square, thin-lipped, grizzled head, he seemed to be scrubbing away in search of some lost puritanical cleanness; and as he left to dry he looked at Carlos and me with an almost regimental reproach. His place was taken by a dal-coloured Indonesian boy with strong yellow teeth, enormous hands and an exceptionally extensile cock, which, quite ordinary in size to start with, filled out lavishly with a few casual strokes of a soapy hand and was burdensomely erect a few seconds later when he grinned across the room – in response, of course, to Carlos's frank appreciation.

O the difference of man and man. Sometimes in the showers, which only epitomised and confirmed a general feeling held elsewhere, I was amazed and enlightened by the variety of the male organ. In the rank and file of men showering the cocks and balls took on the air almost of an independent species, exhibited in instructive contrasts. Here was the long, listless penis, there the curt, athletic knob or innocent rosebud of someone scarcely out of school. Carlos's Amerindian giant swung alongside the compact form of a Chinese youth whose tiny brown willy was almost concealed in his wet pubic hair, like an exotic mushroom in a dish of seaweed. On the other side of me a young businessman displayed one of those long, dispiriting foreskins, which gather very tight about the glans and then bunch and dribble on childishly for an inch or so more. Beyond him the cock of one of the weightlifters, radically circumcised, was in its usual ambiguous form, not quite at ease, not quite at attention. I looked obviously and lovingly at him as he turned slowly from side to side, unaware of me and lost in his serene, numerical weightlifter's world. I couldn't wait any longer, and at the merest word to Carlos took him dripping and giggling to the lav, where we brought each other off swiftly and greedily.

How hopelessly different life must appear to Charles, I thought, as I took the train to St Paul's. When one is beyond love, where does pleasure lie? What does one do, seeing the lustful, disrespectful world going about its business, the young up one another's arse? Was there ever an end to it, this irresistible, normal, subnormal craving for sex? Or did it go tauntingly on?

At Skinner's Lane the door was opened by the new man. He was not unlike Lewis, a plausible ex-con, with regular good looks enlivened by a pale scar running up his left cheek almost to his eye. It touched me as a strange coincidence, today of all days.

'Mr Beckwith?' he said, with the complacency of one who knows just what's going on. 'His lordship is expecting you.'

Charles was sitting in the library with *The Times*. He didn't get up but looked jolly, and chuckled to see me. I went over to him, and he slipped his arm round my waist, as parents shelter and draw to them a tired or evasive child. 'Can you think of anything to go in there?' he asked.

There was one word of the crossword to do, and as I had filled the whole thing in quite quickly that morning I decided I would only pretend to think for a second or two before coming out with the answer. ' "Hurry to start mischief in the women's quarters",' I quoted. 'Well, I should have thought it was "HAREM", but . . .' The three across answers, which gave the first, third and final letters of the word had been uncompromisingly filled in with 'SCREW', 'AZALEA' and 'PRESURIZE' (*sic*).

'C blank Z blank P,' Charles pondered. 'I'm dashed if I can think of anything. I seem to have boxed myself in.'

'I don't think some of these answers can be right,' I said kindly. ' "I hear of a line in a bottle", for instance, must be "PHIAL".'

Charles was pleased that I had fallen for it. 'Oh, I don't do the *clues*,' he said, in a tone of voice and with a little downward slap of the hand which conveyed tired contempt, an almost political feeling of disaffection. 'No, no, no,' he smiled; 'I do the *alternative* crossword, as they call things nowadays. You have to fill in words which aren't the answers. It's much more difficult. It's a kind of solitaire, you see, you have to make a clean sweep of it. And then often, I'm afraid, you get buggered in the last corner.'

I nodded and thought about this. 'You could invent a word, then, I suppose,' I said.

'Oh yes, let's,' said Charles.

'Well how about " CO-ZIP" – to do up your flies with somebody else's help. Or "CO-ZAP" – getting together to blast something.'

'Oh, co-zip! co-zap! Which do you think?'

'Let's have co-zap.' I gave the paper back to him and he wrote it in in biro. His lettering was quavering but emphatic, and he seemed completely satisfied with the whole thing.

'Now, my dear William, some coffee is just coming. It's Graham, by the way, the new man. A model of devotion. And tell me how you've been getting on.'

'You've given me some surprises,' I said, sitting down opposite him as I had on my first visit.

'Pleasant ones, I hope.'

'Pleasantly mysterious, yes. The two lives of Bill Hawkins were quite unexpected. And quite unexplained,' I added.

'Aha!' Charles was diverted by the opening of the door, and Graham's smiling but deferential approach through the broken plinths, the imaginary colonnade of stacked and toppling books. 'Splendid, splendid. Graham. Thank you. From silver spouts the grateful liquors glide, while China's earth receives the smoking tide' – this last said with heavy ironic relish. 'I've been rereading Pope,' he explained, tapping what must have been a very early edition on the coffee-table. 'Such a bitch. As one nears the end, I feel one should only read things which are really most frightfully good. I learnt the whole of the "Rape of the Lock" by heart once.' He looked at the picture-rail as if trying to recall something, but his mind had clearly gone blank again. Graham poured the grateful liquors and withdrew.

'I wanted to ask you about your meeting with Ronald Firbank.'

Charles looked round; he had got what he wanted. 'Sandy Labouchère was fearfully funny about that other thing in Pope, you know, the thing that's Waller. There used to be this place, a vespasienne in Soho he used to go to – which everyone knew as Clarkson's Cottage, because it was just by Clarkson's theatrical outfitters, in Wardour Street. Most of them had sort of trefoil holes in, so you could look out and check if the police were coming, or who was coming in. Not Clarkson's Cottage, until one day, somebody hammered out a little peephole. You can guess what Sandy said.' Charles lifted his cup, and I looked pained and dim, so that he patted it out for me: 'Now Clarkson's Cottage, battered and decayed, lets in new light through chinks that queens have made.'

I grinned excessively and said, 'Of course.'

'I think he may have said "buggered and decayed",' said Charles.

I sipped at my hot, weak coffee and after a bit asked, 'Did you meet Firbank again?'

'You've read about that, then? Most extraordinary creature I ever met. Met him at the Savoy. He belongs to another age – even then he belonged to another age.'

'I've been reading him recently.'

'Do you find him pretty maddening?'

'I'm keen on him, actually. I have a friend who's a great fan.'

'He always had a small following,' explained Charles, as though this were something rather sinister. 'I only met him once, not long before he died. He drank most frightfully and never ate a crumb. Did you want something to eat?'

'No, thank you.'

'That's very much what he would have said. He went off abroad – he liked Africa: that's what we were supposed to have in common. We did write to each other – just one letter each way, I think. Then I was out of the country of course. I heard about his death years later, from Gerald Berners. He was with him at the time as far as I recall.'

'You don't still have his letter?' I asked, preparing for disappointment, and disparaging the possibility in my own mind.

'Perhaps,' said Charles.

I didn't want to bother or bore him. It was something he declined to see the interest in. I thought of how thrilled James would be to know about this: he had once paid hundreds of pounds in an auction for some postcards by Firbank saying almost nothing at all. 'If you go to the bookcase,' Charles said, 'you'll find one of his books.' He went on talking as I scanned the shelves and I interrupted him as I spotted it and pulled open the tall door with its trembling panes of old glass. It was *The Flower Beneath the Foot*, in a still crisp, slightly torn grey wrapper with a drawing of a nun on the front. It felt deliciously light, cool and precious in my hand. Reverently, almost timidly, turning to the frontispiece, which was a drawing of the author protected by that sexy tissue that was strewn throughout Ronald Staines's photographs, I found it to fall open half-way through, where a small cream envelope was packed right into the stitching. I took it out gently. It was addressed to Charles at Khartoum, in violet ink and large round writing, and bore at the top left-hand corner the pictorial device of the 'Grand Hotel, Helouan': a group of palm trees reflected in the Nile, a single distant pyramid, and a houseboat going by. The postmark, orthographically at variance, was 'Hilwan-les-Bains', with a blurred date in 1926.

'What have you found there?' said Charles, with a hint of possessiveness in his voice. I handed him the envelope with some excitement. It was empty. 'Hey-ho,' he said philosophically. 'Sorry to disappoint you, old darling. Why don't you keep the book, though. I'm sure you'll get more out of it than I will.'

I started reading it on the Underground, rattling out eastward in an almost empty mid-afternoon carriage, the sun, once we had emerged from the tunnels, burning the back of my neck. The book was beautifully designed, refined but without pretension, with restfully little of the brilliant text on each thick, wide-margined page. It was a treasure, and I could not decide whether to keep it for myself or to give it to James. Imagining his pleasure at receiving it, and then feeling apprehensive about Arthur, I looked out of the window at the widening suburbs, the housing estates, the distant gasometers, the mysterious empty tracts of fenced-in waste land, grass and gravelly pools and bursts of purple foxgloves. Modern warehouses abutted on the line, and often the train ran on a high embankment at the level of bedroom windows or above shallow terrace gardens with wooden huts, a swing or a blown-up paddling pool. Everywhere the impression was of desertion, as if on this spacious summer day just touched, high up, with tiny flecks of motionless cloud, the people had made off.

It was a false impression, as I found when my stop came and, slipping the book into my jacket pocket and taking up my bag, I went out on to a busy platform and then into a crowded modern high street with mothers shopping, babies in push-chairs blocking the way, traffic lights, delivery vans, the alarming bleep of pedestrian crossings. It was like an anonymous, exemplary street, with a range of nameable activities, drawn to teach vocabulary in a foreign language.

I was amazed to think it was in the city where I lived, and consulted my A—Z surreptitiously so as not to set off with faked familiarity in the wrong direction. The culture shock was compounded as a single-decker bus approached showing the destination 'Victoria and Albert Docks'. Victoria and Albert *Docks*! To the people here the V and A was not, as it was in the slippered west, a vast terracotta-encrusted edifice, whose echoing interiors held ancient tapestries, miniatures of people copulating, dusty baroque sculpture and sequences of dead and spotlit rooms taken wholesale from the houses of the past. How different my childhood Sunday afternoons would have been if, instead of showing me the Raphael Cartoons (which had killed Raphael for me ever since), my father had sent me to the docks, to talk with stevedores and have them tell me, with much pumping and flexing, the stories of their tattoos.

I soon saw where I was going, three squat towers which rose above the rooftops of the street: they were some distance away and the shops had turned to curtained terraces by the time I branched off. At the end of a short side-street a narrow ginnel with concrete bollards led into the surprisingly wide area in which the blocks of flats stood. I wondered why they had been forced up to twenty storeys or so when they could easily have spread across the empty ground which they now overshadowed, where the streets which they replaced must once have run. With surreal bookishness the three towers had been named Casterbridge, Sandbourne and Melchester.

To get to Sandbourne I wandered across the worn-out grass on a natural path eroded by feet and children's bikes. In the odorous stillness of the day I thought of the tracks that threaded Egdon Heath, and of benign, elderly Sandbourne, with its chines and sheltered beach-huts. Away to the left a group of kids were skateboarding up the side of a concrete bunker. I somehow expected them to shout obscenities, and was glad I had come ordinarily dressed, in a sports shirt, an old linen jacket, jeans and daps.

The buildings, prefabricated units slotted and pinned together, showed a systematic disregard for comfort and relief, for anything the eye or heart might fix on as homely or decent. Rainwater and the overflow pipes of lavatories had dribbled chalky stains across the blank panels, and above the concrete rims of the windows weeds and grass grew from the slime. The only variation came from the net curtains, some plain, some gathered back, a few fringed and archly raised in the middle like the hoop of a skirt. Behind them lay hundreds of invisible dwellings, very small and stuffy, despite the open windows from which, here and there, the thump and throb of pop music could be heard. I found myself sweating with gratitude that I did not live under such a tyranny, dispossessed in my own home by the insistent beat of rock or reggae.

Casterbridge, which I came to first, was connected to Sandbourne by a serviceway with, on one side, a double row of garages with buckled up-and-over doors, and on the other a six-foot wall screening, in various compartments, a generator and a number of institutional dustbins on wheels, large enough to dump a body in. At the end of this alley a group of skinheads were playing around, kicking beercans against the wall and kneeing each other in spasmodic mock fights. One of them, slobbish, with moronic sideburns, and braces hoisting his jeans up around a fat ass and a fat dick, was very good. I looked at him for only a second; a phrase from the Firbank I had just been reading came back to me: 'Très gutter, ma'am.'

Perhaps it was he and his friends who had smashed the glass of one of the doors into Sandbourne: it was now blind with hardboard. The lift arrived as I went into the hall, and a very old man with a hat and all his buttons done up shuffled out, looking at me apprehensively. It was a big, functional lift, like a goods-lift, with a battered door that shuddered shut and metal walls sprayed thickly with graffiti, and with the menacing, urchin monogram of the National Front scratched over and over in the paint.

It was only when I got out at the ninth floor that I began to feel anxious. The door closed behind me at once and left me alone. I could hear a television from within one of the flats, and the sound of a police siren outside came from very far off, from some other transgression in the hot summer world below.

The flats opened off the corridor where I stood in electric light; transverse corridors, with windows at each end, formed an H plan, and I went along very cautiously till I found the right number. By the door there was a bell and under it a little plastic window showing a card with 'HOPE' written on it in blue ink. I nodded my head mirthlessly over this, my heart raced as I lifted my finger and held it in the air, wincing with trepidation, before stepping back and slipping quickly round the corner and looking out of the window. I saw the suburban sprawl, the tall windows of a Victorian school, gothic spires rising over housetops, and then immediately below the yellowing grass, the children skateboarding, surprisingly quiet.

I wanted to see Arthur, and make sure he was all right. I wanted to touch him, support him, see again how attractive he was and know he still thought the world of me. I stood very still, hearing the racing on television from inside the flat I was nearest to. I had hardly allowed myself to think what I would actually say, if his mother wanted to know who I was, or his drug-dealing brother; or if he had never returned home since the day of the fight, and had disappeared from their lives as completely as he now had from mine. Perhaps I should abandon the whole thing, the pains I was taking. Perhaps I could see him from a distance, coming across the grass below with friends, and know that he was all right, and slide away.

It is horrible to be cowed by circumstances. I crept back to the Hopes' door, mechanically obedient to my original plan. The doorbell was shrill. I massaged my face into a plausible, friendly expression and stood back.

Oh, the relief as the seconds pounded by . . . and nothing happened. There was a scare as the door of a flat nearer the lift opened and a man in overalls came out without even looking in my direction. A scraping noise, a girl's voice saying, 'No, Wednesday,' and the slam of a door, must have come from within another flat – it was hard to be sure. I turned on my heel, but being so far in I knew I must ring again to be sensible and certain. Perhaps Mr Hope, sleeping out his jobless afternoon, would be disturbed, and come vacantly to the door.

A minute later I burnt off my adrenalin leaping down the stairs – which were bleakly concrete, like the long exit stairways at the back of cinemas. There was a smell of urine, and lines down the walls drawn by running hands. At the turn of each flight 'NF' had been scrawled, with a pendant saying 'Kill All Niggers' or 'Wogs Out'. I thought with yearning of the Hopes, whom I did not know, forced to contain their anger, contempt and hurt in such a world.

It would be best to see Arthur on common ground – in a bar or club or out in the open air which I now re-entered gratefully. In view of the horror of the case it had been rather reckless to go to his home, and I was glad I had got away with it. Ideally, I suppose, I wanted to help, to give money to the friend or consolation to the grieving mother: though I was always hoping, expecting even, to see him, there was an assumption dully gaining ground in my mind that he was dead.

In the charmless passage between the buildings there were at least the skinheads to look forward to. I had once spent a weekend with a skinhead I picked up at a dance-hall in Camden Town; he called himself Dash, though that was not among the qualities of that ugly, passionate boy. I preferred to see it as a polite euphemism for one of the stronger words that were always hypnotically on his lips. They were a challenge, skinheads, and made me feel shifty as they stood about the streets and shopping precincts, magnetising the attention they aimed to repel. Cretinously simplified to booted feet, bum and bullet head, they had some, if not all, of the things one was looking for.

I came by easily, and shot a glance at the big one I had noticed before. He was leaning against the wall, by the entrance to one of the rubbish bays, his ankles crossed, and looking straight at me. 'Got the time,' he said neutrally, hardly as a question.

I virtually stopped, referred to my old gold watch. 'It's 4.15,' I said.

'Let me see,' he said, grabbing my wrist and giving me a strange, private smile. There was a swastika tattoo on the back of his hand, very badly done, almost as though it had been drawn on with a biro.

Another of the group was across the alleyway, his eyes shifting with amazing speed, as if he was mad. 'Give us your watch!' he said, with extreme, petulant vehemence, though never looking at me for a second together. But the sexy one tossed my arm away from him, I gave a nervous gasp of a laugh, and decided I was in control of things. I stepped forward, and around the big boy, who had moved out to block my passage; the other one said, 'Where do you think you're going? We want your watch.'

I said rather crossly, 'Well you can't have it.'

At this point a third youth, that I hadn't spotted in the narrow shaft of the bin-yard on the right, clambered rapidly up one of the six-foot high bins and sat throned on the top among the black bags of rubbish, banging his heels against the side of the container. 'Fucking poof!' he said, with a kind of considered anger.

Angry myself, I wanted simply to get away – but as I tried to do so was challenged with 'Um – excuse me – no one said you could go.'

'You can tell he's a fuckin' poof,' said the one on top of the bin.

It was an old problem: what to say, what was the snappy putdown? Clever, but not too clever. I acted out a weary sigh, and said, tight-lipped: 'Actually, poof is not a word I would use.'

'Isn't it, *actually*?' said the leader, again with a smile that seemed to say he knew my game, he knew what I liked.

'Look, excuse me,' I said tetchily, nervous, hearing my own voice in my ears as though they had played it to me on a tape-recorder. I felt I mustn't flatten it, or pretend, but to them it must have sounded a parody voice, pickled in culture and money.

The jittery one, skinny, pecking forward with his oddly vulnerable neck and gulping Adam's apple, said: 'Yeah! What's 'is game, any'ow? What's 'e doin' 'ere?' His eyes ran up and down over me, as if wondering where to strike.

I knew I needn't answer and blustered inwardly about a 'lawless tribunal'. At the same time I had a terrible certainty that I was lost. They had decided on my fate and were nerving themselves up to it by humiliating me. 'As a matter of fact I've come to see a friend.' I was hopeless at this, and my looking about showed how I wanted to escape.

'Fuckin' shit-hole wanker,' the skinhead on the bin said, then spat, hitting the ground just in front of me.

The leader took in his boys with an ironic glance, and said: 'I think his friend must be one of our little coloured brothers, don't you?'

The other one rocked his head about and punched at the air just in front of me several times. 'Yeah! Fuckin' nigger-fucker,' he said, with an excited little laugh, then froze his features again. On his thin, hairless head he needed the biggest expressions if he was to make an effect, like actors in old silent films. He concentrated his malice in a frown, the lips slightly apart and firm.

My fat interrogator rested his swastikaed hand on my shoulder. He might have been going to give me advice, and checked the passageway in both directions to make sure we were alone. No one appeared, and the sounds of the kids playing went on riotously and unconcerned not far off. Then he glanced up at his friend aloft: it was like a prearranged signal, though it couldn't have been. The boy reached into the bin, fished out a bottle – brown glass, Cyprus sherry, some pensioner's empty – and dropped it down to him. Gripping me more tightly, smiling more broadly, the big boy swung the bottle round and knocked off the foot of it on the wall.

I bucked backwards to get free, to retreat down the serviceway, swinging my sports-bag ineptly round to buffet him. But his skinny mate rushed me, grabbing my jacket collar and shoving me forward into the enclosed space of the bin-yard, where we could not be seen. I lashed around with my right arm, catching him in the stomach with my elbow. He gasped, spat out 'Cunt' – and as the leader held me from the other side, brought up his knee in the small of my back. I lurched forward, but my attacker had hold of my jacket, half ripping it off, and pinning my arms behind me in its sleeves. I was completely helpless and exposed.

The leader passed the broken bottle-end backwards and forwards in front of my eyes and under my nose. 'I don't think we like you,' was his reasonable summary. The two of them pushed me down till I was almost kneeling in subjection, my legs twisted under me. Very carelessly, as if getting into bed or dropping into water, the boy on the bin slid forward, fell for a fraction of a second and hurled me over backwards, my head smacking against the concrete floor, a tearing pain in my knees, and a sack of rubbish toppling after him and bouncing down on us, sodden paper and peelings bursting over the ground. It was actually happening. It was actually happening to me.

I twisted my whole body sideways to throw him off, and he did tumble half over. The other two were standing over me. The skinny boy, as if slyly taking a tag in Winchester Football, kicked me sharply in the stomach. I was tensed and fit for it, but could not help curling up. I saw two things: my beautiful new copy of *The Flower Beneath the Foot* had been jerked from my pocket in the scuffle. It was just in front of my eyes, standing on end, its pages fanned open. There was a peculiar silence of several seconds, in which I thought they might be calling it off. I read the words 'perhaps I might find Harold . . .' two or three times. That must have been enough to show how I cared for it. A boot slammed down on it, buckling the binding, and then again and again, grinding the pages into the warm-smelling spilt rubbish, scuffing to pulp the lachrymose saint on the wrapper. The second thing, as my head was jerked back by the hair, my cheek squashed and grazed on the ground, was a boot drawn back, very large and hard, then slamming towards my face.

'But darling, I was going to give it to you.'

James was terribly upset about the book. 'I haven't got one with the wrapper. It was probably worth £100 – more, if it was as mint as you say.' He sat beside me on the sofa, holding my hand. It was rather awful to see him so cheated of his treasure, his aghast look of cupidity and disbelief.

'I'm afraid the dustmen will have cleared it away by now.' I spoke thickly, as though I were very drunk. By a miracle I had only lost one tooth, but as it was right in the front it gave me the fatuous air of a defaced advertisement. My left cheek was purple, my mouth swollen and lopsided, and my left eye narrowed to a gluey slit in a bed of tenderest black, like an exposed mollusc. Over the bridge of my beautiful nose, broken and cut, an apache stripe of dressing was stuck.

My James was so movingly practical over all this, not repelled, even slightly in his element, somehow vindicated. Deliberately or not, he kept making me laugh, which I could hardly bear, with my bludgeoned head, cracked ribs, and the bruises and contusions on my side and my legs. I had always had such good health – never a broken bone, never a filling, all the household ailments checked off in childhood – that James had had no occasion to prescribe to me for more than a hangover. Because we were always so private with each other he seemed almost to be play-acting when he sounded me and felt me expertly with his still mottled, childish hands, and took my pulse and gave me tiny, painkilling pills. I surrendered to his doctoring, since it resembled the special kindnesses and attentions of an intimate, done for our mutual pleasure. At the same time I knew he was judging me physically and professionally, despite his look of doleful pride at having such a dangerous friend.

Phil came too, each afternoon, fresh from his lunchtime breakfast. Though still hot, the weather had turned rainy and bothersome, and he wore a blue showerproof jacket with a hood. He would look lightly flushed when he came in and took it off, and he concealed his initial dismay at my appearance with a preoccupied, evasive manner. For ten days or so I hardly went out and he sweetly brought me food – tinned soups, fruit juice, bread and milk – which he unpacked on the kitchen table for me to see. But I didn't have much appetite. His catering, out of a baffled desire to make everything better, was over-generous, and I twice found myself throwing bread away – guilty about it as I never would be about throwing out overripe fruit, an unpicked carcass of partridge or grouse.

Despite the pleasant passivity of being a patient, a condition ministered to as by some perverse kind of luxury, I was profoundly shocked by what had happened. I was constantly reliving the sudden sickening panic of it. James gave me things to help me sleep, which left me drowsy and dozing through the morning, running in and out of horrible, sour little dreams. I hated it when Phil had to leave for work, and longed for him to arrive the following day.

James felt that my mother at least should be told, but I was fiercely against it. She was due in town shortly to restock the deep freeze with exquiseria unavailable in Hampshire, and to buy new clothes to fit her ever-expanding figure. When she rang to fix the routine lunch in Harrods (it had to be on the spot so as to minimise the loss of spending time) I told her I would be going to stay with Johnny Carver in Scotland that week – though in fact I had not seen Johnny since the day of his crassly youthful wedding two years before. My mother said I sounded odd, and I said I had just come from the dentist – a lie nearer to the truth.

It took something of an effort to look at myself in the mirror which usually gave me such quick, uncomplicated pleasure. As I stood washing my face with extreme gentleness, even the fronds of the sponge seeming rough on my puffed and tender skin, I found it took that kind of mastery to meet my eye in the shaving-mirror that I had needed, as a child, to look at certain pictures not manifestly horrible in themselves but subtly repulsive or awesome through some accretion of mood. My grandfather had at Marden a portrait of his aunt, Lady Sybil Gossett, by Glyn Philpot. It showed an ivory-faced society woman, of the kind perplexingly referred to as 'a famous beauty,' with bobbed fair hair and large, lugubrious eyes. She wore a misty pale blue frock, cut very low at the bosom, and sat back in a little chair beside a tub of mauve hyacinths. Her melancholy, so intense it seemed almost depraved, and the vulgar sensuality of the colour scheme, were deeply terrible to me as a child, and I could not bear being alone in the dining-room where she hung. It was a family joke that I was 'snubbing Sybil' by having always to eat with my back to her, and I was not unpleased to be the victim of so abnormal and aesthetic an emotion. At times I would steel myself and look. It was just like now, keeping my eyes fixed there until the spirit-lamp of rationality guttered, my gaze flicked away in fear.

James had said humorously that I wouldn't like having my beauty spoiled, and though it could all be remedied I found my injured appearance unbearable. My vanity, which was so constitutional that it had virtually ceased to be vanity, was shown up for what it was; I bit Phil's head off when he blandly suggested that I didn't look too bad. For a while I became the sort of person that someone like me would never look at.

After a few days I took a turn around the block with Phil. Accustomed to daily exercise, I now experienced an aching restlessness which mingled with the pain of my bruises and bones. I couldn't make my limbs comfortable, and had to get out. It was a bright, blowy tea-time. Already people were coming home, the traffic was building up at the lights. The pavements were normal, the passers-by had preoccupied, harmless expressions. Yet to me it was a glaring world, treacherous with lurking alarm. A universal violence had been disclosed to me, and I saw it everywhere – in the sudden scatter across the pavement of some quite small boys, in the brief mocking notice of me taken by a couple of telephone engineers in a parked van, in the dark glasses and cigarette-browned fingers of a man – German? Dutch? – who stopped us to ask directions. I understood for the first time the vulnerability of the old, unfortified by good luck or inexperience. The air was full of screams – the screams of children's games which no one mistakes for real screams as they blow on the wind from street to street. If there were real screams, I found myself wondering, would it be possible to tell the difference, would anyone detect the timbre of tragedy? Or could an atrocity take place whose sonority was indistinguishable from the make-believe of young-sters, their boredom and scares? I had never screamed in my life. Even when the three boys had laid into me I had uttered only formal little oaths, 'Christ', 'God' and 'Oh no'.

There was a lot of time to fill, but I hardly did anything useful. Mainly I closed the curtains and watched Wimbledon, alternately alerted by a breathtaking rally and soothed by the drowsy putterings of Dan Maskell, like some rich stew left bubbling all day long over a low flame. James brought me videos from the rental shop, as well – not the bath-house freak-shows he usually offered, but charming old films to make me feel better. On his day off – which was drizzly, the covers were on at the Centre Court – we sat and watched *The Importance of Being Earnest* together. Michael Redgrave and Michael Denison were such bliss, so brittle and yet resilient, so utterly groomed and frivolous, dancing about whistling 'La donna è mobile' . . . Afterwards James told me his theory about Bunbury and burying buns, and how *earnest* was a codeword for gay, and it was really *The Importance of Being Uranist*. I had heard it all before, but I could never quite remember it.

Charles's books were lying around, of course, and James picked them up and showed curiosity enough to make me feel ashamed that I was not getting on with them. 'What's it all like?' he wanted to know.

'Rather wonderful in parts – when he's having adventures and things. Other bits are rather – earnest.'

'You must have read all of it by now.'

'Good God no. There's so much, it rather puts one off. And then he's so frightfully keen about it himself, and regards it all as a big treat for me. I've got to try and be honest about it.'

James looked at me sceptically. 'You must show me the bit about R. F.,' he said.

'Yes, that is good. Parts of it are – he must have put a lot of care into it. There are some rather Bridesheady bits about Oxford – though some-what more candid than that deplorable novel. They would be good in a book. But a lot of the stuff in the Sudan is very routine – and he has this trying kind of nature-worship thing about blacks. He has only to see the back of a black hand or the curl of a black lip and he's off.'

'I thought you were rather the same.'

'Well up to a point – but I don't go writing about it in this secret, religious kind of way. There's no indication that old Charlie ever actually got it together with any of these tribesmen, bearers, and so on.'

'I think you're going to have to brush up on one or two things, dear. I mean, you could hardly have the District Commissioner riding round on his camel rogering the subject people, could you? I know that's what you would have done, but it would really have been rather frowned on in the Political Service.'

I smiled in gap-toothed, humorous shame. 'I haven't been very systematic about it,' I further confessed. 'I've read bits here and there – just to see if I like it, if I think I can do it. The idea of writing a whole great big book – it's too ghastly. Of course,' I added, 'I haven't got everything here. The diaries stop, I think about 1950.'

'Does he still keep one, do you suppose?'

'I don't know. He could do. He's full of energy, even though he's so old and not, strictly speaking, all there.'

'He's probably writing about you now – the peaches and cream of your complexion – soon to be restored – the well-knit frame.' I aimed a swipe at him with a cushion, and then clutched at my ribs. 'The subject describing his biographer . . . It all gets rather complicated and modern,' he said, frowning and getting up to go.

As usual he had been a corrective, and when Phil turned up later he found me aloof with a volume of the diaries, and hardly interested in his anecdotes about Pino and the hotel lift, and how there was a gay couple staying who had made a pass at him. He unpacked some veal, some ripe peaches, some wine and more bread. He seemed to believe in bread in some literal way as the staff of life.

I watched him moving about, doing a little tidying, neatly stacking up Charles's tumbled notebooks. For all his compact, self-contained ordinariness he was a shape-changer. He was exercising his ability to make himself bigger, stronger, and more beautiful. I could still summon up one image of him when he first came to the Corry – standard material, a bit overweight, uncommunicative. Now he grew better week by week. His whole gait was changing as his thighs became more massive, rubbing together as he walked and so pushing his knees apart and turning his toes slightly in. As a result his ass, even more than before, seemed to be proffered, thrust out ingenuously towards the admiring hand. Whilst I was Impotens he was a great consolation just to hold and touch – like those exhibitions of sculpture that are put on for the handicapped. Instead of the normal brutal rush our lovemaking was tentative and respectful – it was as if we were both of us afflicted by some cruel, slowing illness that made us think everything out from scratch.

'Still reading those books?' he said, with a hint of reserve, as he came and sat on the floor by my chair and activated the remote control of the TV. I don't think he really knew what the books were, and looked on them as some tiresome academic pursuit to which I was snobbishly attached.

'There's no tennis,' I said, as the still of the court welled up in the screen, accompanied by optimistic light music.

'Do you fancy any of the tennis players?' he asked.

'I think tennis the least erotic of all sports,' I lied firmly, 'marbles and pigeon-fancying not excluded. Please turn it off.'

He fairly jabbed down the button, and I could see him forcing back a reasonable riposte and remembering to be tolerant of me. He sat with his head bowed, until I reached down and stroked the side of his neck, pulling his chin back, and running my fingers over his face. When my palm covered his mouth, he kissed it slightly, and I was perhaps forgiven. 'No telly today,' I said. 'I'm going to read to you. Please excuse my temporary lisp. Our hero is just arriving at Port Said, with him three rather keen young men, Harrap, Fryer and, um, Stearn; all are wearing panama hats and too many clothes. The date, September 12, 1923.'

We were all jolly stirred, though we showed it in different ways. Harrap was particularly struck, & gasped 'I say, I say' over & over, taking his hat off & then prudently putting it back on again. I imagine he'll say 'I say, I say' quite a lot more as Africa offers up its wonders. Not that the landfall itself is in the least remarkable: we had shuffled along in & out of sight of land for the last day or more, but it gave nothing of itself away: a certain amount of traffic evidently going in & out of Alex, & smallish freighters passing near enough for us to see our first Africans. Their lack of any sense of occasion was infinitely touching & humbling. Here was your *fellah* at his changeless labours – and us Englishmen, coming to rule & to help, so young & calm. I was in the most delirious mixture of silliness & solemnity, & as we approached the entrance to the Canal, & saw the cranes on the docks, the frankly undistinguished buildings, soldiers too as we drew closer, & crowds in djellabas somehow indifferent & yet in a flurry at our arrival, Oxford and England and Poppy seemed almost giddily remote.

The heat was rocketing up all the time of course, & when the ship finally stopped moving, & we stood along the rail disdaining to wave at the children & waiting for the gangway to be lowered, it slammed in our faces for the first time. We had 12 hours here while refuelling took place, and I was so much looking forward to it that I cd hardly bring myself to go ashore, & had to think hard about deadly serious things to keep myself from grinning like a fool as I went at a canter down the virtually perpendicular gangplank & shot into the melee of people. I longed to look at them & shake their outstretched, begging, greeting hands, instead of marching implacably through, as we had to.

Custom dictated that we go to Simon Artz's emporium to buy our sola topis; Fryer and I stood wearing them in front of a huge dim mirror, which made us look very historic, and rather silly. I found mine uncomfortable, & was afraid it suddenly drew all the character out of my face & turned me into just another hard-hatted, heavy-handed empire-builder.

I wandered alone through the shop, from the clothing department, which is like a designated school outfitters, stocked with the kit which Europeans will need for the term, through rooms with shelves of rolled & folded cloth, with grubby-suited Arab attendants climbing up tapering ladders to get down fabrics – printed cotton mostly – from the top. Occasional lethargic fans stirred the air. There seemed to be no windows, & beyond irregular pools of electric light lay mysterious, abundant semi-darkness. I came to a sort of dead end, a tall, stuffy place like an airing cupboard, a store-room perhaps, with a young boy barefoot, climbing up & down the shelves, checking stock, a pressure-lamp in his raised hand, his black face concentrating, dazzling in the plane of light that he swung about him. I stayed & watched, mesmerised, feeling that nothing else mattered. Down he clambered, his supple child's body comically bursting out of his khaki cotton uniform. When he saw me he smiled. I smiled back – though I was at the very edge of the field of light, & perhaps he cd not really see me. He kept on smiling – an immense, gentle, jolly smile – not yet a vendor's smile, nothing calculating in it. He was a pure Negro, from far south evidently, like the people we are going to, quite different from the crossbred scamps who haunt the quays. I turned & went back, & as I did so he called out, 'Welcome Port Said, m'sieur' – in a heartbreaking voice, its boy's clarity just cracking into manhood.

I was inordinately, unaccountably moved by this—except that I knew it for what it was, a profound call of my nature, answered first at school by Webster, muffled, followed obscurely but inexorably since. Was it merely lust? Was it only baffled desire? I knew again, as I had known when a child myself, confronting a man for the first time, that paradox of admiration, of loss of self, of dedication . . . call it what you will. Back in the sunshine—fiercely hot now, so that I at once put on my topi, & walked out conscious of some inner effort of self-effacement, of humility wrestling with grandeur & compassion—the scamps, repelled from Simon Artz's door by a fearsome old Arab with a peaked cap and a cane, flocked about me, some pushy & assertive but others festive and friendly, trying to take me by the hand. I had the absurd vision of myself as a doting schoolmaster leading off his charges on some special treat, & for the first time I had to assert myself, strike out airily with my hand to repel the little demons. Then I felt childlike myself, very pink & white, laughable in my indignation, & my authority much too big for me, as if bought in anticipation of my 'growing into it'.

I have omitted to mention the smell, which as soon as the ship docked & the wind it made was stilled, rose to the nostrils from the land. 'Ah, the East!' Harrap had said connoisseurially. It is not a smell one could anticipate, or even much care for in itself, but I relished its authenticity at once—a dusty dryness, & a sweetness, a foetor, as it might be near some perpetual meat-market, a smell utterly unhygienic and inevitable.

The other streets here might have borne exploring, but I was thirsty & went to sit in the shade of the tea-terrace. The tea, served impractically in a glass, was refreshing, somehow muddy & more sustaining than tea I am used to. All the while there was Sinai, very hazily apparent in the distance, & near to the spectacle of the ship being refuelled, which is done by an endless chain of Egyptians, some in blue or white djellabas, others naked but for a knotted nappy around the loins, lean, by & large, & sinewy. All the while they pass on baskets of coal, their foreman leading them in monotonous chanting, a call raised, a general echoing response, the words, indistinguishable to my Oxford Arabic, intensifying the impression of changeless pharaonic labour. Meanwhile on the quay, & even for a while from the bows of the ship until an official stopped them, three or four youths, virtually naked & entrancingly wild & fearless, were diving for coins.

As I sat & watched them, my pleasure & fascination evident perhaps in my gaze, a handsome young man with the immemorial flat, broad features of the Egyptian, a blue djellaba & a circular embroidered hat that made him look like an exotic afterthought of Tiepolo, sidled among the tables towards me, half-concealing behind him a battered valise. I had been thoroughly trained to expect him & his inevitable offers of fake antiquities, but as I was still alone – the others not yet having arrived at the rendezvous – & in my mood of exultant curiosity & celebration, I let him approach. The major-domo, I noticed, kept an eye out for my reaction, & when I did not object, looked at the youth in a way which suggested some sinister understanding between them, as if, the protocol of deference having been observed, I was now a legitimate victim of their antique trade.

'You see Lesseps statue, m'sieu,' he said, standing over me solicitously.

'No, no,' I replied tolerantly.

'Is very good, m'sieu. You like. You like, I take you. Only 50 piastres. Is most instructive.'

'No thank you,' I said firmly, but with an amused look, I suppose, which may have encouraged him – if encouragement were needed – to carry on. He hoisted his case up then on to the table, although I raised a hand to promise him it was no use.

'Here is postcard picture of statue of Lesseps, m'sieu. Is most instructive & also relaxing. Also is only ten piastres.' I bought one of these &, since we wd not go there, one of the Pharos & one of Pompey's Pillar. Encouraged, he rummaged inside a cloth bag, & produced a small brown bottle, taking the opportunity too to pull a chair up beside me & sit down. He had a strong, not particularly pleasant smell. 'Here is very special drink, m'sieu. Very good for you & for your lady.' He looked at me keenly & I felt myself colour. 'Is the cocktail of love, m'sieu. Is the wine of Cleopatra.'

'No, no, no,' I said, flustered. To my surprise he was sensitive to this & put the bottle away. He seemed prepared already to give me up, afraid to overstep the mark, & packed up his case again; some other Europeans approached an adjacent table, & I was glad to be seen successfully repulsing this mountebank, fascinating & confidential though he was. Leaning forward as though to rise, & so hiding what he did from our neighbours, he produced, almost prestidigitated, from inside his robe, from somewhere mysterious about his person, a hand of postcards which he quickly fanned & as quickly swept together again & covered. It should not have surprised me that there was a market for such things here. He may only have been taking an inspired commercial guess in showing them to me. But I was keenly dismayed, humiliated, feeling that he had read me like a book & I, in the glimpse I caught of naked poses – all male, young boys, fantastically proportioned adults, sepia faces smiling, winking – had confusedly admitted as much. I declined him sternly, & with an amiable, philosophical bow he withdrew to pester the newly arrived party.

Tonight we travel south along the Canal. I have just walked on deck under stars; it was quite bracingly cold. Beyond the sheer canal walls there are occasional lights & fires: otherwise featurelessness & a distant horizon of hills to the east, and plain to the west, just perceptible as darker than the sky. Like a child I feel far too excited to sleep through my first night in Africa.

A couple of weeks later Charles rang me. As usual he was already talking when I raised the apparatus to my ear: ' . . . my dear, and too appalled to hear that you've been vandalised.'

'Charles! I'm much better now. I've got a false tooth very cleverly sort of welded on at the front . . .'

'I've only just heard about it from our friend Bill.'

'I didn't know he knew.'

'I was most dismayed. I went for a swim, you see. I hoped I might find you there. But I suppose . . .'

'I haven't been going in while I've been looking so hideous, but I hope to make an appearance in the next few days.'

'Were you badly hurt?'

'Well, I've got some cracked ribs, and there's not much you can do about them, you just have to let them mend. The only permanent defect is a broken nose.'

'Oh *dear* . . .'

'It gives me a sort of pugilistic look – quite like one of Bill's boys.'

'Even so . . . Who's been looking after you? Can I send you bouquets?'

'I have a wonderful doctor, and a very sweet friend. I'm fine.'

There followed a typical Nantwich pause, which, heard over the telephone, was more disconcerting than when one was with him. I stood expectantly by. Suddenly he was on the air again. 'Come over to Staines's tomorrow, if you want to see something really extraordinary.'

'I had a fairly extraordinary time there a few weeks ago.'

'It may be a bit vulgar. About seven o'clock.' There were a few seconds of reedy respiration, and then he hung up.

I remembered from something he had said before – about Otto Henderson's cartoons being 'vulgar' – that this was a word Charles used, as I had used it when a little boy, to mean indecent, in the manner of, say, a rude joke. Of course, anything remoter from the *vulgus* than the arty pornography of Henderson and Staines would have been hard to imagine; but it was telling that in his euphemism Charles made the connection, as though his taste for them somehow joined him with the crowd.

It was the crowd in the sense of the little *clan*, the gathering of half-a-dozen queens, that I joined when I went to Ronald Staines's, feeling for the first time restored and randy, and enjoying the breeze that set the chestnuts and cherry trees along the pavements sighing.

Bobby answered the bell. 'Jolly good,' he said, letting me in and then conducting me across the hall with a heavy arm around my shoulder, a kind of gentlemanly muffling of eroticism which also disguised his need for support: he was already extravagant and slow with drink. 'Jolly glad you could come,' he said. 'Not brought your little friend this time then?'

'I'm not sure he has a career as a model.'

Bobby laughed tremendously at this. 'I *liked* him, I must say,' he confessed, as if discussing with colleagues an underqualified applicant for a job.

In the white, selfconscious drawing room Staines sprang up when I entered. He had on blue, baggy workman's trousers but with a very high, belted waist that gave him the look of someone in a Forties film; a checked, camp shirt, the sleeves tightly rolled up around wiry biceps, the pale hairless arms somehow improperly revealed; and blue, rubber-soled sailing shoes, which completed the fantasy image of the man prepared for action.

'My dear, how perfectly perfect of you to come,' he welcomed me. 'We're all so relieved that you're better.' I came forward sheepishly but proudly, like an injured games hero at school, almost expecting sporting applause. Bobby only let go of me to move towards the drinks table.

There was a perceptible conflict of claims on me as Charles, seated monumentally on the sofa, slower on the uptake, half turned to see me and then reached out his left hand for his unconventional and friendly greeting. 'Ah, William. Let me see the worst. Let me see what they've done to my Boswell.' He wore an elderly, Aschenbachish cream linen suit, not unstained.

I went and sat beside him, and he took my hand again as he searched my face, appraised it as he had before. He offered no verdict, except 'Well, at least I saw it before they spoilt it.'

'Is it really so bad?'

But he only patted my hand and then threw it away. 'How's the great work?' he wanted to know.

Staines, unprepared for Charles's possessiveness, cut in here with instructions that we must drink. 'And then there's Aldo,' he said, swivelling with extended hand and producing a small, curly-haired young man in graphic jeans from behind his armchair. As I walked round I saw that he had been looking through a pile of photographs on the floor. I shook his surprisingly large red hand, and he gave a privileged sort of smirk. 'Aldo's my bummaree,' said Staines, 'my John the Baptist.' He had a nice, alert little body, and I realised he must be a part of the planned vulgarity.

The martinis were extremely, almost disagreeably, strong on an empty stomach, and gave me a light head at once. We talked frothily for a while – Aldo, however, saying nothing at all, although Staines spoke for him in a supercilious way: 'Oh Aldo doesn't care for that, do you Aldo?' or, to suggest that under other circumstances the Italian might be a desirable conversationalist, 'That's what Aldo always says.' Then Staines would touch some part of him and Bobby would nod and raise his eyebrows, as if to say there was no limit to what these queens would do.

I was some way through my second drink when Staines asked us all to go through – not to the dining-room ('We will have a special meal later') but to the studio. I got an unpleasant feeling that we were all going to watch a sex film, and that with this company it would be most embarrassing and anaphrodisiac. Charles took my arm, more to connect me to himself than as a prop: he was clipping us together and hardly leant on me at all. There was an odd and rather revolting attitude of suppressed expectancy on everyone's face, and I saw that I was the only one who did not know for sure what was going on.

I was more confused in the studio, where there was a noise of other people, and we hovered for a while as our host rushed off with a great air of professionalism and urgency. The romantic Edwardian backdrop, with its balustrade and overhanging cloudy branches, was in position, and in front of it the fat-cushioned chaise-longue from the garden. A couple of blond teenagers in wing-collars and tight, striped pants were sitting there, passing what was left of a thick joint back and forth, cupped under the hand, as doormen keep their illicit fag from view or from the rain. Lights and reflectors in an arc defined a kind of acting area, divided from us by a clutter of chairs. 'Everybody got a drink?' said Bobby, very heartily. 'For God's sake sit down. This could take hours.'

Charles seated himself on a creaking old carver, and looked around a bit fussily for me to pull up a chair beside him. Aldo sat down neatly on my other side, and drew protectively on his long drink. Beyond him Bobby extended his legs from one chair to another. My ignorance and foreboding added to the social discomfort and I leant over to whisper to Charles: 'Who are these boys?'

He looked startled. 'What, these boys? But . . . you don't know them? I thought . . .' He tugged out a handkerchief from his breast pocket and ran it back and forth under his nose. '*Most* naughty and wicked boys.' He coughed, as if discretion forbade him to say more, and then tucked the hanky away.

'More important, what are they going to *do*?'

'Oh . . .'

I felt foolish, reddened a little; was annoyed too, but really peculiarly drunk. One of the boys, better-looking, I thought, was flicking at the other's fringe with his fingertips. The other smiled woozily, and gripped himself between the legs. There was something familiar about him, some faint blur on the screen of memory. Then they turned to look into the shadows beyond, where a figure was moving, in and out of my view, dark – black. I couldn't see him when his quiet but resonant voice was heard: 'How's you boys feelin?'

'Want a bit?' said the looker, with tartish expressionlessness, holding up the joint.

'I'm stoned, baby,' was the reply, melodious, rather stern. When he came forward none the less to have a pull on the last papery thumbnail's length of the joint I knew his handsome, lined face at once, the huge, challenging, mobile eyes, the pink of his inner lips, as if at any second he would lick them clean of raspberry fool. And then of course I knew the boys.

'Oh Abdul, Abdul,' Charles was calling, in his most invocative and hammy voice. The chef came over, not now with the serious, solicitous manner of the Club dining-room but with a kind of flirtatious nonchalance, as if he were a fellow member. They shook hands, Charles hanging on as Abdul withdrew his long, powerful fingers.

'All right, Charlie?' said the black man genially, amazingly.

'You remember my young friend William.'

'How are you William.' He shook my hand too, in a casual fashion, and gave a drugged grin. 'Come to see the show.' He looked along to Aldo and Bobby, who clearly needed no introduction, and closing his eyes and biting his lower lip ground his hips around slowly, as if dancing to some very sexy music in his head.

I was nearly shocked by this, and dazed and gulping like an innocent. Though he was twice my age I fancied Abdul crazily, was seriously moved by him. I remembered how I had watched those places where his black, black skin disappeared into his white chef's uniform, the wrists and the long, thick neck, and the awareness I had of his body. As he turned away I followed him with what was probably a look of stricken devotion. It was the high, haunted African brow, and the high, rolling African ass, and the long, dangling, fishing, musical hands.

Staines came rattling back in at this point, carrying a camera on a tripod, its legs unsplayed making it tall and unwieldy. I suppose it was inevitable that it would be a film, that this swaying, powerful chef, with all his virile elegance, would be doing something with these common little waiters. I was surprised to remember that Charles had told me there was no dining at Wicks's on a Sunday evening. But I was staggered to think that he — and Staines — could actually lure the staff elsewhere and make them act out those fantasies which they must have fathered in sly glances over their fatty beef, soapy veg and boiled school puddings. What bizarre transactions and transitions must have taken place. The whole thing had that achieved bizarrerie which made it normal to the participants, demonic to the outsider.

Staines's hand was on my shoulder. 'It's the very last bit, dear,' he said. 'It's going to be the most wonderful film ever. We've been doing it for months now — a cast of tens . . . I thought you'd like to see us polish it off in this sensationally sensational scene.'

'I don't know,' I hesitated. The backdrop, cracked in places where it had been rolled up, took on an air of redundant charm as the lights were switched on, isolating an area of tawdry smallness in which the action was clearly to unfold.

Aldo grew confidential. 'Is very old-fashion,' he explained. 'I am in another part, in the garden. There I met the young milordo, and we do all sort of thing, and up a ladder too. Now he is on holiday, and the servant is left — just Derek and Raymond and Abdul.' Aldo fluttered his lashes at me, restoring an illusion of gentility, as if we had been discussing the new vicar, and whether or not he favoured the Series III communion. I couldn't pretend that I hadn't wondered what it would be like to make a porn film. I had cast my own on parched, electric mornings after, putting the boys through their paces; but those were unstable little loops, that oxidised and decomposed in the light of day. I wasn't sure it would be possible to watch these acts, fearing to be aroused, fearing not to be.

Charles laid his hand on my forearm. 'Isn't our chef a splendid fellow? He's devoted to me, you know. Utterly devoted.'

The camera had not yet begun to run, but Abdul, seemingly careless of whether or not he started, strolled back on to the set. He wore a sumptuous calf-length fur coat, and, as one saw when he sat back on the bed and it fell open, nothing else. His flat stomach was crossed by the longest scars I had ever seen, as though long ago, and with the crudest means, someone had removed all his insides. With his scarred black skin inside the thick black fur he struck me, who adored him for a moment, like some exquisite game animal, partly skinned and then thrown aside still breathing. I excused myself for the lavatory, tiptoed to the front door; but then slammed it behind me.

9

No headaches; painless breathing; bruises, with all their touchy, indwelling tenderness, mysteriously fading out: I felt well again, whole, and wholesome. I didn't need the decadent secrecy of Charles and his pals – and as I had left Staines's house I had thought of putting the whole thing behind me. Why be encumbered with the furtive peccadilloes of the past, and all the courteous artifice of writing them up? I wasn't playing the same game as that lot. I looked forward to clear July days, days of no secrets, of nothing but exercise and sun, and the company of Phil. I was enthralled, almost breathless, at the very idea of men, the mythological beauty of them running under trees and sunlight in the Avenue or in the long perspectives of Kensington Gardens. But I was pure and concentrated as well. No longer loathing myself I was once again in love, and turning the full beam of my devotion upon Phil. I dreaded somehow to find that he had grown complicated, that my hatefulness of the past few weeks had left a stain on him, or eroded that ingenuousness which struck me almost as a property of his body, residing speechlessly in his palms and wrists, in his strong calves and ridged stomach, in the crisp hair above his cock, in the pumping heart I laid my ear to, the neck I kissed and bit, the glossy, speckled darkness of his pupils in which I looked and looked and saw myself, miniature, as if engraved on a gemstone, looking.

But no. He was surprised, relieved – like a child released at last from some unfair and arbitrary penance. But there was no resentment in him – and he had I suppose the further relief of finding me pretty again, with only the knotty broadening of the bridge of my nose and the too American whiteness of my ingenious new tooth to remind him of our little season of misery. Unlike recovery from a cold or a hangover this took me forward, not merely back to the old unthinking well-being. It made me romantically ambitious for sweetness and strength, and for the moment I felt all over some seasonal convulsion, quite exhilarated by that grand illusion, that I could make myself change. It was the return of physical strength – and at just the time when, sitting apprehensively, watching those two stoned boys and that beautiful scarred stitched-up man, I had seen myself, with weird detachment, in the society of corruption: the baron, the butcher, the boozed-up boyfriend, and most corrupt of all the photographer.

I went straight to Phil that night, though he was not expecting me. I had not been at the Queensberry for weeks, and as I got out of the taxi a new boy on the door – very thin and formal, not at all my kind of thing – asked me if he could help. I looked in on the staff TV room, where one of the receptionists was watching the news and a commis chef, fast asleep, had fallen half out of his chair. In the corridor I ran into Pino, who was fantastically pleased to see me and shook my hand between both of his, insisting on a complete account of the injuries Phil had told him about. He was keen too not to keep me from my friend. 'You go to see Phil? Is upstairs. Is gettin is beauty-sleep.' We shook hands again before he left me, and I heard him laugh aloud with pleasure as he went on his way.

Up under the roof, in the hot, shadowy corridor, outside Phil's door . . . distant traffic and a creaking floorboard making no impression on the silence, residual, anticipatory . . . dream echoes of childhood evenings, going up to fetch a book, drawn to the open window and the stillness of the elms . . . or at school, waiting for Johnny, knees under my chin on the sill of a gothic dormer, heart thumping, swallows plunging into the darkening court below . . . pushing open the rattling, leaded panes at Corpus Christi, the sky precipitating its blues, its darker blues . . . the surprising, secret moistness of the twilight, sloping down to the Swimming-Pool Library, the faint, midsummer-night illumination of a glowing cigarette . . . exquisite, ancient singleness in moments just before whispers, the brush of lips and love . . . I felt it all again, the romance of myself, for three or four seconds squeeze urgently about me, and my mouth went dry.

I barely knocked, tapped with the backs of my nails. It seemed like a cowardly knock, hoping not to be heard. If he were awake he might just hear, and I listened for an answering rustle or call. But what I wanted was to come upon him as he was, to stream through the keyhole, to be with him without any prosaic ado. One morning, weeks before, when he was asleep I had pinched his key and had it copied in a heel and key bar at the station. Phil was so orderly and cautious that he always dropped the catch, and I envisaged some picaresque occasion when I might need to get in, some about-turn in a sex comedy that called for a surprise entry.

I slid the key into the lock notch by notch and opened the door a fraction. There was no light on, though the last of the day still lingered and without yet going in I could see the room in the dressing-table mirror,

Phil lying on the bed, the white of his underpants. He didn't move as I came forward, silently closed the door, and stood at the end of the bed. His breathing was extremely slow and distant and he was clearly deeply asleep. He was lying face downwards, but slightly turned to one side, his left leg half-drawn up, his mouth squashed open on the pillow, his thighs apart but not widely apart, his ass slewed a little to the right. I wanted x-ray eyes for that, though the barrack-room modesty of his sleeping in his knickers was beautiful too. Beside the pillow, trapped under a slumberous arm, was *Tom Jones* – the fat, squashy Penguin redolent of O levels and essays on virtue.

I could hardly bear to look at him any longer, and shook him roughly to wake him up, falling on him before he knew what was happening and bothering him with kisses.

I hadn't made love like I did then since I was a schoolboy. It was extraordinarily innocent, fervent and complete. By the time Phil had to get to work it had begun to rain, and after he had gone I lay in the dark with the window open and listened to it pattering on the leads. Falling asleep I slid briefly through a zone of luminous happiness, a vision as clear as summer – not the ominous clarity of Hampshire or Yorkshire summer but a kind of desert radiance where rocks and water and scrawny shade, lying by chance together, seemed divinely disposed and glowed in their changelessness.

I more or less forced Phil, who did it with a certain comical reluctance, to take the following night off in exchange with Celso. Celso, it transpired, was anxious to have Friday off to treat his wife on her birthday – a musical and dinner and then, one assumed, some especially Spanish and honourable congress. I'd hoped for a high noon of sunbathing, back on the roof, but it was one of those close dark days when one can never get dry and longs for a thunderstorm that never comes. We went back to my flat and lounged about and I came on rather fierce about wanting sex several times, at which Phil showed at first a demure disbelief though clearly, when it came to it, he wanted it just as much himself. Later we went up to the Corry, which was unmomentous, no one seeming to have noticed that I had been away and the virulent strains of exercise going on much as normal.

It was wonderful though, additionally hot from weights, to plunge into the sombre coldness of the pool. No discipline made me feel more free, or contained me and delighted me within its own element so much as swimming. Even so, when Phil came down the spiral stairs – displaying (some well-judged vanity of his own) new trunks cut high on the hips, black behind and gold in front — I was happy to do things I normally deplore, getting in people's way, doing handstands or swimming between his splayed and sturdy legs. For a while we gloomed Cousteau-like in the depths of the deep end, swivelling our goggled heads from side to side, searching for our locker keys which we had thrown in and left to settle, buffeted and wandering in the choppy water. Where the end wall met the floor of the bath Phil pointed out to me with slowed, speechless gestures the melancholy aperture where the water escaped, and, gathered round it, dozens of sticking-plasters, bleached clean by their long immersion and waving over the filter like albino, submarine plants. Then I saw him give out his breath, the bubbles crowding from his mouth, flooding around his head and up towards the light with baroque exuberance. He himself shot up then and I followed a second or two later. We hung on our elbows to regain our breath.

The plan was to go later to the Shaft and dance and get drunk and have a wonderful time. Phil had never been there with me: our funny routine isolated us from the normal gay world, and what with one thing and another I had not been there myself for a couple of months — though for a year or more before that I was impelled towards it, without any power to resist, every Monday and Friday night. I had been an addict of the Shaft. If I was out to dinner I would grow restless towards eleven o'clock, particularly if I was away in the western districts and had several miles to travel. I would go to the opera very inappropriately got up, and had more than once exploited the privacy of the Covent Garden box to slip off during the last act as the anticipation of sex welled up inside me, rapidly distancing and denaturing the carry-on on stage into irksome nonsense. The Shaft itself I hardly ever left alone, and I had made countless taxi-journeys down the glaring, garbage-stacked wasteland of Oxford Street and along the great still darkness of the Park, a black kid, drunk, chilled in his sweat, lying against me, or secretly touching me. I took home boys from far out — from Leyton, Leytonstone, Dagenham, New Cross — who like me made their pilgrimage to this airless, electrifying cellar in the West End, but had no way, if they failed to score, at three or four a.m., of getting home.

Phil took a practical attitude to his initiation, and we walked from the Corry through dusky, cooling Bloomsbury to have supper at the hotel. In Russell Square, under the planes, there was at last a perceptible breeze. The immense, leafy twilight shivered, and the three fountains, shooting up their forceful jets, reckless and almost invisible, splattered down across the path and caught us in their spray. Phil put his arm round me, remembering too, I suppose, our first terrifying walk here.

The kitchen at the Queensberry was a high, white-tiled hall into which plunged a series of writhing air-ducts, tubes of aluminium, riveted along their joints, and opening out into wide, battered hoods above the loaded and archaic gas-ranges. Even so, it was wearyingly hot in there, and the team of chefs, in their crumpled white jackets and hats and their blue and white checked bags, were testy and pink-faced, shying the portions that were ordered along the metal counter beyond which the waiters waited. As 'staff' we had to wait there too, until there was a convenient pause. I felt awkward, ready to be resented, whenever we visited the kitchen. Its incessant toil, unadorned by the servility and charm of the public parts of the hotel, made me feel a frivolous observer of some truly serious industry.

Tonight Phil got us some whitebait – dull, Rotarian starter – and then excellent beef olives, the fat tongue of veal juicy in its meaty sheath. We ate it in the staff dining-room, keeping to ourselves whilst two of the washing-up women and a leathery old porter smoked fanatically through the last minutes of their dinner-hour.

'Off out tonight, then, young Philip?' enquired the porter, preparing to go, hoisting up his waistband and buttoning his hot jacket. There seemed to be some hint of contempt in his voice, a sarcasm in his civility which showed it to be a challenge, even an insult. As he drew himself up, he was somehow shielding and shepherding the two women – though they themselves betrayed no sense of danger.

'Yes, I'll probably go out for a drink or two.' A subfusc, minimal answer.

'Don't stay in this fucking shithouse anyway,' said one of the women kindly.

'I won't.'

'Don't go breakin' too many 'earts, neither,' said the other with a chuckle.

I said nothing until they had gone. They probably thought me very stuck up, but I felt a kind of duty not to incriminate Phil. It was hard to believe they didn't see me for what I was, but a pretence, a performance, was sustained that we were just pals. Rather like James, Phil cultivated a reserve that grew into a sort of authority. I must have needed their discretion just as they were freed by my lack of it. It was all a question of *bjopti*.

I finished eating and laid my knife and fork side by side. 'Am I a frightful liability to you, darling?' I said, conceitedly and solemnly.

In a swift, unconscious convulsion he clutched together the bevelled glass salt and pepper pots. 'Of course not. I love you.' He looked up for a split second and then went on very quickly and quietly, pushing the last French beans around his plate with his fork, 'I really love you, I don't think I could live without you. I couldn't bear it when you were ill, and . . . I don't know . . .'

It was much more of an avowal than I'd asked for, and the tears came to my eyes and I grinned at the same time. I covered his hand that was coupling the cruet with my own, and looked anywhere but at him – around the horrible, narrow but disproportionately tall room, which had obviously been made by splitting some more generous space in two.

Afterwards we got changed upstairs and shared a tooth-mug of vodka, which made me if anything more amorous, though in a generalised way, as if it were not just Phil but the whole world that was in love with me. I put on some very old, faded, tight-loose pink jeans and a white T-shirt with no arms and side-seams ripped open almost to my hips. Phil squeezed into other new acquisitions – some hugging and rather High Street dark blue slacks with a thin white belt, and a gripping pale blue T-shirt.

When we were clear of the hotel I took Phil's arm. It moved me to do this, to insist out loud that he was mine (he himself, keen to be so claimed, didn't quite flow with it, butchly somehow held himself apart – though I locked my fingers through his). At Winchester one summer day I had run across a couple of queens – one perhaps an old Wykehamist showing his friend the places where his honour died. They had wandered over to Gunner's Hole, that curving canal-like backwater, drawn off and returning to the Itchen, where in Charles's day swimming had taken place. Now, of course, there was a beautiful indoor pool – where I was soon to establish my freestyle record – and the Hole had surrendered, as it must always have promised to do, to crowding cow-parsley and heavy seeded grasses, while in the water itself long green weeds curled to and fro in the current. I came scuffing past through the meadow, hot, shirt undone, and saw them gazing, one pointing at the rioting May-time flowers, then spotting me, giving me a glance – very brief but I felt it – and then the two of them turning back towards College, arm in arm. I mastered a frisson of shock into pleasure – not at them individually (they seemed hopelessly old and refined) but at the openness of their gesture. I wanted men to *walk out* together. I wanted a man to walk out *with*.

Well, I had one. My heel was suddenly tacky, and I stopped – though Phil kept going and almost pulled me over. I hopped forward, supported by him, and turned my sole upwards under the yellow street light. A tongue of white chewing-gum, rough with grit, had welded itself to the rubber and squelched into a curl under the step of the heel. It was surprisingly difficult to detach – and I had a certain revulsion from it, and reluctance to touch it. So with drunken insouciance I remained, leaning on Phil's bunched shoulder, one flamingo leg drawn up, and spoke quite seriously about the British Museum, outside whose bleak north entrance we were standing. On a huge pillar above our heads a poster advertised the Egyptian galleries, with a number of aproned, broken-nosed pharaohs standing stonily, but rather pathetically, in a row. As I spoke of Charles's relief of Akhnaten Phil actually started giggling, and only giggled more when I told him to fuck off.

'If you really cared you'd get this stuff off for me,' I said. 'At the one time I need help, you refuse it to me.'

He was not quite sure of the rhetorical conventions now, but muttering 'Oh give it here' grabbed my foot and jerked it upwards, so that I hopped round involuntarily and hung on his neck. I don't know how slow I was to realise that we were being watched. Certainly my eyes dwelled incuriously on the far pavement for several seconds and though I took in a figure waiting under one of the gently stirring young trees I did so abstractly, and focused all sensation in my hands on Phil's cropped neck. To the watcher we must have been a well-lit and enigmatic group. I looked away as Phil flung down my foot, but still embraced him while he groped for a handkerchief, a quiver of protective anxiety ruffling my sexy, complacent mood. Two seconds later, the figure had moved. I was slow again to spot him, now further off, under the next tree, and screened to chest height by cars parked at meters along the middle of the street. His act was to be going away, disarming the suspicion he had aroused in me. Or perhaps he did not know he had been seen. He was looking back again now, but still moving, sidling inexpertly under a street-lamp. Then I quickly led Phil away, keeping him turned in towards me, my arm and hand oppressively around his shoulder, so that he was squashed and stumbling against me. But there could be no doubt who it was.

It gave me a shock but also the pleasure of a bitter little nodding to myself in recognition of what was afoot. 'Right!' I thought, and then, after turning quickly at the corner to look back – but there were other people on the street now, and the distance was all a pattern of shadows – more or less forgot about it for the rest of the night. I was too taken up with the honest but slightly unworthy excitement of coming back to my old haunt with such a luscious piece of goods as Phil.

It was the half-hour after closing time and the narrow grid of Soho was rowdy with people, some shutting up shop, some stumbling from pubs, and others performing the awkward, drunken transition from one place of amusement to another, where money would pour off them into the early hours of the morning. There was a small crowd outside the Shaft, a gaggle of excited boys, and others waiting, staring challengingly at the arrivals. The thump of the music, like some powerful creature barely contained, came up out of the ground and gathered around us as we went in at the door. On the stairs it began to be really loud, the whole foundations humming with the bass while a thrilling electronic rinse of high-pitched noise set the ears tingling. From now on talk would be shouting, or confidences made with lips and tongue pressed close to the ear: we would be hoarse from our intimacies. The medium of the place was black music, and even the double-jointed spareness of reggae came over the dance floor like a whiplash.

At the foot of the stairs, in his pink-bulbed cubbyhole, Denys took our money. 'Hey Willy, I thought you was dead, man.'

'I've been resurrected, just for tonight.'

He grinned. 'Whatever did happen to your nose, eh?'

I pinched the broken bridge with my fingers. 'Ooh, a bit of trouble with some boys – a bit of rough, you might say.'

'Well you take care man – because you, are, *pretty*.' He fluttered his long lashes, but kept the straightest of faces. 'And I hope you will have a pleasant evening too sir,' he said to Phil, who thanked him apprehensively. So we passed on, waved in to the pounding semi-darkness by the impassive Horace, whose twenty-stone bulk, toiling and yet stately in a Hawaiian short-sleeved shirt, was reflected in floor-length mirrors that flanked the door and repeated him *ad infinitum*, like exotic statuary surrounding a temple.

The mirrors and pink lights were reminders that this place, which to me was purely and simply the Shaft, was other things for other people on the intervening days and nights. Indeed, the club went back a bit and under different names had been a modish Sixties dive and before that a seedy bohemian haunt with a pianist and alcoholics. The décor, of what was essentially an arched, brick-walled cellar, was correspondingly eclectic, the bar overhung by a thatched roof, and the sitting-out area screened from the dance floor by a huge tank of flickering tropical fish. On first acquaintance these features seemed hideous or absurd, and gave me the sinister feeling that nightlife was still run by an elderly, nocturnal, Soho mafia who actually thought such details were smart. Soon, though, they became camp adornments to the whole experience, and I wouldn't have had them changed for the world.

The heavy hotness of the day, which had begun to drain from the streets, was redoubled in the thickly crowded club. Some people had come all innocently in shorts, and on the floor a trio of black boys had already removed their singlets, which swung, like waiters' towels, from the loops of their jeans. I propelled Phil to the bar for the sharp, gassy lager, not in itself pleasant, which was the economy fuel of the place. We leant together at the counter, his arms bulgingly crossed, and I splurged my tongue up his jaw and into his ear – he turned to me with a grin and gave me, too close to be in focus, a look of the tenderest trust.

We perched for a while by a little shelf, drinking quite fast, feet rocking to the music, more or less silent though I pointed people out to him and he looked and nodded in a factual sort of way, not feeling, perhaps, that it was quite right to rave adulterously about other men. Even so, he was enthralled when Sebastian Smith moved through the crowd at the heart of his own little crowd, who touched, supported and congratulated him. He had come fresh, exhausted, from Sadler's Wells, was still on the serene, unpunctured high of adoration and acclaim, still sustained, as in some sugary Spanish Assumption, by the pink clouds of triumph and the tumbling black putti of his entourage. Still wearing, too, his leotards (though now with little patent, winking pumps), his torso rising in a naked black triangle to the glitter-sprinkled, ballerina-hefting shoulders. Everyone wanted him to dance, and he came forward, considering it, to the floor's edge – one foot set before the other as if on a gym bar, the long, taut thighs chafing, all the effort instinctively keeping his body steady, as though it were his discipline to carry a glass of water on his head or to propel without obscene lurching the contents of his high, prancing basket. But he decided against it, paced back to a darkened corner, leaving me with a faint ache of adulation and inadequacy.

Phil I found had that look of relished, vulgar curiosity which from time to time reminded me that he was as prone to sudden lusts as the next man. Not for you, dear, I thought, as I gestured 'Let's dance', he carefully finished his drink, and we felt our way through the gay throng. I turned, we sculpted out a little area on the edge of the mass of dancers, and were drunk enough to be dancing already, Phil too (who I thought might selfconsciously jiggle), going into a kind of mood, hardly looking at me and swivelling chunkily to left and right in a tight, fashionable style he must have picked up somewhere. I sprang about in my own reckless way. In a sense we had nothing to do with each other, though I kept an eye on him and grinned with pleasure when his shy dark gaze held mine. Then I would whirl him round once or twice, and hold his handsome head and kiss him clumsily, bumping noses.

I kept him at it for about an hour, never stopping as, under the DJ's gurgling patter, the rhythms of one track, clean and fierce, cut across and then went under the rhythms of the next. It was a sport, where exhaustion was only a spur to more effort, the blood-opiates sang through the system, lap succeeded lap. On the floor there was competition, more athletic than sexual, and I would find myself challenged, magnetised by strangers, drawn into faster and faster action, though no words were said, we affected not even to look at each other. And some of the kids there could dance. Sometimes a ring would suddenly form around one or two of them, and we hung on each other's shoulders to see them – their brief, fizzy routines of backward handsprings, jack-knife jumps and other crazy things. Boy after boy would follow, explode in action, stumble back into obscurity; and then the ring would dissolve, the crowd would repossess the floor.

At last Phil rocked to a stop and gestured for drink. I gasped 'Lager' in his ear. Both of us were parched – and all wet outside, so that his hair, when I roughed it and sent him off, stood up, and the bristly back of his neck glistened as if it had been dressed. I lurched off the dance floor and into Stan.

Stan was a colossal Guyanan bodybuilder, not only gigantically muscular but six feet six inches tall. 'Love the arse on your chum,' he said. 'I've been watching him.'

'Heaven, isn't it?'

'Yeah. Where d'you find that then?'

'I took him under my wing at the Corry.'

He craned to see where Phil had got to in the further spotlit half-dark. 'Still go there then?'

'Daily. You should come back. We all miss seeing you.'

Stan smiled sweetly and said, 'I bet you fucking do.' His mouth, like the rest of him, was vast, so that when he laughed it seemed his whole head would open up like a canteen of cutlery. I had met him at the Corry during my first Oxford vac and fooled about with him rather unsatisfactorily in an alley off the Tottenham Court Road. I remember how struck I was by the contrast of his rocky physique and the beautiful, almost smothering softness of his lips. A term later he had left, for some north London gym more suited to his championship needs. But I would run into him from time to time in clubs and bars, and though we had nothing much in common I seemed to charm him somehow, so that despite his super-human body he was slightly in awe of me. I rested a hand on the side of his neck, whose shaft, thicker than his head, was buttressed by the gathered, sloping muscles of his shoulders.

'You're looking very big, Stan,' I said, smiling at him teasingly. He was a hard man to clothe and at night often went out as he was now, his torso draped in the tatters of some sweat-scorched singlet, a broad leather belt (which he assured me *came in handy*) needlessly supporting pale old jeans rubbed thin under his bum and along the thick bolt of his cock. He once showed me a picture of how he looked at fifteen – tall and uncertain, and indifferently built. I think some sort of crisis about being gay had got him to the gym, which gave him both lovers and a new body. An element of defiance had made him a now almost unconscious exhibitionist. A lot of sex went on in the lock-ups of the Shaft, but one evening I had stumbled in for a piss to find Stan fucking a boy just inside the door. He had him with one leg cocked up on a washbasin and as he laid into his ass the bracket of the basin was breaking free of the wall, and the kid, who looked the younger and slighter in his giant grasp, rode up and down against his own breath-smeared reflection in the mirror. An ever-growing group of admirers deserted the dance floor and stood around feeling themselves and muttering encouragement.

Phil was back with the much-jogged pints of beer. I craved liquid, and as I drank my dry palate seemed to admit the alcohol straight to my brain. 'See you, sweetheart,' said Stan, realising we would be no good to him – the endearment, as always when spoken by a real man, a virtual stranger, moving me for a few seconds intensely.

Phil watched him amble off. 'Some bloke grabbed my cock, at the bar,' he said, in a tone which strove to combine pleasure and resentment and came out, neutrally, as a statement of fact. I drank and then kissed him, squirting cold lager into his mouth, though much of it, in his surprise, ran back down his chin. As I held him I could squeeze the sweat from his shirt where it clung down the channel of his back – so I took his drink from him, and helped him tug the wet garment off. The atmosphere was more and more liquid. Everyone was stripping off, and those who touched each other could cream off the sweat with a finger.

I took his hand and led him away. There were corners of the club, removed from the dance floor, dead-ends of cellars, crypt-like areas, dimly lit, faintly damp, with a limey dampness quite distinguishable from the tropical humidity the weather and the dancers made. We ran into John and Jimmy, a sweet black and white couple who had been together for years, John a cuddly blond, Jimmy handsome to tears, with lingering, ironical eyes. We stood and shouted some banter, Jimmy as usual hugging his friend from behind: they would shuffle around for hours like that, coupled and domestic and yet giggling, party-going. They might have been the beginning of a conga, ready to sweep everyone away in silliness and fun, but their devotion to each other made them at the same time inaccessible. I knew they had something which I had never had. They felt Phil a bit, ooing as he looked bashful but knew he couldn't object, and Jimmy lifted up his hand as if he'd won a fight and made him flex his biceps and triceps, and then in a little showery cadenza of laughs and nonsense they were on their way.

We went into the section beyond the fishtank, with a comfy bench running along the walls, very low, with knee-high tables crowded with beer glasses. From where we sprawled the fishtank formed an unreliable window on to the dance floor, its water threaded by bubbles up one side, and the tiny fish, neurotically it seemed, twitching from one direction to another as the music shook the thick glass. The floor of the aquarium was at eye level, and laid out like a miniature landscape, with picturesque rocks tilting up out of the pinky-brown sand, and a little pink house like a French country railway station with gaping doors and windows which the fish never deigned to swim into. The subdued lighting made the surface gleam when one looked up to it, and gave the water an unnaturally thick appearance, like a liqueur. Through this entranced, slowing medium the dancers could be seen spinning, rocking and bouncing, freakishly fast and disconnected.

'All right darling?'

Phil nodded. 'Bloody hot,' he said, running his hand over his chest and stomach and then looking at it admiringly. It was one of those occasions when I couldn't think of much to say to him: we lolled stickily together and slurped our lager. They kept the lager so chilled that the glasses were slippery with their own cold sweat. When Phil slid his hand through the slit side of my vest I gasped at the shock – like cold water thrown in horseplay in the showers, or the touch of hands under clothing in winter out of doors.

A short way off I made out a couple talking about us in a way meant to be noticed, heads together, with long glances and point-weighing smiles and nods. I raised an eyebrow, recognising the boy, Archie, whom I'd taken home a few months before. He had one slightly sleepy eye, which gave him a lewd and experienced air, though he was only a kid, sixteen or seventeen, illicit and the more queenly for it. He had trashed up his appearance since he'd gone with me: hair slick with a jar-load of gel, black lips queerly glossed with lilac lipstick. He said something to his companion, then got up and came over to us, surrendering himself confidentially to the seat beside me.

'Hello dear!'

'Hello Archie.' We looked at each other for a moment with that strange disbanded intimacy of people who have once briefly been lovers. 'This is Phil.'

'Mm. I'm with Roger. He says he's seen you in the gym. He was well jeal when I told him about you and me.' I glanced over to where Roger was affecting an interest in some men in the other direction. He was someone I was half-aware of, a morose middle-aged fellow who appeared at the Corry in a suit on weekday evenings but on Saturdays and Sundays was transformed by heavy boots, jeans and biking jacket, the ensemble looking just a trifle too much for him.

'I'm not sure that I'm not jealous of him,' I said with arch courtesy. 'Are you seeing a lot of him?'

'Yeah, last couple of months I've been stopping over at his place, Fulham, quite posh it is. He's got a video and that.'

'I can imagine.'

'No, he's really sweet though.'

'I think he's perfectly hideous, but I suppose it's nothing to do with me.' He might have been hurt by this remark, but he seemed to quite admire me for it.

'Yeah – still it's nice having someone to look after you, know what I mean?' He slid his hand between my legs, and I felt Phil go tense on the other side of me. I said nothing, but stared at Archie in an existential sort of way, my cock quickly thickening under the light pressure of his fingers.

'Not today dear,' I murmured, shifting away and slipping my own hand on to Phil's thigh.

'P'raps you're right,' he said, with his typical experimenté air, and looked round to find out what had happened to Roger. Roger was smoking a cigarette and gazing at the ceiling, a model of tense insouciance. 'Your mate looking for a friend, is he?' Archie asked, as if it were the 1930s.

'Phil you mean? No, no: he has a mate.' Archie looked at me, expecting me to say something else as it sank in.

'That's not like you,' he said. 'I thought you only went with black boys. Sorry love,' he said to Phil, needlessly enlarging on his error; 'I thought you must be down here after a bit of beige. That's what most of the white guys come here for.'

'That's all right,' said Phil gruffly.

'D'you hear about Des?' Archie asked in tones of gossipy shock. I had to think for a second. There was a Desmond at the Corry; but he must mean 'little' Des, dancing Des. It was yet another sentimental history salvaged from the nightclub floor.

'You mean little Des?'

'Yeah, you know. You had that threesome with him and that bloke from Watford.'

'You seem to know a lot about my sex life.'

'Yeah, well, he told me. Anyway, he got involved in some other really heavy scene. This taxi-driver that tied him up and whipped him. Anyway, one night things got well out of hand and this cunt goes off and leaves little Des tied up in some garridge, with rats and stuff, and he's got burns all over him. He was there for three days till some old bird found him. He's in hospital now, and he don't look good.'

Archie was pleased to be able to tell me this horrible news, but I saw him swallow and knew he was as shocked in the retelling as I was, hearing it for the first time. While he was speaking the lighting system had gone over to ultra-violet, so that the dancers' teeth and any white clothes they were still wearing glowed blueish white. Seen through the tank these gleaming dots and zones themselves seemed to be swimming and darting in the water and to mingle with the pale phosphorescence of the fish.

There were two or three sickening seconds. The vulnerability of little Des. The warped bastard who had hurt him. A face passing beyond the glass, turning to look in, mouth opening in a luminous yawn.

I got up with such suddenness that Archie and Phil, leaning on either side of me, tumbled together. 'Must have a piss,' I said. But I was hardly thinking of them: my heart was racing, excited relief rose in a physical sensation through my body, I felt angry – I didn't know why – and frightened at my own lack of control. Over and over, under my breath, or perhaps not even vocalised, just the shouting of my pulse, I said, 'He's alive, he's alive.'

I caught up with him on the far side of the dance floor, was on him even before he recognised me, and flung my arms round him; we fell back against the wall, where he held me off a moment to look at me. 'Will,' he said, and smiled only a little. I was kissing him and then bundling him down the passage and through the swing door. A couple of guys were rolling joints on the edge of the washbasin and looked up nervously. A lock-up was empty and I pushed him in in front of me, falling back with amazement against the door when I had bolted it. I had almost no idea what I was doing. I prised open the top stud of his trousers – maroon cords, just as before – yanked down the zip, pulled them round his knees. Seeing again how his cock was held in his little blue briefs I was almost sick with love, fondled it and kissed it through the soft sustaining cotton. Then down they came, and I rubbed his cock in my fist. I knew it so well, the thick, short, veined shaft. I weighed it on my tongue, took it in and felt its blunt head against the roof of my mouth, pushing into my throat. Then I let it swing, went behind him, held his cheeks apart, flattened my face between them, tongued his black, sleek, hairless slot, slobbered his asshole and slid in a finger, then two, then three. Long convulsions went through him, indrawn breaths. Tears dripped from his chin on to the stretched encumbrance of his trousers and pants. He was sniffing and gulping.

Slowly I came to my senses, slid my wet fingers from his ass, stood up behind him and pulled him gently to me. 'Baby . . . Arthur . . . sweetest . . . love . . .' I kissed the back of his neck, half turned him against me and kissed the submerged pale filament of his scar, cool tears over a burning face.

He was reaching down, tugging up his clothes again. I helped him maladroitly. He said nothing; sniffed. I felt abjectly unhappy. We leant awkwardly together in the narrow, stinking box of the lavatory, and I ran my hand soothingly up and down his back.

'Will . . . I got to go. My brother's here. He's waiting. I got to go with him.' He looked at me with unspeakable sadness. 'To do stuff for him. I got to go.'

He let himself out of the lock-up and left me standing stupidly in it. Someone else was hovering to get in, saying, 'Have you finished?' I almost fell past him, wandered out in a torment of confusion and self-disgust into the flashing darkness of the club – and then stood, looking on, but drowning in a world of my own.

This must have taken several minutes, until some outcrop of objectivity rose again from the flood. Out on the street it was surprisingly cold, and I ran a little way in both directions. There was no sign of Arthur. I was loitering, dithering, craning around at the nothing that was going on. It was nearly two o'clock. A taxi came slowly past, its yellow light burning – and then just behind it a yellow Cortina, with tinted windows and the wheel-arches flared out over gigantic customised tyres. It came almost to a stop at the entrance to the Club and as I walked up quite fast a thick-set black man stepped out from the pink glow of the doorway, the car's rear door was flung open for him as a voice inside said 'Come on, Harold.' Then the door slammed, and the car surged away past me and down the street. I saw its bank of rear lights glare on as it braked at the crossroads, and then it swung to the right and was gone.

Perhaps only the drink enabled me to sleep, tucked in behind Phil, my hand on his heart. I woke feeling cold, even so, pulled a sheet over us without waking him, and curled back again into the same body-warmed space. But I couldn't sleep now, and as the incident with Arthur flared up over and over in my mind my heart would race and thump against Phil's back in panicky counterpoint to the dreamless slowness of his own pulse.

I got up about six and moped around in my dressing-gown, the very dressing-gown that Arthur had liked to wear, maroon, full-length, shabby, stained and cordless after its school career, and which had hung so poignantly, threadbare and exclusive with memory, on his young shoulders or tumbled open about his sprawling thighs. I had the feeling I was imitating him as I made tea: it was something he was always doing, the only domestic thing he could do. He had made tea as if it were instinctual to him, unasked, uncomplaining . . . I took a mug of it to the drawing room and lay on the sofa with my eyes open, thinking. There was a section of Charles's diary I had been reading, and I picked it off the floor and made myself concentrate on it again.

May 26, 1926: At Talodi there were complaints, a dispute over two water jars (both parties seemed equally implausible, so it was a doubtful decision, I fear) & a girl with a septic foot. There are many more of these medical problems this time, several shot-gun wounds in the legs, mysteriously – but the Nuba will hang on to their ancient firearms, &

there seems little we can do about it. After what has been done to them they deserve some means of self-defence. Today those things in Palme's book were constantly in my mind, the terrible stories of slavery, mutilation, castration: how they weighed the boys down with sandbags, razored off their balls & patched them up with – melted butter, I think it was. I believe many of them died. And all this going on nearly in my lifetime! The sheer evil of it oppressed my heart as I went through the village, putting things to right, rewarding & punishing & laying down the law. At least our justice is felt to be justice. Even so, these days I halt the lash in mid-air, am ready almost to extend a comradely hand instead. *Not to be too friendly* – that was poor old Fryer's constant caveat. There's a great deal in it – not to be the schoolmaster mocked for his absurdity who only wants to be loved.

At sundown I went up to the little police parade-ground to see the famous stones – famous, at any rate, to us, & talked about from time to time in Khartoum. There they were, most unmomentous like many famous things, two short pillars of reddish rock, buffed up, & often *touched* one felt, so that they have a glow like marble. The story as I had heard it was that an Egyptian officer, posted out here for a long time, had gone crazy with the sun & the isolation, shot a colleague & then turned his revolver on himself. It was viewed, certainly, as a warning, but in fact it intrigued me & made me the keener to come, partly because I thrive on the very solitude & emptiness it was meant as a warning against; but also because I never believed the story. Heat & loneliness may have played their part, but for the young man to kill his comrade there must have been some deeper, odder, fiercer reason to it. I see it romantically – one of those intense, amorous Mohammedan friendships that no one talks of or even guesses at in England, but which flourish here with an almost startling luxuriance. One sees them everywhere, in town, among the tribesmen, in my own little retinue, of course . . . poetical, chivalrous *amitiés* which none the less must operate on some principle quite beyond the European mind. Perhaps it is just my European mind that insists on this heated little *mélodrame* – but I see a passion & a festering discontent, a flaring noon-day of violence, the remoteness of these stony hills, these fingers & fists thrust up out of the desert, threatening the unspoken balance & courtliness of the affair . . . Well, we shall never know. The stones were erected in their memory, which suggests that their fellow officers responded to something deeper & more poetic in the case. I liked the stones for their enigma, & stroked them, & wanted them to keep their secret for ever, illegible and dignified. They were still, naturally enough, uncomfortably hot, standing as they do all day long in the parade-ground's shadowless glare.

May 29, 1926: . . . These friendships . . . In my happiness here it never strikes me that I have no friends. There are the long monthly letters from home, but like *The Times* which comes, folded, yellowed and elderly, six weeks late, they seem like reports from a fictional world, improbably stuffed with circumstance. Sitting last night before dinner with a pink gin & listening to Hassan coughing & kicking round the kitchen, my strangeness here suddenly appeared to me, a kind of agoraphobia, a continent wide – just for two or three seconds I had an objective vision of myself, unsheltered by the glowing trance, aerial & romantic as the sunset then was, that at all times absorbs me. I saw how singular I must be for Hassan, & for the new houseboy, Taha.

Now Taha has gone from the room & I hear his low murmur of song as he crosses the yard, & then his talk with Hassan, who will be telling him what to do & preparing to serve the supper. They talk as usual in the Nubian language – I grasp only the occasional word or name, and from here it is anyway all indistinct: it gurgles on as in England a stream might at the bottom of an orchard, easy, colloquial & yet ineffably ancient & impersonal. And then Hassan's voice is raised, & he vents his little jealousies & proud possessiveness on the boy.

Hassan, being with me so long, is part of my life, and whenever there are new boys there is trouble of some kind. It is remarkable to think that they are both of the same race – the old cook with his aquiline, sallow look, those brown betel-stained teeth, the utter absence of physical grace that somehow recommended him to me & guaranteed his honesty; and the boy, a supple, plum-black sixteen, with his quiet nervous movements, dreaming eyes & occasional smile, so inward & yet candid . . . Him I chose for quite contrary reasons, so that his charm, however fickle or professional, wd be an adornment to each day. And here he comes back now. He has the most lyrical hands, and as he reaches out & takes my glass to refill it the action of his long graceful fingers suggests to my woozy fancy the playing of the harp.

There is something which charms me utterly about this house. It is whitewashed & square & has four rooms, each of the same size. It is a house reduced to its very elements, with empty holes for windows and doors, so that one looks from one room into the next – & through that to the outside, the surrounding shacks, the clustered peaks of the huts or the bald, enigmatic rocks. The house is a kind of frame for living in or discipline for thought – so that its few furnishings, the book-case, a rather hideous rug, the photograph of the king, seem unnecessary embarrassments. I find myself quite as austere as a hermit for those hours when I am alone, & I want nothing. Or if I have been with the chiefs, eating & drinking & reciting to them, as they seem relentlessly to require, from the *Thousand & One Nights*, I return to this little box of shadows, to the fringed globe of the *shamadan*, the little folding captain's chair, with a sense of enchantment. And Taha is waiting, never snoozing or yawning, but squatting in perfect, illiterate silence. His beauty is enhanced by his watchfulness, which is never impertinent or burdensome; it is an almost abstract form of attention, a condition of life to him. Though he only joined me for this tour I feel already with him, as I imagine long-married couples do, a complete freedom from self-consciousness, & as I sit & write, or merely gaze at the moon & stars, his eyes, which are always upon me, are weightless, demand nothing, are themselves dark globes in which lamp & stars are distantly reflected!

And then I remember that he knows nothing of this, as I know nothing of him. I look across at him & smile, & after a second he smiles back, begins to rise, but I gesture to him to stay put. There is a momentary uncertainty, but as he settles again it disperses & is forgotten.

May 31, 1926: Terrific drama yesterday, as Taha was bitten by a scorpion . . . I was just coming home: the heat had become too intense & I had failed to resolve a contention between two men over a pig – a pig which had been given to one of them as a reward for his prompt payment of taxes. I was in no doubt of that, & the pig was branded, but the other chap, a rather svelte character with a distinctly flirtatious manner, said that this admirable tax payer had owed him a pig – indeed, owed him two pigs, & he thought it was only his right to take it. The whole issue will need further attention. Both men tucked their hands under my elbows as if confident that I wd side with them against the other. As I approached the house I had the startling sight of Hassan, that most immovable and cynical of men, limping across the little sandy piazza at a dangerous speed, a large wooden spoon still clasped in his hand like a weapon or the emblem of a guild. 'Sir, Lord,' he gasped, 'the boy is very very stung.'

For a second or two, half-stupid in the heat as I was, I thought decorously, Englishly – or possibly Arabicly – only in metaphors. I actually thought I had committed some frightful *faux pas*, some mortal infringement of an obligation, & that *the boy*, my Taha, had made off in a dust cloud of enraged propriety or was at least in a mutinous sulk somewhere & giving Hassan an angry fright. But he did a funny little jabbing gesture with his spoon, & I realised he was speaking 'without music'.

It seems Taha had been sitting on the wooden step of the kitchen, engaged in no less an occupation than polishing my shoes, when, dropping the brush by accident, he had antagonised a scorpion which happened to be sauntering past & which had promptly stung him on the calf (his bare feet being doubtless too tough for a mere scorpion to pierce & his djellaba, as I saw it in my mind's eye, being drawn up, bunched up between his knees). All of which, of course, was nothing uncommon, & I knew clearly enough what I had to do. Yet I was almost shocked to see how I took on Hassan's panic, how it touched me myself & left me suddenly short of breath. I ran down to the house, with Hassan following on & making lachrymose interjections in Nubian, the words of each outburst bubbling and shrinking away like water thrown out from the house over the stones.

Of course I have dealt with snake bites & so on several times before, & managed to master my sympathy & anxiety & present an impassive doctorly face. The poor boy was still sitting, but half lying back, in the kitchen doorway, motionless with fright or caution, but breathing heavily, salivating, sweat on his upper lip. He knew enough to be holding his leg tight in both hands just below the knee.

I shd have gone straight to the house, & darted over to it now to get my medicine case, fumbled to check it & close it, bounded out across the yard. My change of role made it possible for me to push him around, to enter with brusque disinterest into a kind of closeness to him that otherwise wd have remained unattainable—though it beckoned & was approached through a thousand hints & formalities. I tugged him, & he half slithered, to the step's edge, & tugged at his hands too which were locked with desperate tightness around his leg. The sting was some way below, on the shallow, boyish incline of the calf—just where one *would* have stung, I thought—& looking pretty nasty. I whipped out the tourniquet & drew it to its tightest notch around his upper leg (I was severe as a matron with that stiff rubber strap). And fussily, necessarily, I shoved back the gathered folds of his djellaba, baring his thighs, glancing at them as well—though with a curiosity almost annulled by the ethical transfiguration I was enabled for a few minutes to undergo. Not so Hassan, however, who had been hovering excitedly behind me, in a state somewhere between despair & delight, & leant forward all helpfully at this point to draw the djellaba up tidily and expose the child's private parts to his greedy glance – though after a second or two Taha brushed the folds of cloth forward again & gave Hassan, I noticed, a pained, abstracted look. As well he might, for the old lecher had hardly chosen the best moment – indeed it was a prurient piece of advantage-taking, & since it also satisfied a curiosity of my own I admonished him & sent him back indoors, before (& all this was only the matter of seconds) taking my scalpel to the boy's inflamed leg and cutting out the sting with such delicate suddenness & firmness that he was amazed when I showed it to him between my fingers, & when he sat up & saw the blood trickling down his calf.

I squeezed & cleaned & dressed the thing as best I could. Though I had been quick enough, some damage had been done & he was already a little feverish; so I picked him up – he was quite heavy & hung on to my neck with both arms, like a child not fully awoken – & took him in & laid him on the camp-bed in the room next to mine.

He is there now, almost better I think, though I have put him to sleep. Hassan has been bringing in meals for us both – Taha cd manage for the first time this evening some broth, & I sat with him & ate some gazelle & some beans – excellently done, though I was stern with the cook & told him Taha was very ill & that he must treat him with consideration & not bother him. I thought this was important, as I was out for most of the day & the invalid has been more or less in his hands. Yesterday he was very bad & I spent much of the night with him, huddling on a stool under the mosquito net, giving him analgesics & mopping his brow. It was terribly hot & he seemed to be on fire: the sweat stood on his brow within seconds of my sponging it away, his long eye-lashes fluttered, his mouth hung open. He drank literally gallons of water. When at last he slept – murmuring and shifting incessantly – I felt again for a moment alone, weary & longing for sleep myself, yet sick with anxiety that I had not done it right, that he wd not recover. Of course when I went to bed I lay awake & tossed about & sweated as if it had been me that had been the scorpion's victim. Then almost at once the dawn came up through the shutters, the heat, that seemed only to have faded for a moment, built up alarmingly & for once the beautiful simplicity of the house revealed itself as a menacing bareness, a kind of trap in which to escape from one room was only to be imprisoned in the next. I felt my responsibility weigh on me, at the same time as it buoyed me up – an asphyxiating feeling. More strictly it was like a cramp when swimming – a sudden challenge in a friendly element, threatening where before it had only sustained.

Everything in this job is personal: it is government on the ground, journeys of many days with a band of men across deserts or through sudden floods & then the instantaneous fields of flowers. It is not sitting at a desk: it is standing in scant shade & deciding between one naked tribesman and another. It is not bookish & bureaucratic: it takes place in open spaces almost without end, in which the rare, unobvious & beautiful people materialise out of the quivering heat. Their beauty of course is neither here nor there: their heads could grow beneath their shoulders . . . But when I went back through the doorless aperture into the room where Taha was, asleep, unaware, & yet tormented, like some saint in ecstasy or martyrdom, I felt all my vague, ideal emotions about Africa & my wandering, autocratic life here take substance before my bleary eyes. He lay with his head back, half off the pillow, an arm flung out, the fingers twitching with his pulse, only an inch above the floor . . . At once I saw he *was* my responsibility made flesh: he was all the offspring I will never have, all my futurity. He became so beautiful to me that my mouth went dry, & when he woke he found me staring at him. I'm not sure if he was the one I prayed for or the one to whom I made my intercession.

I am very, very drunk. It is half past two in the morning. I tiptoe in with fantastical caution, & see him sleeping quietly. Everything I have an impulse to do wd wake him – & that wd be inexcusable. All my love to him goes out in a sweet bedside gesture of self-denial, a kind of blessing, a sweeping of the arms that comes from I don't know where and is lost into the air. And in a mood of complete certainty & faint ridiculousness, I stagger to bed.

June 1, 1926: A terrible head this morning. I cancelled all engagements, such as they were, & fell into a routine of parallel convalescence with my boy. Hassan evidently foully jealous.

This evening, as he was much brighter, I sat with Taha in close & utterly irregular comradeship & had him tell me about his family. I even told him a bit about mine, until he said that being British I must know Mr Mills, a missionary apparently, who comes from New York, & I recognised that our understandings were a trifle out of kilter. Finally I told him the story of Prince Ahmed; it was the one I had learnt most recently to tell after dinner, & a strange amusement & entrancement came over his features to hear me recite to him in my painfully correct Arabic, as if he had been some dignitary. But then the story too held him like a revelation. I made use of various props for the three magical gifts of the princes: for the flying carpet the old rush mat on the floor, for the spying-tube which showed whatever one desired my field-glasses, & for the apple which cured all ills the lime on the tray with my drink. He laughed with that delight which children show at certain well-worn jokes whose very repetition is a guarantee of pleasure & security, & I capered around, squatting on the mat, peering out of the window through the binoculars – though I saw not the Princess Nur-al-Nihar but birds coming down into the nim-trees, a stupendous sunset above the rocks, a girl loping home with a dog at her heels – & then wafting the lime under my nose & rolling my eyes as if it smelt divine. But all the gifts were of equal wondrousness, I explained, sitting solemnly down on the edge of the bed: and then, as I went on about the shooting of the arrows, & how the Princess wd be given to him who shot the furthest, the most exquisite thing happened. Taha slid his hand shyly across the blanket & clasped my own. I scarcely faltered as I spoke of Ahmed's arrow, which going so far was assumed to have vanished so that he lost the Princess to his brother Ali, but I felt a squeezing in my chest & throat & hardly dared look at him as, all unconsciously, I made our two hands more comfortable together, interweaving his long fingers with my own. By a simple gesture I wd never have dared to make & without words which neither of us cd have said, he conveyed his trust in me, & holding my hand held on to a simple faith that all wd be well with Ahmed, wretched though his current state now was. And when the others had all turned home, I went on, saying that the arrow wd never be found & that they must make haste for the wedding-feast of Prince Ali & the Princess Nur-al-Nihar, Ahmed went on alone & lo he encountered the radiant fairy Peri-Banou & fell in love with her & married her & lived in happiness with her all the days of his life. Then Hassan was scuffling & waiting at the door, & Taha with less than innocence drew his hand away –

The phone was ringing. Phil, I knew, would never answer it, though it was at the bedside, and when I came in he was sprawled over the sheets, pale, bleary and tumescent. 'Leave us out with the phone,' he groaned. I half sat on him and picked up the receiver.

'Darling, it's James. You couldn't come over, could you?'

'Sweetest, I've got a pretty frightful head and it's only seven o'clock. Can't it wait?'

'A bit, I suppose. I'm in a terrible mess. I've been arrested.'

10

As I came up he was dithering on the doorstep and had a look, not uncommon with him, of bitten-back anxiety and determined self-control. He gripped my arm and said, 'God, this is intolerable. I've just had a call.'

'Don't worry, old girl, I'll wait for you.' I patted him on the shoulder and smiled with a quiet confidence that I didn't altogether feel after this traumatic night. A gorgeous summer day was unfolding and as James went off flapping his car keys I stood at the gate and let it sink in. The steady rumble of far-off traffic, the thinning haze, the suited people hurrying past, all seemed invitations to some wearying and majestic happening. I almost seemed to see, above the houses across the street, an immense golden athlete stretching into the sky like the drop-curtain of a ballet or a gigantic banner at a Soviet rally, full of appalling promise. It was a relief to go indoors.

James's flat was *quite* nice – clean and roomy and safely sandwiched half-way up a house of geriatrics and absentee Greeks. The little cosmopolis of Notting Hill, its littered streets, its record exchanges, its international newsagents, late-night cinemas, late-night delis, was to hand. The elegant vacancy of the Park was admirably near; you could walk to the museums, to Knightsbridge even, and a little later in the year, to the Proms. And at the back, a block away, you were in Carnival country.

Even so, the very convenience and accessibility of James's house gave it a bleak and transitory feel. The shelf in the hallway was always stacked with post addressed to former tenants whom nobody knew – bills, circulars, mailing-shots aimed with desolate regularity at a population of migrants. In the small carpeted lift (which this morning I allowed myself to take) one would meet strangers who were just polite, incredibly well dressed, sometimes carrying tiny fancy dogs.

James liked the insularity of his flat, liked having a place all to himself, but was clearly affected by this mood of transience, a sense of valuelessness despite the climbing prices and the mortgage. He could never bring himself to do much to it, and though he loved pictures seemed not to notice the half-furnished bareness of his own few rooms. He had a fine Piranesi – all tumbled masonry and sprouting bushes – that he had bought years ago in a sale but had never framed. It was propped, sagging in its mount, on the mantelpiece, above the dusty and ornate black ironwork of the blocked-off grate. There were comfortable, nondescript armchairs, and a heavyweight stereo system. He was obsessed with Shostakovich and had innumerable records of baleful quartets and sarcastic little songs. They put me into a gloom and a fidget within seconds but I think their bleakness met some otherwise inarticulate inner compulsion of his own, of a piece perhaps with the featurelessness of the apartment and his fatalistic disdain of possessions.

I heated up some coffee in the kitchen. James's life – like Phil's in a way – followed such awkward and demanding patterns, was so thrown out for the service of others, that ordinary things like mealtimes and provisions obeyed a quite different logic. Often he would live for weeks on three-minute snacks, and he was used to breakfasting at five in the morning or lunching at five in the afternoon. The fridge and cupboards were always full of little items to eat, many of them bought from the local Japanese supermarket. I riffled through packets of seaweed, red-hot crackers and the sprouts of various beans before deciding that coffee alone, perhaps, would be the thing.

There were two kinds of specialist publication James took. As I sat on a stool and leafed through to the end of the *Guardian*, I was alarmed to find one of them underneath, lying on the kitchen work-top. This was *Update*, a medical monthly that kept GPs abreast of the latest in sores, goitres, growths and malformations of all kinds. The articles were sober to a fault, and cast an assumption of disturbing normality over conditions which the accompanying photographs showed to be quite revoltingly unusual. This effect was worsened by the colour spectrum used, a flashlight glare which lent to the contorted limbs, the misted-over eyes and weeping wounds the high tonality of well-hung game. It was hard to imagine looking forward to the arrival of *Update* as one might to that of *Autocar* or *Hampshire Life*.

The other mags were not left lying about. The fact that even in his own home he kept them neatly hidden away (under some jerseys in the second drawer of his dressing-table) showed I suppose the secret and illicit power they still had for him. I hauled them out to see if there was anything new – though it was actually hard to remember. He dealt largely in material put out from Chicago by the Third World Press – a title which might have been thought to chasten rather than excite the exploitative urge, though

James was clearly unabashed. The Third World Press specialised in blacks with more or less enormous cocks, and in leaden titles like *Black Velvet*, *Black Rod* or even *Black Male*. James was no bigot, however, and other publications such as *Whoppers* and *Super Dick* kept up with big boys of other creeds and colours. Often enough these were sexy men towards whom one could feel a notional sort of warmth, but the premium on the massive member resulted in some weird inclusions: skinny little lads, stout middle-aged men, a boy with one eye. Turning the pages of the new *Nineteen-Inch Pipeline* I half expected to come on illustrations of boil-ringed sphincters and mis-set bones.

And then what the hell had James done? Though he had his mischievous side he was a conscientiously good citizen. He parked on yellow lines, but he always displayed his 'Doctor on Call' sticker. He was a member of CND, but when he went on demonstrations was ingenious at lending support without actually sitting down in the road or being dragged away. The obvious thing was some sexual hitch: I didn't know what the dear boy got up to, but as I assumed it wasn't much, the idea of him procuring in a Gents or interfering with a minor seemed desperately unlikely. He would surely have had to have been in a crisis, a crack-up, to do anything like that: for whatever his eccentricities James was wonderfully well-adjusted to being ill-adjusted. I hated to think of him in the sudden scary spotlight of an arrest, the humiliation and the shock of its being for real.

Odd how, in the space of a few weeks, the police had come twice into my life. After the business with the skinheads they had been at the hospital, and I had been to the station and looked at photographs. It was a surreal thing, to look through several pages of criminal skinheads, all, apart from those with tattoos on their foreheads and necks, doing their utmost to look the same. Like the unfortunates in *Update* they squared up to the camera with an odd mixture of pride and reluctance. And I too, though angry and in great pain, was almost afraid to find the culprits and to throw my weight behind the whole machinery of prosecution. The policemen themselves were very businesslike: they were adamant against crime. But they weren't prepared to be friendly, to be such suckers as unreservedly to take my part. What, after all, had I been doing at Sandbourne? And as I could not mention Arthur I had been a little vague and capricious, and taken refuge in my bandages. An amazing number of other things were going on at the station too, and I was encouraged not to consider myself special. It took a senior officer, seeing that my father was an 'Hon', to make the connection with my grandfather, to enquire if 'by any chance' I was related to the former Director of Public Prosecutions whom he remembered, and thence to soften into cautious sycophancy. What was most horrifying, though, was how, in the company of the police, my vulnerable, brutalised state was not soothed but exacerbated; the feeling that anyone might turn on me came over me again as I worried about James. To show my confidence and calm him I had suppressed my vulgar need to know what had happened. Now I began to want calming myself.

James's diaries were always a good read and at Oxford I had made no pretence of not knowing what was in them. Nowadays he kept a more spasmodic record, was often weeks behind, and I found less opportunity to keep up. This was a shame, since they had for me the famous fascination of containing a good deal about myself. They pandered to my heart-throb image – 'Will adorable', 'W. looked fabulous' – though there was always a certain risk, as in hesitating at the door of a room where one is being discussed. There were pages – 'W. insufferable', 'What a jerk! No regard for my feelings' – where I was obliged to see myself from another point of view. It was like suddenly finding out that someone I knew quite well had been leading a double life: the delectable blond super-stud I loved so much was really a selfish little rich boy, vain, spoilt and even, on one stinging occasion, 'grotesque'.

None of this was quite innocent. Like all diaries it envisaged a reader. The odious Robert Smith-Carson had read long sections of it about himself when James was so infatuated with him, and was both pleased and alarmed by the Wagnerian pitch of the entries (whole paragraphs delirious with exclamations: 'Weh! Weh! Schmach! Sehnsucht!' and so on). Other passages had an obscure biblical fervour: one which began 'His thighs are like bronze doors' I had subsequently annotated with exclamation marks of my own. My readings were also somehow allowed for, and the baroque candour of the diaries enabled James (who could never bear an argument or cross words) to tell me what he thought of me, without ever letting on in so many words that he was doing so. Between us we enacted a secret charade, a charade whose very subject was 'secrecy'.

The sober, maroon-spined notebooks, drink-stained, rubbed and buckled, took up part of the very special shelf where the Firbank books were, those pocket-sized first editions with their gilt lettering or torn wrappers wrapped again in cellophane. Now that I was reading them myself I looked at them with more interest – *Caprice, Vainglory,*

Inclinations, though not, alas, *The Flower Beneath the Foot* – and patted their backs encouragingly. Along from them the current volume of the diary was neatly in place, history already although only half-filled. Fairly a professional now at reading other people's private bits and pieces, I settled down with my mug of coffee to find out what had been going on.

Reading Charles's journal I could be confident that nothing in it, however boring on the one hand or touching on the other, could ever implicate me; whereas in James's there was the uneasy excitement of some certain entanglement and my eye would skip down the page in search of myself. He had that elegant, art-nouveau kind of writing which many architects still use on plans, and the Ws were very strong and conspicuous, like a pair of brick-hods side by side. How annoying it was when he was going on about *Rheingold* or *Parsifal*: Wagner and I shared an abbreviation, which cropped up pretty often – though in general it was possible to tell which of us he meant.

I discovered that he was hopelessly behind, and realised that I would find no clues here to last night's events. The latest entry was from several weeks before: 'To Corry 6.30. The boy Phil, W's new thing, was in the showers. Fantastic body, disappointing little dick. Still, felt quite a pang for it – smiled at him, but he looked straight through me. Humiliation! I had made such an effort when we met to be charming, but now I wish I hadn't bothered. Perhaps all lovers resent such old friends, who know things that they don't? Either that, or they really court them. But again it was that terrible feeling that no one ever notices me or remembers me.'

I felt a mixture of shame and cruel pleasure in this, that my little Philibuster was not giving anyone else a foothold on his hard, soap-slippery self-possession. And the unvoiced envy, vainly denied in the disparagement of Phil's cock, came through good and clear. I worked back to the evening of *Billy Budd* with a masochistic sense that I wouldn't come out of it well, though I was sure there would be very beautiful and insightful stuff about the music. It began: '*Billy Budd* – box – Beckwiths – bloody! Not the music, but W. impossible. What poor Ld B thought I don't know – he, of course, urbane & charming, tho' at moments somehow steely & abstracted: one wdn't want to be on the wrong side of him, & so one becomes faintly sycophantic (but that I'm not sure he likes either). W. has taken up with some boy at the Corry – it sounds to me as if it's that gorgeous little tough with red trunks I'm half-crazy about. He told me as soon as we met & so ensured an evening of tortuous envy, regret & failure for me, which the music both soothed & inflamed *à la fois*. There *was* something rather infuriatingly consoling about the opera – struck by the mystery that comes from its not being about love but about goodness, and the way Britten channelled what he felt about love away into some obscurer, less appealing theatre of debate. We kind of mentioned this in the interval – Ld B it turns out knew E M F – perhaps quite well. For the first time ever I got the sense that he might like to talk about these things which are so difficult for people of his age and standing. As usual one was all discipline & good manners – *unlike* Miss W., who smirked & simmered & did her "Great Lover" number. Home. Miserable supper of old tofu-burgers; listened op. 117 & felt much worse. And then, what are these affairs? I thought of W. doubtless already back with his boy & made myself madly rational about it all, how it wdn't last, how it was just sex, how yet again he had picked on someone vastly poorer & dimmer than himself – younger, too. I don't think he's ever made it with anyone with a degree. It's forever these raids on the inarticulate. Appallingly tired, but cdn't sleep. Lay there longing for someone poor, young and dim to hold me tight . . .'

I think I preferred the envy unvoiced. I sidled into the entry across the page. ' . . . Surgery. Then to swim – 40 lengths, exhausted but good. Hung around in the showers – full of mutants & geriatrics. About to go when that heavenly Maurice came in & took the shower next to mine. His skin, close to, exquisitely fine & silky – & his great lazy cock, half-erect, with that thick vein meandering down it, the dull purple head when he pulled back the skin . . . *Extase*! Then on call. Out at once to a basement flat that time forgot, the stinking dereliction most people know nothing about. Miserable, thousand-year-old husband & wife – she senile, he incontinent. She had slipped on the stairs, he cdn't lift her, pissing himself. A great fat dog that kept getting in the way. Huge malodorous furniture, photographs, war-time wireless. I was so businesslike – its utter & absolute seriousness to them. Once I was outside in the car again I breathed freely – feelings of pity & misery, but no longer moony about Maurice. And this was only the beginning of a really useful night.'

This touched me far more than the attacks on me – which I read as a kind of flattery – and humbled me with a true sense of my uselessness. James was like Charles in this: without in the least intending it they exposed my egoism by the example of their goodness, by all their sweet, philanthropic sublimations.

There was the jolt of the lift being called, and its whining descent. I jumped up and put the diary back, but not quite in line, so that it would be clear that I had looked at it. I nipped into the kitchen for the *Guardian*, sprawled on the sofa and then – since there was something farcical and implausible in this – decided I would be asleep. I pretended to surface as James came in: 'Dearest! Sorry, I'm so tired – frightful night. Down the Shaft till *all* hours.'

He didn't seem too thrilled about this. 'I hope it was fun.'

'Up to a point. I went with my little Philpot but ran into Arthur . . .'

'So you had them both, I imagine?'

'Well . . .' – I left it in the realm of possibilities.

He slammed around the kitchen, ground more coffee, put bread in the toaster almost as if to complain that I should have done all this for him already; but to fend off what had to be said, too. 'You'd better tell me what happened,' I said. He hugged me suddenly and hard.

'Yes; do you mind if I tell you the whole thing? At the risk of sounding rather foolish.'

'My darling.'

'Let's go in the other room.' We did so and he opened one of the big windows on the faint summer roar, and walked about and gazed into the rooms across the road while I sat attentively. 'I suppose I've been feeling a bit wretched lately,' he said, and then stopped.

'What sort of wretched?'

'About love and sex and life in general.' He put down his coffee mug as if it were a nuisance. 'I don't know, I just feel so out of it. I'm working so hard I can scarcely do anything I want – I never see anybody. Well, I see hundreds of people, but never anybody I want to see. When did we last meet, for instance? I know you're busy with your boys and what have you – but I would like to see you darling a bit more often, you know? You are one of my oldest, dearest friends, fuck it.'

'I do feel the same, James. I'm always thinking of you and having conversations with you in my head and imagining what you would say about things. You're my most constant companion, even though I'm so pathetic and never get in touch with you.'

He smiled: 'You see, just talking to you now makes me feel better. Which proves we should meet more often.' He turned away. 'How's it going with Phil?'

I wasn't sure if he wanted the gratifying news that it was all over, a mere flash amid the long day of our relationship, or the mortifying assurance that it was all going fine. 'I must say, we do rather adore each other,' I offered, with a modesty that may have sounded like bragging. 'He's really cuddly.'

'That's it,' James said, with nodding recognition. 'It's cuddling I want really as much as everything else. It'll sound stupid to you, Willy, but over the last few weeks I've just felt . . . *so out of it.* I've gone so long without love and I've become simply so accustomed to it all, as if that's how life is and evermore shall be – death – horror – amen. It struck me that I've turned into that archetypal middle-class intellectual out of touch with everything, just like someone in a Forster novel, and that was eighty years ago . . . It's all very well being ironic, but then it keeps coming over me that no one wants me, the summer's burning away, and no one makes a move for me, I don't preoccupy anyone . . .' He wailed a little but was unable to cry.

I went over and held him. 'Darling heart, of course people want you. You're so adorable.' I kissed away the tears that weren't there. I found him very slightly repellent.

'They don't. No one ever wants to fuck me.'

I chuckled almost. 'I'll fuck you – here and now, if that's what you want,' and I let my hand drift down his back and over his big schoolboy bum. He smiled shyly.

'That would never do,' he said.

It wouldn't of course. I held him away from me, looked at him frankly. 'Last night,' I reminded him.

'Oh last night. I was driving home, full of all these kinds of thoughts. I'd just been on one of those really appalling calls, to certify someone dead – suicide – at least three weeks ago – locked room – in this weather. You can imagine – no, I think you can't imagine actually. One could hardly go into the room . . . I was coming along the Park, about nine o'clock – it was very heavy and still, you remember. *The Creation* was on the wireless, the Karajan from Salzburg last year, you know, with José van Dam, gloriously good. And suddenly it was that unspeakably sublime bit 'Seid fruchtbar, Alle' – go forth and multiply, fill the heavens and the seas and so on? I thought I'd never heard anything more beautiful and profound – I was in hysterics – I had to pull over and put on my hazard lights and I sat there weeping and weeping until it got on to a jolly section, which it always does with Haydn, bless him.'

'It is a good bit.'

'Unutterably great. Did we use to listen to it? I felt as though I knew it but hadn't heard it for a thousand years. Anyway, back here, I thought what does this all mean? It means we must be as creative as possible – even if we can't actually have children, we must give ourselves completely to whatever we do, as I've always sort of thought, we must *make* something out of everything we do.'

'Quite so.'

'And I thought, I must have a man.'

I was relieved that he saw the funny side of it. 'Of course, I was still on call. All the same I put on some sexier clothes and a bit of mascara and really looked quite nice – a bit bald, but clearly an exceptionally nice guy. I had that old shirt with the button-down pockets that I put my bleep in – it looked like a packet of fags, I hoped. I went off down the Volunteer. I knew I couldn't get drunk or anything, but I sipped my way down a Pils for about half an hour and then fell quite naturally into chat with a fellow – a Scotsman, but pleasant, black hair, jeans, sweatshirt, that sort of bruised look about the eyes, vulnerable, but dangerous: you know the type. You've probably had him, indeed.'

'Oh, *him* . . .' I played along.

'I bought him a drink, we talked about music: he said he played the violin. I said did he know *The Creation*? He did not, needless to say. I was trying to decide whether to accept a drink if he offered me one when another Scot came up and slapped him on the back and off they went.'

'I hope you weren't put out.'

'The resolve did wobble a little. But I knew what I had to do, or rather what I had not to do. I hung about for a minute, but as can happen there it dawned on me dismayingly that I was by far the most attractive person in the room, and I wanted something ravishing and epic. I was about to go, I thought I'd tootle down to the Coleherne perhaps, then I wouldn't be too far away if the bleep went. Then I saw this guy come out of the loo – lean, tanned, denim top and bottom and, what I noticed first of course, a big curving prick sort of lolloping about. He walked through the bar in a very come-and-buy fashion, looked at me, then looked away at once and went out on to the street. I realised who it was, that bloke I was once rather worked up about at the Corry and you were horrid about, very thin but quite muscled and somehow incredibly sexy.'

Out of an unaccustomed sense of decency I had never told James about the afternoon I had had this boy, Colin, had even cut him when I ran into him at the Club with James a week or two later. 'I think I know the one,' I said.

'He was what I really wanted, though the look he gave me wasn't very encouraging. And then, naturally, having seen what I wanted I came over all incapable, and faffed around at the bar, and then I went to the loo. But when I finally left the pub, it must have been about five minutes later, beginning to feel a bit miz, there he was outside, leaning against the pillar at the corner, one foot raised behind him – very rent-looking, actually, which should have made me wonder, but I found I was talking to him. Really tat stuff about haven't I seen you at the Corry et cetera, but I know you've told me it doesn't matter what you say as long as you say *something*. In spite of my earlier doubts, he was amazingly keen and responsive, said where shall we go, I was completely practical and said I had a car just round the corner, we could go to my flat, and suddenly the whole thing had just taken off and I didn't feel apprehensive at all, just happy, almost, and sexy.'

'Fantastic,' I said. 'Really good.' I hadn't liked him much myself but I even felt a shade possessive now about him, and then decided to be generous, and wished James well with him.

'Anyway, we got in the car, put on our seatbelts; I made a little grab for him, which he didn't seem to mind – I just had to get a feel of it, you know. Then he calmly reaches in his jacket pocket, as it might be for a fag, and hoiks out this kind of fob, and says, very pleased with himself indeed, "You might as well drive round to the station, I'm a police officer."'

I was quite speechless and James was shaking from the recollection and from having brought off his story. I had been with him all the way at a nodding, trainer's distance and then he had knocked me out. But it wasn't quite over. 'I didn't say a word, but started the car, and of course just as I did so my bleep went. Then I saw the evening was inevitable in a different way, and the irony was all working overtime in that hideous way it can do. So it was my turn to grope in my breast pocket for my little professional accoutrement. I tried to make something of this with what now seems a fantastic gallantry and said how neither of us was what he seemed. I needn't have fucking bothered. He changed completely and became all textbook – not actually taken down and used in evidence et cetera, but calling me sir and not giving an inch (as it were) . . .'

'James,' I had become angry. 'I'm sorry. I didn't say anything about this for obvious reasons. I have had that man – Colin he's called, isn't he?' He nodded. 'I picked him up on the Tube, ages ago, just after we'd seen him at the baths. He followed me off the train, almost invited himself back to my place. I fucked him. He fucked me. He's as queer as – whatever is very, very queer: me, you. He can't possibly get away with this pretty policeman thing.'

James looked at me very closely. Under no other circumstances could all this have been good news to him.

I carried on being angry all day. My tiredness made it harder to resist and as I went into town later I was muttering audibly about people around me, and when they showed signs of offence, deviating abruptly into sarcastic good manners. I was full of outrage at an act in which the brittle shoppers in Liberty's (where I went to buy socks) and the incurious drifters of Oxford Street (who got in my way) seemed all to be careless conspirators. At the Corry, I did a few ferocious exercises and then flaked out and dropped into the pool with more than usual relief. But even there the slowness and clumsiness of others enraged me, and I was becoming the victim of one of those premature oldsters who bump into one on purpose, just for the muffled charge of contact. I wondered what I would do or say if I saw Colin. Was the whole matter strictly speaking *sub judice*? Would it have been any service to James to deal angrily, even ironically, with the officer who had charged him? I had all sorts of plans, not necessarily the wiser for their violent neatness.

James's experience, like mine with the skinheads, made me abruptly selfconscious, gave me an urge to solidarity with my kind that I wasn't used to in our liberal times. In the busy one o'clock changing-room, cross though I was, I looked at the others, the bankers, the teachers, the journos, the advertising johnnies, the managers of hamburger outlets, the actors, the consultants, the dancers from West End musicals, the scaffolders, the rack-renters, queuing for the hair dryer and clouding the air with Trouble for Men, with a kind of foreboding, as an exotic species menaced by brutal predators. It was outrageous that Colin should have joined the brutes. I could see him clearly in memory, his tan and his weird eyes – hungry and yet chilly – and his habit of hanging about, the feeling he gave that something might happen.

Afterwards I went to have my hair cut. A while ago I had affected an old-fashioned barber in Neal Street, who would keep me trimmed and tidy for £1.05 – a guinea, as he always insisted. In the window were black-and-white photographs of men tipping their heads forward, and inside, where one waited, a colour poster of the Prince and Princess of Wales simpered above the boxes of Durex. The shop was an outpost of neighbourly simplicity amid the chic revamping of Covent Garden, and Mr Bandini, who ran it with his middle-aged bachelor son Lenny, would talk with motiveless fluency about boxing and about life during the war, and the hard time he had had then. Unlike modern studios, where each haircut has the pretensions of a work of art, Mr Bandini's shop, with its floral linoleum, its clippers and ivory-handled razors, gave me the reassuring feeling that exactly the same thing had been happening in it for half a century. There was something melancholy but entrancing in imagining the hundreds of thousands of identical, routine haircuts that Mr Bandini had given as the decades slipped by. Though, like other Soho Italians, he had been interned in the war, he had been at work on this spot for almost forty years. I could easily imagine Charles, in handsome middle age, popping in for his fortnightly short back and sides and a friction of *eau de quinine*.

Wartime London, which I had always imagined half bombed to bits, the rest of it keeping going on five-shilling dinners and a lot of selflessness and doing without, emerged quite differently in Charles's journal. It appeared (and I suppose this was the other side of my apprehension about war) as an era of extraordinary opportunity, when all kinds of fantasy became suddenly possible, and when the fellow-feeling of allies and soldiers could be creamed off in sex and romance.

September 26, 1943: My birthday . . . It's so dull being as old as the century, it makes one's progress seem so leaden & inevitable, with no scope for romantic doubts about one's age. However, a beautiful, hazy pre-war sort of day — lunch at the Club with Driberg, who was very flattering & said he thought I only looked 42. He told me about some of his exploits, though I was perhaps a shade reticent about mine: with him one simply doesn't know where they'll end up — careless talk etc. We lamented the still frequent attacks & insults meted out to coloured servicemen, by the English though mainly of course by the Yanks. It seems all Driberg's attempts to counter the foul American laws, in Parliament & out, have been unsuccessful. Never mind, he said, he tried to make it up to them personally.

Afterwards I wandered through Soho & then in Charing Cross Road saw three black GIs loitering along rather idyllically, smoking cigarettes & looking at girls. They had that touching quality which off-duty soldiers so often do have, as if they knew they ought to be up to something but didn't quite know what it was. There was a fat one, a thin one & an inbetween one with a lost, ingenuous expression which was decidedly heart-stopping. He was clearly the butt of his two smart friends' humour & had an infinitely tolerant, good-hearted glow about him. I walked beside them to pick up their talk, & then went on & took up an insouciant pose on the other side of Oxford Street, by the Lyon's Corner House.

By some sublime, birthday miracle they split up on the corner opposite, Fat & Thin turning back down Charing Cross Rd as if to have a second, more determined go at something they had funked or got wrong the first time, while my friend crossed over & then crossed again, to the far side of Tottenham Court Road. When I strolled over myself he was looking at the posters at the little cinema there. He appeared uncertain about the prospect of an afternoon of *This Happy Breed* and something else with Jack Hulbert in. He asked me if I'd seen these films, & I said I had (which I hadn't) and that they were unutterably tedious. It seemed to me that if he cd be kept out of the cinema then there were possibilities: I wasn't going to go in with him & sit it out expectantly in the dark for hours on end, smoking American cigarettes. I said why didn't he come & have a swim at the Corinthian Club, that's what I was going to do. Like a child who had been hoping for guidance, & with only the faintest hint of adult irony or doubt, he came along, & when he saw the bombed-out far end of the building under all its tarpaulins & scaffolding reacted to it as though it were a cause for personal sympathy and congratulation.

I cd hardly wait to get him in the showers, but I hired him some drawers & a towel & drew out our time in the pool as if I were only there for the exercise. Roy (his name, Roy Bartholomew) was a clumsy swimmer, but jolly fast, soldier-fit & divinely constructed. I tested him gently by saying how muscly he was, & he flexed his arms & had me punch him in the stomach – at the same time saying how I shd see so-and-so in his regiment, who evidently has the biggest muscles imaginable. I discovered he likes to box, & wished for a moment I was twenty years younger & cd have taken him on.

In the showers he was all I cd have hoped for, flawed only by a little appendicitis scar; but he was selfconscious – not, I realised, about nudity, but about showering with whites. He was like other American negro servicemen I've seen in the Corry, used to segregation & despite their often transcendent beauty & presence somehow cowed or fearful of rejection. The regulars, however, were impressed, & Fox was very pointedly doing his 'Get a bunk on last night, Charlie?' patter, while young Andrews lathered his conversation with my Lord this and my Lord that – which of course impressed Roy in turn.

I took him back to Brook St & opened a bottle of champagne. Taha looked at me very knowingly before going off to see his uncle, & then, having the place to myself, I more or less did what I wanted. There was a statutory preamble of remarks about girlfriends and what-have-you, but that out of the way we started kissing & stroking each other pretty uninhibitedly, & stripped off & had it away on the sofa & then on the floor three or four times. I must say he was absolute bliss, with that kind of innocence that so appeals to me, & very manly & friendly – nothing affected or girly about it. I've never known anyone ejaculate such quantities. Even the last time, when I brought him off by hand, it shot right up into his face.

September 27: In a moment of foolishness I'd given Roy my telephone number. I was out most of the morning & didn't return home until 5 or so, when I asked Taha if there had been any calls & he said 'No Sir' with a noticeably self-satisfied air. It wd have been wonderful to have had Roy again, but I found I was glad not to, & decided that if he shd get in touch I wd not see him. Any repetition wd lack the spontaneity & beauty of yesterday, & I wd rather remember it as one of those rare & wonderful days when two strangers come together in deliberate ignorance of each other for their mutual pleasure.

September 28: A fairly terrible day, which seemed to have been designed as the counterpart to Tuesday, all choking catastrophe instead of the sentimental camaraderie & avoided intimacy of that brief afternoon. Taha went out for me after lunch to deliver some papers to GS & to find me if he cd some flowers – I had a sudden yearning for those great bronze chrysanthemums. As I sometimes do, I imagined him going through the streets on my behalf, saw him by some supernatural, aerial sixth sense moving among the people, pointing to the flowers, taking the long, top-heavy cone of paper in his hands . . . I knew how people noticed him, sometimes were rude or cruel, all of which only deepened my pride in him. It was a mystery – for as he ambled about the prosaic London streets he moved too in the realm of my imagination, inviolable, invested with my love.

He took an age to return & when he finally did come in with the chrysanthemums in a vase I asked him if everything had passed off all right, feeling a little anxious at the confidentiality of the things I gave him to carry – not on his account, whom I trust utterly, but lest he shd be waylaid. He said he was very sorry and cd he ask me something. I said of course. He said he wanted to marry Niri. I congratulated him, shook his hand, wished him every happiness, & said I looked forward to meeting his intended. He went out & shut the door, & a minute or two later I heard him leave the house.

It was only then that I allowed myself to absorb the news, or rather to be transfixed by it, for it filled me with the most piercing anguish, & as he went out, wearing – I knew – his comical broad-brimmed hat, it was as if something within me had been released & I found myself gasping for breath, tears rolling down my face & the whole room & its furniture & pictures & books somehow sodden & heavy with the misery of it. It is true that the announcement of any marriage, however dear to me the couple & however perfectly suited to each other, invariably fills me with the blackest gloom; it may lift after a day or two, though not before an enduring sense has been instilled, not of the beginning of something new, but of the irrevocable ending of something innocent & old. But when the innocence is that of my own Taha . . . I felt it almost as if he had died – or worse, been magically translated into some other element. It was as if I saw him through field-glasses dancing & singing in a place so far away that when he opened his mouth, when his lips moved, no sound disturbed the silence.

I went round & round the room, mastering my feelings & then yielding to them again. I fetched up in front of the chrysanthemums, which he had arranged in the tall Tang vase that used to be in the hall at Polesden. They were utterly immaculate, ripe yet dry & glossy, the colour of their great clustering heads autumnal while their leaves were green. They might almost have been lacquered art-works, & one had to squeeze them or pinch their petals to prove that they were perishable. I ran over the brief scene of a few minutes before again & again in my mind, each time with renewed pain, & recognised the unspeakable deference with which he had as it were offered the flowers & suppressed his own excitement. He showed, as so often, his tender & acute intimation of my feelings while not altogether being able to contain his own. I understood too in time why he had been so cocky for the last few days, pulled as he must have been between gaiety & apprehension. So the chrysanthemums – in that way that inanimate things have of implicating themselves in moments of crisis – swam before my eyes like emblems of his years of fidelity, and festive tokens of his future, now elegiac, now heartlessly splendid.

I pulled myself together & went into the study & swallowed a large glass of whisky. I tried to get on with the proofs of my Sudan book, as a mechanic exercise, but of course the merest table of figures seemed to speak of my sweet Taha & our past together, & sent the memory ferreting

around for the tenderest spots, the purest moments of selflessness &
mutual service. Perhaps these inspired me in a way – for I wrote him a
cheque for £200, then thinking better of it wrote him one for £100
instead; then I tore them both up & wrote another for £500 and put it in
an envelope, and trotted up to the attic to leave it in his room. It's a room
I've so rarely been into, & I had to hold myself back from maudlin
pillow-stroking reverie. It reminded me too of a room in the Sudan, since
there is nothing in it save the bed covered with its beautiful shawl, a rug on
the bare boards, & a little table with a photograph of Murad, and that
other taken just before we left Khartoum, outside the Sudan Club – he & I
standing side by side, smiling against the sun. But I cd scarcely bear to
look at it, & hurried out again. Such simple, reassuring things were
turning against me.

So many changes will come about, things that I haven't even begun to
think of, can't think of. Will Taha stay with me, will they want to live
here? Niri, I believe, lives with her mother and an old uncle out west
somewhere . . . I thought of the appalling magnanimity I will have to
show & realising I wd not be able to control myself if I saw him again so
soon I went out, had a further drink or two at Wicks's & then as evening
came on found myself wandering somnambulistically towards
Clarkson's Cottage. It was welcome enough: I needed some narcotic,
some soulless distraction.

The broken light has been replaced, so it was rather bright in there.
There was a sort of businessman at one end in a raincoat & that thin,
anxious little chap who's always there & keeps Cave at the other. He
reminds me of a college servant, making sure that the gentlemen are
happy – his payment, I suppose, being the dubious pleasure of having a
jolly good look. I took up my position in the middle & fiddled about for a
bit as my brief mood of anticipation dwindled & then there was a familiar
clippety-clop & Chancey Brough came in & *force majeure* took the stall
on my right. He had the most tremendous & businesslike pee – he must
have been saving it up for hours so as to seem (vain hope!) an authentic
convenience-patron – & then weighed his immense tackle in the palm of
his hand for a while. We obviously cdn't remain where we were, but I
knew his sticking-power & so I buttoned up & slipped off, tipping my hat
with a polite 'Good evening' & best wishes to his wife.

I went along Old Compton Street, wishing Sandy were still there, &
rather wanting a pal to get drunk with. The Leicester Square lavs seemed a
possibility, so I popped in, but there were all the usual faces turning

expectantly, Major Sprague & that butler from Kensington Palace & a few anxious youngsters on the make. Andrews tells me you can have a wonderful whirl at Victoria these days with all the tommies & tars; he picked up a couple of the latter there some time last week & had the night of his life, if he is to be believed. I wandered down towards Trafalgar Square, thinking I might get a bus, but the sunset came on & I was suddenly flooded with misery again & just gave it all up & went back to the Club for a chop & a glass of beer & was wretchedly rude to anybody who approached me.

It was with a mind worried by the gloom and misfortune of my friends and with my appearance newly toughened, Marine-style, by Mr Bandini that I went that evening to the view of Ronald Staines's little exhibition. Normally I would have kept away, but James's news made me realise I must put in an appearance. I had had to go through the rubbish bin to find the invitation again, a purple card with, scrawled on the back in white ink, the note 'Sorry to lose you so soon the other evening – Ronnie'. I could quite happily have remained lost, but I needed to keep in with him and to secure from him those moody but surely incriminating photographs of Colin.

The exhibition was called *Martyrs*, and was hung at the Sigma Gallery in Lamb's Conduit Street, a home, or at least a stopping place, for many 'alternative' figures. Founded in the Thirties by Rycote Prideaux, it had catered in its earlier days for left-wing artists, and Prideaux's Sigma Pamphlets had been launched there with readings and exhibitions. In my lifetime, though, it had been run by Prideaux's much younger friend Simon Sims, who had diluted his late mentor's style, showed a lot of banal mystical art interspersed with often embarrassing gay and ethnic shows, and opened an austere vegan café, with harpsichord music and wooden plates, in the basement. The whole establishment was tinged with a mood of high-principled disappointment.

Through the front window I saw the few early arrivals, clutching wine glasses, frowning selfconsciously at the pictures. To one side Staines, dressed in black and white, was talking to a man with a notebook. He had that look of insincere good behaviour that people have when they are working on their own public relations. As I came in the coppery clack of the shop-bell had all heads turning – it was like the showers at the Corry – and Staines twisted round to smile at me and give me a presumptuous wink before carrying on with his interview. I signed the book and made for the drinks table.

I wasn't warmly disposed towards the pictures, but knowing about their background I felt a slight anxiety on their behalf, as I do when I see a friend on stage. I hoped that their tawdry Smithfield muses would be sufficiently glamorised by Staines's lens and the finery of the studio. By and large, I should not have worried. The photographs were intensely professional, the lighting and tonality were beautiful, and the silkiest of purses had been made from even the hairiest of sows' ears. I spotted young Aldo at once, in his role of the Baptist, his naked torso broadening into brightness, his stiff little pennant at an angle over his head, an expression of faint surprise about his sleepy dark eyes and stubble-roughened jaw.

The controversial conversation piece in which Aldo appeared with the as yet unmartyred St Sebastian hung alongside. Sebastian was a boy of tedious, waxen beauty, with a little loincloth about to tumble down. They had been cleverly posed against a projected backdrop taken from some Tuscan master, but for all the quattrocento piquancy of their gestures they reminded me of nothing so much as those queeny fashion spreads in *Tatler* and *Uomo Vogue*. The impression was reinforced by a surge of Trouble for Men across my nostrils and the appearance at biceps level of the luminous pink spectacles of Guy Parvis. For a second I thought I might actually be caught up in one of his *Alternative Image* TV programmes, and prepared to sidestep the cameras as they zoomed in on Sebastian's Gillette-smooth profile. But it seemed he was there in a private capacity. I distanced myself even as I was perversely drawn to stare at him, keen to pick up any absurd and memorable remarks.

I finished my glass of wine and downed most of another while I looked at the handsome bearded St Laurence with his dinky little gridiron, and the St Stephen who crouched appealingly in a shaft of light while above him the shadowy form of an immense black whom I would have liked to meet held a stone aloft. St Peter was Ashley, who worked out at the Corry, but he was not seen to best advantage upside-down.

The bell clacked frequently now and we early browsers became subsumed into the crowd of callers, who greeted each other, kissed, caught up on their news, walked backwards into other guests without apologising and generally, as if they were in a private house where such curiosity would have been unseemly, ignored the pictures. Those who had equipped themselves with a price list were forced into the crude necessity of asking the drinkers to move so as to get some distance on the martyrs or to squinny at the numbered labels. I took another drink and moved downstairs.

Here there was a series of life-size nudes, in a sculptural Whitehaven style – martyrs only to the bench and the Nautilus machine – and a set of plates made to illustrate a limited edition of John Gray's *Tombeau d'Oscar Wilde* along with Stephen Devlin's setting of the poem for tenor, string quartet and oboe d'amore – a martyrdom with a whole teeming afterlife. The photographs were balletic and metaphorical, with a good deal of emphasis on the slim gilt soul aspect and a number of images, in Staines's most typical style, crossed and half-obscured by the shadows of prison bars.

I was following a line of the music – a sort of Mahler-and-French which came as close as sexless music could to being explicitly homosexual – when there was a nudge, and Aldo himself was standing beside me. He didn't say anything, but announced himself in this physical way as some people do in clubs and bars, or as boys do abroad, when there is a language problem. I smirked at him and carried on reading, and he seemed happy to stand by. 'Ronnie didn't think you'd come,' he said after a minute.

'I'm a bit of a martyr myself,' I said. 'One day one of Ronnie's little *jeux d'esprit* will finish me off altogether.'

'You don't like the pictures?' Aldo looked cast down.

'Oh they're all right. I like these ones here.' We turned and ran our eyes over the plated athletes. 'They aren't martyrs, are they? I don't like the martyrs so much – they're just soft porn. You look very pretty in them . . . but I honestly prefer to have hard porn – or no porn at all. It's all pretending, that stuff.'

'Still, you didn't stay long at Ronnie's house the other day,' he objected. 'It was very good fun. We made this great scene and then at the end everyone joined in.'

'That was just what I was afraid of.'

'Even Lord Charlie had a feel.'

'Please!'

'Those boys Raymond and Derek were so tired,' he had to go on. 'Not Abdul, though. He could have kept at it all night.'

'They should be showing the film here,' I suggested, and Aldo was full of giggly shock. I looked him over candidly. In his tight white jeans and red-and-white checked shirt he reminded one vaguely of an Italian restaurant.

'Is that all you?' I asked, my question loitering around his groin. He seemed not to get it, and chuckled vacantly rather than asking me to repeat or explain. I pressed past him, squeezing his heavy bulge as I did so – it seemed real enough – a situation which my brother-in-law Gavin's expression, as he suddenly reached out to me over several people's heads, seemed to suggest he found tolerably typical.

'Gavin! Wonderful to see you.' We shook hands warmly and he said, 'Good to see you, my dear,' in that agreeable, almost nostalgic way that straight men sometimes flirt with gays. 'How are things?'

'Things are rather sort of emotional and peculiar . . . fortunately *one* is in good shape and can cope.'

'Sounds fascinating!' He looked quickly aside to Aldo, wondering perhaps if he could be the source of this peculiarity, and I hastened to introduce them.

'Gavin, this is Aldo, he's in some of the pictures upstairs, he impersonates John the Baptist – Aldo, this is Gavin, who's married to my sister.' The two of them shook hands, and Gavin bumbled on about how in that case he must know Ronnie. What puzzled me was how Gavin himself knew Ronnie, and I asked him.

'You know, some of us lot do have contacts with some of you lot.' He waggled a finger. 'You may like to think that you live in a world all of your own, but in fact you live considerably further away from Ronnie Staines than we do. *We* were together on the committee about the traffic and the one-way system, and a very useful committee member he was too.' I stood in mock-penitence. 'I won't ask how *you* met him.'

I saw no reason not to say. 'I met him in a rather less grown-up and public-spirited way. Do you know an old boy called Charles Nantwich? He introduced me to him – at Wicks's, I should add: all madly respectable.'

Gavin raised his eyebrows and nodded several times, then took a sip from his wine glass and allowed a faintly sinister pause to continue. 'I'd no idea you knew Nantwich,' he then said briskly.

'I've only got to know him over the last few months. He's terribly nice – and he's told me a lot about his past . . .' (how far should I go?)

Gavin smiled. 'I'm just surprised that he should want to strike up with one of the Beckwiths.'

'Well you did,' I reasonably observed.

He laughed, overlong, so that I saw his embarrassment and knew I shouldn't pursue the subject, on which he swallowed further drink and shut up. 'How is my ugly sister?' I asked. 'She's not here?'

'No, it's not really her *tasse de thé*, is it? Not that it's much mine,' he added cautiously.

'Roops, though, I imagine, would have loved it. It's right up his street.'

'Roops, as you rightly surmise, was extremely keen to come. When Philippa told him all the reasons he wouldn't like it he got very excited: but he had to go round to a children's party at the Salmons' instead – it's Siegfried's sixth birthday, you see. Roops, being a sophisticated child, naturally holds all the members of the Salmon shoal in unqualified contempt – so it's been a rather difficult afternoon. Apart from that we're fine!'

'You must give them my love.'

Aldo, who had been happily listening in, nodded as though to add his love to mine, and Gavin, good chap that he was, took a nervous gulp of wine and plunged into the unknown waters of male photography: 'Do you do a lot of modelling?'

'No, this is the first time I have done it.'

'Really! I wonder how on earth you get started.'

'In my case I was very lucky. Mr Staines discovered me.' Aldo looked modestly down at this, giving the impression that some vast show-business career had sprung from that ordinary but fateful encounter. 'Do you like the art?' he appealed.

'Um, some of them are rather striking, aren't they? I haven't really had a chance to see . . . the ones upstairs . . .' – he craned round – 'some of them are rather strong meat, *perhaps*, for me!'

Aldo was delighted to be given a cue and produced a remark of the kind that pass for jokes among people who can barely speak the same language: 'Ah yes, you see, I am a butcher.'

Gavin smiled and I explained that Staines had found him while doing some studies of working people in Smithfield. 'I was carrying half a cow,' said Aldo, 'all covered in blood. Ronnie said I looked like bacon.'

There were a few seconds of puzzlement before I worked it out: 'I expect he meant that you looked like *a Bacon*.' But it was going to take too much explaining. Aldo continued pleasantly with an account of portering opportunities in offal and the many under-the-counter benefits of his trade (some nice heart or brains one day, the next perhaps some good fresh liver). I found my eyes resting with momentary respect on the chalked-up menu of alfalfa-sprout salad, chickpea casserole, lentil and parsnip pie . . .

'*Sorry*, William, Gavin Croft-Parker, what an honour, Aldo poppet . . .' – Staines was among us, clutching at hands, emphatically friendly and humble on his great night. 'Do forgive me. There was that dullest of men from the whatsit, Bright City Lights, whatever it's called. Apparently everyone's opinion is simply made by consulting his organ, so you have to be dreamily dreamily compliant and answer all his dreary dreary questions. So ignorant,' Staines whispered, 'he'd no idea what a pyx was; and as for a scapular . . . he said, "Do you mean the collarbone?" I said "I don't – and anyway it isn't the collarbone, it's the shoulderblade." Clearly he was never a Catholic, and then I've ticked him off and he'll say something vile in his article just because I've made him feel small.' He took a swig from his glass. 'Still, I suppose it'll only be half an inch under the "Gay Listings"' (a prophecy with which I was bound to agree).

'I must have a look upstairs,' said Gavin, weaving away from us, and I nodded to him, realising he was going altogether. When I turned back Staines was negligently fondling Aldo's muscly shoulder and gazing distractedly around the crowded room. It was probably better to catch him while I could.

'Excellent show,' I said.

'My dear, do you like it. I'm not utterly utterly displeased with it myself. But of course other people's praise means more to one even than one's own!'

'You've managed to find some fascinating models. I like your St Peter particularly – but then I have known him for some time.'

'Old Ashley! – or rather Billy, as he calls himself professionally.'

'I'd no idea.'

'Mm – he thought Ashley was too girly, especially after *April* . . . But I still think of him as "Old Ash" – Ash on an old man's sleeve, dear . . .'

'Fabulous tits!'

'*Don't!*' Staines shivered, and looked at me with a new, suspicious curiosity.

'There's one of your models I'm sorry not to see stretched on the rack tonight.' I looked about and tried to keep my manner sluttish and casual. 'One of your most intriguing ones, I should say.'

'My dear, I'm sorry. Not all of my boys were ready, or indeed eager, for divine sacrifice.'

'He's called Colin – thin, short curly hair, blue eyes, permanent tan, permanent everything else pretty well too.'

'Oh Colin. You like him do you? He *is* rather extraordinaire. But he's

234

not really a regular of mine. He doesn't have the sort of innocence I needed for this . . . cycle.'

I agreed. 'He does look pretty naughty.'

'Oh he's wildly naughty.' Staines lowered his voice. 'And you know the most ridiculous thing about him. What do you think he does?'

'Absolutely everything, I should imagine.'

'True, true,' Staines almost boasted. 'But I mean as a job?'

'He's not one of your butchers, is he? I don't know – a florist . . .'

'No!'

'I can't guess.'

'My dear, he's a policeman. Isn't it wonderful?' I blinked and then rolled my eyes in a way I would never have done if I had been genuinely amazed. 'In fact I first spotted him on the beat – you could see at once he was something special. But what I say is, with boys like that in the police force, things can't be all bad!' He began to move off, but returned to his subject. 'Not an eyelash, though, not a teardrop, of innocence. The one I'd have loved to do, the really *innocent* one, was your little friend Phil . . .'

I wondered at first if I was going to have to strike a bargain. 'I'd like to buy one of your studies of Colin.'

Staines had virtually left me, so that he called out to me as Guy Parvis pressed himself upon him, 'Dear, I'm far too dear!' And then mouthed, in a kind of grimacing secrecy: 'I'll give you one . . .'

Now I was alone with Aldo again. I wasn't utterly utterly uninterested in doing something with him afterwards, but the social work was a strain, so I struggled back upstairs. I planned another drink before escaping, and looked round the main gallery too to see if there was anyone else I wanted to escape with. It was as full as it sensibly could be now, and there were some interesting punky-looking boys with public-school voices as well as real leather queens and a sprinkling of those dotty types with monocles and panama hats who seem to exist for ever in some fantastic Bloomsbury of their own.

I was excited by a heavily built man with thick slicked-back hair, and was showing an implausible degree of interest in the picture hanging just by his right shoulder, when the bell went again. We both turned, though he looked away at once while I, seeing Charles shuffle in, felt my mood lighten with friendliness and a flicker of guilt. I had been neglecting the old boy, and seeing him now in this noisy, confusing place recalled my responsibilities. I went to help him.

'Ah . . . ah . . .', he was saying, looking regretfully to left and right.

'Charles! It's William.'

He took my arm at once. 'I know perfectly well who it is. What an orgy . . . Good heavens.' He gave off, close to, the elderly smell of sweat and shaving-soap. 'We almost didn't come,' he admitted, with what I took for humorous grandeur.

'I'm very glad you did. I haven't seen you for ages.'

He was prodding his other hand behind him, like someone searching for the armhole of a coat. 'This is Norman,' he explained, as another man, thus encouraged, came forward from his shadow. 'The grocer's boy.'

Norman reached round Charles to shake my hand. 'I'm the grocer's boy,' he confirmed, very happy, it seemed, to be remembered by his juvenile role. As he was a man in his mid-fifties I found it hard to place him at first. 'I used to work in the grocer's in Skinner's Lane,' he said, smiling, nodding, 'years and years ago, when Lord Nantwich first moved in.'

I cottoned on. 'And then you joined the merchant navy and sailed all over the world.' He smiled again, as at the successful recitation of an old tale.

'I left the service some time ago now, though.' Service, one could see, was something he was proud of, and his whole manner spoke of it. He was soberly dressed, in an ill-fitting grey suit and shiny casual shoes of a kind that had been fashionable in my earliest childhood (my father had worn something very similar on family holidays). The suit, which was broad in the shoulders and stood off the neck, was the sort of thing that students bought in second-hand shops, and on one or two of the modish boys in this room could have had a certain chic. Norman's wearing of it was without irony and he reminded me, as the man in the lavatory had reminded Charles forty years before, of a College scout, habituated, stunted by service. His face shone.

'Norman dropped in this afternoon,' said Charles. 'Quite amazing. I hadn't seen him for over thirty years.'

'I sent him a picture of me from Malaya, though.'

'Yes, he sent me a picture from Malaya.'

'I was surprised Lord Nantwich recognised me, even so.'

Charles puffed and muttered something about a tifty. 'Come and have a drink,' I said to both of them, and took Charles's wrist to lead them through the crowd. I could see, as I swivelled round to pass Norman a glass of wine, that he would always be recognisable. His broad cheekbones, large mouth, grey eyes and blond hair, now indistinctly grey, were elements in a formula of beauty, whatever disappointments and desertions might have taken place. Charles was politely inscrutable, but I sensed that he was pained to be disabused. He turned away from the 'grocer's boy' who had needlessly returned to destroy the sentimental poetry with which he had been invested. I felt sorry for them both. And then, drunk again, hated the past and all going back.

'I share a house with my sister,' Norman was explaining to me. 'It's very near the middle of Beckenham, quite convenient for the station and the shops.'

'You should have brought her today,' said Charles loftily.

Norman flushed at this, and looked around hectically at the straining torsos and ecstatic mouths upon the wall.

'Can I come and see you soon, Charles?' I asked. 'I've been picking my way through the books, and I've almost got up to the end. I need some briefing.'

'Briefing, tomorrow?' His eye had been caught by Staines, and I watched his attention waver and then switch abruptly away. Staines reached a ringed hand to him and I heard Charles saying ' . . . splendid evening, most memorable . . .'

I kept up with him and squeezed his arm: 'I'll come for tea, as before' — and he patted my hand. Then I was talking to the thick-set man, laughing overmuch so as to charm, and with my shirt half unbuttoned, running my hand over my chest. He was keen on photography, had his reservations about Staines — I agreed with him brutally — but liked Whitehaven. I told him Whitehaven had photographed me, but I saw that he thought I was taking a rise out of him. 'Well, have you done any modelling?' I asked.

Aldo came up and said, 'Oh, let's be going.' He looked tipsy and abandoned. It was only when the three of us were virtually through the door that I realised his words had been addressed to the thick-set man rather than to me.

'Nice meeting you,' said the thick-set man; and other perfectly pleasant remarks were exchanged before the two of them strolled away, arm in arm. I lurched off furiously to the hotel.

11

'Sugar?'

'I don't, thank you.'

'I rather *do* these days. I've given in.' Charles discarded the tongs, and
shovelled up roughly half a dozen sugar-lumps in his bowed, flat fingers.
We sat and sipped as Graham came in again with more hot water, and
Charles watched his manservant with confident gratitude. At Skinner's
Lane everything was running like clockwork. 'I have my own teeth,' he
added.

We sat, as before, in the little library, Charles's den, the only part of the
house which did not come under Graham's orderly care. Each time I
visited it there were signs of new disturbances, books moved from table to
floor, old Kalamazoo folders stacked or scattered, as if some task of
sorting and searching were being executed, leaving only greater confusion, like a site turned over for coins and amulets by amateurs. Books
whose titles had caught my eye last time atop their teetering plinths were
now cast down or overlaid by other strata: atlases with cracked spines,
popular sheet-music (the 'Valse' from *Love-Fifteen*), magazines whose
colour printing had freaked with sun and age and, Gauguin-like, showed
brown royalty, pink dogs, pale blue grass.

I felt at home there. As we sat on either side of the empty hearth, I was
reminded of my Oxford tutorials, and the sense I often used to have of
inadequacy and carelessness in the face of my tutor, whose hours with me,
he came to imply, were needless distractions from his own, decades-long
work on succession and the law. There was a similar maleness and
candour to it, that scholarly inversion of the rules of the drawing room
that allowed one to talk about sodomy and priapism as though one were
really talking about something else. There was a similar toleration of
silence.

'Most tiresome,' Charles enigmatically resumed. 'One lives in the past
fully enough as it is, without people coming *back* like that.'

'Your grocer's boy. Yes, I confess to having been a bit disappointed.'

'He couldn't see that he only had meaning in the past, poor fellow.'

'I think *Martyrs* were perhaps a bit much for him.'

Charles smiled wistfully. 'I thought they'd scare him off, but he rather took to them.'

'I can see that he must have been pretty hot stuff once,' I conceded. 'And the shop-boy thing is so glamorous, all the whistling and the boredom, and the way they're trapped there, on show.'

'He used to go out on a bicycle,' Charles corrected my overwarm reconstruction. 'He did the deliveries with an apron on.'

I lifted the fluted shallow teacup to my lips, and my eyes rose again, as they inevitably did in this room, to the chalk drawing above the fireplace. Taking a risk on it, I said, 'Is that Taha in that picture?'

Charles was looking at it too, and repeated the name, but stressing it differently. 'Yes, yes, that's him,' he said, with a sad breeziness.

'He's very beautiful,' I said honestly.

'Yes. It's not an especially good likeness. Sandy Labouchère did it soon after we got back from Africa – you can see he had a rather brilliant line when he wanted to. But he hasn't brought out the child's gaiety, a kind of radiance . . . He was the most beautiful thing on earth. You just wanted to look at him and look at him.'

'Is he still alive?' I asked, unable to imagine him going the way of the grocer's boy into banal middle age; but Charles muttered 'No, no,' unanswerably, and then bashed on: 'So you've read all the books I gave you.'

'Yes, I have. Well I haven't read every word, but I've taken a pretty fair sample.' He nodded reasonably. 'I would read them really thoroughly, of course, if I decided to take on this . . . job.'

Charles was quite quick and tactical. 'Quite so, quite so,' he said. 'But tell me, I don't know what sort of impression those books give. Do they appeal at all to, to a young person?'

'Oh I think they're very interesting indeed. And you've done so much,' I obviously went on, 'and known such extraordinary people.'

He sighed heavily at this. 'I ought to have been able to make something of it myself; but it's too late now. As you get near the end of your life you realise you've wasted nearly all of it.'

'But that's not the impression I have at all. I'm sure you don't really think that,' I said, in the way that one blandly comforts those whose torments one cannot imagine. 'I mean, I really am wasting my life, and it's not like what you were doing.'

Charles took this up directly. 'I've no time for idleness,' he said. 'I want you to have a job.'

'I just don't want the wrong one,' I said, sounding spoilt even to myself. 'I'd like it if I could simply disappear, like you did. It was wonderful how you could disappear into Africa.'

'One disappeared,' Charles admitted. 'But one also remained in view.'

I came back to it carefully, weighing the weightless teacup and saucer in my hands. 'What I rather got the impression of is that you were lost in a dream. It's very beautiful that feeling the diaries give of a constant kind of transport when you were in the Sudan. It's like a life set to music,' I said, in a fantastic impromptu, which Charles ignored.

'We were doing a job, of course. It was exceedingly hard work: relentless and exhausting.'

'Oh, I know.'

'But you're right in a way – of me, at any rate. It was a vocation. Not all of them in the Service saw it in quite the same light as I did, perhaps. Many of them hardened. Many of them were dryish sticks long before they reached the desert. They write books about it, even now – fantastically boring.' Charles shot out his foot and sent a book across the hearth-rug to me. It was the memoirs of Sir Leslie Harrap, privately printed and inscribed to Charles: 'With best wishes, L. H.'. A photograph of the author, in puzzled superannuation, took up the back of the dust-jacket.

'He was one of the people who went out with you, wasn't he?'

'He was a good administrator, loyal, fair, stayed on longer than me, went back in fifty-six to help with the independence arrangements: utterly sound – Eton, Magdalen. Not a breath of imagination in his body. It was reading his book – what's it called? *A Life in Service* – that made me realise I didn't want to write anything of that kind. There is a book in my life, but it's almost entirely to do with imagination and all that. The facts, my sweet William, are as nothing.'

I looked on abashed. 'You have published something about the Sudan though?'

'Oh – yes, I did a little book in the war; part of a series that Duckworth brought out on various different countries, I can't quite remember why. It wasn't much good. Fortunately almost all the stock was destroyed when a bomb hit the warehouse. It's probably worth a fortune now.' He laughed hollowly; and then lapsed into a vacant half-smile. I was trying to decide whether or not he was looking at me, whether this lull was an enigmatic part of our intercourse or merely one of Charles's unsignalled abstentions, a mental treading water, 'blanking' as he called it. I thought, not for the first time, how odd it was to know so much about someone I didn't know. A person could only reveal himself as Charles had done to me in love or from a deliberate distance. For half a minute, as I took in his heavy frame, the eyes dark and somnolent in his pink, slightly sunburned head, either reading seemed possible.

'If you've looked at the diaries for when I first went out,' he said, 'then you'll understand how young and aspiring we were. We were quite sophisticated in a way, but with that kind of sophistication which only throws into relief one's childlike ignorance. It was a bizarre system, when you think about it. There was one of the vastest countries in the world, and they sent out to govern it a handful of boys each year who had never in their brief lives experienced anything even remotely comparable. It wasn't like India, of course, there wasn't the same element of domination – indeed, the whole enterprise was utterly different. Anyone could go to India, but for the Sudan there was this careful selection, screening don't they call it nowadays. They got some worthy Leslie Harrap types of course, and plenty of sprinters and blues to keep things running on time, and they also got their share of cranks and unconventional fellows. There were possibly more of the latter. It was an absurd system and yet very, very subtle, I've come to believe. It singled out men who would give themselves.'

'They didn't make objections to people's – private lives?' I carefully queried, reaching across with the teapot.

'Thank you, my dear. No, no, no. On the gay thing' (he unselfconsciously brought it out, seizing a lot of sugar again) 'they were completely untroubled – even to the extent of having a slight preference for it, in my opinion. Quite unlike all this modern nonsense about how we're security risks and what-have-you. They had the wit to see that we were prone to immense idealism and dedication.' Charles sipped his tea excitedly. 'And of course in a Muslim country it was a positive advantage . . .' We laughed at this, though the implications were not quite clear.

'I'm sure you weren't such innocents as you make out,' I said. 'You must have been trained, after all.'

'We read a book about the sort of crops and stuff, and did a bit of Arabic.' Charles shrugged. 'And then they sent us up to the Radcliffe Infirmary to watch the operations. The idea was that if you saw a lot of blood and severed limbs and so on it would prepare you in some mysterious way for the tropics. They'd bring in chaps who'd been run over, or undergrads who'd tried to do themselves in, and we all had a jolly good look. Fascinating, in a way, but of no obvious benefit for a career in the Political Service.'

Charles was in knowingly good form. 'So you simply followed your instincts much of the time?'

'Mm – up to a point. There was a tendency to treat Africa as if it were some great big public school – especially in Khartoum. But when you were out in the provinces, and on tour for weeks on end, you really felt you were somewhere *else*. If you'd had the wrong sort of character you could have gone to the bad, in that vast emptiness, or abused your power. I expect you know about the Bog Barons in the south – truly eccentric fellows who had absolute command, quite out of touch with the rest of the world.'

'It sounds like something out of Conrad.'

'So it is often said.'

'I must say, I see you as more of a Firbankian figure – or at least that's how you seem to see yourself.'

'I don't know about that . . .' Charles rumbled.

'It's this idea that rather appeals to me, of seeing adults as children. His adults don't have any dignity as adults, they're all like over-indulged children following their own caprices and inclinations . . .'

'Well, I don't know!' Charles gave a brusque laugh of disagreement.

'Don't you feel that, though? I'm always being struck by it, especially with very grand and humourless people who can't afford to see that they're behaving just like prefects. And men are often like that together – I don't mean . . . gay men particularly, but the sense I have that men don't really want women around much. I think most men are happiest in a male world, with gangs and best friends and all that.'

'I believe I've always conducted myself with dignity,' said Charles.

I let a properly respectful pause be felt. 'I suppose what I'm trying to say is that you were very lucky in being able to turn your caprices into a career.' I was slow to realise how carefully Charles would measure everything I said against his wish that I should write his life. My slight nervousness, frivolousness, trying to be clever, perhaps put him off.

'There was this absolute adoration of black people,' Charles said, 'you could say blind adoration, but it was all seeing . . . I don't know. I think it was more of a sort of love affair for me than for most of the others. I've always had to be among them, you know, negroes, and I've always gone straight for them.' He put down his cup. 'I've been jolly lucky with them, too. All my true friends were black,' he added in a desolate imperfect. 'Oh, I tangled with a few cads and sharpers, bar-room heartbreakers –' he broke off actorishly.

'But all your true friends . . .'

He was bound to slight me just a shade in replying: 'Unwavering loyalty, you knew you would die for each other you were such pals.'

'I hope you see me as a true friend, Charles,' I said with half-pretended hurt. 'And I know people – white people – who are immensely loyal to you. Old Bill Hawkins or whatever he's called; and all these servants who fight over you.'

'I do command loyalty,' Charles assented. 'In Lewis's case perhaps too much loyalty.' He sighed and chuckled. 'Did I tell you about when he locked me in my dressing-room while he fought it out with Graham?'

'Oh, I was there, if you remember.'

'My dear child, I'd entirely forgotten. And all that sort of black magic stuff? Most unacceptable, I think, in a gentleman's companion. He thought I'd betrayed him – but he'd been troublesome for a long time, and when he'd flogged off half of my beautiful Georgian cutlery I could no longer turn a blind eye. He's inside again, now, I hear. He does these very artistic, kind of *symbolic* burglaries – with effigies of the people, and little arrangements of things. So there's never any doubt about who did it.' Charles chuckled and sighed again. 'He had a way with him, though.'

'How did you take him on in the first place?'

I was not surprised when he hummed 'Oh . . .' and wandered into his stratospheric vagueness, broken only by heavy, widely spaced, sibilant breaths: it was like the end of some visionary anthem by Stockhausen. The little gilt carriage clock whirred and chimed five.

'One quite interesting episode,' he said, 'which I think would make a telling bit of the book, was about Makepeace. Did you read that in the diary?'

'I don't think I did.'

'It was a little romance of mine, back in London. I was most frightfully smitten with a young Trinidadian barman at the Trocadero, who went under the charming name of Makepeace. The Troc was a very big, rather vulgar restaurant in Shaftesbury Avenue, with masses of mauve marble – long since gone now, of course. I don't know quite why I was in there, but one evening in the cocktail bar I was served by this fabulously handsome boy, and I stayed on and got him talking, though he was madly shy, but then I've always liked that. It turned out he'd had a rather extraordinary experience, as he'd worked his passage over on a ship – this was long before West Indians came in any number, of course – and then, missed the boat home. He walked into town from the Docks and as it was rather cold and rainy and not I suppose at all what he'd hoped for he went into the

National Gallery to keep warm, and there he was found by an artist called Otto Henderson, who was a madly *musical* type as we used to say – and also a third-rate painter by the way – and he sort of picked him up. He lived with Otto for a bit, but Otto was a terrible drunk and it got rather difficult, so Otto found him a job in the Trocadero, where, as it happened, he knew the head barman who was very Scottish and respectable *apparently* but underneath, according to Otto, wore ladies' knickers. Scottie was terribly jealous, needless to say, when I hit it off so with his black Adonis. Later on, he even threatened to expose me, but he changed his tune when I promised to tell all about the knickers.' Charles laughed, and waved a hand in the air, as if shaking a tambourine.

'How did it all end up?'

'Oh, Scottie had him dismissed for drunkenness (he did put it away rather) so I took him on myself for a bit. *That* didn't really work out, what with Taha in the house as well, so I farmed him out to a friend.' His face clouded. 'There was quite a lot of talk about it at the time. Of course in a way it helped being a lord – the English have such a superstitious awe of the aristocracy. But it also had its disadvantages, in terms of gossip and what-have-you – the English having such prurient and priggish minds. As you will find out, my dear, when you succeed' – words which seemed to anticipate not only my succession but my success.

'I suppose black people were comparatively rare then – in England.'

Charles half suppressed a burp of agreement. 'There were a few seamen – they had a hostel out at Limehouse. I had some good friends there, brave, reckless fellows, many of them. There were jazz players in London, of course, who had quite a following. But I suppose most people in the country didn't see a black person in all their lives. It was impossible to imagine the hatred that would be unleashed against them later on.'

'You've seen a lot of that.'

'You could say so.' Charles nodded, staring fiercely at the carpet as if caught by some bitter and ironic memory. I started to speak but he cut across me: 'There are times when I can't think of my country without a kind of despairing shame. Something literally inexpressible, so I won't bother to try and speechify about it.'

'I know what you mean.'

'Only last year out at Stepney there were hateful scenes – precisely hateful. Oh – National Front and their like, spraying their slogans all over the Boys' Club, where, as you know, a lot of . . . non-whites go. Every day there were leaflets, just full of mindless hatred – I'm sorry to keep saying it. The horrific thing was that several of those boys were boys who used to come to the Club themselves. It's the only time I've seen our excellent friend Bill get truly angry. He threw out a boy by main force, simply picked him up, carried him to the door and hurled him into the street. He's as strong as an ox, old Bill. I remember the boy – but boy is too beautiful a word – had a Union Jack pinned to the back of his sort of coat, and Bill had torn it off, accidentally I think, as he ejected him, and was left scowling absolute thunder and holding it in his hand. I was very frightened as I'm not the man I was in a fight, but all being cowards in the bone these louts sidled away when they saw they had met their match. And I wondered to myself what on earth that flag could mean now.' He paused, mouth agape. 'We had an outstanding young Pakistani boy, a genius at badminton, who was horribly beaten up last winter – much worse even than you, knifed in the arm and also completely deafened in one ear. Those youngsters feel they have to go about in groups now. And then of course the police think they're out to cause trouble.'

'Will it ever get better,' I said, hardly as a question.

Charles puffed helplessly. 'I'm beginning to feel a kind of relief that I shan't be around to find out.' –

It was graceless of me to put Charles on the spot but I said I found it hard to reconcile his views on race with the film that Staines had made and he himself – according to Aldo – had paid for. But I did it with as much cheek and charm as possible. He was bemused.

'I don't think *race* comes into it, does it? I mean, Abdul is black and the others aren't . . . but I don't want any rot about that. Abdul loves doing that sort of thing – and he's actually jolly good at it. He's a pure exhibitionist at heart.'

'I must say I was rather amazed by the whole affair – you know, seeing half the staff of a famous London Club about to copulate in front of the camera.'

'I think you'll find a good many of them do it – though not always on film, I agree. They're a close little team, there at Wicks's, and they like to do what I want. But then I got them all their jobs,' he added. It was one of those moments when I had the feeling, chilling and flustering at the same time, that Charles was a dangerous man, a fixer and favouritiser. In the world beyond school, though, perhaps one could have what favourites one wanted.

'Even so . . .' I shrugged. 'Do you have any idea what will happen to the film?'

'Well, it'll have to be edited and everything of course, which is actually frightfully difficult with blue films, the continuity, and putting the close-ups in the right place. We have some contacts – well, friends really, who do all the technical side. We made a few mistakes in the last one we did – filmed over several days so that the boys could come up with the goods, but then you found, if you had an eye for such things, that they'd somehow mysteriously changed their socks in the middle of a fuck or whatever.'

'I didn't realise this was such an established business – I'm astonished.'

'This is our third,' said Charles, with the personal satisfaction of the amateur. 'Much the best. It should be ready quite soon; and then we'll put it out to one or two of those little basement cinemas in Soho where there are people we know. I don't suppose you ever go to such places.'

So now my rather prickly line sprang back and snagged on my own moral woollies. I was embarrassed and laughed. 'Well yes, I have sometimes been to them.'

'I think they're jolly good value,' Charles went on in candid, reasonable tones. 'I mean, you pay your what is it, fiver, and nine times out of ten you'll see something that really takes your fancy.'

'I confess I go to them more for the off-screen entertainment,' I archly bragged.

'Ah yes . . . well . . .'

'In fact, I first got off with my current friend in a cinema in Frith Street. He was very shy afterwards about admitting that it had been him – in the dark, you know. He's a very shy boy, actually, but in those places people seem to lose their inhibitions.' Charles was not paying attention, and perhaps I shouldn't have been telling this story. I still wasn't wholly sure it had been Phil that I had felt up that day in the basement of the Brutus. Blushing, abstruse, he would not, when I put it to him, confirm or deny it. If it had been him, then he seemed to want it forgotten; if not, then he showed an odd readiness to be incorporated into some half-apprehended fantasy of my own. If it had been him, that squalid and exaggerated little episode must alter my understanding of him, open up the faintly sickening possibility of there being another Phil, whom I could not account for. He might have been at the Brutus at this very moment – or at the Bona or the Honcho or the Stud . . .

'It's always gone on, of course,' Charles recalled. 'We had little private bars, sex clubs really, in Soho before the war, very secret. And my Uncle Edmund had fantastic tales of places and sort of gay societies in Regent's

Park – a century ago now, before Oscar Wilde and all that – with beautiful working boys dressed as girls and what-have-you. Uncle Ned was a character . . .' Charles sat beaming.

'I'm always forgetting how sexy the past must have been – it's the clothes or something.'

'Oh, it was unbelievably sexy – much more so than nowadays. I'm not against Gay Lib and all that, of course, William, but it has taken a lot of the fun out of it, a lot of the *frisson*. I think the 1880s must have been an ideal time, with brothels full of off-duty soldiers, and luscious young dukes chasing after barrow-boys. Even in the Twenties and Thirties, which were quite wild in their way, it was still kind of underground, we operated on a constantly shifting code, and it was so extraordinarily moving and exciting when that spurt of recognition came, like the flare of a match! No one's ever really written about it, I know what you mean, sex somehow becomes farcical in the past.' Charles looked at me very tenderly. 'Perhaps you will, my dear.'

'Are you finished, my lord?' Graham was enquiring in his complaisant *basso*.

'Graham, yes, yes. Do clear away. And William, I must give you just before you go something else to read.' I hopped up, alert to these covert stage directions in Charles's talk, and helped him up too. He shuffled round his chair, and looked about for whatever it was. I was convinced he knew where to find it, and had politely and theatrically introduced this air of uncertainty. He handed me a document of several pages, the size of a pamphlet of poems, bound in black shot silk boards and tied legalistically with pink ribbon. 'Don't read it now,' he cautioned. 'Read it when you get home.'

Graham had gone out with the tray, and we followed a few moments afterwards, Charles's hand on my shoulder. 'Thanks so much,' I said.

'Thank you, my dear.' He leant on me and – which he had never done before – kissed me on the cheek. I clumsily patted him on the back.

On my way home I stopped at the Corry for a swim. It was that transitional half-hour before six o'clock, and the last of the afternoon customers – oldsters, college boys, the unemployed – were combing their hair and wringing out their trunks as the evening crowd, the workers, began to pour in and down the stairs. In twenty minutes every locker would be taken, and those who had been held up in traffic, late for their fitness classes or for a squash booking fast elapsing, would come cantering through the swing doors flushed and swearing. Like restaurants and Underground stations the Corry had its times of day, and to come in on a weekday afternoon or a Sunday evening was to find it in the unhindered possession of a small number of people – like a school at half-term, when only the masters and those boys who live abroad are left. The pool, the gym, the handball court had the grateful calm of places only briefly reprieved from habitual clamour. As I arrived the calm was yielding fast.

I took advantage of the crowd, and of the need I always felt on leaving Charles to be childish and naughty. In the showers were a gaggle of Italian kids, in London on a language course. The Club often played host to these groups, and though their bored ragging was a nuisance in the pool the members by some unspoken agreement forgave them everything for their sleek brown bodies, the tiny wet leaves of their swimwear and all their posturing and tossing back of curls. I halted under a fizzing nozzle before going down to the pool and looked them over frankly. It was impossible, with my opera-goer's Italian, to understand what they were saying, but as they took notice of me I heard their chatter sprinkled with *cazzo* . . . *cazzo*, slurred, whispered and then called aloud, almost chanted, so that they fell about in coarse, lazy giggles at their audacity.

When I got back to the flat I was half expecting Phil to be there, and remembered as I slouched sulkily and randily around the kitchen taking a glass of Scotch in great hot nips that he had arranged a couple of nights 'off' to see some South African friends and, tomorrow, to go to a leaving party at the 'Embassy'. In the sitting-room, remote control in hand, I tripped from channel to channel on the TV, trying to find something attractive in the personnel of various sitcoms and panel games. Abandoning that forlorn pursuit, I put on the beginning of Act Three of *Siegfried* and conducted it wildly, with great tuggings at the cellos and stabbings at the horns, but without, after five minutes or so, having made myself feel the faintest interest in it. It was in a reluctant mood that I finally settled down at my writing-desk to read Charles's precious document. When I untied it I found it to be, unlike anything else of his I had seen, an elegant fair copy, from which a compositor could easily have set type.

Although it would have been allowed, I did not keep a journal over those six months. From the start I saw that what I wanted to say, although 'hereafter, in a better world than this' it might find other readers and do its good, would have brought nothing but scorn and salacity at the time. And later, long after the start, when I thought writing might earn some slight remission of my solitude and pent-up thoughts, I shunned it, mistrusted it like one of those friends to whom one is drawn and drawn again and yet each time comes away cheapened, wasted or over-indulged. My journal has always, since my childhood, been my close, silent and retentive friend, so close that when I lied to it I suffered inwardly from its mute reproach. Now, though, it seemed to hold out the invitation to something shameful – self-pity, and, worse, the exposure of my narrow, treadmill circuit of memories and longings.

There was too my catastrophic change of station. I had fallen, and though my fall was brought about by a conspiracy, by a calculated spasm of malevolence, its effect on me at first was like that of some terrible physical accident, after which no ordinary thoughtless action could be the same again. The fall had its beginning in that very fast, dazed and escorted plunge from the dock after the sentence had been given, down and down the stone stairs from the courtroom to the cells. I had the illusion – so active is the faculty of metaphor at moments of crisis – of being flung, chained, into water: of a need to hold my breath. In a sense I kept on holding it for half a year.

Chaps did keep journals there – little Joe his childlike weekly jottings for his wife eventually to see, 'Barmy' Barnes his notebooks of visions and apocalypses – but they were licensed by their childishness and barminess; whereas I had been violently removed from my rightful lettered habitat, and as an invisible and inner protest refused to write a syllable. Now that I am home again I may write a few pages, merely to attest to what happened – and perhaps to feel my way towards recovery, to patch up my forever damaged understanding with the world.

One thing I notice already is that since leaving prison I have had long and logical dreams of being back in it, just as when I was in it I dreamt insistently and raptly of happy days long before and also of a day – now, as it might be – when I had been released, and various longed-for things would happen, or promise to happen. Dreams had a powerful and sapping hold on me there. I am the sort of sleeper who has always dreamt richly, so perhaps I should have been prepared for the futile mornings, sewing mail-bags, filling infinite time with that cruel simulacrum of work, but whelmed under in the world of last night's voyagings, their mood of ripeness and reciprocation. These – and other waking wishes – had such supremacy over the prison's abstract, cretinous routines that to tell the story of those months with any truthfulness would be to talk of dreams.

When, after evening Association – at some infantile early hour – we were sent to our cells, I gained a kind of confidence from the certainty that another world was waiting, a certainty, if you like, of uncertainty, the only part of my life whose goings-on were subject to nobody's control. The prisoner dreams of freedom: to dream is to be free.

Perhaps the strangest dream I had was one which recalled the evening of my arrest. The frequency with which it recurred could of course be explained by the frequency with which I anyway dwelt on those few crucial minutes. What puzzled me was the variations on the actual events. Always the sequence began with my leaving a group of friends and walking off briskly and excitedly, as I had done, towards the cottage. Which cottage it was, however, altered from night to night, much as it did, of course, in my actual routine. Sometimes I would make for the merry little Yorkshire Stingo, sometimes for the more dangerous shadowy dankness of Hill Place. Sometimes I would find myself going out to Hammersmith, intent on one of those picaresque 'Lyric' evenings; and this involved a cab, or bus or train, inevitably subject to diversions, wilful misunderstandings by the driver, or bodies on the line. Even if I was only walking a few hundred yards to a spot in Soho or that ever-fruitful market-barrow, the Down Street Station Gents, I was liable to lose my way or to be caught up in other business, other people's demands, which only served to increase the frustrated urgency of my quest. Often I would arrive at the correct location to find that the cottage had disappeared, or been closed down and turned into a highly respectable shop. And in reality the places that I sought had in some cases long been closed or demolished. Down Street was shut up before the war; and the station at the British Museum, although I recall no lavatory there, was another imaginary rendezvous, that now is an abandoned Stygian siding; so that my dream dissolved one nostalgia in another, and showed how all closures, all endings, give warning of closures, greater yet, to come.

I enter the narrow, half-dark space – again certain that there will be something for me there, but always uncertain what. In the dream it is only the acrid, medicinal scent that is missing – but the excitement from which it is almost indistinguishable survives. It is a smell as remote as can be from supposedly aphrodisiac perfumes, but its effect on me is electrifying. I unbutton at once, or in the dream remove most or even all of my clothes; my mood is optimistic and youthful – and my body too puts off half a lifetime of weight and care.

After a few moments a handsome young man comes in, his eyes obscured by the brim of his hat; or the lightbulb in its wire cage is behind him, so that he is a figure of promising darkness. I realise that of course I had seen him in the street on my way here, and had had the impression that he returned my glance. He must have followed me in.

He stands well back from the wall and the gutter as he eases his bladder, his penis is preternaturally visible and his attitude encourages me to look at it. Sometimes he seems to drop his trousers round his knees or to undo a wide fly with buttons up both sides, like a sailor's. In the light of day I can discern elements of many people in him, some of whom he may for a few seconds become, so that I whisper in welcome 'O Timmy' or 'O Robert' or 'Stanley!' At each moment he embodies a conviction of happiness, of a danger overcome. His penis is not quite that of any of the ghosts of whom he is compounded: it is not either large or small, thick or thin, pale or dark, but has an ideal quality, startling me like some work of art which, seen for the first time, outwits thought and senses and strikes in an instant at the heart.

He puts his arms around my neck, and I lick his face and push back his hat, squashing it down urchin-like on his springy black curls. His features are serious and beautiful with lust. We two-step backwards into what is no longer simply the cottage but a light-filled space whose walls alter or roll away like ingenious stage machinery in a transformation scene. We make love in the drying-room at Winchester, or in a white-tiled institutional bathroom, or the white house at Talodi, bare of my scraps of furniture and revealed in all its harmonious vacancy: simple places whose very emptiness prompts desire. In one version we are in a beach shelter of poles and canvas – the sides, luminous as screens of shadow-plays, thrum in the wind, while overhead tiny white clouds are blown across the radiant blue.

In another version, of course, it is not like this. I enter the lavatory and within a few seconds hear the click of metal-tipped shoes approaching the doorway, and look casually across at the young man who takes his place next to me. He is so gorgeously beautiful, in American jeans and a flying-jacket, that I can hardly believe, as he vigorously shakes his prick and with his other hand pushes back his lustrous hair, that his act is aimed at me, a man of twice his age, an old gent in an old Gents. In a cottage one takes what one is given, and is thankful; but none the less I am fifty-four – I hesitate before such golden opportunities. I am looking down intently, paying no attention, though my heart is racing, and then I hear other footsteps outside. I have missed my chance. But oddly the footsteps stop, recede, and then after a few seconds start back again. Somebody is waiting there. I glance quickly at the young man and his thick erection, and find he is looking at me steadily. I take a deep breath, and my heart sinks like a stone as I realise I am about to be robbed, more, perhaps badly beaten. If I try to leave I will be caught between the lovely boy – whom I see now for what he is, a steely young thug, perhaps the very one there has been talk of lately in the pubs – and his companion nervily keeping watch outside.

It is a horrifying moment, and I button up hastily and step back, all my instinct being to preserve myself as far as possible from the physical and moral outrage which almost visibly gathers itself to strike. There is a thumping silence, and the light of the one lamp across the wet tiled floor seems conscious that it will illuminate this and many other atrocities, just as it will go on shining through days and months of sudden speechless lusts, and all the intervening hours of silent emptiness. The boy, seeing I have begun to escape, himself adjusts his dress, but says nothing to me. As I go out at an ungainly scuttle he is behind me, almost beside me, and I see the other man, in a dark overcoat, step forward and look interrogatively past me. The boy lets out a little affirmative grunt, the man raises his hand to my lapel and speaks: 'Excuse me, sir . . .' but I am slipping past him, dreading to become involved in their insults and sarcasms. It is only a second later when I hear a car approaching and make for the opening in the bushes, beginning or meaning to cry out, that I slam full length to the ground, my arm is jerked behind my back, the boy is astride over me, and the man in the coat says: 'We are police officers. You are under arrest.'

My months in the Scrubs were a kind of desert in time: beyond their strict and ascetic routines they were featureless, and it is hard in retrospect to know what one did on any day or even in any month. I had had, of course, some experience of deserts, even a taste for them, and knew how to fall back, like a camel on its fat, on an inner reserve of fantasy and contemplation. I was a kind of ruminant there. Even so, it did not turn out in quite the way that – in the first numbed and degraded hours – I had imagined it would. Indeed, for several weeks the time rushed by, and it was really only in the final month, when freedom grew palpably close, that every minute took on a crabwise, cunctatory manner, came near to stalling altogether. I was haunted then by an image, a visionary impression of young spring greenery – birches and aspens – quickened by breeze but seen as if through frosted glass, blurred and silent. But by then a real atrocity had happened, something more than my freedom had been taken away from me.

My early days there called on my resilience. It was like being pitched again into the Gothic and arcane world of school, learning again to absorb or deflect the vengeful energies which governed it. But a difference soon emerged, for while the schoolboys were bound to struggle for supremacy, and in doing so to align themselves with authority, thus becoming educated and socially orthodox at once, we in the prison were joined by our unorthodoxy: we were all social outcasts. The effects of this were often ambiguous. Many of the distinctions of the outside world survived: respect for class, disgust at certain violent or inhumane crimes, and the ostracising of those who had been convicted of them. But at the same time, since we were all criminals, a layer of social pretence had been removed. There could be no question of pretending one was not a lover of men; and since many of the inmates of my wing were sex criminals – or 'nonces' in the nonce-word of the place – there was between us a curiously sustaining mood of sympathy and understanding. Of course guilt and shame were not magically annulled by this, but a goodish number of us – by no means all first offenders – had been caught for soliciting or conspiring to perform indecent acts, or for some intimacy (often fervently reciprocated) with underage boys. And many of the prisoners themselves, of course, were little more than children, old enough only to know the dictates of their hearts and to be sent to prison. The place was fuller than it ever had been with our people, as a direct result of the current brutal purges, and many were the tales of treachery and deceit, of bribed and lying witnesses, and false friends turning Queen's Evidence, and going free. Such tales circulated constantly among us – and I added my own mite to this worn and speaking currency.

My case, on account I suppose of my title, had been the subject of more talk than most – though nothing like as much as that of Lord Montagu, which shows all the signs of iniquity and hypocrisy evident in the handling of my arrest and prosecution, but wickedly aggravated by police corruption. In the prison my fellows felt sure that we two must be acquainted, and imagined us, I think, swopping young men's phone numbers in the bar of the House of Lords. It was hard to convince them that not all peers – just as not all queers – know each other. Even so it appears that his case – and in its little way mine – are doing some good: even the decorous British, with their distrust of the life of instinct, their pleasure in conformity, are saying that enough is enough. Some of them, even, are saying that a man's private life is his own affair, and that the law must be changed.

My dim lavatorial notoriety became in the prison a kind of glamour, and helped me, as I looked about and learnt the faces and moods of the men, to make friends. Covert gestures of kindness saved me from trouble, or explained the punctilio of some futile but unavoidable chore. Matchboxes and half-cigarettes were slipped to me as we jostled together for Association. Warnings were given of the foibles of particular screws. And so the nonce-world, which became my world, closed about me, offered me its pitiful comforts, and began to reveal its depths – now murky, now surprisingly coralline and clear.

My guide and companion in this was a young man I met after a week or so, a well set-up, rather tongue-tied little chap called Bill Hawkins. I had noticed him early on, and was not surprised to find that he spent a lot of time in the gym: he had a fine torso and packed shoulders. We played a few games of draughts together on my first Sunday evening. He clearly wanted to talk to me, but was uncertain how to go about it, so I drew him out. It transpired that he had been for over a year the lover of a teenage boy who trained at the sports club in Highbury where Bill was employed. They saw each other every day, and were blissfully happy, though Alec, as the boy was called, avoided his old friends and caused concern to his parents by his singular behaviour. Twice Bill and Alec went to Brighton and spent the weekend in a guesthouse owned by a friend of the sports club manager: if anyone asked questions they were to pretend to be brothers, for Bill himself was only eighteen, and Alec was a couple of years younger. After a while, though, Alec became more distant, and it soon became clear that he was involved with another man. Bill, in all the torments of first love, took precipitately to drink, and would make a nuisance of himself banging on the door of Alec's parents' house. Then foolish, intimate letters were written: and found, by the parents. They showed them to Alec's new friend, an insurance salesman with a Riley whom they, in a fine hypocritical fashion, considered more suitable and respectable than poor, passionate, uncontrollable Bill. Together the salesman and the parents took the letters to the police. Bill, when questioned, did nothing to conceal his feelings. He was sent down for eighteen months with hard labour.

Bill and I became great friends, and he, who was regarded as a kind of mascot by many of his fellows, and entrusted with secrets in the way that one might pour out one's feelings to one's dog or cat, knew a great deal about almost everybody, and seemed to feel keenly their various trials and tragedies. He pointed out to me a number of relationships between the men, confirmed my suspicious interpretations of odd gestures and habits, and revealed what was fairly a structure of submerged bonds and loyalties. There were half a dozen longstanding affairs going on, and various other men and boys were available if properly approached, or shared their favours with a satisfactory polygamy between two or three of their companions. In a way what had happened was a comic reversal of the circumstances which had put us all in there in the first place, with the prison authorities bringing us together, admitting our liaisons, and protecting us from the persecution of the outside world. The screws themselves were by no means indifferent, it transpired, and two of them at least were having sex on a daily ration with prisoners – though those prisoners were treated with the greatest suspicion by their fellows as being probable grasses. One of them was provided with lipstick and other maquillage by his officer, and his femininity, at least, was tolerated as it would not have been outside.

Bill drew me out too, and I have a clear and rather touching picture of him sitting opposite me, his powerful, stocky young frame transforming the stiff grey flannel of his uniform so that he looks like a handsome soldier in some poor, East European army. He concentrates on me closely as I tell him about my childhood, or about life in the Sudan; and he is interested to hear about my house and my servants. I have promised him that when he is released, early next year, I will find him something to do: a job in a gymnasium, if possible, where his feeling for men and physical exercise can be fulfilled, rather than baulked and denied in some clerkly work. It was rather desperate to see him toiling for weeks over detective novels from the prison library: he doggy-paddled through books in a mood of miserable aspiration, but they were not his element.

I took to the prison library with more duck-like promptness. It was a bizarre collection, made up almost entirely of gifts. Ordinary well-wishers and a number of voluntary bodies gave miscellaneous fiction and popular encyclopaedic works on technology and natural history; an outgoing governor had presented a collection of literary texts, some deriving from his own schooldays but also including French classical drama and the complete works of Wither in twenty-three volumes; and the *Times Literary Supplement* had charitably for some years sent to the prison all those books it felt no interest in reviewing, a body of work ranging from bacteriology to handbooks on historic trams.

I picked on something which must have come from the ex-governor's bequest: a schools edition of Pope, with notes by A. M. Niven, MA – one of those frustrating near-palindromes with which life is strewn. It had seen active service, and words such as 'zeugma' filled the margins in a round, childish script. I had not read Pope since I was a child myself, but I had a sudden keen yearning for his order and lucidity, which was connected in my mind with a vision of eighteenth-century England, and rides cut through woodland, and Polesden and all my literate country origins. The book contained the 'Epistle to a Lady' and various other shorter poems; of the longer works it gave only 'The Rape of the Lock' complete, and I fastened on this poem, and on Mr Niven's account of how it had been designed to laugh two families out of a feud, as the flashings and gleams of a civilised world, where animosities were melted down and cast again as glittering artefacts. I determined to learn it all by heart, and put away twenty lines a day. The discipline, and the brilliance of the work itself, were a kind of invisible enrichment to me – though, lest I should feel like an actor learning a great part with no prospect of a performance, I had Bill hear my lines each time I mastered a new canto; and he seemed to enjoy it.

Tempting though it was to retire into this inner world, there were always visits to look forward to – and to regret, for their cruel brevity and for the new firmness with which, afterwards, the door was shut, the walls of the cell confined one. The visitors carried their horror of the place about them and for a while after they had gone left one with an anguished vacancy of a kind I had never known before. All one's little accommodations were laid bare.

My first visit was from Taha – a 'box-visit', a reunion conducted through glass. I was wildly shaken to see him, so that I could not think of much to say. He smiled and was solicitous, and I looked at him closely, masochistically, for signs that he was ashamed of me. It was extraordinary how his confidence was undimmed: he spoke very quietly, so as not to be overheard by the guards or the other prisoners, and told me a score of sweet, inconsequential things. The second time he came, a few weeks later, we were allowed to sit at a table together: he had his little boy with him now, who seemed very excited at being allowed into a prison but frightened too of being left behind. Taha told him to hang on tight to my hand, and as he himself was holding my other hand we sat linked in a triangle, as if conducting a seance. The day before had been Taha's birthday – and of course I had nothing to give him. He was forty-four! I can honestly say that he was no less beautiful to me than he had been when I saw him first, twenty-eight years ago. His brow was higher, his face scored with lines that had been mere charcoal strokes on the boy's velvety brow and cheeks. His eyes, though, had deepened their immensity of melancholy and laughter, and his exquisite hands too were lined and shiny as old leather, as if he had done far more than merely polishing my shoes and silver.

That night I lay long awake, caught up again, with a vividness of recall, in the life we had spent together. Despite a thousand differences it was like a marriage, a great, chaste bond of love and tact – which made it all the odder that he had really married and become a father. I was gripped again by my mood of awful falseness and despair on his wedding day, when I *gave him away* into that little house in North Kensington and into a world more unknown and inaccessible than the Nuba Hills where I had found him first. Since then I have seen this period simply as a test, challenging our bond only to affirm it again. The terms were different, his independence, as each evening he went off on the Central Line, took a concrete, dignified form; but his loyalty was unaltered. Perhaps his distancing even endeared him to me more, and showed me afresh a devotion to which we had both become over-accustomed.

Such thoughts were still uppermost in my mind when I was called to see the governor a couple of days later. We had not met since the cursory talking-to of my first day, an occasion when I was strongly aware of the unease that his brief and accidental superiority had given him. Dressed though I was in my deforming prison bags I was made to feel wickedly sophisticated. He knew the disadvantage I suffered under would not – even should not – last. Today he was absent, and one of the senior officers took his place, pacing behind the desk but starchily resisting the temptation to sit down. I was not asked to sit myself, and as I refused to stand to attention, I adopted a rather decadent kind of slouch, which the officer did not like, visibly suppressing his criticism. I wondered what was up and had faint expectations of some kind of remission.

'I have some' – he seemed to hesitate to choose and then reject an adjective – 'news for you, Nantwich. You have a servant, a houseboy. What is his name?'

'I have a companion. He is called Taha al-Azhari.' I spoke with assumed calm, suddenly afraid that Taha had done something stupid, something he thought would help me.

'Azhari, exactly. He came from the Sudan, I believe?'

'Yes.'

'How old a man?'

'He is just forty-four.'

'Wife and children?'

'I really don't see the point of this. Yes, he has a wife and a seven-year-old boy. I think you saw the boy yourself,' I added, 'when he came to visit me last week, and Taha himself of course . . .'

The officer showed no recollection. 'Azhari will not be coming to visit you again,' he said. I shrugged, not out of carelessness, but out of a refusal to show care, and in a mute lack of surprise that to my current deprivations others were to be added.

'Have I done something wrong?' I suggested. 'Or perhaps he has?'

'He's dead,' said the officer, in a tone overwhelmingly vibrant and severe, as if this event were indeed a proper part of my punishment and as if to Taha too some kind of justice had at last been done.

'I confess,' I said, 'I am surprised you should find it fitting to convey such news, even such news, in the form of an interrogation.' I stepped with a kind of blind resolve from word to word, and it was only my utter determination to deprive him of the sight of my agony that kept me pressing on. He said nothing. 'Perhaps you will tell me how this happened. Where did it happen?'

'I gather he was set on by a gang of youths, over Barons Court way. It was late at night. I'm afraid they showed no mercy: stones and dustbins were used as well as knives.'

'Is any . . . motive known?'

'I wouldn't know. The police have no idea of course who did it. It seems not to have been for money – he still had money on him. Did he usually carry money?'

I ignored the lazily loaded question. 'There can be no doubt that this was an act of racial hatred and ignorance.'

'I'm afraid so, Nantwich. I think there will be more of them, too.' He looked confident of vindication, almost proud. I was still standing in the middle of the room, though by now I was beginning to shake, and had to force my knees back and grip my hands together.

'Your opinion is of no interest to me,' I said.

He gave a little smirk. 'You will be allowed to attend the funeral,' he said, as if I had been wrong to judge him so harshly.

And so the light of my life went out.

The morning of the funeral was ragged and squally, and I was stunned to find how readily I returned to the Scrubs and hid myself away: even if a car had been waiting to drive me home I would have been incapable of accepting it – and throughout the first few days of choking grief the hermit bleakness of my cell served to contain me in the fullest sense. In my own house I would have fallen apart. The other men, my friends, too, helped me and held me, and showed in their laconic condolences an understanding I could never have received in the world at large.

It would be unedifying to describe as it would be needless torture to recall those days when the world first changed, and became a world without my Taha. It was a terrible destitution, and my knowledge is all bound up with my physical experience of the hard coir mattress where I lay, the few properties of my cell, the bladeless razor, the little framed square of looking-glass in which I caught my tear-blotched face, the steady night-time smell of the chamberpot. As the autumn drew on it grew colder in the prison, but if one held one's hand to the black iron vent through which warm air was supposed to issue into each cell one felt only a slight chill stirring, which seemed to come from far away.

It was a time of incessantly recurrent images of my sweet dead friend, and of a thousand memories fanned into the air by this cold draught. I haunted and interrogated the past even as it interrogated me. London, Skinner's Lane, Brook Street, the Sudan – how had we passed all that time? Why did we not burn up every moment of it, as we would if we could have it all again? The journey back to England surfaced in dreams and occupied my days, the train to Wadi Halfa panting across the desert, reading old newspapers in the white, shuttered carriages while Taha, alas, was obliged to travel with the guard; and the stops, which had no names, but only a number, painted on a little shelter beside the track; and the steamer to the First Cataract and the visionary beauty of Aswan.

And I went further back, prone and defenceless, to Oxford and Winchester, shrinking from the world, curling up in the warm leaf-mould of earlier and earlier times, drawing some wan, nostalgic sustenance from those dead days. My life seemed to go into reverse, and for a month, two months, I was a thing of shadows. It was in vain to tell myself that this was not my way: I was impotent with misery and deprivation.

Then, as the end came in sight – it was the dead of winter – something hardened in me. I saw the imaginary verdure beyond the frosted glass. I began to think of the world I must go back to, with its brutal hurry and indifference. I would have to take on a new man. I would have to move again in the company of my captors and humiliators and be glanced at critically for signs of the scars they had inflicted. I would have to do something for others like myself, and for those more defenceless still. I would have to abandon this mortal introspection and instead steel myself. I would even have to hate a little.

I see in *The Times* today that Sir Denis Beckwith, following calls in the House for the reform of sexual offence law, is to leave the DPP's office and take a peerage. Oddly typical of the British way of getting rid of troublemakers by moving them up – implying as it does too some reward for the appalling things he has done. Perhaps I will have the opportunity to argue with him over law reform in the House – perhaps the only occasion in Hansard when a Noble Lord will have challenged another such who more or less sent him to prison. And he is a man I could hate, the one who more than anybody has been the inspiration of this 'purge' as he calls it, this *crusade to eradicate male vice*. Though one always treated him with contempt, he will now be a powerful voice in the Lords, with others like Winterton and Ammon – though beside their ninnyish rant he will be the more powerful in his cultured, bureaucratic smoothness. I have the image of him before me now in the courtroom at my sentencing, to which he had come out of pure vindictiveness, and of his handsome suaveté in the gallery, his flush and thrill of pride as I went down . . .

It was Graham who answered the phone. 'Oh Graham, it's Will Beckwith – is Lord Nantwich there?'

'I'm sorry, sir, he's dining at his Club this evening.'

'At Wicks's? When will he be back?'

'I don't expect him until late, sir.'

'I'll try again tomorrow.'

But tomorrow was too far away. I was so confused by this digest of disasters, I felt so stupid and so ashamed that I walked around the flat talking out loud, getting up and sitting down, scratching my crew-cut head as if I had lice. It was impossible so quickly to formulate a plan, but I felt the important thing was to go to Charles, to say something or other to him.

It took me ages to get a cab, and as at last it locked and braked its way through the West End closing-time crowds, I found all my ideas of what I might do rattling away, leaving me in a queer empty panic. I left the cab in a jam a block from the Club and ran along the pavement and up the steps. The porter emerged from his cabin with an expression of moody servility and told me Charles had left quarter of an hour before. I hardly thanked him, but dawdled out again, realising that at this moment he was probably roaring along the Central Line on his way home. I drifted around in front of the Club as if waiting for somebody, hands in jacket-pockets, chewing my lip.

Between the high neo-classical façade and that of the adjacent office block was a narrow chasm, gated from the street. The gate opened, and Abdul emerged, evidently also on his way home; he had on a light anorak over a T-shirt, and cheap grey slacks. I went up to him, surprised him as he locked the gate, greeted him with the conviction that he somehow held the answer to my problem.

'Hey, William,' he said, 'all finished now.' He gave a flashy smile and was ready, I think, to move off and abandon me, so that I said recklessly:

'Oh Abdul, did you know that Lord Nantwich had been to prison?' He turned back and looked at me and I looked back at him closely, his lined face, pink inner lips and fierce eyes slightly bloodshot, more guarded in the street's shadow.

'Of course,' he said lightly. 'Everyone knows that.'

I pursed my lips and nodded three or four times. 'Have you always known?'

'I have always known. Of course. I went to see him in there when I was a little boy. No place to take a kid,' he added. It was a detail that gave my evening a sickening completeness, like an orchid seen in a nature film brought in a few seconds from bud to heavy perfection.

I was laughing nervously as he turned back towards the gate. 'Hey, come in here,' he said. I followed him with a kind of absent-minded excitement and waited as he locked the gate behind us and went along after him past bins and milk-crates that were hard to make out in the alleyway's blackness. He opened a door and the flickering of the strip-lights was dazzling.

It was the Club's kitchen, abundantly old-fashioned, with many pantries and offices, windowed partitions and white-tiled walls. Cleaned and swabbed for the night it tingled in the fluorescent glare as if I was drunk. It had about it the discipline of institutional life and beyond that, for all its emptiness, something of the melancholy and teeming sense of order of an Edwardian country house. Abdul, who had sauntered to the far side of the room, came back to me where I lounged wondering against a table. He put his hands on my chest and sliding them up pushed my jacket back off my shoulders; it was then I realised that I had no tie on, and could never have been admitted to the Club proper, even if Charles had been there.

Abdul tugged my shirt out at the waist, and ill-temperedly opened my fly and pulled my trousers down about my knees. I saw his cock curving and buckling in his pants with anticipation before he turned me round and spread me out. It was one of those worn, foot-thick chopping tables, eaten away by incessant jointings and slicings into a deep, curved declivity. I waited greedily, and yelped as his hand came down, and again and again, tenderising my ass with wild, hard slaps. Then he crossed the room in front of me and yanked down from a shelf a catering-size drum of corn oil. It fell cold on my skin as he splashed it from a height then slicked my cheeks and slot, driving a strong unhesitating finger in. I heard the graphic rustle of his clothes, his trousers dropping to the floor with the weight of the keys in his pocket. He fucked me with a thrilling leisured vehemence, giving each long stroke, when it was in to the balls, a final questing shunt that had me gurgling with pleasure and grunting with pain, my cock chafing beneath me against the table's furred and splintered edge.

It was quickly finished, and he slurped out of me, and slapped me again. 'Hmm,' he said noncommittally; then, 'Fuck off out of here, man.'

12

I was woken by Andrews crossing the wide expanse of the bedroom and tugging back the curtains with a cruel flourish, shouting, 'Good morning, my lord.' Behind him came the naked Abdul, pushing a trolley on which his cock, perhaps three feet long, was supported, curved and garnished like an eel. He wheeled it to the bedside and I looked at it anxiously: it had a dull grey-black sheen to it, and a slight pile, like wet suede. 'I'm going to be very late,' I said, sitting up abruptly and kicking back the bedclothes. 'I have to give my maiden speech in the House at ten o'clock.' Then other sounds broke in, and I woke up, heart racing, in the pink penumbra of my own room.

It had gone eleven, but I had not slept until four or five, turning over the uncomfortable revelations of the previous evening. If Charles had been orchestrating his campaign, as I sometimes believed he had, then he had brought it brilliantly and comprehensively to a head. The prison was the key. The one unspeakable thing that no one had been able to tell me threw light on everything else, and only left obscure the degrees of calculation and coincidence in Charles's offering me his biography to write – a task he must have known I could never, in the end, accept.

And as for my grandpa . . . As I shaved I looked at myself quizzically, yet his image was also in my mind, the groomed, sharp-eyed, authoritative face, 'handsome suaveté' . . . I remembered the rather frightening figure of my childhood, the trenchancy and reserve, and what I could now see as a slow softening of outline as he left politics and received his viscountcy. In retirement he had grown more accommodating, and with the arrival of Philippa's children and the death of my grandmother had taken on something of the remote glamour of abdicated monarchy. His power was exercised with deference, calling on remembered allegiance. Yet his dynasty was not, in any strict sense, secure. Perhaps his fear that I would never have children explained the nervy familiarity of our relationship these days, the sense I had of being encouraged and yet kept at a hygienic distance. Perhaps it explained my own wariness of him, and the exaggerated obligation I felt under for the help he had given me. Oh, I wanted the flat and everything, but I was irked, graceless, I knew, and coltish about recognising its provenance. I loved my grandfather, too. Whether by the hoped-for sunbursts of our childhood holidays or the more watchful indulgence of his old age, he made one feel part of something superior and precious.

All that could hardly change now that he turned out to be in part a tyrant and bigot – not just the elder statesman I had been so proud of at my tother, but (the first saddening strands of evidence suggested) a kind of bureaucratic sadist, a man who had built his career on oppression. Perhaps his precious and superior coterie was not so desirable after all. I was at a loss what to do. I wanted somehow to record my dissent but without callow scenes. I needed, without altogether wanting, to know more.

I gave Gavin a ring, and was relieved when the long-suffering Spanish maid answered the phone: I didn't want to bring it up with Philippa. After a few moments Gavin came amiably through.

'Gavin, you must think me the most frightful fool.'

'Good heavens . . .' he laughed.

'About Charles Nantwich – I hadn't the faintest idea the other evening what you were talking about.'

'Oh yes.'

'I have now, though. It's so ghastly – have you known for ages?'

'Mm – quite some time. I mean that whole episode is more or less forgotten now, it was what? – thirty years ago. You must feel pretty awful about it, I suppose.'

'You're right. And was grandpa really the driving force of all this sort of anti-gay thing?'

'I'm afraid he probably was. With the Home Secretary, I suppose, and the police.'

'I'm so appalled by people knowing all this, and me going prancing around making passes at anything in trousers and not having the remotest inkling. And Charles and his friends leading me on . . .' Gavin laughed nervously. 'I don't know what to say to him, to either of them. Is Philippa aware of all this?'

'She might be. She probably wouldn't take it as seriously as you. I guess it was before either of you was born – I mean it's another world, *thank heavens*,' he hastily emphasised.

'But if you met Charles Nantwich, who's the dearest and most extraordinary old boy, you would see that it isn't another world. He was sent to prison and it's obviously scarred him or whatever – *and* he was set up by some pretty policeman, and that's really not another world, Gavin, it's going on in London now almost every day.'

After a moment Gavin said: 'I have met him actually; I think it was more than just the soliciting, there was a conspiracy charge and they raked up all sorts of other stuff. I heard about it originally from old Cecil Hughes when we were doing the London Bridge project. As you perhaps know, Lord Nantwich's house has a remarkable first-century Roman pavement under it.'

'Yes, I've seen it – why didn't I ask you if you knew it?'

'Cecil took me to see it then. It's exceptionally beautiful, don't you think, with the swimming figures and the Thames deity? It really ought to be removed to somewhere safe.'

'I don't see Charles taking to that idea. But it must be rather damp.'

'It's not only that,' Gavin said in a strange, camp tone of voice. 'There are other things. I remember Cecil and I had the distinct impression that orgies or something went on down there: there were candles and old leather-bound books going mouldy, and the queerest smell. And of course those outrageous Otto Henderson doodles on the walls. I must say it was more than a touch embarrassing – though Cecil I think quite enjoyed it.'

'I wish I'd talked to you before. There is a whiff of black magic sometimes at Skinner's Lane.'

'I'm not surprised. It's not my kind of thing. Henderson was said to be mixed up with some sort of spiritualist society himself, and Cecil said something about Nantwich getting in touch with I think a friend who had died tragically. I must say it rather gave me the creeps, as did Nantwich himself. Worth it for the pavement, though.'

'This was before you were married.'

'Actually it was just about the time that P. and I started seeing each other. The irony was not lost on Cecil; he very much came from that world, and it was he who told me about Denis. Very tight lips, as you may imagine. Of course, the irony's rather worse for you, being, you know, gay, and – I'm frightfully sorry, Will.'

'My dear Gavin. Anyway, I must think a whole lot more.'

I looked around my untidy bedroom, and was surprised to find I missed the invitation that the Nantwich book had offered for the past few weeks. I had played hard to get without ever envisaging an outcome such as this. 'I'd love to see you, too. We must all get together. Now that I'm not writing a book I'll have so much more time.' Gavin made a miraculous little humming sound, in which sympathy and scepticism were perfectly combined. 'He must have known gay people – he was a cultured man. What did he think he was playing at?'

'Well I'm too young to know. But I suspect it really was a different world – not only the law, of course, but political pressures, and we just don't know. It's Uncle Will. Yes, you can. Hold on, Will, I've got your nephew here to speak to you. Very important, right . . . See you soon, my dear!'

There was a plonk and a series of rustlings and a protest of '*Daddy*' before Rupert came on the line: 'Hello, this is Rupert,' in his serious treble.

'Roops, how nice to hear you. How are things.'

'All right, thank you. I've got to wait before Daddy goes out of the room.' This took a while, as apparently he came back for something, and was, as I pictured it, being expelled from his own study and his important work on Romano-British drains.

'It must be jolly secret,' I said encouragingly.

'It's that boy,' he hissed.

'Arthur, you mean? Have you seen him then?' And looking across the empty bed and out into the hazy sky, chimneypots among still trees, I felt a sudden plunging need for him, a Straussian phrase sweeping from the top to the bottom of the orchestra.

'Yes, I have. It was in the road, yesterday.'

'It was jolly clever of you to spot him.'

'Well, I've been keeping my eyes peeled for him, you know.'

'What a good spy you are. What was he doing, did he recognise you?' I tried to repress my eagerness and anxiety: to think of him being so close to here . . .

'I saw him walking along the road first of all, and I thought it was him, so I followed him.'

'Good boy! Now what did he have on?'

'Um – trousers. And a shirt.'

'Terrific.' I wanted to know if his tight cords cut into the crack of his bum, if you could make out his nipples through his T-shirt; but I made do with the more general answer. 'Go on.'

'Well, he went along our road, and then turned right, and when I went round the corner he was coming *back again*. So I went into a house and hid behind the hedge, I was pretending that it was my house, you see. I'm sure he didn't recognise me. Then he shouted when he was just outside the hedge, and there was another man.'

'Did you see him?'

'I saw his legs and hands. He was a black man too, and I think he was called Harold.'

'Harold, yes, that's Arthur's big brother. Arthur sort of works for him sometimes.'

'I think he was very cross. He said he was going to give him a smack.'

'The idea!' I exclaimed, as the real idea – which I had never seriously been able to disallow – seeped inexorably through my system.

'It was so funny being where I was, because he had something hidden in his sock, all wrapped up in silver paper, and when he got it out he didn't know I was there!' Rupert sounded very excited by this bit. 'What was in the paper?' he asked, a shade cautious now.

'I wouldn't know, old boy.' His silence told of his disappointment. 'Did they say anything else?'

'Yes. Arthur said, "Where's fucking Tony?"' He giggled.

'Mm – there's no need to do the accent and everything.'

'And Harold said, "He's in the car," or something, I can't *quite* remember . . . And Arthur said something about "That Tony was lucky to be alive" and Harold said "Watch your – um – lip" – does that mean mind your ps and qs?'

'Yup, more or less. That's very interesting Roops.' I pictured Arthur's lips, and imagined Tony, and wondered if it could possibly be the same one. 'You didn't get to see Tony, then?'

'No, he was in the car. Actually, they walked down the street a bit, and then there was a car going parp, parp. When I came out again they were just climbing into the car.'

'Was it a big yellow car?'

'It was a quite big yellow car – and *all the windows were black*.'

'That's the one. Darling, you are a great genius. One day I shall have to give you a medal.'

'Well I promised I'd tell you. Will?'

'Yes?' I sensed some more probing question was coming.

'Does Arthur and Harold still live in England?'

'Oh I think so, yes.'

'He didn't escape then?'

'It doesn't look like it, my old duck.'

I spent a lackadaisical afternoon, sprawling in the window-seat half-reading the paper, then closing my eyes, as the sun came round. I drifted in and out of sleep, took off my shirt, woke to find the coarse stitching of the tapestry bolster had patterned my slightly sweating back. I thought about Arthur, and how minutely brief our affair had been, and difficult to understand. I saw him again licking my balls; or swallowing as he slowly sat down on my cock; or helpless beneath me, locking his dry heels behind my neck. I hated to think it was over – yet dawdled half-awake in a maudlin, jealous reverie. I imagined him servicing the scarred and despotic Tony as they rolled towards the West End in their black-windowed Cortina.

So much had ended, so many things gone crooked and bad – and yet the high June afternoon lasted and lasted, grew stiller, more crystalline. There was no friendly darkness in it. I shifted and slept again.

At about drinks time I began to want to do something. I wrapped up my trunks in a towel, flung them in my sports bag with my goggles and soapbox and an American 'gay thriller' I had been loaned by Nigel the pool attendant, and trotted off out. The pavements and gardens were exuding their summer smells, and as I approached the Tube station I walked against the current of people coming home, youngsters in pinstripes from the City fanning out from the gates, jackets here and there hooked over a shoulder, smart clippety-clop of old-fashioned City shoes. They were quite handsome, some of these boys, public-school types with peachy complexions and contemptuous eyes. Already they commanded substantial salaries, took long, overpriced lunches, worked out perhaps in private City gyms. In many ways they were like me; yet as they ambled home in the benign and ordered vastness of the evening, as I fleetingly caught their eye or felt them for a moment aware of me, they were an alien breed. And then I was a loafer who had hardly ever actively earned money, and they were the eager initiates, the coiners of the power and the compromise in which I had unthinkingly been raised.

My disaffected mood persisted in the sweaty train. *Goldie* was one of the poorer accessions of the swimming-pool library. It was not, alas, about the Cambridge second eight, but about rent-boys, blackmail and murder in Manhattan; Goldie was the gay police officer who got to buy the favours of the chief suspect, and seemed bound to fall in love with him before the sorry end. The book's formula was to alternate blocks of fast, bloodthirsty action with exhaustive descriptions of sexual intercourse. Nigel, night-sighted in the pool's subterranean gloom, had said it was a good one; but I resented its professional neatness and its priapic attempts to win me over. The trouble was that, as attempts, they were half-successful: something in me was pained and removed; but something else, subliterate, responded to the book's bald graffiti. 'Fuck me again, Goldie,' the slender, pleading Juan Bautista would cry; and I thought, 'Yeah, give it to him! Give it to him good 'n' hard!'

As we slowed towards stops I looked around at the other passengers, wary slumpers and strap-hangers who never met each other's eye for more than a fraction of a second. Half-heartedly playing the game James and I used to play I tried to select which person in the carriage I would least object to having sex with. Occasionally the choice could be made difficult by the presence of too many scrumptious schoolboys or too many dusty-handed navvies. Normally, as now, the problem was to choose between that businessman, regular and suited but with a moody something about him, and the too-tall youth in the doorway giving off a tinny, high-hat patter from his headphones, and looking flightily around through a haze of Trouble for Men. It was James's theory that everyone had about them some wrinkle at least of lovability, some peculiar and attractive thing – a theory which gained poignancy from the problems in applying it.

Consoling and yet absurd, how the sexual imagination took such easy possession of the ungiving world. I was certainly not alone in this carriage in sliding my thoughts between the legs of other passengers. Desires, brutal or tender, silent but evolved, were in the shiftless air, and hung about each jaded traveller, whose life was not as good as it might have been. I remembered for some reason a little public lavatory in Winchester, a urinal and a couple of cubicles visited by bandy-legged old men going to the market and at night by ghostly fantasists who left their traces. It was up an alley where the College turned one of its high stone corners against the town – not a place for boys, for scholars, though I went there once or twice with an almost scholarly curiosity. The cistern filled for ever, the floor was slippery, there was no toilet paper, and between the cubicles a number of holes had been diligently bored, large enough only to spy through. Talentless drawings covered the walls, and wishful assignations, and also, misspelt in laborious capitals, long unparagraphed accounts of sexual acts – 'they had her together . . . 12 inches . . . at the bus station'. In between these were fantastic rendezvous, often vague to allow for disappointment, but able sometimes to touch you with their suggestion of a shadowy world in which town and gown pried on each other. I had read: 'College boy, blond, big cock, in here Friday – meet me next Friday, 9pm.' Then: 'Tuesday?' Then: 'Next Friday November 10' . . . I had thought almost it could have been me, until I just made out, bleared and overwritten, the date '1964': a decade of dark November Fridays, generations of College blonds, had already passed since those anonymous words were written.

At the Corry life was going on full blast. I swam more joylessly than usual, hoping I might catch Phil, starved of him, longing to have and to hold him: I wanted the solidness of him in my arms, and for a moment excitedly mistook another swimmer for him as he lounged at the shallow end. He had trunks on just like Phil's and when I surfaced grinning in front of him he gave me a bothered look before pushing off in a panicky, old-fashioned sidestroke. I felt keenly about the discipline of swimming, and then was suddenly bored by it, and by the taste of chlorinated water. When I hopped out I had a few words with Nigel. He was sprawling in those viewing seats erected long ago for matches and galas which never now took place.

'Hullo Will – good swim?'

'I'm not in the mood, I'm afraid, today. I can *do* it, you know, what's the point?'

'Mm, still, good for you. How are you getting on with that book then? Good one, isn't it?'

'I'm a bit disappointed by it, actually. You've lent me better.'

'Mm, but that Goldie, is it, I'd like to meet him. He can give me a taste of his truncheon any time.'

I shook my head sorrowingly. 'He doesn't exist, love. It's just a silly book.'

'Get out,' said Nigel, tutting and turning his head away.

'I could show you something really sexy – and true,' I said, in a sudden treacherous bid for his interest – he who didn't interest me at all, handsome and idle though he was. 'I've got some private diaries of a guy' (Charles a guy? some affronted guardian spirit queried) 'with amazing stuff in them. It's even got things happening here – years ago . . .' I had doubts and petered out.

My true come-uppance came not from a fascinated insistence I should tell more but from a deliberate lack of attention, as if to endorse my self-reproach. 'You still going with that Phil?' he wanted to know.

'Yup.' I squared my shoulders and tried to appear worthy.

'He's looking good.' Nigel smiled at me slyly. 'He was down here earlier on, splashing about, diving and that. Showing off. I wouldn't mind a bit of that, I thought. Gave me a really fresh look too.'

'You little slut,' I said, and flicked at him with my towel as I darted off. But I was reassured by how he had got it wrong, for though Phil was taken with his own body he almost stubbornly never tarted. His love was all bottled up and kept for me.

I thought of him with such tenderness in the shower and the changing-room that I was hardly aware of the bustle around me. I had not been good enough to him. I had often been sarcastic, and used him as a kind of beautiful pneumatic toy. He was the only true, pure, simple thing I could see in my life at the moment, and I wished I was with him, and wanted to thank him, and say I was sorry. I decided I would go up to the Queensberry and hope to catch him before he went out. Then I would go to James, who was true and pure too of course in his way, and worrying about his looming court appearance.

I went through the deeply familiar streets and squares through the equally intimate cooling and soft-fingered evening. Then there were the high plane trees and the bold splashing fountains – my mood escaping all the while from its bleak morning pacings and ambling into a more romantic melancholy. I became somehow picturesque to myself, prone as ever to the aesthetic solution.

I was about to go round to the side of the hotel, where I was well enough known now, but I was suddenly tired of my laundryman's-eye view of life, and swung up the main shrub-flanked steps and into the hall. I had become so used to the back stairs that I was quite surprised to see svelte couples coming down for pre-dinner drinks, others checking in, their anxieties melting as uniformed boys magicked their monogrammed luggage away. One or two people, waiting to meet friends, half-concentrated on the lit showcases where scarves, watches, perfumes and china figurines were displayed, or revolved the squeaking postcard racks, soothed by the customary London views.

I loitered too for a minute, charmed – or at least amazed – by all this bought pleasantness. And then I saw a wonderful young man, perhaps about my age, and with just that air of bland international luxury about him, come from the lift and saunter towards the cocktail bar. He was tall and graceful but gave the impression of weighing a great deal; as he approached I was startled by his deep-set brown eyes, long nose and curling lips and his trotting, swept-back hair; as he walked away I took in his maroon mocassins, his immaculate pale cotton trousers, through which the shadow of his briefs could be seen, the cashmere slip cast around his shoulders. I felt he must belong to some notable Latin American family.

It hardly required thought to follow him, though I gave him a second or two to get settled. I feared he might have gone to sit at a table or have joined his diplomat father and ragging, adoring younger brothers and sisters. But no, he was perched at the marble curve of the bar, and I was able to greet Simon – all in braid and tumbling his cocktail-shaker – as I took up a convenient high stool.

'What are you having?' Simon wanted to know. He was a skinny Lancashire boy who loved fucking girls and should ideally have been following a career as a pianist. He played extremely well, and had a long, long tongue with which he could easily lick the tip of his nose. He knew all about my little ways.

'What's *he* having?' I said, as I watched the wild pink liquid rattle from the shaker into the inverted cone of the glass.

He raised an eyebrow and murmured disgustingly, 'Cunnilingus Surprise.'

'Mm. Not quite my kind of thing perhaps.'

Here the notable Latin American said: 'It's really good. You should try one.' And then smiled immensely so that I went funny inside.

His lips curled back in a friendly primitive way, and gave an unexpected animation to his dully beautiful face. I realised he reminded me of one of the sketches of Akhnaten on Charles's stele – not the final inscrutable profile, but one of the intermediate stages, half human, half work of art.

I watched incredulously as the various ingredients, some exotic, some European, were measured into the shaker. Simon gave me a smirk of lewd surmise as he agitated it. Mr Latin America and I glanced at each other and then found it proper to look around the lofty bar, with its concealed lighting, reproductions of Old Masters and vulgarly gathered blinds half down against the westering sun. Across the road were the boles of the great trees in the square into whose upper branches I had so often gazed; and that did remind me of Phil, and how I must not take long over this drink.

'Perfectly revolting,' I pronounced after taking a sip. 'If that's what cunnilingus tastes like, I think I've done well to stay away from it.'

'You like?' said my new friend.

I nodded, as if to say it was nice enough.

'You are staying in this hotel?'

'No – no, I've just come in for a drink. After my swimming.'

'Oh you like swimming. I am a very bad swimmer.' I smiled politely; perhaps in his country, which I believed to be poor and old-fashioned, there were few swimming-pools. Even in Italy there were few: hence the fondness of the language children for hours of bombing and showering. 'Do you have a girlfriend?' he asked.

'No, no,' I said, actually slightly shocked at his naive forwardness. I let a minute or more pass in silence, but had to grin when Simon started humming *Tristan*. I wasn't sure what to do. The boy was undoubtedly a find. I swivelled on my stool so that we were sitting with our legs apart and knee to knee. He looked frankly at my crotch before meeting my gaze and we smiled enquiringly at each other as he ran his finger up the back of my hand where it dangled from the bar.

'If you come to my room, I will show you something very interesting,' he said. 'Do you want to finish your drink?'

'Um – no.' I started to reach in my pocket for change, but he stopped me with a firm hand.

'Number 205,' he said curtly to Simon.

'I must have got the name of that one wrong,' said Simon perplexedly as I followed my conquest – my conqueror? – out.

Room 205 was a small but grand suite – a sitting-room with a flower arrangement in front of a mirror, a gloomy bedroom looking on an inner well, and a neon-bright bathroom with a roaring extractor fan. The thick double-glazing on the front gave the rooms a strange feeling of remoteness. I walked around in them for a bit before Gabriel – as he was fetchingly called – said, 'Hey, Will, look at this,' and flung open a suitcase on the bed. It was stuffed with pornography – videos and magazines, many of them still in their rip-off cellophane wrappers. The buying had been prodigal and indiscriminate.

'You like it?' I was asked, as if it were a triumph of his own.

'Well up to a point – but I thought –'

'In my country these things, these dirty pictures, do not exist.'

'I should be highly surprised if that were the case. What is your country anyway?'

'Argentina,' he said, with a neutrality of tone which showed that this news was likely to have some effect. It made me want to apologise to him; at the same time I could have castigated him for buying up all this trash. Surely if any British self-esteem could have been thought to have survived the recent war it must be something to do with our . . . cultural values? The top magazine in the suitcase was a tawdry old thing I could remember from schooldays, called *Latin Lovers*.

'But what about the war?' I said dismally, seeing a TV news map of the Southern Atlantic and imagining too the customs-check at Buenos Aires.

'That's all right,' he said, putting his arms around my neck. 'You can suck my big cock.'

He stood patiently while I unbuttoned his trousers and slid them down over brown hairy thighs. The black briefs I had glimpsed before turned out to be leather. 'I suppose you bought these today as well,' I said; and he nodded and grinned as I prised them down and saw the studded leather cock-ring he was also wearing. He had clearly wasted a small fortune in some Soho dump. His assessment of his cock had not, however, been wrong. It was a sumptuously heavy thing, purpling up with blood as the cock-ring bit into the thickening flesh. 'I'm not a size queen, but . . .' would have been my classic formulation of the affair.

I hadn't had anything like it all summer, and gorged on it happily. But Gabriel's own performance was becoming off-putting. Every few seconds he would make some coarse exhortation, some dumbly repeated catchphrase, and I came to realise with dismay that this trick too he had picked up from crudely dubbed American porn films. 'Yeah,' he would croon, 'suck that dick. Yeah, take it all. Suck it, suck that big dick.'

I took a pause to say, 'Um – Gabriel. Do you think you could leave out the annunciations?' But it wasn't the same for him without them, and I felt unbelievably stupid appearing to respond to them.

'Okay,' he said brightly, as I abandoned the job. 'You like to fuck with me?'

'Of course.' There was after all some charm in his childlike openness. 'But in silence . . .'

'Wait a minute,' he said and kicking off shoes and tugging off trousers and pants, ambled into the bathroom, his dick bouncing with a kind of mock-majesty before him.

I slipped off my own shoes and jeans and lay playing with myself on the bed. Gabriel took his time getting ready and after a couple of minutes I called through to ask if he was all right. He came in almost at once, now completely naked except for his cock-ring, the pale gold wafer of his watch and – which I should somehow I suppose have expected – a black leather mask which completely covered his head. There were two neat little holes beneath the nostrils, and zipped slits for the eyes and mouth. He knelt on the bed beside me and was perhaps looking to me for approval or amusement – it was impossible to tell. Close to I could see only his large brown pupils and the whites of his eyes, blurred for a split second if he blinked, like the lens of a camera. It was hard and disturbing the way the eyes could not vary their expression isolated from the rest of the frowning or smiling face. I felt that childhood fear of rubber party masks, and of the idiot amiability of clowns who you knew, as they bent down to pinch your cheeks, were fearful old drunks.

Gabriel held my head to look at me closely, and I unzipped his mouth and breathed in his hot breath and the expensive smell of leather. His body was supple though slightly gone to seed – but I liked it and bit it. There wasn't much he could do in his mask, and when I had nosed around him for a while he hoiked me over and pushed my legs apart. I was anxious not to take all that raw, and had begun to complain, when I felt something cold and wet, like a dog's nose, trailing up my thigh. I looked over my shoulder to find that from somewhere this madman had produced a gigantic pink dildo, slippery with Crisco. I heard him giggle tensely inside the mask. 'Do you want to smell some poppers?' he asked.

I rolled over and sat up and spoke in a strange tone of voice which I seemed to have invented for the occasion. 'Look pal, I'd need more than poppers to take that thing.' It was all very well to be violated as I had been last night by Abdul, but I did not like the idea of inanimate objects being forced up my delicate inner passages. He turned and walked across the room – angry, hurt, careless, I couldn't tell – and threw the great plastic phallus into the bathroom. I imagined the maid finding it there when she came to tidy up and turn down the bedclothes. 'Okay, so you don't like me that much,' he said, thickly, from inside the leather.

'I like you very much. It's just the moving toyshop I can't be doing with.' And I decided I had better go, and reached for my jeans.

'I could whip you,' he suggested, 'for what you did to my country in the war.' He seemed to think this was a final expedient which might really appeal to me; and I had no doubt he could have provided a pretty fearsome lash from one of his many items of luggage.

'I think that might be to take the sex and politics metaphor a bit too seriously, old chap,' I said. And I could see the whole thing deteriorating into a scene from some poker-faced left-wing European film.

When I was dressed and had my bag again slung over my shoulder Gabriel was wandering around the sitting-room, his huge erection barely flagging, but somehow no longer of interest to me. I stood and looked at him and he grasped and grunted and writhed out of his mask. His hair was moist and standing up, and his clear olive complexion was primed with pink – as it might have been if we had just simply made love. I went over to him and kissed him, but he closed his teeth against me, kept his hands at his sides. I left the room without saying goodbye.

Well it served me right, I thought, as I wandered with a vague sense of direction along uniform carpeted corridors – Phil's terrain, where he did his job. All this had certainly got me in the mood and now I would be too late to catch him and the uncomplicated solace he could give. Surely hotels must be hotbeds of this kind of carry-on, easy encounters at the bar or unlocking the doors of adjacent rooms. My little Philanderer could make a fortune out of escorting truly glamorous men – and not all of them would turn out to be as weird as the eye-catching Gabriel. It was quite likely, wasn't it, that Phil had already caught Gabriel's eye?

I found the corner by the service lift and the steep flight of stairs up to Phil's attic. It was a drab, cheapjack little area, unambiguously removed from the public, and yet I had come to love it in a way I never could the rest of the monstrous edifice. The little room – and above it the lonely roof – were nothing really, but like the lovers' cottage in 'Tea for Two' they had been wonderfully sufficient for our romance. I knew there was no chance of finding him in – he would be well off on his laddish booze by now – but it would be comforting to sit there for a bit with the window open and surrounded by his empty clothes. When I put my key in the lock, though, there was a muffled call of surprise, I thought, from within.

Phil and Bill were kneeling face to face on the bed. Bill's hand rested on Phil's shoulder, and it looked like some College jerk-off job. Their tilting dicks, alert as orgiasts' on a Greek vase, withered astonishingly under my expressionless stare. Not for them the witless priapism of Gabriel; but there was enough defiance in their confusion for them not to blabber excuses – not to say anything at all. And I couldn't think of anything much to say. I know I swallowed and coloured and took in, as if I needed to satisfy myself, the circumstantial details. Certainly there were no signs of passionate haste. Bill's trousers were neatly folded and his vast smalls were spread like an antimacassar across the back of the chair. I nodded repeatedly and slowly withdrew, closing the door as if not to disturb a sleeper. Before I had reached the top of the stairs I heard a gasped 'Oh my God' and a loud frightened laugh.

And so to James's. By the time I got there my anger, hurt, care were welling up under the frigid discipline I had instinctively assumed. I smeared away stupid tears. Thank heavens at least no crass, unforgettable words had been spoken. 'Darling, whisky' was my own first utterance – and I thought, none of your namby-pamby Caribbean aphrodisiac nonsense.

James was eating scrambled eggs standing up and listening to some fathomlessly gloomy music. 'Bad day dear?' he enquired maritally.

'The last twenty-four hours have actually been quite extraordinarily hideously awful.'

'Oh darling.'

'I thought I was just about managing it until half an hour ago, when I went up to Phil's room at the hotel – I don't know why, just on some sentimental whim, I thought I'd put on some of his clothes and lie there for a bit and just *be* him, you know – he having arranged to go off drinking with some of his appalling friends. Well they may not be appalling, I've never met them. I say we couldn't possibly take this music off? It's driving me insane.'

'It's Shostakovich's viola sonata,' said James pettishly.

'Exactly . . . That's better. And the drink?' He poured a generous Bell's. 'Dearest – thank you. So I opened the door, to which as you know I have a key, and find Phil in there with old Bill Hawkins, from the Corry, messing around stark naked, etc, etc.'

'Fucking hell.'

'I do find it very terrible actually.' I flopped on to the sofa and gulped at my drink. 'I mean, I absolutely hate the thought of Phil going with someone else. But one would understand if it were just some spur-of-the-moment fling – some sexy guy staying in the hotel or something. To go with Bill, who is anyway a pal of mine and what? three times his age . . .'

'No?'

'Well, just about.' I stared at James, through him, as I realised how slow I had been. 'You know, I should have been on to this. I've seen Bill hanging around near the Queensberry before now – and of course I knew he was sweet on Phil, sweet on him before I was. Indeed it was really Bill's interest in him that got me going, made me see how good he was. And then last week, when I took Phil to the Shaft, I knew something funny was going on. We were sort of horsing around outside the B M and I realised someone was watching us from across the road. I don't think Phil saw him, but I'm convinced it was Bill.'

'Kind of creepy, *n'est-ce pas*?' said James, wandering off and looking out of the window. He was my only friend but I knew that he would take a kind of wistful satisfaction in things having at last – *at last*: it was what? two months? – gone awry. 'This needn't mean it's all over, though, surely?' he said.

I stared some time into my glass. 'I don't know. No, it needn't. It will, I think, mean that whatever's going on between those two is all over. What you don't know, and what Bill doesn't know I know, is that he has already been inside for interfering with young boys.' But these were the kind of real-life details that never shocked James: it was only on the fantasy level that one got to him. 'He'll be pretty scared about all this.'

'Well, you're hardly going to shop him to the police, are you?'

'Ooh, I don't know,' I said with a rueful laugh, finishing my drink and getting up to splosh in another half-tumbler full. I walked over and hugged him from behind, resting my chin on his shoulder. 'It's like one of those frightful seventeenth-century epitaphs: I've had my Will, I've had my Fill, and now they've sent in my Bill. Or something like that.'

'Do you want something to eat?'

'I think I'll just stick on the booze, actually. Darling, can I stay here tonight? I just don't fancy going home – and I'm sure he'll try and ring up and it will all be too appalling.'

'Yes, of course you can.' I sensed his nervous pleasure at the certainty of companionship. He turned round in my arms and gave me a tight squeeze and a kiss on the blunted bridge of my nose.

'There's actually something in a way much more awful that I've just found out,' I began, sliding off and taking to an armchair. 'It all came up in old Nantwich's papers, you know? He led me on a long way and then he sprang his journal on me for 1954, from which it emerged, in brief, that he'd been sent to gaol for six months for soliciting and I think conspiracy to commit indecent acts, I'm not sure about all that. As if that wasn't hideous enough it turns out that the person behind it all – there was a whole sort of gay pogrom apparently – was my grandfather. When he was Director of Public Persecutions.'

James sank to the chair opposite me and looked at me intently. 'Lord B,' he said, quietly and calculatingly.

'Lord B, as you say. Did you know anything about this? Of course it just fucks up absolutely everything, it's soured everything. It seems Lord B, as he was yet to become, was so successful in cleaning up the perves that he was whisked off to the Upper House. His whole career was made by it.' We held each other's eye. 'Of course it turns out that when Charles was in gaol he met up with Bill Hawkins, doing his aforementioned stretch for being in love with a kid. He was a kid himself at the time, needless to say. And there are all sorts of other connections with people I know. It's all come horrifically at the same time. And we're only kids ourselves,' I huffed.

James felt entitled to draw on professional language. 'I guess if those things are building up and building up, when they erupt there will be a bit of a mess. There will be pockmarks,' he seventeenth-centurily went on.

I got him to play me some more positive music, some courtly, phlegmatic Haydn; and I turned the conversation round artificially to more general subjects. We watched a mirthless comedy on the television from beginning to end. It was only when we were in bed, and I was now dry-throated and woozy-headed from the drink, that I came back to the subject.

'It's the way we didn't know about it,' I murmured. 'The gruesome incongruity of it.'

'Isn't there a kind of blind spot,' James said, 'for that period just before one was born? One knows about the Second World War, one knows about Suez, I suppose, but what people were actually getting up to in those years . . . There's an empty, motiveless space until one appears on the scene. What do you know about your own family anyway? They're such secretive organisms, I can't be doing with them.'

I felt his erection – the idiot emblem of the day – yearning against my thigh, and waited resignedly as his hands wandered down towards my own. It was a curious experience, for while he stroked he seemed instinctively to be feeling for other symptoms, exercising that slight pressure which discovers a tender kidney or a swollen gland. He was rather fastidious when he reached his objective too.

I turned on my front, and he gave a little humorous sigh and tipped his forehead against mine while I told him of a thing that had happened on the train. It was while I was coming to see him and had taken place just in front of me, an ordinary thing and yet calmly beyond the turmoil of my own mood, in fact wonderfully self-sufficient and entire. Among the crowd that got on at Tottenham Court Road were a black couple with a baby: they took the two places against the glass partition, so that the man and I sat – as I had done with Gabriel shortly before – knee to knee. Once he had looked at me politely as I shifted to make room for him he had no interest in me at all – and I hardly took notice of him. His wife held the impassive and very young child in her arms: despite the heat it was dressed in a quilted one-piece suit, but with the hood back. My thoughts were all elsewhere, though I saw the man, about thirty, I suppose, lean over the baby's open flawless face, and smile down on it, out of pure pleasure and love. His fingertips moved from his own softly bearded lips and gently stroked and almost held within their span his child's lolling wispy head. His other hand lay loosely in his lap, and it took me a while to

279

see that he was hiding and coaxing – yes – a hard-on in his respectable grey slacks. I was not aroused by this; but did I dwindle, if only for a moment, in the face of their glowing, fertile closeness? I felt perhaps I did.

Last thing of all before sleep we muttered about the charge against James, though he was shy of my ruse not only to get him off but to bring Colin down. He had pleaded not guilty to the magistrate on the morning after his arrest, and so gained time, the case being deferred. He had a good lawyer, one of his Holland Park patients, who was gay himself and knew how to fight and what such fights could mean if lost. We wondered if it depended on whether the court would accept works of art as evidence; and besides, whether they would accept that Staines's photographs were works of art. It was a shaky idea, and I fell asleep and dreamed that they confiscated all Staines's pictures and sent him to gaol instead. When I woke before dawn, parched and aching, I felt lost. I decided that if necessary, and if it might save James, I would testify in court to what I had done with Colin – and so perhaps do something, though distant and symbolic, for Charles, and for Lord B's other victims. I had that most oppressive of feelings – that some test was looming.

James was off to work early, so I walked home through the awakening streets. I moped about in the flat, now furious with Phil, now reproachful, and held a hundred imaginary conversations with him, in which I would often speak out loud – 'What do you mean, you did it out of pity?', 'How could you imagine that I wouldn't find out?', 'I've never heard anything so absurd in my life . . .' and on and on. But when the phone rang I was terrified to answer it and embroil myself in the meanness and misery of arguments. I sat on the bed looking at it and summoning my resolve; but when I did pick up the receiver it was someone I had been at Winchester with – one of those City youngsters – informing me of the memorial service for a not-much-liked don.

I was apprehensive about going to the Corry too, but after a day of fretting, squalid inactivity, I decided to take the chance. It was Phil and Bill who were the naughty ones and I refused to be cowed by them further. My mood was all torn, and had not been helped by my finding, when I was in the bath, a single dark hair (too dark to be mine) trapped on the soap in a long looped wiggle like Corporal Trim's flourish with his stick. It wouldn't just wipe off, and I had to scratch at it and gouge at the soap with a fingernail to get rid of it, all knotted up as I was with revulsion and pathos. It was the most thoughtlessly intimate of all the reminders of Phil in the flat – his trainers, his throw-away razors, his bits of paper – insisting it could hardly be over. The Corry too, of course, was running with the idea of him – but he was nowhere to be seen, and Nigel, who would have noticed, assured me he had not been in the pool. I looked abruptly into the weights room, but Bill's worried features were not to be made out either.

I did, however, run into Charles on my way out. He was sitting in the melancholy cafeteria, looking through the plate-glass windows at the gym-floor below. He was finding it difficult to drink hot coffee from his flimsy plastic beaker. I sat down heavily opposite him.

'Fascinating athlete, that young man down there,' he said.

I followed his gaze to the shirtless figure dancing at the punchbag. 'Yes, that's Maurice. He's a dream, isn't he. Not, however, musical.'

'Quite so, quite so. I must get him a job.'

'I think you'll find he's got one already,' I said with a little fading snigger. Charles was looking at me closely, and I looked down, and then away again to Maurice, cutting and jabbing in wonderful ignorance of his spectators and their quandary.

'I've made a mess of things, haven't I,' said Charles.

I shook my head. '*You've* made a mess of things! Dear Charles. I've been thinking about this all the time but I still don't know what to say. But you have not made a mess of anything. Except, of course, that I can't do the book.'

'You could.'

'I can't.'

He followed Maurice again. 'You've no idea of the quite extraordinary, powerful and – my dear – entirely kind conviction of rightness I had when I discovered who you were. It was such a perfect idea; too perfect perhaps to be enacted by decent human beings. Good punching! Marvellous boy! But perhaps, when your grandfather . . . is dead – and I'm dead – you'll come round to it.'

'All I could write now,' I said, 'would be a book about why I couldn't write the book.' I shrugged. 'I suppose there are enough unwritten books of that kind to make that of some interest.'

Charles was not following me. 'It was naughty to keep back so much – though I kept thinking you would be bound to learn about all that from other people. I felt sure our friend Bill, for instance, would spill the beans.'

'Bill's a pretty careful, secretive character,' I said, my benign and contemptuous views of him appearing to me suddenly at the same time.

'We'll still be the most terrific friends, won't we? I mean, it has been worth it, even if, you know . . .'

'Of course it has.' I didn't want to get caught up in all this today. 'What brought you into the Club?'

'Oh – a meeting. Very dull, I'm afraid. And you've been swimming, I imagine. Gosh how I envy you,' he unnaturally rushed on. 'There's nothing like it, is there? It's one's real element. It was a thing one missed most frightfully inside – you know.'

'Yes.'

'I must say this coffee's quite revolting. I must get them to do something about it. Maurice you say? I've seen him before, of course. And now I think I'd better shuffle home. You couldn't, my dear . . .?'

I gave him my arm, and we made our way slowly up to the hall. I knew that, although he came to meetings and could get the coffee changed, he valued being seen with some young thing more, as a sign that he belonged and was wanted. I felt my familiar bafflement with him, and that our meeting had not been at all as I hoped. It was so brief and profitless.

'You won't kind of believe me when I say this,' he began. 'But old Ronnie Staines has found something most frightfully interesting. *Not* what you're thinking; indeed quite the opposite, by all accounts. I'm going to go and see it tomorrow after lunch. Ronnie said actually he wondered if you would come. And I think – I daren't tell you more – that you should bring that friend of yours you've told me about, the *Prancing Nigger* buff, you know.'

'It's an invitation I could normally resist – but Ronnie has promised me some pictures, which I must go soon to collect. I suppose I could do it all at once.' It was typical of my friendship with Charles that I told him nothing about what really mattered to me while he had laid himself bare, systematically, decade by decade. 'I was going to mention it to you: my friend James, the Firbank buff, has got into a bit of trouble with the law, picked up by a policeman who just happens to be one of Ronald's porno models. I don't know, I thought it might be useful to get hold of the photos.'

Charles absorbed this information with the narrowed eyes and thoughtful nod of someone beyond surprise at human duplicity; but he said nothing.

'So I will come. But honestly Charles, I'm not on for any more bellboys-get-it-up-the-bum stuff. I've had it up to here with all that lately. If not to here.'

'I promise you, my dear,' he said, with cloying candour.

James had expressed an interest in Staines, and a dirty-minded and vengeful interest in the pictures of Colin: I liked him in that mood, when he got rid of his selfless wretchedness and we could drunkenly slag people off together. I knew he would be ready to visit the photographer's house.

There was no word from Phil that night. I was in a tense, vacant condition, but I drank a bottle of wine, and managed to sleep. Dreamlife was wildly disturbed, however. There was a barely remembered sequence in which I met Taha, who was a very old but beautiful man, and began to interview him about Charles and their life together. And there was another, more vivid, in which Phil and Bill were going off on holiday. They were loading up the roofrack on my old Fiat with tentpoles and buckets and spades, and standing about in the road with various other things they had brought from my flat. I wanted to help but kept getting in the way. 'Be careful where you put that,' I said. 'Don't forget about the blind spot.' Phil was already in tiny swimming-trunks and Bill gave him a saucy slap on the rear, leaving a large oily handprint. Across the top of the windscreen the sticker read 'PHIL and BILL'. It was funny, I thought, as I came round, how you never did see cars saying 'GARY and CHRIS' or 'LANCE and DEREK'. They would probably have got smashed up.

James came to lunch with me, and I had taken special care to stuff some aubergines and make a bitter and original little salad. I felt something of that homely, maternal impulse which would occasionally surface in me at times of strain. One could potter pathetically with one's chicory and watercress and enjoy an almost *creative* feeling. James, of course, had been hard at work for hours, and I thought what a great narcotic a job could be; and then one earned one's own money.

'How are you getting on?' he asked.

'I feel pretty helpless. I thought it was a good thing there had been no sordid row or anything, but one would like some kind of contact. It's so stupid. I don't know what's going on. Why doesn't the little fucker ring me? I feel furious for a while, and then – well, I love him *so much*. I want to be with him again. And then at other times I feel like a sort of Pantaloon figure, who's been hoodwinked. Actually I don't see how any of us can do anything without a certain loss of dignity.'

'You could just go round to the hotel.'

'What, and find them frigging away again? I'm not into that.'

'I thought you thought it couldn't possibly still be going on.'

I opened the oven door and shoved my hands into the linked asbestos pockets of the oven-gloves, slapping them together a few times as if I were a lunatic in some restraining garment. A good garlicky smell blossomed. 'I don't honestly believe they can be having an affair,' I said carefully. 'On the other hand, I do believe that the heart, and more particularly the willy, have some very strange ways. It's just possible,' I allowed as I squatted down, 'that a handsome eighteen-year-old could prefer a waddling fifty-year-old to someone as beautiful and well-endowed as me.'

James embarrassedly ruffled the top of my head, but I shouted 'Out of the way!' as I made for the table. The oven-gloves were never as efficient as they should have been.

After lunch we popped into James's Mini and made the two-minute journey over the avenue to Staines's house. These were the very streets where little Rupert had seen Arthur and Harold at their miserable business: I looked out for them, in a fairly ridiculous and superstitious way. I wanted to save Arthur. At least, I think that's what I wanted to do to him. It was a strange conviction I had, that I could somehow make these boys' lives better, as by a kind of patronage – especially as it never worked out that way.

Staines was on his very best behaviour, though it didn't fool me. One could perceive his slight polite disappointment that James was not more beautiful. The ego was smartly suited, buttoned up, and though at any moment I expected some rude eruption, a comic photographer's surprise the split second before the flash, the most explosive thing about him was the pink of his socks. Charles was already there, glass in hand, at the end of lunch, and I introduced him to James, whose enthusiasm was precisely modulated to disguise the intimate knowledge he had of him from me. We strolled through at Charles's pace into the studio, and I heard him saying to James: 'So you're the Firbank fellow, eh? I knew him, of course – though not well, not well . . .'

Staines let down a roll of white paper from the ceiling and had us sit in a row in front of the projector on its high table. As he turned the main lights out and began to speak I was reminded strongly of those scenes, early on in thrillers, when the agent is briefed and shown film clips of leading suspects, taken largely from the back of moving cars.

'I'm going to show you a short piece of film which I believe will interest you all. It's part of a whole lot of home-movie stuff I've just bought at Christie's. Most of it's too madly dull for words – you know, gay young things arsing around with no shame. I just thought it might be fun, and give me some sort of ideas for some Twenties and Thirties – er – pictures I want to make. And then in amongst it there was this fragment – quite exceptional . . .'

The bright white square at which we had been looking was convulsed with running black and grey, and white flashes. The first thing we could make out was a brief and static view of a lake with steep woods around it. The light in the picture was strangely bleak, and a hundred little lines ran up and down the screen. Even so there was something mysterious about that seemingly black circle of water. Remembered books suggested it was an extinct volcano. 'Aha,' said Charles, very smugly. The camera angle jumped to include, possibly by mistake, the bonnet of an early-looking motorcar.

'You know where we are, Charles,' said Staines from behind the purring projector.

'Oh yes – Lake Nemi. Unmistakable.'

There was then a shot, held unnecessarily long, of a tin sign saying 'Genzano – Città Infiorata'.

'I think we all know where we are now,' Staines added patly. An old peasant in a hat and carrying a stick as tall as himself limped into view, looking troublesome.

The following sequences took place presumably in the precipitous streets of Genzano. Here was the car again, drawn up outside what might have been the town's smartest café. The citizens, some aware of the camera, some at least showing no awareness, went stiffly up and down the pavement, turning flickering smiles or frowns. Some of them were getting up from the tables outside under the awning, couples bustling off, while others, with raising of hats, went into the absolute blackness of the interior. One side of the picture was then obscured by a man's back. He half-turned and wavered in evident response to the cameraman's protest, and shuffled away to the left. Then he reappeared full-length further off, and took up a position against the car, full of Chaplinesque fidgets, crossing his arms, cocking an ankle on the running-board, turning his head in ladylike parody from side to side.

It clearly wasn't Charles, though even a sensible person, I knew, might act up like this when a camera was running. It was a taller but thinner man. Moreover it was a bona fide queen. He had on elegant, unEnglish light suiting, with a bow-tie and a broad-brimmed straw hat which gave him a sweetly arcadian character, at the same time as shadowing his face. Then, overcome with embarrassment, he walked rapidly towards the camera, loomed in it with peculiar closeness for a couple of seconds, high cheekbones, a long curved nose, funny little mouth.

James was gripping my arm. 'It's Ronald Firbank,' he said.

'I don't think there can be any doubt, do you?' said Staines.

'That's certainly him,' pronounced Charles.

'If it's what I think it is,' said James, 'it must be at the very end of his life.' And in the next little bit he was laughing and suddenly it was going wrong: he had started to cough and cough, doubling up, his long hand gestured the camera away.

I understood then, in the next scene, why he looked so frail, had the air of a man nonetheless confronting a threat. He was tackling a steep cobbled hill at the top of which a church was outlined in the late afternoon sun. His whole walk was anyway extraordinary, not best calculated for getting from one place to another, a business of undulating hands and picked tiny steps, and yet obviously inescapable: that was how he walked. A couple of small children at the roadside watched him pass and then started to follow him. One understood their sense that anything so conspicuous must be done deliberately, as an entertainment or as the origin of a procession. A taller boy, a ten-year-old in ragged clothes, joined them, imitating the novelist's walk. The little ones, emboldened, skipped round him, running ahead as well to see him coming on, openly curious, asking questions, it seemed, of two or three syllables. The hectic jerkiness of the film lent them all a fantastical twitching energy. Then Firbank's hand went into his pocket and flung backwards a scatter of nickel coins.

Unsurprisingly the next scene showed the crowd about twenty strong. They were reaching the brow of the hill, capering around, others almost marching, but in a volatile Firbankian way, like some primitive disco dance. They were calling and waving their hands, and then chanting something together — a name, an epithet. The camera, with a certain artistic flair, concentrated on the youngsters: tots and urchins with a droll seriousness to them, rowdy pubescent boys bursting out of children's clothes, and others, with their wide-eyed Italian faces, gazing into the lens as they half-strode, half-loitered with the crowd, plucking at the sleeve of the heart.

And yet it was the mood which fascinated. This marionette of a man, on his last legs, had been picked on by the crowd, yet as they mobbed him they seemed somehow to be celebrating him. He became perhaps for a moment, what he must always have wanted to be, an entertainer. The children's expressions showed that profoundly true, unthinking mixture of cruelty and affection. There was fear in their mockery, yet the figure at the heart of their charivari took on the likeness not only of a clown, but of a patron saint. It was a rough impromptu kind of triumph.

There was a brief tableau in which order had been more or less imposed. The children gathered round Firbank and glared and grinned at the camera; Firbank flapped his hat in his hand and looked hot and bothered. A little girl tugged at his trousers and he pulled his pocket inside-out with a drooping and muffled gesture to say he had no more to give. He smiled too, but showed that he wished it was all over: it was a tiring situation for so childless and singular a man. In the final few seconds he was walking away by himself: there was something decisive and businesslike about him; in spite of everything he was in a hurry, he had work to do. Then a fat boatered man and a woman with a parasol were parading past a tent with the word STEWARD on it. 'Ah, that's the end of our film,' said Staines, and put out the projector's bulb. We were in virtual darkness for several seconds, and James squeezed my hand and I felt his charge of emotion.

'It's the most wonderful thing I've ever seen,' he said, in the way that one does to a host, but he meant it.

'Quite a find, eh?' Staines agreed, putting on the light. 'I want to turn it into a little feature, with a commentary perhaps by you, Mr Brooke, if you would care to.'

'I've got some ideas about it,' said James.

'I've been to Genzano, of course,' muttered Charles, who did not want to be left out. 'They have this festival of flowers, and the main street is carpeted with . . . er . . . with flowers.'

'Very Firbankian,' I put in my obvious bit.

'You mean, on another day,' said James, 'if it only had been another day, we would have seen the flowers beneath his feet.'

Chatter about this went on, and I asked Staines surreptitiously about the Colin pictures. 'Oh, I'd forgotten,' he said, hand raised chidingly to brow. 'Will I ever be able to find them?'

'Is it a frightful bore?' I said courteously. 'I just thought as I was here, and you had kindly said . . .'

'Oh, I *know*. But there's no system, as you doubtless recall.'

'Actually I think I can remember roughly where they were.'

He allowed me to take out the huge print drawer that Phil (ouch!) and I had shuffled through weeks before. 'You're welcome to *look*,' said Staines, as if he held out little hope.

But it was the right place. I recognised the Mayfair portraits, the louche studies of Bobby — Bobby who today was nowhere to be seen, banished doubtless under the good behaviour clause — and all the randomness of it was right to me, as that was how it had been before. But when I got to the bottom, and peeled back the last piece of protective tissue, I had to acknowledge that none of the pictures of Colin, those artfully lewd compositions, was there. I searched the drawers above and below as well, but with dwindling hope. Charles called out, 'What's he looking for?' and when Staines replied, 'I promised him some photographs of a boy called Colin, but I just *don't* know where they are,' I knew he was lying.

'Colin?' said Charles. 'Oh, I don't think I know that one. Do I know that one?'

I nodded at him to signal that this was the boy I had told him about, the thing that mattered to me; but he was quite inscrutable, full of diplomatic ignorance. Half an hour later, when we shook hands and parted, he wouldn't meet my eye.

'Well, that was a mixed success,' I said to James, as he climbed down into his car, and I leant over the open door.

'Don't worry about the Colin thing,' he said.

I drummed on the roof. 'I want to get him! I don't seem to have anything else to do.'

'Do you want a lift?'

'No, I'm going home. Then I'm going to have a swim: one must keep the body if not the soul together.'

'See you soon.'

'See you my darling.'

It was very quiet at the Corry, when I arrived mid-afternoon. The few people there looked at each other with considerate curiosity rather than rivalry. There was a sense of various different routines equally overlapping. There were several old boys, one or two perhaps even of Charles's age, and doubtless all with their own story, strange and yet oddly comparable, to tell. And going into the showers I saw a suntanned young lad in pale blue trunks that I rather liked the look of.